“THIS IS AN EMERGENCY. . . .

This is not a test . . . repeat . . . this is disaster. . . . This is no dream!”

Hanna looked at the displays but she could not see the enemy. She cried out and tried to run. All the others aboard were dead, yet still they screamed in her mind. They took too long to die and dragged her down, down, and death ate at her. Smoke of burning flesh, ship metal screeching, and beyond the enemy she knew, beyond the true-human foe, something evil and unseen hunted through the darkness. Closer, closer it came, deadly, unknowable, unstoppable—and reaching out to claim only her!

Books by Terry A. Adams
in DAW Editions:

SENTIENCE
THE MASTER OF CHAOS

SENTIENCE

TERRY A. ADAMS

A Novel of First Contact

DAW BOOKS, INC.
DONALD A. WOLLHEIM, PUBLISHER

1633 Broadway, New York, NY 10019

Cover art by James Gurney.

DAW Book Collectors No. 661.

To Barry, Leveda, Linda, Lisa, Robin and Stan; to my mother; and above all, to John.

First Printing, February 1986

3 4 5 6 7 8 9

PRINTED IN THE U.S.A.

PROLOGUE

The millefleurs sang a melody of ending. Clouds of twilight dimmed their thousand colors; rainbows faded into grayness, peace and longing mingled and black were there. Singing into silence:

Hallucination, she thought. Desperate battle to think. *Oxygen loss*.

She struggled for breath and lost the thought in Tirane's screams.

But he was dead—the strength of that ego to survive in memory still!

Dorista leaned close and said aloud, "Not lack of air."

Shock made Hanna stupid. "But—?"

"The flowers. They're Gabriel dying."

Dorista wept. Hanna felt hot wetness, tasted salt. Tears of the living: Dorista, Martin, Antonia, Roly, Hanna herself. She knew these few were alive because she saw them here in Auxiliary Control.

There were also the tears of the dead.

She thought of getting up and decided against it, remembering dimly how a few minutes ago she had struggled to pick herself up off the floor and regain her seat. With clearing eyes she saw that Auxiliary Control was untouched, even though something like the heart of a star had smashed into the corvette *Clara Mendoza* and rammed it through space without effort. Pretty *Clara* with her rainbow passages, garlanded for battle: she had never had a chance against the Nestorian cruisers, nor had any of her mates.

(I want to go home oh please I'm lost lost alone and it's dark—)

Dark-eyed Pamir. Dying too his final thoughts echoing in her mind.

Hanna lifted her right hand and brought it down hard on the edge of the console before her. The surface was curved but she hit it with all her strength and the sharp personal pain filled her and blotted out the ghosts. In the reprieve she began calling Main Control. No voice answered. Gabriel of the millefleurs faded. Had anyone survived?

"Smashed. It was smashed." Dorista still wept. "There can't even be any bodies."

"Gabriel's, anyway." The personal essence disappearing from the cooling flesh . . . the strongest took hours to go.

Voices rose round Hanna. Instinctively they were reverting to speech, the old way, the true-human way. To enter each other's thoughts was to lose their way in the mental chaos of the injured, the dead and the dying. Not many left injured, not now. The second assault had finished the patients from the first, along with sickbay and the medics and the drugs for pain and the drugs for dying. The third had finished everything.

"Report," Hanna said over her shoulder, but nobody did. She turned and screamed at them, "Report!"

(Agony staggered them and stopped. They put a name to it. Don trying to keep pain to himself so it would not defeat them. Half the ship was crushed between them and he said: *Don't even try*—)

"I am—"

(Ash, dead or dying, mourned the son he would not have—)

Hanna said through the wave of darkness, "I'm the senior officer. If Main Control is gone, I must be. Report! *Concentrate!*"

Ghosts moved among them, nearly visible: scraps of childhood, loving faces, the detritus of ebbing consciousness. She gave them something to concentrate on: white hatred of Nestor. *Nestor, Nestor!* she cried to them, and shaped the images, fanning hate. The crazed old general, the bleak warrens of an ill-managed colony world. The Polity worlds had closed ranks and done nothing for Nestor, and it was the ancient story: find an outside enemy to hate. D'neerans were easy to hate, telepaths; true-humans considered them only quasi-human. And D'neera was a peaceful world. With more love for flowers than for defenses.

Hanna kept her mind—

(*Oh God, I'm so afraid, his blood, oh God, oh God*—)

"Who's—?" someone said.

She said over the swelling panic, "Alia. Not even hurt. Roly, find her and calm her down. It's clear to Engineering."

—kept her mind on the reports.

Main Control gone. She knew that. The few secure modules of *Clara* were on local life support. The reactor heat wasted into space, irretrievable; soon the cold of space would creep in. Of the twelve ships D'neera had been able to muster, only two answered now, and they were fighting, falling back. They could not come to *Clara*'s aid. The guns were out. Such as they were. And the shields. And Hanna's head was spinning and her stomach lurched; gravity was erratic, it would be free fall soon.

"They want surrender," Martin said. He snatched the link from his ear as if it had caught fire.

"Give me the link."

But it fell to the floor as a mental howl from somewhere stopped them, and somewhere a failing heart stopped.

"Willi!"—that was Martin—"Willi!"

Hanna was stuck in a nightmare where nothing could be done. Through dimming eyes she saw Martin crawling, his frantic fear for Willi (but too late for fear; time for grief) heavy as her head.

I told them. The slow thought ticked over. I told them no lovers on the same—

The mental weight suddenly lifted. Martin sobbed and collapsed. The arm Hanna had stretched out to him hurt. She snatched up the link, fumbling it, put it to her ear and picked out the words that meant disaster.

Surrender. Immediate. Destroy.

Enough. It was too much effort to sort out the Standard words from the uncouth Nestorian accent.

"Let me see them. Tonia, what can you get?"

Her head was empty and quiet now. She supposed the living were unconscious or calming themselves. Roly had not gone after Alia; she assumed Alia had fainted. She risked a thought to Tonia that took in every sensor the *Clara* possessed, and an order to Dorista to evaluate their chances of escape through the unspace of Inspace. And an order to Roly to count, if he could, the living. For hand-to-hand fighting, if it came to that.

You know we're all there is you're good at this too good as true-human, Roly said, and it was hateful, a signal for a purely D'neeran catfight. There was no time for one. She stared him down and he bowed his head and started the hopeless job, dropping into himself and reaching out.

Tonia said unsteadily, "No visual. Nothing."

"What about the rest?"

"I think—wait."

Smoke began to drift through the ventilators with, oh God, the smell of burning meat.

Hanna clipped off her own horror and made them do it too.

"This is bad," Dorista muttered.

Hanna looked at the computer's relentless judgment. Not just bad. Fatal. Inspace systems were working, in a manner of speaking. They could Jump out of here. But incoming space-time data was getting garbled somewhere in the system, and if they Jumped—

Dorista's vision was almost soothing. Particles fanning at random through infinity like fine gray dust . . .

"We'll have to surrender," Tonia said.

"You don't want to surrender," Hanna said, and Roly came out of the silence where silence should not be and stabbed her with a picture of herself as the quintessential soldier, fighting mindlessly to the end.

"Giving up is better than dying," Tonia said.

"Come on! They want to question us. They want to find out what can hit them from the surface. And it's an all-male army, Tonia."

Roly looked at her blankly, the two women with growing unease. Innocent, innocent, Hanna thought in despair, how innocent we are! We feel one another's pain and cannot harm each other. And are helpless before our brothers who are our enemies.

Tonia had forgotten the sensors. She was examining things caught from Hanna's mind, shocking lessons in events that happened in places that were not D'neera. Third-hand memories, fourth-hand; they had not happened to Hanna. She had only brushed against them, and imagined how it would be. But they made Tonia tremble. Giving up did not look so good.

Hanna got up and went to her and pushed her aside. There were faults in the pictures the sensors drew, colors changing for no reason, lines flickering and re-forming. But Hanna said, *"What's that?"*

Her hands worked at Tonia's controls. She knew two of the shapes—Nestorian cruisers, not as fast as *Clara* in realspace but bigger, better shielded, better armed and scarcely damaged. *Clara* was their prey. But something new was there, and when the mass readout came she looked at it with disbelief.

"Data error," Roly whispered.

"No." She coaxed the library for a guess.

"Cit—," its vocal circuit said, and expired.

Citybuster, said the legend on the screen.

Gravity rocked and they fell against each other.

"It's not after us," Hanna said, single-minded. The others did not speak but watched the lumpy thing grow as sensors built up a pseudo-visual pattern.

"Havock," the library said suddenly. "*N.S. Havock* commissioned ST 2808 drydocked . . . ST 2809 . . . under . . . terms . . ." It sighed and died again.

"You could stuff a hundred *Claras* into that," Dorista said.

"Uh-huh. More than that. And look at those shields."

Hanna sank into Tonia's seat. Weight flux or defeat tore at her stomach, and she might have been watching herself go through the motions of command from a distance. She had never taken Defense as lightly as most of her comrades, who thought danger meant pirates and knew the existence of their elegant little fleet was deterrent enough. The news that Nestor would attack had not surprised her—nor should defeat; yet defeat did not seem real.

And we are all so young, she thought. Parents cannot serve. . . . I should have had Max's baby when he asked me.

Roly mumbled, "I don't believe it. Mass sensors would've warned us."

Hanna presented him with her memory of the third and last assault. Every alarm on *Clara* had been screaming, and even those sounds were dim; the voices in their minds, the soundless terror, had drowned them out.

The cruisers were beginning to move toward them. They did not have much time.

"We took them on," Dorista said suddenly. "We did that, anyway."

Her palpable pride annoyed Hanna. "Too little and too late," she said.

She got up and turned away and paced the tiny chamber, leaving them to stare at the *Havock*. She felt resentment spreading through them at the unfairness of this giant's coming when they could do nothing to it. It felt better than Alia's panic, anyway. It did not occur to her that her own control strengthened them.

The lights in the room seemed dimmer. She did not bother to check the power.

Dorista said, "What are they going to do?"

Hanna looked around, remembering the others had not heard the ultimatum. She told them, but she added, "I think it's bluff. I still think they want prisoners. They won't put that buster in place till they're sure we're finished. That—" She pointed at a signal for an incoming message; it had been flashing since she threw the link down. "That's probably an order to stand by for boarding."

"We can't," said Tonia. "I won't. I'll kill myself first. I'll kill them."

There was an overtone of wonder in what she said, as if she could not believe it of herself. Hanna looked at her thoughtfully.

"Me too," she said. "Dorry?"

Dorista hesitated. Faint voices, visions, the traces of death, but at their minds. Dorista and Don had been friends. Don was still conscious and paralyzed with his back broken and the fire coming close. The reeking smoke had begun to choke him.

Dorista said, "I want to fight. I want to kill one for him."

"Roly?"

He opened his mouth and shut it. He had liked Defense exercises; he had liked free fall and riding the clouds and the little band's camaraderie. He had never expected to fight. He did not want to fight anymore and he was ashamed of not wanting to. He let them see it and Tonia touched him sympathetically, accepting it.

"Doesn't matter," Martin said. He pulled himself up and set his back against the wall. His grief for Willi filled the room, the world, the universe, and then he shut it in again.

"Oh, Martin," Dorista said, and went to him and took him in her arms.

"I guess we don't give up," said Roly, looking sick. "But what's the use?"

"No use," Hanna admitted. She wandered back to her place, veering here and there as gravity wavered. It was safer sitting down. She got into her seat and stared at the outline of the citybuster. D'neera had nothing dangerous on the surface. Nestor would find that out soon enough. And then this thing would move into orbit, ungainly, unbalanced, but efficient enough in space. It could blanket fifty square kilometers with fast or slow death. Its presence would guarantee there would be no resistance.

She said softly, "The Polity's got good intelligence. They must have known Nestor refitted that thing."

"Why didn't they tell us?" Roly said. He was cross. He could not get used to what had happened or what was coming, and with the end nearly here he could only be querulous.

"I don't know. Yes, I do. They only told us to prepare for an attack. They thought we'd ask for help and then, you see, when they had us where they wanted us, they'd tell us all the rest. I don't think they were even going to tell us where the strike force was coming into realspace without an agreement. But they did. Somebody must have thought the ambush was our only chance. It was, too."

Don's control broke in a wave of death-fear that stopped breath and thought. Hanna clung to her seat and her sanity riding it out— It lasted only an instant before the smoke knocked him out, and when it ended the others were choking. Alia was awake and screaming in their heads.

"Roly! Will you go shut that bitch up!"

"Yes. Yes." He stumbled into a wall and righted himself and made it out the door on the second try.

"She's too dumb to get out of Engineering," Dorista muttered.

"Why'd we put her there anyway? Never mind. At least there's air there," Hanna said, and rubbed her face with weary hands. After the first two attacks they had been spread too thin to be selective.

They waited in silence. Alia modulated to shock and pain and was still. It was like having a siren turned off, something that squawked just at the end when you touched the switch.

"Sharp right to the jaw," Hanna said.

I think I'll stay here, Roly said to her, half-present. *To be here when Alia wakes up. For the end.*

He felt acquiescence and let the mind link go, and Hanna forgot him. She ought to be thinking of sidearms, some form of futile deployment, but she could not stop staring at the citybuster. There was something at the back of her mind and she could not dig it out, and it was getting harder to think, to go on trying. Roly and Martin were passive dead weight, the future another weight of apprehension. *Clara* had set out with a crew of thirty-six and the survivors had died, in effect, thirty times in these last hours. The dead spoke to them still with ghostly voices their ears would not hear again. Perhaps the voices were even real. To let herself and the others believe so would reduce them to shadows for Nestor to take with ease.

And she could not keep from thinking of how she would die. Small-arms fire if they boarded, perhaps. A single blast of heat and radiation if they didn't. If she were taken alive there would be the half-world of stripdope, irresistible. And other indignities; but perhaps she would be drugged and would not care; and perhaps she would live and someday get revenge.

The patterns before her eyes grew and shrank and burgeoned again as the computers adjusted for real motion. They had settled on red and yellow, and the lines that showed the cruisers coming in on *Clara*'s flanks were lengthening. When they met the uncertainty would end. The thought had a kind of seductiveness.

"H'ana," said Dorista from the floor. She still held Martin's hand. He looked indifferently at nothing; with Willi gone he waited patiently to die.

"H'ana?"

Wildfire, whispered her thought, the intimate image that meant Hanna in happier times, laughing and ready and reckless. It woke Hanna, a little.

"What?"

"They tried this once with Lancaster, didn't they?"

"I think so. . . ." She was not good at history, recent or not. "Years ago. About the time they built *Havock*, I guess."

"And the Polity stopped them."

"Must have. Lancaster's got fewer defenses than we have. Than we had."

"Why didn't they stop it now?"

Hanna said wearily, "They thought we'd ask for help. We didn't ask."

"Why?" Dorista sounded merely curious, but behind Hanna's eyes she floated the shadow of D'neera encased in implacable stupidity.

"The magistrates couldn't agree. Stiff-necked as usual. That's all."

Hanna saw that her hands were unsteady. It made her angry. She knew, distantly, that Alia was conscious and huddled in Roly's arms. Tonia sat unspeaking near the door; she had caught Martin's mood of relinquishment. Only Hanna and Dorista on this dying ship were thinking, and Hanna did not know how much longer her own endurance would hold. She was a D'neeran, after all, though she knew D'neera's faults better than most. D'neerans gave and took comfort freely, and readily believed against all evidence that wrongs could be cured with love. They were stubborn and joyous anarchists who could not make a common move without arguing the direction for years, and they did not like emergencies, did not know how to meet them. There were men and women still alive and vigorous who remembered the time when D'neera had nothing to do with the rest of the human species. Many wished it were still that way. They had argued too long about asking for help.

The cruisers were closing in, in no hurry. Perhaps they thought everyone on *Clara* was dead. The *Havock* was closer too; *Clara* could not hold herself steady, and she would drift near but not into the monster's path. Hanna put her chin on her hand and watched the course and mass displays, resisting an impulse to let herself sink into the pretty colors. The idea was coming by itself. Think of something else and let it be born.

Dorista said in a desultory way, "They wanted to help, didn't they."

"Umm-hmm. One of the commissioners talked to the magistrates personally. Jameson of Heartworld, in fact. Isn't that funny?" The ghost of a smile twitched at her mouth. "Of all people."

"What did he say? Did Lady Koroth tell you?"

"There wasn't time for much. She thought he was angry because she was the only one who'd listen."

"They'd listen now."

"It's too late."

"To call for help now? Why? Even if we're finished, the Interworld Fleet would just come in and kick Nestor out of the system."

"It would take too long for the Fleet to get here. By that time the buster would be in place. Over Koroth, probably. It's got the biggest city and its House has the best ties with the Polity. Then—well. City Koroth alone gives Nestor two hundred thousand hostages."

Dorista sighed and did not speak again. Hanna watched the citybuster coming closer. She thought of City Koroth with its fountains and its ever-blowing wind and the slow clean river rolling toward the sea, and its white splendid House gleaming in the sun, and how in winter the scarlet stoneveins grew up its walls from the snow. She thought of the sky as she had seen it last, so crisp a blue she could almost touch it, and how this abomination would dirty it with threat.

The idea was there, born whole.

What wasn't? Suicide.

Dorry! Hanna said, showing it to her all at once. They were almost close enough to *Havock* to make it work. Closer would be better.

Fear and approval wrestled in Dorista. This was different from deciding to fight; no human being believes in his death, and there is always a chance of winning if he fights.

But look, Hanna said, concentrating on *Havock*'s end, displaying it: yes, only dust left of *Clara* and, yes, her people dust too, but also much of *Havock*, the rest crumpling and folding like soft plastic and a fireball at the end—

Hanna looked at her friend. "Well?" she said.

Dorista hung back. But the logic was irresistible. With *Havock* gone Nestor would find it hard to press the Polity for terms of occupation.

"Yes," Dorista said.

Martin focused on Hanna and smiled.

Tonia sighed and got up. "Where do we start?" she said. She added, "Don't ask the others."

"I have to," Hanna said. "Start figuring it out, Dorry."

The ghosts sang to her more loudly: Come to us. I am not doing this, she thought, it is against nature; but her hands moved, her voice was clear, even Roly somehow did not hear the ghosts. Roly was relieved. He did not mind dying so much, only fighting. The picture Hanna showed him comforted him: *Clara* drifting helpless, harmless, near *Havock.* A last burst of conventional power to throw them straight at *Havock,* crashing with luck right through its shields. And a last Jump to anywhere shredding *Clara* and *Havock* together through all of space-time. Roly would not have to fight. He would just be here, and then not here; and he settled on what his death would buy with a fixity of purpose that shamed Dorista's hesitation. And Alia took courage at last, took it from him.

"Are you smiling?" Tonia asked. She looked at Hanna strangely.

"It's everything they warn us about," Hanna said. "Random terminus, undescribed mass, we're not clearing dimensional topography for any point—we're doing it all wrong. Every last thing."

They had had the same solemn instructors, and Dorista smiled too.

For a while they worked very hard, sabotaging failsafes and destroying *Clara*'s automatic inhibitions against what they were going to do. They worked with an air of astonishment at themselves and also, because they were D'neerans, some of the pleasure of clever children getting away with the forbidden. Hanna fixed on the pleasure to keep her thoughts from other things. She would key the Jump herself. There was no time to program the computers for every contingency, and they might be unreliable in any case. She thought about the final key, the last thing she would touch. She pushed the dead away so the others would not hear, and went machine-like through her tasks. Past a crystal wall the shadows waited, urging her to farewells. Farewell to sun and sea of youth, the lure of stars and strangeness, bright future so much, so much wasted—

(*You are our future*, Lady Koroth said. The white faces of a non-human emerged from the past. The F'thalian Hierarchus had chuckled at humanity's useless squabbles. *You were right, Progenitor*, she said. *But did you see my only own end?*)

"Ready," Dorista said, but something in her wavered. Hanna put aside her memories and the alien Heirarchus diminished into the past. She had strength for Dorista and steadied her. Where did the strength come from? The ghosts, perhaps. In a kind of exultation she saw the wills of her friends as separate threads and took them in her hand. H'ana ril-Koroth faded with the ghosts. She had become an instrument.

She drew a lever through its course, and *Clara* shuddered and began to move.

And the cruisers moved fast; but not toward *Clara*.

"*What the hell?* What have they got up their sleeves?"

Hanna stood up suddenly. She felt very light; gravity had stabilized, but not at norm. She pushed at her hair and rubbed her hands, too nervous to keep still.

"They're heading out," Tonia said.

"Where? What to? There's nothing out that way. Why aren't they defending *Havock*?"

Clara picked up speed. Dorista said, "Maybe *Havock*'s going to finish us off and they're getting out of the way."

"Busters don't track moving targets. They depend on warships for defense. *Clara* masses enough to get through its shields. Get us more speed, Roly."

One of the cruisers started back in a wide turn.

"That's for us," Hanna said. "That was a command error before. Why? What happened?"

"Now," Tonia said suddenly.

"What?"

"I can't get the evasion program going. They're going to fire and it'll catch us before we do it."

"I want to be closer."

"There isn't time!"

Hanna's hand crept toward the key. She said, "A second. A few seconds. Marty, can you hear what they're saying? Let us hear."

The loop was still going, mindless. On another band someone shouted at them to halt. The same on still another.

They were close enough to *Havock* and the cruiser would fire. Now. Now.

A new voice boomed out in clear strong Standard, not at them.

"This is Commander Andre Tirel of the Interworld Fleet Warship *Willowmeade*. You are ordered to lay down your arms and vacate the stellar system of D'neera at once. Do not attack. We will return fire—"

Dorista caught at Hanna's moving hand. She looked at

Hanna's face, slipped in front of her, and set about changing course. *Clara* responded slowly, pulling up, up, on a course that would clear *Havock*. The calm voice went on.

"Any hostile act directed toward a D'neeran vessel will be considered an act of war against the Interworld Polity and we will take appropriate action—"

Martin shut off *Willowmeade*. "We could get them on sensors," he said.

Tonia's fingers flew. "There they are." Her voice shook. "We weren't looking there. What's the other one?"

After a minute Martin said, "*St. Petersburg*."

"There's more. What happened?"

"They must have been waiting. They must have been close. For days maybe. Waiting for the magistrates to yell."

Dorista said, "H'ana? H'ana. Are you all right?"

Hanna slowly took her eyes from the shifting forms. The cruiser was not coming after them. Sweet ballistic curves of life. She said thickly, "All right."

All right but wounded. All right; but there was no joy. Shock held them silent and guilt gnawed them already. Others who deserved to live were dead. The world was changed and they were changed forever. They could not yet know how. Hanna felt them touch her, seeking comfort and offering it. She did not want comfort. She did not know what had happened to her. It seemed she had pressed the button after all; that the decision had been the reality and all of them were ghosts, chattering in the dust, and the fireball which she saw vividly, sharp-edged and real, in the lesser reality of this crippled chamber.

She moved at last, slowly. Dorista had canceled the Jump order; but she looked once at Hanna, and checked it again.

Hanna said, her voice dragging, "Get *Willowmeade*, Marty."

The choice came unconsciously from memories of Willow. She had been met courteously there.

"Got it," Martin said.

She did not bother to identify herself. "Polity force," she said, "we need help."

She put her head down and thought about darkness. Dorista took over.

PART 1

CHAPTER I

The art of personal combat, like every other human endeavor, is transmuted on D'neera. Combatants abstain from the use of telepathy, presumably in order to retain the element of surprise; but in compensation, by a curious inversion of logic, each movement is announced before it is made by the tiniest of gestures, nearly subliminal, so that no one is hurt unless he is incompetent or undisciplined or distracted.

Hanna nearly got hurt; she was unexpectedly flat on her back, looking up at Master Ling through the indignation of pain, the sun-warmed boards of the studio floor very hard beneath her. The big dusty space swung round her once and stopped.

Ling thought: *Soldiers!*—a piercing image of destructive, undisciplined children. "They send me," he said aloud, "soldiers, who of all human animals are least suited to this art."

Hanna sat up and carefully rubbed her spine. She did not point out that D'neera's tiny defense establishment hardly qualified as an army, or that its handful of part-time fighters had, on the whole, a profound distaste for the job, or that if it were not for them Ling might have been blown to atoms a few months ago. He knew all that; he was only relieving his dissatisfaction with her performance.

"I was thinking of other matters," she said humbly.

"That is more-than-enough for today," Ling said, permitting himself a sharp edge of sarcasm.

"Yes," said Hanna, still aching. She got to her feet and went to the railing that in summer was the only thing separating the studio from the space over City Koroth. Ling's next student sat cross-legged near the edge, meditating; he had not seen her fall, nor had he seen anything for some time except the non-images deep in his own soul, where, according to

Ling, all the universe was discernible. Hanna had never seen the boy before. She leaned over the railing to let the summer breeze dry her sweating skin and wondered if Ling had arranged for the stranger to be present as a lesson to her. She had been coming to Ling for four Standard years, and for four years he had been scolding her because of her—

"Youth," she said. "That's all. Consider what distracts me, Master. Travel and sex and curiosity—maybe in forty years, or a hundred and forty, I'll be an apt pupil."

"You are facetious," said Ling, whose worst fault in Hanna's eyes was his lack of humor. "I teach children who are less easily distracted."

"Yes," Hanna said submissively, but she was distracted again, looking out over City Koroth.

Ling had his studio on the fourteenth floor of the tallest building in City Koroth. The child H'ana Bassanio, occasionally towed here by her mother from the little seaside town of Serewind, had looked up it seemed forever at this structure with its sometimes transparent, sometimes vanished walls, where artists played in the sunshine and Ling (not much younger then) taught something that might be combat or dance, and at the very top in a space as bare as this the Development Committee argued the future. The committee had now withdrawn to more comfortable quarters—after fighting about it for years—and to the woman H'ana ril-Koroth, who had traveled, who had seen the cloud-piercing towers of Earth and the spires of alien F'thal, this box of a building was very small. But not many D'neerans had traveled, and to most of her compatriots it was still tall.

Ling came up behind her and laid his hands on her bare shoulders. He knew what she was thinking, and would not be drawn into it.

"Nevertheless, you have what is necessary to become Adept," he said. She shivered a little in the sunlight, caught in his vision of the precise, inhuman control of the Adept.

"To what end?" she said.

"The no-end of the inward journey, which is the beginning of all others," he said.

"I haven't the time," Hanna said, "or the patience," but that was as close as a D'neeran could get to a lie or an evasion, and the rest of the truth was as visible to Ling as if it stood before them: the silver spaceship and the starclouds.

Ling's hands tightened for a moment and withdrew.

"Go," he said. "You are impatient for news. Pursue it."

Hanna turned from the railing, drew her small figure upright, and made him a formal bow. He returned it courteously.

"We meet again in three days' time," he said.

"In three days, Master," she said. But she hoped, and he knew it, that soon she would be nowhere near D'neera.

The bathing rooms of Ling's establishment were uncompromisingly bare. It was a condition of working with Ling that on his premises, at least, his students share his asceticism. Hanna stood under a fall of cold water until she felt clean—it did not take so long to feel clean in winter, when the water was icy—cupped some of it in her hands and drank to ease her dry throat, dressed and left quickly. It was a considerable walk to her House, and she was eager to be there.

The answer's got to come today, she thought. This morning. But it's midnight at Polity Admin. But no, dammit, he's not even on Earth, I don't know what time it is where he is. Why doesn't he make up his mind?

Much of her way was uphill and the day was growing hot, but she was in superb condition and City Koroth seemed to flow backward around her. City Koroth: first city of D'neera, center of the first province, site of the first governing House. The founders leaving ravaged Luna had sworn not to repeat history's mistakes. They had favored beauty over utility, trees over convenience, flowers—a tiny side street caught Hanna's eye, and she glanced appreciatively at its blaze of blossoms—flowers over almost everything. Sometimes the ground trembled under her feet as heavy machinery moved beneath it, but the ground itself, in this stretch, was surfaced with beautifully painted and well-maintained tiles. It was true that the midyear sun heated them so they stung her bare feet; but the next part of her way was through a shade garden where birds swooped low and sang piercingly and snatched at her ears until she thought soothing shoo-away thoughts at them. And how odd, she thought, looking at their tiny paws, that we call them "birds." When first I saw true-birds on Earth I said no, that can't be a *bird* . . .!

After the garden there were neighborhood markets which sold, absurdly, flowers. She bought one with her good name and tucked it into her coiled dark hair. There were cool thick-walled dwelling places, a place for the manufacture of clothing—she skidded to a stop and looked through the open door in astonishment. A woman passing by inside wheeled and came toward her, already angry.

"It's just," Hanna said weakly, "that last week they grew foodstuffs here."

But the woman only met her with a vast certainty that none of the too-numerous regulations were being broken, nothing was being polluted, and not even the House of Koroth—here her finger waggled emphatically in the hot breeze; Hanna's head began to ache—could find anything wrong!

But the produce balance, said Hanna, trying to remember whether the ponics people had reported a move and if so to where, but the woman was having none of it, and took her rather forlorn thought that she would have to check into it as a threat.

Hanna left, and ran the next block or two.

Governing any part of D'neera was not easy.

There were more gardens, including a stark patch of desert which she circled carefully because it grew spikes which would hurt her feet. There were plenty of people about, many noisy children and their quieter adults, but snatches of song and the music of fountains came to her plainly on the wind. A child came with her for a time, chattering confidentially and practicing his budding faculty for projection until her head ached again from his efforts. When he grew tired of walking she handed him over to the nearest willing adult; when he was ready to go home, someone would make sure he got there. Once she passed an adolescent boy and girl leaning together against a tree, eyes closed, barely touching, deep in that mutual inner exploration which for a season obscures all other concerns. Likely enough they had forgotten where they were and would begin making love right here, unless they got hungry first. No one would disturb them. Hanna was twenty D'neeran or twenty-four Standard years old and she had not felt this sort of attraction, as of particles of opposite charge, since adolescence; and in spite of her protest to Ling, even the purely sensual encounters were increasingly far between. I'm getting old, she thought in a moment's panic, and I'm still young. A hundred and fifty years to go, and already no time for love! There was too much else to think about: produce reports, facilities-use reports, the New City being built past the wilderness, the aftermath of war. And, when she could manage it, her private work in exopsychology, shabbily neglected. And the decision in the far-away Polity. And its consequences. If it came out the way she wanted it; she and the Lady of Koroth.

She reached a wide stone avenue that broke up at the end into greensward, and beyond it the white walls of the House rose into the clear blue sky. There was not much traffic to the House today, though as she ascended the final hill she met a freight carrier, festooned with banners and piloted by two men deep in half-spoken, half-thought conversation. On Earth the machines drove themselves. Was that what she wanted for D'neera someday? The machines thinking and the people tending to them? Towers founded on crystal and held up by aggies? Anti-gravity mansions in the sky, anchored by fragile-seeming cables and swaying—but only for effect—with the wind. . . .

"But I didn't really like it there," she said a little guiltily, and plucked a handful of many-scented millefleurs and carried them with her the rest of the way to the House, holding them as if they were a talisman against change.

When she passed into the House its ambience closed over her like water, cool and dim in the summer's fierce heat. The walls and floors and ceilings and furnishings testified to a peculiarly D'neeran passion for the decorative arts, and the whole vast warren always smelled deliciously of flowers and baking. But its essence was the people who lived and worked here. There was always an undercurrent of activity, less a matter of sound than the hum of many brains thinking all at once, and the flavor was decidedly female; this House was traditionally female, and had been since Maria Koroth started building it six hundred years ago. A hundred and fifty people worked here (when they felt like it), and all but a handful of them lived here. There was room for all of them; the House had been growing by fits and starts for hundreds of years, and Hanna still could get lost in it after five years of residence.

She did not have to ask for news. Cosma ril-Koroth, who, like Hanna, stood high in the house, sensed her presence and met her in a scarlet-draped hallway with a shake of the head. They made faces at each other, sharing disappointment in silence, and Hanna went on to her workspace. The first thing she saw when she came into the room—plainer than most, by her choice—was a message from Iledra, Lady Koroth, winking at her from a computer terminal:

"The Design Arbitration Committee at the New City site has failed to settle the Central Garden question within the lawful ninety-day negotiation period. I intend to invoke magistrate's privilege. Will you go there tomorrow and settle the matter? Choose a design that appeals to you and *do not* let them persuade you to grant an extension of the arbitration period. This project *must* be started this year. At least half the committee members, to my certain knowledge, are expectant parents. Ask them where they think their children will live if we do not build. . . ."

Hanna stared at the message for a little while. Grimly, trying to ignore disappointment, she rearranged her thoughts. She had hoped to disinter her notes on Girritt tomorrow, and try to make sense out of them. But perhaps it was just as well; perhaps she would never make sense of them without the Polity archives. And the archives were closed to her, unless. . . .

She thought of the silver spaceship, the library it would carry, the ancient eyewitness accounts of the first contacts with Girritt and F'thal and the Primitives. Surely the evidence she needed was there. Without it how could she prove to contemporary true-humans that they were wrong? How could she show them that the charming, monkeylike Girrians had not knowledgeably rejected high technology but were simply incapable of thinking past a certain level of abstraction in technical matters? True-humans would have it that Girrians lived as they did for noble motives. They had passed into the mythologies of certain religious and social movements as the embodiment of non-technocrat virtue—and the Girrians fostered the myth, having learned to enjoy the respect it brought them from the smooth-skinned beings called humans. But they did not understand telepathy, either, and had permitted Hanna to examine the contents and blank spaces of their minds (so many and such very large blank spaces!) with the generosity of naïveté. True-humans would take a lot of convincing, however—and more and more it looked as if Hanna would never have a chance to convince them.

She sighed and sat down and wiped Iledra's message, and called up the ever-growing list of questions to answer, tasks to perform, reports to read and write, requests to fulfill, disputes to arbitrate. Two landkeepers of Riverine Sector were quarreling over a stand of falseoaks on their common border, which one wished to fell. A nearby village had entered the dispute. I will have to stop seeing Ling, Hanna thought, I just don't have the *time*—

The Lady of Koroth came into the room without a sound. She had a trick of making unexpected entrances, and Hanna jumped at this one, seeing herself without warning through Iledra's eyes—

(*Brown-skinned and blue-eyed and growing into beauty but always too thin since the war, too apt to see the shadows beyond sunlight, hear silence in the intervals of music*—)

"Stop it," Hanna said. Her hands made fists on the keyboard. A trace of shadow lingered for a moment, and the intrusive presence withdrew. Hanna said without turning around, "I wish you wouldn't think such things, Lee. Not at me, anyway."

"A week ago your nightmare woke half the House from sleep. Must I order you to visit the mindhealers?"

"You already did. They've done little enough for other survivors. I don't want to talk about it, Lee."

"Very well," Iledra said. Her composure was unaltered; Hanna thought of it as unalterable. She said without a change of tone, "You know I've heard nothing from Jameson?"

"Cosma told me."

Hanna tapped a familiar sequence on her keyboard. The opening page of what had become a large file flashed onto the screen. "The *Endeavor* Project," said the title page. "A proposal for renewing the organized search for sentient life on the borders of human space." At the head of the list of names of those who had prepared the document it said: "Starr Hollin Jameson VI, Commissioner-Heartworld. Chairman, Committee on Alien Relations." Near that was a flamboyant, illegible signature. The proposal was dated a Standard year before, and Hanna knew it by heart.

She said, "I have to get on that ship. I just have to."

"Heart's desire," Iledra murmured.

"Yes. Oh, yes."

"It never pays to have them," Iledra said.

She moved at last to Hanna's side, and Hanna looked up a little apprehensively. Iledra was well into her sixties, but she looked only a little older than Hanna; D'neera's first concern upon reopening relations with the Polity a century before had been to appropriate, with unbecoming eagerness, every available advance in anti-senescence techniques. On that score there had been scarcely a dissenting voice. The tall Lady of Koroth, smooth-skinned, gray-eyed, golden-haired, was proof of their efficacy. Hanna could not imagine anything changing her. At some time in the past Iledra had unbent sufficiently to give birth to a daughter, and afterward had given the golden child to its father and forgotten it. Once, when Hanna asked her about that time, she had tried with D'neeran honesty to answer, but she could remember little about so brief and unimportant a contretemps. She had been Koroth's Lady for twenty years and might be Lady a hundred more. She spoke sometimes of the advisability of early retirement, and was fond of pointing to the stagnation of true-human societies as evidence that the young-seeming old gripped power too tightly and too long; but Hanna rather thought that "early" would always be a point somewhere in the future.

Iledra looked over Hanna's shoulder at the *Endeavor* proposal. She said, "I think we should begin giving more attention to alternative ways of proving our usefulness to true-humans."

"That's what you were doing before this came up. It didn't get you anywhere."

"True. But the choice is not ours."

"I don't want to keep plowing away at something I know is hopeless."

"You know no such thing." She touched Hanna's shoulder and the girl looked up again, rebellious and reluctant. "Patience," Iledra said softly. "Patience is everything. . . ."

Behind the gentle words were images of many rivers, of waters flowing, shifting, changing, slight perturbations repeated for centuries and gradually changing the contours of earth and sky till the whole mighty network was changed. Continents and climates shifted. Hanna rode the imaginary waters—and shook her head as if it were wet, came back breathless to the quiet cool room, and said loudly, "All the same. The data I need so— And to have a telepath at a first contact. They must see what it could mean!"

"They do," Iledra said. "But they would rather put it off for a century or two. . . . Here is the ring."

She never bothered canvassing subjects she felt had been

sufficiently discussed. Hanna was used to it. She looked at the gem in Iledra's hand and said hesitantly, "I'm still not sure."

"It is not an absolute commitment. It is an honor, however, and the formality gives, well, some weight to one's authority. I remember that when Penelope gave it to me I found those I dealt with were suddenly more cooperative. It is one thing to defy an administrator-delegate of the House, even knowing what she is likely to become. It is another to quarrel with its acknowledged heir."

The ring that lay in her white palm was a plain gold band set with a blue stone. After a minute Hanna took it and slipped it onto her hand.

Iledra glided to the door, unhurried. Hanna stared at the Heir's Ring of Koroth, but when she spoke it was not about the ring. She said, "Lee? Why hasn't Jameson called you?"

"Rudeness," Iledra said succinctly.

"What?"

"The privilege of power. We have no power. We need the Polity, but it does not need us. Whatever courtesy a commissioner shows us is ours by his sufferance." She gave Hanna a long gray look and said, "I would like to see that change before I die."

Hanna, left alone, looked at the ring's blue fire. The bauble felt heavy on her hand.

Stanislaw Morisz went to see Starr Jameson about the *Endeavor* project a day or two later. He did not know that the House of Koroth had given up its hopes of participating in the project. If he had known he would not have cared; he had other things to think about. Jameson made Morisz nervous, and Morisz was finding out to his consternation that even approaching Jameson's residence was enough to produce the symptoms.

"I thought," he said, "this was all wilderness," and looked out the window of the aircar again at the great fields brown with stubble in the weak afternoon light. He felt lost.

The flier who had come to meet him at Arrenswood's only outport said, "No wilderness here. Farther on."

"Where does Commissioner Jameson live, then? Closer to the forest?"

"No. Here's Starrbright," said the man, and the aircar

dove to the left and down. There was a knot of trees there and in the center half a dozen structures that grew rapidly as they went down. They went down fast. Evidently, Morisz thought, Jameson required speed from his subordinates when he was at home just as he did on Earth. They talked less here, however, if this pilot was a sample.

Morisz stood a little helplessly by the aircar when it landed, not sure of the protocol. You might or might not be expected to carry your own luggage, depending on where you were on which world and also on who you were. He did not know how Heartworld's respect for status applied to him; Jameson's status was very high indeed, and presumably so was that of his guests. On the other hand Morisz was a subordinate of any commissioner from a Polity world, and Terrestrials were not highly regarded here.

But the pilot began getting the bags out without a glance in his direction, and Morisz had a chance to look around. He had been on Heartworld before, even in Arrenswood province, but only in the cities, which were grim. This was a little grim too, he thought: windswept prairieland, further flattened to increase the efficiency of machines.

Morisz was a man of crowded Earth, not used to being far from centers of population even though his job had sometimes required it before he moved into Polity Administration. He was not sure how far the aircar had brought him, but he knew he was some distance from any town. Beyond the trees, fields stretched to the horizon. Everything he could see would belong to Jameson; the term "landed family of Heartworld" suddenly took on new meaning.

The main house was made of brick, and no doubt the bricks were handmade, though somewhere, probably underground, there must be agricultural robots of great size and power. The house was three stories tall, shingled with wood—shingled? Yes—and also trimmed with wood. It was gaunt as the bare trees surrounding it. Nothing about it suggested it was the product of a star-traveling civilization. On the other hand it did not have the patchwork look of settlements on poorer planets, none of which were Polity worlds. The latter fact was largely due to Heartworld; its representatives to the Coordinating Commission of the Polity made a good case against letting underdeveloped societies enjoy Polity perquisites. Jameson had been the commissioner from Heartworld for eight years. And after all, Morisz thought, why should he want to sell the produce of these fields for less than the market would bear to customers who had nothing to offer but money?

He was still looking out over the fields, fallow in the dying year, when he heard a footfall behind him and realized his status was settled; Starr Jameson had come out to meet him in person. He turned a little hesitantly. Morisz was director of Polity Intelligence and Security, and knew more about Jameson than almost anyone else did. He rather liked the man, but did not understand him and had never seen him in this setting. He thought Jameson might be different here.

But the only difference he saw was that Jamesom was smiling, the rare sunburst of a smile Morisz had seldom seen.

"Stan. Glad to see you," Jameson said, and they shook hands and Morisz relaxed. There was no difference. It was just like Polity Admin on Earth, except for the smile and also that this was partly a social occasion.

Morisz, not thinking socially, said, "I thought you'd be glad. This is it, isn't it?"

Jameson seemed not to have heard him. He said, "You've come prepared for big game, I hope?"

"I don't know," Morisz said cautiously. "How big?"

"Medium, I should say. Earth import. Nothing difficult."

"I thought of bringing a combat laser," Morisz said a little wistfully.

"Not here. Here you hunt with spears or bows or not at all. It'll be good for you, Stanislaw. Come on up to the house."

Morisz wondered if he should pursue the matter of the report he carried or wait for Jameson to bring it up again. Well, that was like Admin too. He supposed ambiguity was a sort of immutable attribute, which Jameson practiced with guests as well as professional associates.

The house had a great central hall that made Morisz look around in wonder. The floor was made of polished wood. Of course; Heartworld was famous for its exotic woods. It would require a great deal of human, not robot, care, and Morisz was sure Jameson did no polishing. The rugs scattered on it would be handwoven. He stared at a gleaming brass chandelier and Jameson followed his gaze.

"F'thalian glowpods," he said. "It only looks incandescent."

"Doesn't that spoil the authenticity?" Morisz was surprised into bluntness.

"The Authenticist movement is very vocal but very small. And its spokesmen travel in aircars."

He took Morisz to a room where a fire blazed in a stone hearth. Morisz did not like open fires but sat near it anyway. He took the drink Jameson handed him and without making a display of it stole a more careful look at the other man's face. Was he spaced? Did he, on vacation at home, indulge himself as he did at his leisure on Earth, with whatever interesting drug the purveyors to Polity VIPs might provide? With, of course, the tacit consent of Earthside Enforcement officials who did not like to antagonize men like Jameson.

But Jameson sat down with a sigh, said, "How does the roster shape up, Stan?" and Morisz might have been back in the big riverside office on Earth, preparing to report in the ordinary way.

He took a cassette from a locked pouch under his shirt. It was wafer-thin and almost weightless in his hand, and it held the final I&S reports on the proposed crew of the exploration vessel *Endeavor*. It contrasted so sharply with its surroundings that Morisz suddenly wondered if there were a reader in the house to put it in.

"It's not a bad list," he said. "I question a couple of the names."

"You've already had one shot at it," Jameson said.

Morisz smiled faintly. "You're still showing a couple I could do without."

"I know," Jameson said. He brought a reader from a drawer built into the wall, reassuring Morisz, and slipped the cassette into it. He said, "Make yourself comfortable. This might take a while," and began reading.

Morisz was not comfortable. The room was too quiet, except for the fire, which made distressingly irregular sounds. The place was full of light that seemed warmer than glowpod luminescence; presumably the shades around the pods accounted for the golden cast. The shades were made of glass. Glass? Yes. Morisz had not been to Jameson's Earthside home. He had heard it was something like this; not nearly so extreme, however. He would bet this house didn't even speak. It was free from the subliminal sounds of machines and the energy transformations that ran them, and it felt too much as if it had a life of its own. Occasionally human voices sounded through it; one was a woman's, and Morisz wondered who she was. Jameson's recent companion in Namerica, a spectacular creature, was still there, which was not to say Jameson had no companions during his rare visits home. But Morisz knew of none at present, and he would know. No doubt whoever it was was at home here. Jameson had relatives nearby, a steward to manage the great estate, a housekeeper—the whole arrangement reminded Morisz that Heartworld's first families still had things pretty much their own way, especially in Arrenswood.

Jameson glanced up at Morisz once, his face expressionless, and went back to reading. Morisz watched him covertly. Jameson was a big man whose face seemed to have been put together without regard for consistency. There might be Amerind blood in the jutting bones and dark hair, but his eyes and skin were incongruously light. His mouth was sensitive when he let it be, the strong face surprisingly pleasant when he smiled; but he did not smile often. By Standard count he was forty-six and, Morisz thought, aging well. Rapidly, but well. He looked—

Morisz hesitated, wondering not for the first time about standards for judging age. Jameson stubbornly kept trying all the usual anti-senescence procedures, and probably looked younger than the forty-six of earlier centuries; but he seemed older than Morisz, who was near eighty but might have been an untreated thirty-five. Today Jameson also looked pale and very tired—unexpected in a man supposed to have been vacationing for eight weeks. He's tried A.S. again, Morisz thought, and it hit him hard. He looks like hell. And now he's waiting for the rest of the verdict.

Presently Jameson put the reader aside with an economical, final-seeming motion. Morisz came to attention.

Jameson said, "The alternate for Liuku. That's the only change."

Morisz estimated his chances of prevailing and found them small. *Endeavor*'s crew list had been thrashed out over several months by the Coordinating Commission, the Interworld Fleet, Alien Relations, and all the other components of a living bureaucratic network whose separate parts had their own goals to consider. I&S probably had exercised all its options. Nonetheless Morisz said, "Liuku's a hell of an

Inspace technician. I'd rather see her out there than the alternate."

"She's a Technocrat," Jameson said. Without giving the word special emphasis, he managed to make it sound distasteful. Morisz was a man of moderate views, and he did not care for Earth's Technocrat enclaves either. Their children were machined and augmented to something more or less than human, and they came out of the enclaves slighly or severely bent. But Liuku had bent in the not-uncommon direction of becoming a superb technician. Morisz's report said so, but now he said so again, emphatically.

Jameson said, "I know. But any person on the *Endeavor*, including the engineering staff, might have to talk to whatever's out there. How do you think a Technocrat would get along with something like a Girrian?"

"Heartworld prejudice," Morisz said.

"Possibly. But I won't risk it. Liuku's out," Jameson said, and Morisz knew he had lost.

He hesitated, wondering if he should bring up his personal reservations about the man who would command *Endeavor*. Their sum, however, was only that at thirty-nine—half Morisz's age—Erik Fleming was too young. You never got anywhere arguing age with Jameson, and in any case it was Jameson who had bullied and cajoled Fleet into leapfrogging a handful of young officers upstairs.

Morisz decided to skip Fleming and move on to surer ground.

"The D'neeran woman," he said. "Hanna Bassanio ril-Koroth. Whatever they call her."

Jameson leaned back and put the tips of his long fingers together. He said politely, "Yes?"

"I think she's a very unwise choice."

"I know you do. I believe she is the only person you strongly protested who will be making the voyage."

It was a pointed reminder that Morisz had gotten nearly everything he wanted, but he said anyway, "They're erratic. D'neerans in general, I mean. This one's reckless. You saw what she almost did against Nestor?"

"Courageous," Jameson remarked.

Morisz eyed him doubtfully, wondering just how much Jameson knew about it. He certainly knew the basic facts of D'neera's half-day war with Nestor—the only war in D'neeran history. There would have been no D'neeran defense force to fight it if Jameson, unofficially and personally, had not talked the D'neeran magistrates into creating one when Nestor's militarism had begun concentrating on the despised telepaths. It was supposed to be coincidence that D'neera was lush and prosperous, while Nestor's settlements were bleak and tired. Morisz believed in that coincidence just about as much as he believed the Interworld Fleet's timely intervention in the incident meant that the Coordinating Commission had acted on a wave of spontaneous, unanimous altruism. Jameson surely had been behind that too. But the official record included only a bare outline of Hanna ril-Koroth's part in the engagement, and there was no reason for Jameson to know the details.

Morisz said, "Let me tell you what really happened. This woman was left in command of the—the—"

He hesitated, searching his memory. Jameson's eyelids drooped; he looked half-sleep, or bored. He murmured, "The D'neeran corvette *Clara Mendoza.*"

"Uh—yes. She was in command because she was the only rank left among the survivors. The *Clara*'s arms and shields were out, life support was half gone, gravity was fluxing, the thing could just barely wallow around in realspace. She's called on to surrender. She decides not to. What does she decide to take on?"

It was a rhetorical question. Jameson said, however, "She goes after a citybuster. The *N.S. Havock.*"

Morisz knew he had made a mistake. "Right," he said.

Jameson said sleepily, "The *Clara* appeared to be drifting into *Havock*'s path. She was not considered a threat. It seems to have occurred to Lady Hanna, however, that a switch into Inspace mode and a random Jump at the point of closest approach would take *Havock* out. It would have worked, Stanislaw. It would have worked, you know."

"And killed everybody on the *Clara*. It wasn't smart," said Morisz, who believed in the wisdom of living to fight another day. "Not even so brave. Just crazy. They were all half-crazy on that ship. Your typical D'neeran doesn't like violence. He starts talking about how he's too empathic to stand it. Then he gets stomped. That won't go over with the Fleet personnel."

"It's an experiment," Jameson said mildly. "Let's give

her a chance, shall we? Naturally there will be personnel changes at the end of the first year."

"A year's a long time," Morisz said. "Something might—"

He stopped, but too late. Jameson looked at him narrowly and said, "Something might happen sooner. Was that what you were going to say?"

Morisz did not answer. He was half ashamed of his interest in *Endeavor*'s projected route. There had been unexplained communications blips for centuries. The experts said the last few years' reports from Sector Amber were not really disproportionate. Officially they had no connection with *Endeavor*'s course through Amber. Officially the name was arbitrary too. Not amber for caution. Just Amber.

Jameson said casually, "Amber's out in the direction some church used to fulminate about, isn't it? The Church of the Coming from the Stars, I believe. Quite a mouthful. What do the brethren think of the project?"

"I wouldn't know," Morisz said. He felt his face getting hot. He was too honest to expunge anything from his own I&S file, and anyway his life so far had been blameless. But if his youthful fling with that nutcult disappeared from the record by itself, he wouldn't reinsert it.

Embarrassed into silence, he watched Jameson pick up the reader and a stylus, note Liuku's replacement and sign the report. He had entirely forgotten Hanna ril-Koroth; when he remembered it was too late. He had been smoothly, ruthlessly diverted for just long enough.

Jameson handed back the cassette without a sign of smugness. "Behind schedule," he said, "but close enough. How about a drink and early dinner? We've got a long flight in the morning. Have you ever hunted with a spear?"

"No," said Morisz, wishing he hadn't come.

"You'll be learning the hard way, then. It's the only way to learn, however."

"What are we hunting, anyway?"

"Tigers," Jameson said, and almost smiled.

CHAPTER II

The exploration vessel *Endeavor,* carrying a crew of two hundred, left terrestrial orbit on the first day of March in the year ST 2835. There were ceremonies. Starr Jameson appeared in the *Endeavor*'s common room and made a practiced and inspiring speech about mankind's destiny to seek new horizons. With him was Commissioner Andrella Murphy of Willow, who looked at everything about her with an air of friendly interest and spoke to no one except Jameson. The commissioners from Colony One and Co-op were not there. Their schedules did not permit them to attend: not by accident. Katherine Petrov, Earth's voting commissioner, made a few formal remarks in a flat voice and disappeared—literally; she was a holo projection.

Jameson and Murphy were real, however. Hanna stood unsteadily on tiptoe to see them from the rear of a too-dense crowd. She wished she could catch a glimpse of their thoughts, but without prior personal knowledge of an individual's ''flavor'' it was impossible with so many people about. She liked Murphy's looks, but not Jameson's. When he was not exerting himself he looked, she thought, cold and indifferent; but she could not see anything very well. The ceremonial circle included Erik Fleming, and Hanna knew he must look like a model officer in his forest-green Fleet uniform, because he always did. He also was admirably handsome—a golden-haired sunchild, Hanna thought, though she was not given to poetic flights. Partly because of this she was favorably disposed toward Fleming, and in the hectic month of training before launch, they had become more than friends. This had advantages besides the obvious ones; for one thing it smoothed Hanna's way with her crewmates, who did not know what to do with D'neerans but knew how to behave toward their captain's friend.

After the formal leavetaking *Endeavor* proceeded to Alta at the edge of human space, a passage that took it an infinitesimal distance into the spiral arm that was Earth's home. The journey took many more days than such a routine trip required, and every minute was used for systems testing. There would be no help near if anything went wrong after Alta.

At Alta, the monks came up to bless them. Hanna was fascinated. It was her first experience with one of the little splinter colonies founded on religious principles, and she imagined penitents stuffing their robes into spacesuits and performing rituals in free fall, firing little globules of blessed liquid that would splat on *Endeavor*'s sensitive hull. Or perhaps they would use a pressurized stream of it?

They did not. They went round *Endeavor* in a vessel begged, borrowed or stolen from whatever secular government Alta had and shook holy water in the general direction of the ship as it drifted in orbit. Hanna found them prosaic.

Afterward the abbot drank wine with Erik Fleming in the captain's quarters.

"A peculiar experience," Erik said to Hanna later.

"What did you talk about?"

"You, among other things."

He said it teasingly, but Hanna, not mind-listening, missed the overtone. Her sketchy knowledge of history was biased toward the paranoid. The genetic experiments that had created D'neera's founders had been prohibited and outlawed everywhere. There were dreadful tales of what the founders had fled, and some of the nastiest concerned measures taken in the name of holiness.

She said with some alarm, "Is this one of those groups that thinks D'neera is demons' work?"

"Oh, no, he thinks you're all right. He's a very intelligent man, actually. He said he was looking forward to further revelations of God's glory."

But Erik had a quizzical expression, and Hanna, sprawled ungracefully on the lounge that was the only visible luxury in the captain's spartan suite, said, "But?"

"He seems to have some idea that Inspace transit is a matter of being picked up by God's hand and thrown across space."

"Well, that's as reasonable as some of the other theories. I lean to the one that says there's no such place as 'Inspace,' myself."

"Why not?" said Erik, and went off to approve another checklist. No space captain was so unimaginative that he did not wonder how he annihilated space and time without himself being annihilated; but meanwhile there were checklists.

Even on the customary routes space travel required caution and, past Alta, the last human outpost in the direction *Endeavor* now took, there were no customary routes. One could go from Earth to Alta in a matter of two Standard days, the actual transits taking no measurable time but data processing requiring a good deal. The equivalent distance through unexplored space would take weeks or months. In a comfortable room on a long-settled world it was easy to speak of great Jumps "through" Inspace that gobbled light years. Alone in immensity you thought instead of limitations: one unsuspected gravity well in your (theoretically nonexistent) path, one unsuspected wrinkle in space, and you would not be heard of again. Under these circumstances you did not gobble space but nibbled at it, felt your way with probes, and concentrated on looking very, very carefully for what might be between you and where you wanted to go. If you got there, others could follow at speed; but someone had to be the plodding first, and out here *Endeavor* was the first.

Hanna settled rather cautiously into shipboard routine. As an exopsychologist she would not be needed until and unless *Endeavor* found intelligent life, and meanwhile she was assigned to Navigation. Unknown-space techniques were familiar to her in theory, new in practice. She was entrusted with little responsibility and did not expect much. Mostly she helped with preliminary studies that would be checked and re-checked and double-checked and checked again. The work was tedious, the sense of community she remembered from D'neeran spacecraft was missing—or at least withheld from her—and at the end of each six-hour shift her ears rang with the constant noise of true-humans who communicated only out loud. Her only wish at those times was to escape to the quiet of her tiny cabin, where she measured the gap between herself and her companions and thought it might be unbridgeable.

Nonetheless, the spacegoing experience was priceless. In these times there were few ways to learn the navigational skills of space exploration. The worlds of the Polity, concerned with internal development and consolidation, had done little exploration for three hundred years. Other human settlements, a scattered fringe marking the outer limit of the first wave of expansion through space, had many problems, little money, and no reason to move on. The roughly spherical volume of the universe known as human space was still limited in content. There were the Polity worlds—Earth, Willow, Co-op, Colony One and Heartworld—five jewels of prosperity. There were D'neera and Lancaster, which were doing well enough, and a handful of settlements like Nestor which were not. There were many apolitical or quasi-political units like Alta or its infamous converse, Valentine, for the most part single-purpose colonies carved out of hostile environments and barely maintaining themselves. They did not matter much to the Polity, or to anyone except their more or less wretched inhabitants, and if they had any curiosity about what lay past human borders, they could not afford to satisfy it.

Also inside human space, though collectively called Outside, were F'thal and Girritt and two worlds that were home to species of uncertain status known as Primitives A and B. Hanna's personal interest in the *Endeavor* lay with the beings Outside. By the time the ship left Alta, she had investigated its library and found that it contained masses of material she had never seen before on all four species. There were minor works and papers and reports from countless governments and scholarly projects, all written during the centuries of D'neera's isolation, all archival matter considered so obsolete or unimportant that it had never been collected in one memory before. There were long-defunct journals, autobiographies of forgotten researchers, obscure essays, operational holos of rituals no human had attended for hundreds of years. There was data on the F'thalians, the only star-traveling species humanity knew of besides itself, whose existence Hanna had not suspected, accessible now because it was newly declassified to this expedition. Much of it was poorly organized, having been poured into *Endeavor*'s memory with no attempt to order the chaos of centuries; but before the first Jump into unknown space, three weeks into mission, Hanna already had seen—not how the data would combine with her own observations, but that somehow it would.

This was exactly what she had hoped for, and she began to spend all her free time reading. She had perhaps one Standard year for research, and she would not waste it. Research was what she had come here to do. To be present when *Endeavor* made a contact was, she thought, a dream, Iledra's dream; space was too vast, full sentience too rare, for contact to come soon. Her presence here was enough to set a precedent so that when *Endeavor* achieved its goal, one D'neeran or another would be there.

What she thought she could do with the archives was of more immediate interest.

Sentience showed different faces to true-humans and to D'neerans—more precisely, to Hanna. If she could synthesize them, the achievement would do more for D'neeran status in the community of man than the whole last century of tentative rapprochement had done. This was her reason for being here, and all the rest—token participation in true-human society, navigational skills, even the slight chance of a first contact—was insignificant beside it. She was so absorbed in her own concerns that she hardly noticed when *Endeavor* made its first halt to signal a likely star system, three months into mission. Later she knew she ought to have paid attention, because that was when the dreams began.

A loudspeaker said: This is an emergency this is not a test. Repeat. This is disaster. This is no dream.

She looked at the displays but she could not see *Havock* because the displays looked back at her with great yellow eyes. She cried out and tried to run from them. Tirane was dead and screaming and all the others too. They took so long to die and dragged her down, down, and death ate her. Smoke of burning flesh sucked at her knees and tripped her. Metal screamed: the *Clara Mendoza*'s dying wails. Death and more death and *Havock* waited with her to die in a life become night. The Nestorian cruisers stalked her and she could not move. Something huge hunted behind them in the dark. Closer. Closer. The smoke choked her screams.

She woke up snorting and struggling, tangled in sheets smooth as water.

Managed to sit up. Couldn't remember the voice code for

light. Fumbled with numb fingers until she found a switch and light blazed. Her heart thudded brutally and her muscles were weak.

"Erik," she said. He didn't stir.

"Erik. Wake up. Please."

She shook him once and rubbed his chest. Her brown hand, tremulous, looked alien against the white skin and coarse gold hair. He opened his eyes and smiled, then reached up and pulled her down to him.

"No. No. That's not it, Erik. That's not what I want."

She struggled again and he let her go. The smile faded. He was puzzled and vaguely annoyed.

"What's wrong?" he said.

Her heart quieted.

"The dream. Something after me."

She showed him what she could—not the immediate horror, because the dream was receding after the fashion of dreams, but the residual fear she knew would not let her sleep again soon. Before she broke the quick contact she felt a flash of anger. He did not like telepathy, like most true-humans, and she had given him no warning this time.

She lay down and put her head on his chest. She wanted him to put his arm around her. Instead he said, "You ought to get some help."

She looked from a pool of light into darkness and thought of Iledra's advice, stubbornly ignored.

"But the other dreams stopped," she said. "It's different this time."

He said after a minute's silence, "If you say so. But talk to Peng tomorrow, will you? That's what he's here for."

"It won't help."

"Hanna. . . ." He patted her shoulder finally. His voice was carefully tolerant. "I'm getting a little tired of this."

She was instantly guilty, and resentful too. And she could not show him her resentment without angering him again. And she did not know how to tell him about it. She had never learned to filter emotion through words. That was a true-human skill.

She eased off the bed, feeling a tug at her stomach as she slipped from its half-gee field into normal gravity. She had discovered long ago where the disciplined officer liked his luxuries: right here. She was one of them.

"I'll see you tomorrow," she said inaccurately, since it was well past ship's midnight.

"Turn out the light before you go," he said.

Hanna's pullover and pants and sandals were scattered between the suite's outer door and the bed. She put them on and slipped out into a quiet corridor. Its lights were dimmed in deference to the arbitrary hour. More doors led to other officers' suites, and she hesitated outside one of them. Tamara—but she knew communications chief Tamara Hweng well enough to know that Tam was not inside.

She began walking, not toward her own room but drawn by an intangible thread toward the woman she sought. Not even Erik could quell the D'neeran impulse to seek understanding, and gentle Tamara at least would listen. The aftermath of the dream oppressed her. She finally found Tamara sipping coffee in the crew's mess hall, not alone. Heads turned casually and away again. Hanna was used to being ignored, almost unseen.

Tamara waved at her. "Sit down," she said. The man with her, Ludo Brown, did not look pleased.

Hanna sat, sharply sensitive to Brown and feeling like an unwelcome child.

"I had another one of those dreams," she said.

Even as she spoke, Hanna saw that Tam looked tired and preoccupied.

"Was it the same thing?" Tamara said.

"The same as it's been lately, yes. Not like the ones I used to have."

"Well, I can't tell the difference, from what you say," Tamara said, but Hanna felt her quick sympathy. She patted Hanna's hand. "You had an awful experience and you still dream about it. You ought to talk to Peng about it. You really ought to. You'll get over it quicker if you ask him to help."

"But it's not *like* that, Tam. It's not just living it over. It's like there's really something out there."

Brown, to her astonishment, looked at her sharply. "What is?" he said. "Out where?"

"Out—" She stared at him, taken aback. "I don't know. Out there."

"Well?" he said not to Hanna but to Tam.

"No. Ludo, don't be silly." Tamara began to laugh.

"Is she talking about the same thing?"

"It's not the same thing at all. She's been having bad dreams. What we've got is something else. Prob'ly means less than a dream. I mean, it's altogether different."

Hanna might as well not have been there. She looked from one to the other doubtfully and said, "What are you talking about?"

"Spooks," Tamara said. "An incoming Inspace signal. Very erratic. We've been debugging and defogging all night and we can't get rid of it. *I* think the last relay we planted is defective."

Hanna, distracted, considered it. Communications through so-called inner space were subject to the same uncertainties as travel and could not be maintained without closely spaced signal relays. A tenuous chain of them now connected *Endeavor* with the established networks of human space.

"Is it a message?" she said.

"No, it's not. Random energy, random timing. That's what makes it so frustrating. If there were some structure we could use for diagnosis—but there's not. And Mister Imagination here keeps telling me it's not in the system."

Brown looked up and grinned at Tam. Hanna wished he liked her better, because she liked him. She liked looking at him, too. There were many D'neerans of Hanna's coloring and some who were darker, but Brown's rich darkness was rare where she came from. But he did not like her, because he did not like D'neerans, and he only tolerated her for tolerant Tamara's sake.

"All the same," Brown said, "you can't get away from it. They think there might be something out here. You can't help thinking about it."

"I can," Tamara said, and Hanna said again, "What are you talking about?"

"The Amber signals," Tam said. "We pick them up sometimes around Alta. They don't say anything, they don't mean anything, and, Lord knows, they're not focused on Alta. They're ordinary glitches, only more of 'em. They're nothing. Some natural source we haven't pinned down yet."

"Or maybe not," Brown said. "That's why we're out here, isn't it? And not out past, say, Heartworld?"

"I don't understand this," said Hanna, beginning to feel desperate. It would be so clear if she could just peek into Brown's thoughts. But that wasn't polite, and his native human faculty for projection, the foundation of her own ability but uncontrolled, was not operating at the moment.

"There's nothing to understand," Tamara said, but Brown said simultaneously, "They told us to track down the spooks. You know they did, Tam."

Tamara raised her fingers to her lips in a comic shushing gesture and breathed, "Unofficially. . . ." She added, "The relay's defective. If we can't eliminate the noise we'll have to censor it. Or go back and replace the relay module. I'll talk to the captain, but I'm sure he'll go for the censor."

"We could do it through the DeCastro program—"

They were going to start talking shop. Hanna stood up and said. "Well, good night."

"Good night," they said without even looking up.

She tried talking to the true-human psychologist Peng, as she had been advised. He said laughingly that he could hardly succeed where D'neeran mindhealers had failed. Were they not supposed to achieve remarkable results with trauma victims? Even with soft psychology?

Hanna gathered this meant they did not use biochemical intervention. She thought she felt a trace of condescension.

She said apologetically, to Peng's amusement, that she had expected the matter to take care of itself.

He approached his task with some enthusiasm, but Hanna was so inarticulate that she did not have to read his thoughts—just his face—to see his enthusiasm wane as quickly as it had come.

He gave her a little flask of something called Dreamdust and told her how to instruct herself to dream that the dead were at peace and the hunters vanquished. It was, he told her, all a matter of suggestion.

Hanna looked at the flask doubtfully and said, "But what if there's another source of suggestion?"

Peng beamed on her and said, "There can't be. That's the beauty of it. Dreams are entirely your own creation. It all comes from inside you."

"But I'm a telepath."

"Oh," said Peng. He frowned.

"We'd never dream—I mean, think of using something like this. We don't project when we're sleeping, unless we're very sick or very drugged or it's enormously stressful, but things creep in."

"You mean," Peng said after a pause, "you dream other people's dreams?"

"It's been known to happen."

"Well," he said after a further pause, "try it."

She tried it. The Dreamdust was effective, all right, but the effect was that the thing hunting behind the cruisers was bigger and closer than ever. She could almost see it. She *would* see it. She had to see it, this thing of terror, though she trembled in reality as well as in the dream. But it was shrouded in cloud and when she crawled trembling into the cloud, every instinct screaming for retreat, it solidified before her and was an impenetrable wall behind which the thing faded and was gone.

She didn't want to see it anyway.

There was nothing about peace or vanquishing at all.

She gave the Dreamdust back to Peng and told him she would not trouble him again.

The dreams receded to their former level of tolerable horror, and she was no nearer understanding their significance than she had been before.

Hanna was not on duty when the excitement began. She must have felt it sweep through the ship, but she got it mixed up with her own enthusiasm. She had discovered "Enchanted River: Notes on a Non-Terrene Evolutionary Process." The work was seven hundred years old, but she had seen that river, and Marshall Ho, dead half a millennium, spoke to her as to a contemporary. Her mind was not on *Endeavor*'s quest but in a steaming forest on the world of Primitive A, where the hot thick air lay heavy on her hair and mud squelched at every step and a fault in her breathing mask would mean death.

She had never learned to whom she owed the privilege of being so uncomfortable. Her request for Polity permission to visit A had been turned down repeatedly, and then one day was granted. She had gone to the planet at once, before They could change Their minds again. A bored Fleet guardian hovered at her shoulder and thought about patting her behind. She watched the sinuous leathery A creatures for days without seeing a single piece of behavior to support her conviction, immediate and direct, that they had already entered the gray area between bestiality and sentience.

"Enchanted River" was a treasure.

Ho, working under the auspices of a rough coalition of Earthly nations, had been unhampered by the stringent regulations developed later by the Polity. He had gotten right down in the beings' midst, and at considerable personal risk watched every detail of their lives for months. He thought their intelligence was on a level with that of certain extinct terrestrial primates, and he held out great hopes for their future.

No one paid much attention even then. Colony One and Co-op had just been established, and there were enough strange things in places where the air was safe to breathe. The contact with F'thal came a few years later, and Ho's ambiguous pets were forgotten. The infant Polity remembered to interdict the place—after the Co-opers decimated a population of potentially future-sentient mammals on their own planet—but the act was neither necessary nor daring, since no one wanted anything on A. Marshall Ho became a footnote in the history of exploration, and then disappeared altogether. "Enchanted River" was never translated into Standard. Hanna did not know why; the translation program was still available, and she had done the job herself by pushing a button. She supposed no one had ever been interested enough to push the right buttons.

She skimmed the work in a couple of hours, her attention so concentrated that when she was done she could have repeated long passages from memory. Then, just to be sure, she ran a search for any mention of something she had seen on A. There was nothing.

("When did they start building dams?" she said to the Fleet sentinel.

"They've always made 'em. Instinct. Read Rutherford. Twenty-six fifties," he said, looking longingly at her breasts. It was a long and lonely tour of duty out here, and he was nearly at the end of it.

"I've read Rutherford. I've seen his pictures. What they were building then wasn't as sophisticated. And it was confined to a limited area."

"That's very interesting," he said, edging closer.

She never had to hit him. Her blast of anger straight into his head was enough; and taught her for the first time what true-humans thought of telepathy. It was all mixed up together in memory: the discomfort and his bitter resentment and the—pups, she supposed she must call them—learning to build. The vague stirrings of extension of the learning skill to other things. Inchoate, as yet. Unrealized. When need called it would happen. But no telepath had gone there before, and no one else could have sensed it.)

The dams created quiet deep pools where the beings lounged and played. Ho described their environment in exhaustive detail; but he did not mention dams. His photographs showed no dams. Now the structures were everywhere, wherever the A Primitives lived.

It was negative evidence. It was better than saying: I am a telepath and I know. But would it be enough?

She had been still for so long that her muscles were cramped. She got up and the heat and stench faded. Her memory of sunlight filtered through leaves vanished, and her cabin seemed cold and dark. It was standard issue; she had brought little with her from D'neera, and regretted the omission. It seemed noisy, as if many voices were talking very loudly nearby.

After a minute she realized there were no voices. But somewhere on *Endeavor* were some very excited people.

She went out into the corridor and followed her instinct toward the source of excitement—Communications. The suggestion of noise grew stronger as she focused her attention. The walls seemed to carry it like a vibration, and the unsound pricked at her scalp. Something was happening, something important. People stood in clusters talking about it, but she did not ask them what it was. She went on toward Communications, moving faster, her breath short for no reason.

It was controlled, crowded chaos inside, but everyone's attention was focused on instrument readings and—something else: something mind-conjured yet so shapeless, shadowy, hidden in cloud that her dream came upon her in a great rush and she drew in her breath harshly, for an instant thinking all of it a dream, and almost turning to run.

Nearby Brown called, "Tamara! Hey, Tam!"

Tamara looked across bent heads. Brown said, "Secondary traces negative. Exclusion from the relay pipeline confirmed."

Tamara said, "Check it again." She plunged back into conversation with Erik.

Hanna was shivering. She was not dreaming, but still everything seemed faintly unreal. She looked for someone to talk to. De Assis, the linguist, was speaking with animation to McCarthy of exobiology; but Marte Koster, chief of exopsychology, stood silent and a little apart. Hanna went to her, picking her way carefully through a larger crowd than the space was designed to handle. Koster was a pudgy woman who made Hanna think of an ill-tempered duck, but her face, Hanna saw with shock, was transfigured, and she caught at Hanna's arm with plump hands.

"It's wonderful! Wonderful!" she said. A clean pure note of excitement made her almost likable.

Hanna said—with an edge of reluctance that made no sense—"What is it?"

"You haven't heard?"

"No. No. I was busy. Heard what?"

"Contact! A first contact!"

"What?" Hanna said. Koster kept talking, but Hanna did not hear her. She looked at Koster's shining eyes, at the bustle around them, as if all of it would collapse now, immediately, any second. Humankind knows one star-traveling race and that is F'thal. Elementary knowledge you knew it before you knew what stars were—

She stood perfectly still. Koster patted at her nervously. "It's a shock, I know. I don't believe it yet myself. But it's true. It's true!"

Hanna said with an effort, "What happened?"

"They got a message a few hours ago. They're still checking to make sure it's not of human origin. It's a series of prime numbers and a location. Clearly intelligent."

"From the system they've been signaling?"

"Where else?"

"But there's no power generation there!"

"You mean not that we recognized. No heat or radiation. We've got to find out how they do it. Think of it!"

Koster was ecstatic; more than ecstatic—bordering on hysteria. "Don't," Hanna said, trying to soothe her. "Don't. For heaven's sake—" She felt giddy. Everyone seemed to be shouting, but that was an illusion; it was only that they could not help projecting. She shut them out as well as she could and tried to think sensibly.

"That's the location they gave? That system?" she asked.

"No. No. The rendezvous is a week away, I think. In deep space."

"Why?"

"Who knows?" But the questions calmed Koster. She took a deep breath and said quite rationally, "I don't suppose you've felt anything, have you?"

"Felt—?"

"Felt anything telepathically that might have come from them."

"I wouldn't. There are too many people on this ship. The aliens would have to—"

She stopped abruptly. Koster said, "They'd have to what?"

"I was going to say, they'd have to be telepaths themselves. But if they touched us I wouldn't necessarily know it was them."

"You let me know if there's anything. Anything at all. Any slightest possibility."

"I will," Hanna said, but she was glad Koster was not looking at her too closely when she said it, because she did not want to be questioned about possibilities. She did not want to talk about the one that had just occurred to her, which was preposterous anyway, but then it was all preposterous. It was too new, she could not believe in aliens yet and half these busy people could not either. History was being made but it wasn't, for those making it, real. Not yet. So the possibility wasn't real either, and besides she did not even want to think about it because—thinking about it made her afraid, and if she thought about it she would have to do something about it; the fear would not go away until she knew she was wrong.

CHAPTER III

Endeavor came to the appointed place nine days later, and found no one there.

The journey ought to have taken longer, and Hanna, like everyone else in Navigation, was tired when the push for speed was over. She was not at once concerned with the silence that answered *Endeavor*'s homing beacon, nor were any of the others. Species X had not specified a time for rendezvous. Perhaps the aliens were still on their way. If this area of space was familiar to them, they might have started for it later, underestimating *Endeavor*'s pace through unknown space. They might think less like humans than like F'thalians, who were universally tardy. As long as the creatures were an enigma there was no point in speculating about their punctuality or their notion of a timely tryst.

Besides, there was the micro factor to consider. From the macroscopic point of view, an interstellar location could be pinpointed with high accuracy; but on the scale of two small ships seeking each other in perpetual night, there was room for error in even the most precise equations. The *Endeavor*'s beacon had its limitations, too. Inspace signals did not travel, but came into existence more or less at the point of reception, the more or less being a matter of probability. The beacon therefore consisted not of one Inspace signal but of billions, fired in a series run at subatomic speed to an array of points within a radius of one light-year in any direction from *Endeavor*. This left sizable gaps in the reception pattern, so it was customary to shift the whole thing in space for each repetition of the sequence of signals. If you were in a crack at the beginning, you had only to wait until a point in the pattern was close enough to register on reasonably sensitive instruments.

Of course, the aliens would not know that; but as the days wore on and stretched into a week of silence, the fear that grew on the crew of the *Endeavor* and the project's Earth-based managers was that they did not care.

Starr Jameson watched the conference and doodled.

He had positioned himself so that he could see past the video screen that showed a dozen members of *Endeavor*'s complement at their conference table, and look instead at the brilliant June afternoon outside. He had gone even farther than his Heartworld predecessors in making his Central Admin quarters at least appear utterly unguarded, though the appearance was deceptive. This room had no visible outer wall, so that the broad river running past the administration complex lapped at its edges, and he could walk straight off the thick carpet into the water if he chose. He never would; a Polity commissioner did not do such things, and in any case Jameson would not have done it because he had seldom done an impulsive thing in his life. But sometimes he thought about it, especially at times like this.

In front of the conference screen floated a smaller screen which displayed the conferees' words as they spoke. Jameson had lowered the volume of the dialogue. He kept half an ear on it and half an eye on the readout, and in his lap he held a notepad and stylus. He would appear to the *Endeavor* personnel, and to the other Earth-based participants whose disembodied voices joined in from time to time from Admin and other locations, to be taking studious notes. He never took notes, but a lifetime of conferences had taught him the necessity of doodling to have something to do besides look at interchangeable faces and listen with diminishing concentration to interminable voices going on and on.

This meeting had been going on half an hour and he had already filled and wiped the notepad's screen once before something on the readout caught his attention.

He leaned forward and said, "One moment, please."

All the voices stopped immediately. He said, "Lieutenant Hweng, back up a moment, please. What did you say about confirmation of the source of the original signal?"

Tamara Hweng said without hesitation, "It took some time to refine the parameters of transmission, sir, probably because of equipment incompatibility, and we've only just pinned down the ambiguity margin. The signal we received didn't originate in the target stellar system. It came from perhaps a third of that distance from *Endeavor*. Unless you accept the possibility of our being directly in line with an established relay system, that means they answered us from a spacecraft."

"Thank you," Jameson said. He waited for the voices to take up their theme before he leaned back and considered the news. It must fit into a pattern somewhere; but there were not yet enough facts to form a discernible pattern. There were only the signal to a distant new world, the answer from a spacecraft close at hand, a meeting set for an unspecified hour—then nothing.

He appreciated the irony of the situation. All the laws of chance and logic argued the impossibility of *Endeavor*'s first effort drawing an answer. Hundreds or thousands of efforts with no answer had been the likely scenario. The impossible had most gratifyingly happened, however—and now was slipping out of reach.

Why had species X not answered from the system that received the signal? To draw *Endeavor* away from it? To avoid being caught on the ground? If they had answered from a spacecraft, why had they not simply made physical contact with *Endeavor* at its original, well-described position?

The readout said: "—suppose we scouted the target system just went there maybe used one of the shuttles or—"

Jameson said, "No."

The speaker was McCarthy. He was a Heartworlder and not over-fond of Jameson. He looked up and said with a familiarity most of the others would not have dared, "Why not?"

"You have no shuttles with Inspace capability, Harry," Jameson said. "You'd have to take the *Endeavor* into the gravity complex. If you took nine days to get to your present location, in deep space and working flat out, you would need—how long, Captain Fleming, to chart a safe path to and through the target system?"

Fleming nodded. He said, "At a guess—and this is just a guess—a month. At least. Probably longer."

"Yes. And you would relinquish the chance of contact where you are."

First Officer Ito Hirasawa said, "What about getting a

smaller Inspace vessel out from the closest base? We could stay where we are while somebody else charts a course."

Jameson said, "We don't know yet that they don't consider one ship an invasion. We don't want them worrying about two. Gentlemen and ladies, we have no idea what we're dealing with. It has been seventeen days since Signal Alpha. Seventeen days may be only a moment to these beings. I suggest maintaining your position for a time. There are other reasons, but at present let's just assume that your time can be best employed in waiting."

Marte Koster said rather plaintively, "But how long, Commissioner?"

She looked woebegone. Jameson did not like her expression, and he did not like Koster. Sheer weight of Fleet seniority had earned her this choice assignment. There had been no valid reason to reject her, and he had not tried to do so. But he did not like her. He said, "I don't know how long you should wait. But as an exopsychologist you're certainly aware that curiosity is a prime trait of sentient life. They'll come take a look at you sooner or later."

She tapped the table restlessly and said, "It might speed them up if we gave them more information. We could add to the beacon content."

One of the disembodied voices—an I&S man from Morisz's office—said immediately, "No!" There was a pause during which he must have considered how his haste looked—a little too paranoid, perhaps—and he added more smoothly, "I'm not an exopsychologist, but surely what we've already told them is enough to stir up any reasoning creature's curiosity. What if we got a message out of nowhere from somebody identifying himself as an intelligent, oxygen-breathing biped? I know how we'd react. Wouldn't we, ma'am?"

Koster said, "You can't generalize—" and was quickly interrupted. Jameson listened long enough to be sure the I&S man was carrying his point, and tuned out again.

The conference started to disintegrate, its business done. Jameson began to think of the long cool evening ahead, of catching up on his endless reading in the sweet-scented garden of his nearby home. Presently Henriette would come to be beautiful and compliant over drinks at twilight, and later all warmth in the dark.

But once he looked again at Marte Koster, and wondered if

she were making any use of the D'neeran girl who was somewhere on *Endeavor*. A long time ago he had given Koster a gentle hint of the possibilities there. Too gentle perhaps; but his was a very private experiment.

Heartsong of the beast. We are (it sings) intelligent star-yearning star-earning. . . .

We know. And knew. Eversought since one day's seeking. . . .

Here. Here. Give no warning.

Wait . . .

"What?" Hanna said.

"Umm?"

"Did you say something?"

"Heaven knows. I don't think so."

"I thought you said something about—" Hanna fumbled uneasily. Water? Waiting? "Never mind," she said.

"Good," said Tamara. "Don't ask me to remember anything I said two seconds ago. Please."

She sat on Hanna's bunk with her capable hands, a little unsteady, wrapped around a mug of steaming coffee. There were hollows under her brown eyes, and the lids drooped from watching too many readouts that did not change. Signal Alpha now was twenty-four days in the past. Tamara had told Hanna that her ears were even wearier than her eyes; that she listened always for an audible voice, although it was absurd; that in her rest periods she lay still and awake because she could not stop listening. It had become her habit to meet Hanna in her short breaks from Communications, because Hanna knew little of the field. With Hanna, Tam could, she said, stop listening.

Hanna said, "They set the damn meeting place. They've got to be close."

She sipped tea and waited for Tamara to say the next thing; they had had this conversation before.

Tamara said inevitably, "Well, maybe they're not."

"Huh?"

"Not close."

"And if they're not we either did something wrong or—"

"Or they never meant to show up at all."

"Which is ridiculous."

"Ridiculous."

Tamara got up with a sigh. She said, "I guess it's time to go back and make sure we're set up for the conference."

"What conference?" Hanna said with half-hearted curiosity.

"Alien Relations. At sixteen hundred hours. Another session with The Man himself listening to every word and jumping on anything he doesn't like. I'm not used to operating on that level, Hanna."

Hanna frowned at her. "What man?"

"What?"

"Wait a minute." Hanna sorted it out. True-humans sometimes used a verbal shorthand that seemed to make up for the vivid images D'neerans exchanged to supplement language, and she was not good at it. "You said the man listens to every word. What man?"

"The commissioner."

"Which commissioner?"

"Jameson," Tamara said patiently.

"Oh. I see. Alien Relations. Erik won't let me in on those meetings, you know."

"I know," Tam said, but she left without saying anything else. There was nothing more to say. Hanna had told her all about it: the bitter argument, the truth coming out at last that even Erik thought her not quite human, a threat, a freak to be kept away from important *human* work.

"You're lucky to be here at all," he had said, and that had been the end of it. She had done as she was told. Erik was the captain and orders were orders; the implications would not be self-evident on D'neera, but there were no other D'neerans here. So she had stayed in her place in Navigation, downing stimulants and working endless hours like everyone else, with little room in her mind for anything else; the stimdope she and the rest of the crew were taking had given her no choice, because they concentrated your mind on whatever task was set it. Her head was filled with mathematical symbols that danced around each other in closed circles and ran together until they made no sense. She was stuffed with them and befogged by them, and her baffled crewmates made another fog around her. Their search went round and round in circles too.

She wouldn't think about it any more. She couldn't bear to. There was no way out of the fog, but at least she could sleep and forget about it for a little while.

She yawned and hovered a moment behind someone's eyes in the command module with its bright displays and telltales and the human beings monitoring a sleek machine whose trillion nerve endings made it a nearly living thing. She drifted, soothed, through the ordinary detritus of humankind, a hundred separate universes of greater or lesser charm, self-contained though admirably bridged. Her tension eased. For after all, D'neeran she was human, at home, at rest among the—

Beasts, said a whisper in her head. She whimpered but the whispering went on without words; she struggled to move limbs that had no strength; she was trapped in the smoke again, and the first flicker of apprehension swelled into fear. The whisper crept closer and called her. Wrong, wrong, no good at all; dark and ashes and an eye like the sun watching pitiless and the shadow looming without mercy, new, new, something new and terrible and that was all she knew, that was all she would ever know but it knew *her.*

I come. I come to you—

She heard herself with terror. *N.S. Havock* filled her eyes. Her hand moved toward a key and Roly, who did not want to die, cried, "You're too good at this!" But still her hand crept on to the last thing she would ever touch. "You're mad!" Dorista said and seized the dreaming hand but it seemed she had gone on: dust of *Clara* and, yes, her people dust—what waited past that end? The whisper said: *We wait.*

She shouted and the shout woke her up. She sat up shakily, sweating.

(*"But you were saved," Peng said reasonably. "The Interworld Fleet, wasn't it?"*

"Yes. Heavy cruisers. The Willowmeade *under Tirel—I remember* Willowmeade*—"*

"These dreams, then. Do you want to die?"

"Me?" she said with disbelief.

"What else?"

"If they come from outside—"

"They don't come from outside," he said.)

She said out loud, "It's the drugs."

The words fell into the cabin's dead air without conviction. She turned over and pushed her face into the thin blanket that covered her bunk. Her thoughts shot off in all directions:

the numbers danced in the puzzled fog and Erik's fear and unkindness underlay it all. If only she could talk to Iledra—really *talk* to her, not record a message that would be censored anyway and wait for a reply to clear Earth. Or to her mother; but Cassie had taken up with a mood poet and gone to live on a beach in the tropics.

The thing that pulled her thoughts in all directions was something she did not want to think about. It had been easy to avoid, with the dreams gone and the stimulants at work.

Suddenly she wanted very badly to go to the conference, to find out what somebody else thought. The heads out here were numbed with drugs and anticlimax. What would the outsiders say? What did the omnipresent Jameson think of the mire his pet project had gotten into? Maybe he knew what was going on. Maybe somebody would say something that would make it unnecessary for her to think about her scraps of surmise. If she went, would Erik throw her out in front of all those important people? What would be the harm in just listening?

She reached out and turned out the light, and sought the greenish glow of a chronometer across the room.

The conference would begin in thirty minutes.

In forty she would go.

. . . and knew. Found today
found yesterday
found at last
tomorrow ends
today . . .
Wait.
Watch.
Wait . . .

It was more than an hour before she stood outside the door and stared at it as if she could see through it.

She had fallen asleep again, just for a little while, and waked feeling profoundly uneasy. Had she had the dream, or not? She couldn't have; she hadn't had it since *Endeavor*'s frustrating chase began; but in her fitful nap it had returned to memory at least, and now it haunted her and teased her as if something known yet not known hovered waiting for a word to make it real.

The polished door showed her nothing but her own reflection: thinner than ever, the dark blue eyes too big, her hair a shaggy mane. She ran both hands through it to tame it, but she did not move yet to open the door. She heard nothing behind it and reached through the wall into mist. There were too many people thinking unfocused thoughts; they slipped from her grasp like the dreams' unseen thing.

But there weren't any more dreams.

Finally she touched the switch that controlled the door, and it opened.

The room beyond was dark, but in a central blaze of light that seemed to float without foundation, Erik sat at the end of a long table whose other end she could not see. Hirasawa sat at his right and Tamara at his left, and Koster and Brown were in her line of sight. She sensed other presences and all of them, seen and unseen, looked at something hidden by a jutting corner at her left.

She edged into the dark edge of the room, feeling like a spectator at a drama arranged by an invisible director. The wall at her side made an alcove from which she watched in shadow. But what were the actors watching?

A male voice she had never heard before was saying, "—your point, of course, but the project calls for keeping on the move unless you have definite results. You've got too much ground to cover to waste time. You're off course and stretching optimum scheduling now."

Hanna felt a jolt of anxiety. Marte Koster's. She knew what Koster would say before the woman spoke, her voice more tranquil than her heart.

"We might stay on course twenty more years without results. Either of the other options would be more acceptable to me than giving up."

The others murmured programmed agreement—Hanna shook off the thought in irritation.

(The white faces of a F'thalian Hierarchus emerged from the past. The thought of the Hierarchus soared and dipped and dizzily she caught at the flashes of light which were scintillating nodes of intersection, though she could not follow his spirit's flight.

Observe the water-breathers, he had said. Move a leaflet,

so, and they rush eagerly to feed, though on this world to which they were not born they have no prey that moves so. Yet they do it, and their offspring will do it, and thus with all their generations. Thus with thee, Little One—)

She shoved the Hierarchus back into memory with an effort. Damn the drugs, they weren't working as they were supposed to work, she was more and more easily distracted and divided. Erik was saying, "—a combination of efforts. I think we could do it that quickly; it's a matter of refining Communications' data. But you said, sir, that you were opposed to that course of action on grounds other than the time it would require?"

She had heard the voice that answered once before. It was deep and precisely inflected and instantly recognizable. Starr Jameson said, "The likelihood that this system is the home of a star-traveling species is small, gauged by chance alone. The absence of any sign of artificial power generation settles the matter, to my mind."

Koster said, "We signaled it and somebody answered. Somebody who was breathing down our necks."

"Quite." Jameson again. "You were then two and one-half light-years away from—let's be specific and say from the life-bearing planet of that system. Your data on the planet itself, therefore, is two and one-half years old. Certainly no native species has developed Inspace techniques in that time. The beings who responded to you therefore came from elsewhere—"

"Yes," Hanna muttered, and froze: how had she known that? She stood in the dark and heard the voice going on, a deep music without meaning, her thoughts paralyzed. She made herself breathe again, and think of what it meant. She knew it; never mind how, for now. She *knew* it. It meant something—

"—should say they prefer to keep their business there to themselves since they invited you to a meeting not in that stellar system but some distance in an opposite direction. I still agree with Kwomo that you ought not to spend time visiting the system. You might do something with an unmanned probe, if you can do it quickly enough—"

Hanna slid without volition into Koster's frustration. Marte reached out, reached out, for something unseen she saw slipping away. Her need for comfort was so strong that

Hanna moved forward automatically. Her eyes were drawn to the end of the room, visible now, where most of the wall was a video screen that showed Starr Jameson and two other men bigger than life, dominant and unreal. The little group of spectators was tense.

Something nagged at the back of her mind. She ignored Koster, with difficulty, and stopped and dug for it in silence.

Koster was talking again: "—backtrack to our original point of contact? If we got our signals mixed up and they're looking for us somewhere else, they'll go back too. There's been a mistake."

"Assuming they exist," said one of the strangers on the screen. "Lieutenant Hweng, are you sure the signal's source was nearby? Couldn't it actually have originated within the system, maybe an automatic device set in place long ago? Something important might have been where you are now and be long gone."

Tamara said with absolute conviction, "There has been no mistake. The margin of ambiguity was too tight for the origin to be in the system. It was far more clear than ours must have been at reception."

Koster said, "Then there's been some kind of accident. We've missed each other. They must want to meet us as much as we want to meet them."

She expanded on the theme, but Hanna was not listening anymore. The receding shadow stood for an instant in the light.

"Oh, they don't," Hanna said out loud. "They don't want us to see them. They don't."

After one frozen instant all the heads turned in her direction at once. Someone said from the video screen, "Who is that?"

Hanna did not move. She did not even feel the eyes; she was looking inward, watching pieces slot into place: the dreams and the tracking shadow always just outside her perception, the Dreamdust experiment whose results had reflected no suggestion of hers, the conviction that she had already known Jameson's theory to be true without knowing, until she heard it, that she knew it. It fit together so simply. It was as simple as—

—as killing *Havock* would have been.

She shivered and looked up.

Jameson said across fifty light-years, "Would you come into view, please? And identify yourself?"

She stood on the edge of light and saw that Erik's face was scarlet. His anger was a tangible barrier she would have to push through. Tam watched her with surprise and approval. She concentrated on Tam; the barrier vanished and she stepped into the light.

Erik said tightly, "I'm very sorry for this interruption. Ms. Bassanio wasn't supposed to be here."

Jameson said, "The proper title is 'Lady Hanna,' is it not? Is that correct?"

She turned to face the screen. She did feel the eyes now, and someone was thinking with sarcasm of her kludge of a title, and someone else was thinking *GO AWAY*. The faces borrowed from Earth were not half so unfriendly. The man in the center knew exactly who she was. That was odd, but she could not spare much thought for the oddness, because she was still thinking hard and she was frightened. She was not good with words, and she was willing to make a fool of herself by being wrong, but it would be terrible to do it by being right and not being able to explain. *WE DON'T WANT YOU*, somebody thought, and it stabbed her. Jameson had asked her something but she could not remember what it was and could not answer. Now he was saying, "Would you repeat your remark?" She took a deep breath, trying to tell herself this was no worse than the Arbitration Committee. But it was.

"I said—" She fastened her attention on the video screen. She couldn't remember what she had said. "I meant maybe Marte is wrong. Maybe they don't really want to meet us."

"Nonsense!" Marte Koster said so violently that Hanna jumped. Her hands trembled with self-consciousness, with fatigue, with the impact of Koster's hostility. She felt an urge to hit Koster's puffy face.

But Jameson did not look hostile. He did not even look surprised. She concentrated on him with a kind of gratitude.

"It's not nonsense," she managed to say. "There's something wrong about the whole thing. What were the odds against making a contact so soon? I know—I've heard—there's a reason we came this way. I'm not a statistician, but still it only makes sense if they were looking for us too."

"That's what I said!" Koster almost rose in her frustration.

Hanna would not look at her but felt the movement in her own limbs, which jerked in unwilled sympathy.

She said, "No. No. It's not the same thing. They might—they might want to do other things besides meet us. They might just want to know where we are. They might want to study us. They're watching us. I think they're watching us."

She did not take her eyes off Jameson. She had never seen so guarded a face in her life. He might have been thinking anything. She waited for him to say something, but it was one of the strangers at his side who said with open skepticism, "Do you have any evidence to support this—this very remarkable hypothesis?"

Hanna glanced at him, but then she looked back at Jameson and said, "I think I do. It's not objective. It's not on a readout anywhere. It's all inside my head. But I started, I started feeling it about the time we sent the first transmission. And it's come and gone and it's taken different forms, but I think it's real."

She waited for a response. Nothing, for a few seconds that seemed much longer. *GET RID OF HER*, Koster thought. Then Jameson said, "Go on," and just as she relaxed in relief, "Please be brief."

She tried, but it seemed to go on for a long time. It was hard to keep it in order, hard to put it all in words, and she could not show the Polity's men directly what she meant. They watched her without expression as she talked. Jameson moved only once, to put down the notepad he held, and Hanna stumbled because she heard Koster think savagely: *NOT WORTH TAKING NOTES ON!* On the wall in far-away Namerica there was a lambent glow as of sunlight reflected from water, and when she noticed it she faltered again. All the *Endeavor*'s clever design tricks failed, and she was vividly aware that she inhabited a metal container lost in darkness. But she recovered and went on.

She finished, "It has occurred to me that they might be telepaths. If the things I've noticed are significant, they have to be. I'm not a telepathic Adept. I couldn't possibly be aware of a distant non-telepathic presence when I'm surrounded by so many people and—I don't think even an Adept would be, unless he were deliberately reaching out to something and had a pretty clear idea what it was. That means they must be touching us in some way, though I'm the only one equipped to feel it strongly."

She thought of Tamara listening always for the voice that did not come, of the goal at the edge of Marte's sight. She added, "Maybe some of the others feel it a little. But if that's true, the only possible interpretation is that they have, have gone partway toward contact and are avoiding completing it. For some reason. I don't have any idea why they would do that. I don't—I don't know why it would take the form of something from my own experience. Yes, I do. I mean, that's because I pattern it unconsciously, because I don't have the, the templates of their experience. But why it should be *that*—"

She stopped abruptly, unwilling to approach the question more closely. She had said everything she had to say. There was no reason to go on.

They were waiting for more, however. They waited until Erik said, "Thank you, Ms. Bassanio."

It was a dismissal, and his voice was rough. He had only gotten angrier while she talked. She looked at him uncertainly.

Jameson said, "Lady Hanna."

"Yes?"

She looked back at the wall with some anxiety. Nobody up there looked inviting, but it was a better view than Erik's fury.

"Do you think it would be worthwhile importing an Adept?"

"Why—I don't know. They've got skills I haven't, of course, but on the other hand. . . ." She pondered.

She must have thought about it too long, because Jameson said patiently, "On the other hand what?"

"Oh. I'm sorry. Adepts don't have any training. My experience. I mean, I think I'm the only D'neeran who's been to F'thal, for example, Adept or not. The Adepts I know, they'd have some very interesting mystical things to say about aliens, but it wouldn't be much use from your point of view. There's something I could try," she said, and regretted it instantly.

It was too late, however. Jameson said, "What is that?"

She said unwillingly, "I could try to touch them without the interference. I'd have to be separated from the ship."

Jameson moved abruptly. No, not abruptly; it was just that her attention was caught because he had been so still until now. He said, "Telepathic reception is not a matter of proximity, I understand."

"Not really. But practically speaking it's like—like—"

She couldn't find the words. Jameson said, to her surprise, "Like Newtonian physics and Inspace. Direction is a perceptual construct, but things still fall downward."

"Yes," she said, understanding him perfectly. "Yes, that's it."

"Suppose you were, as you put it, separated from the ship? What then?"

"I don't know. I don't think," she added, utterly forgetting propriety, "I would like it much."

Jameson blinked. Out of the corner of her eye Hanna saw Erik make a violent gesture, instantly controlled.

"Why not?" Jameson said.

Automatically, because it was her custom to let emotion speak for itself, she visualized herself alone in nothingness, knowing the thing that hid behind Nestor's warships was nearly upon her. The persons around her stirred uncomfortably, and someone made a sound of protest. But Jameson could only hear her words, so she said simply, "I think I would be scared."

He looked, for the first time, mildly surprised. He surprised her by saying, "How did you feel the first time you made telepathic contact with a F'thalian?"

"What? Why?"

"How did you feel?"

"Well. . . ." She tried to remember. The dizzying sweep of infinite circles was familiar to her now. She couldn't think of F'thalians without them. But at first it had been like falling, and at every attempt she flinched away until the Hierarchus showed her the circles intersected everywhere, and she would always fall to a momentary resting place.

She said at last, "It was strange. It frightened me."

"The novelty?" he suggested.

"Well—"

He made a gesture with one human hand that would have meant, if the Hierarchus made it, Similarity of the First Order. She stared at him, disconcerted. How did he know so much about it? Or about her trip to F'thal, for that matter?

She said, "All right. It could be the novelty."

She had forgotten Erik. He could not restrain himself any

longer. He said suddenly, his voice furry, "Even if there's something to this, I don't know how practical it is to separate her from the *Endeavor*. She couldn't get very far in a reasonable time in the shuttles we carry. They're not Inspace transport."

Jameson made a barely perceptible gesture, and one of the men with him took up the discussion.

"You could Jump and leave *her,*" the other said. "The shuttles are equipped as lifeboats and have Inspace communications capability, am I right?"

Erik said stubbornly, "It would take us away from ground zero for an indefinite length of time."

They went on talking. Hanna, finding herself extraneous, looked for a place to sit down. Her knees felt uncommonly weak. There was no vacant place near Tam, but she found an empty spot next to McCarthy and felt under the table's edge until she touched the button that made its associated chair unfold from the floor. McCarthy looked at her in astonishment, as if seeing her for the first time, but he did not speak to her.

She was shaken and apprehensive and she did not try to hide it. A true-human would have tried, but Hanna had not been among them long enough to adopt the habit, even if there had been any sense in it; and here, anyway, some of the surfaces were wearing so thin that her anxiety was not overly conspicuous. Erik was a stranger. He had a right not to take her seriously, she supposed, but she had thought that was because Marte Koster did not take her seriously. Surely if these men did, Erik would? But he did not, or adamantly refused to, and she watched something that she finally understood was a duel of words until Erik lost. When the man with Jameson was done—it was Kwomo Thermstrom, she discovered, and remembered his name from the *Endeavor* Project proposal—Erik had agreed to the experiment at some unclear point in the future. That was all. As if she had never been there they talked of other things, of staying and going and unmanned probes, and finally Hanna realized no one was going to talk to her again, and stopped listening.

She stayed until the end, but not with pleasure. Too many questions had come to her in the last half hour, and she kept thinking of more: of what it might mean to Iledra and to D'neera if she came back from the forthcoming vague mission with something to show for it, and what it might mean if she came back with nothing. She was used to acting on the basis of direct mind-to-mind communication, but could she have made a mistake? Here in this strange world of true-humans, might she have misidentified as alien a complex of her own past and fears?

Once she looked up and saw Jameson looking at her so closely that she stared back at him in shock. For an instant she felt naked—not as an object of sexual interest, but as if she were being stripped right down to the bone and implacably assessed.

It lasted a second or two, and then he looked at someone else. She might have imagined the whole thing. But she knew she had not; why should a commissioner of the Polity watch her that way? What possible importance could she have for him?

She could not think of any, but later, as she filed out with the others, she thought suddenly: Whatever it is I will not like. Whatever he's doing, I wish he would not.

CHAPTER IV

She would not even try to transmit the letter. It would not get past the censor. She went on with it anyway, speaking softly, watching words form and lines flow on a square of light in her darkened room.

"I don't understand what I feel, Lee. It's new. Is it fear? Today I told the commissioner F'thal frightened me once. That wasn't the same. It was strange and exciting. And I was so curious about them! I couldn't have been very afraid. And, oh, what people said to me after Nestor! How brave I must have been! Was I? I don't remember feeling like this. I don't understand this. I don't. I don't. Am I imagining it? I have to get off the stim boosters. . . ."

It was deliciously quiet in the tiny cabin. Hanna should have had the booster implant renewed some hours ago. She had not; she would not. It seemed to take a great deal of energy to move even a little. Her mouth tasted of metal.

"This might be the chance we talked about. I have to be good enough. Don't I? I never thought it would happen. But I thought, if it did, I'd show true-humans how to do it right. Do it right from the beginning. I'm not even curious about them, Lee. Why? How can I not be? Why am I afraid? I have to get off the boosters and think. We're not going anywhere. We're staying here a couple of weeks more. I'll have time to think. . . ."

The room's sparse furnishings seemed to move in the dark.

Hanna fell asleep with her head on the computer keyboard.

She spun through the thought of the Hierarchus, pursuing a meaning that just eluded her. It was essential that she find it, because behind her was something that pursued *her*, and what she sought was her defense against the seeker.

The terror was so familiar that it bored her.

"Hanna?" said a soft and urgent voice.

She swam toward the voice, up through dark waters. Pursued and pursuers receded.

"Hanna? Wake up. Wake up."

She straightened, surprised to find herself not in bed. The cold light of the text display hurt her eyes. Her back hurt. She was cold.

Tamara said, "What's wrong with you?"

"What?"

"You're shaking."

"Wake fast. Happens."

It came out in a mumble. Tam touched her shoulder anxiously.

"Did you hear the alert?"

"Yes. I did. What alert?"

"You and some of the others. Briefing Room Two. I've only got a minute, I have to get back."

"All right," Hanna said vaguely.

"Promise? You won't go back to sleep? Promise."

"Promise."

"I have to go. Hurry."

"Thank you," Hanna said. She heard the swish of the door as it closed.

She got up, feeling heavy and unwieldy as a statue come to life. It seemed that she could only think one thought at a time, very slowly. There was a weight of nothing tangible in the pit of her stomach. When she started for the door, she stumbled.

The walk took forever.

When she entered the briefing room all the heads turned toward her—again—as if the scene from a few hours ago were being repeated. Her stomach lurched and she stopped dead. But there were only three people there—Erik, Koster, and Hanna's chief from Navigation.

"You're late," Erik said, not quite in a snarl.

"I'm sorry. . . ." She pushed a hand through her hair and looked at them blankly. It struck her that the discontinued stimulants were taking their revenge. The thought did not console her.

"Dismissed. Except you," Erik said, looking at Hanna. "Sit down."

She did. She was acutely aware of the hard seat of the

chair. The pale blue of a wall was garish. The others' footsteps thudded loudly as they left. Koster gave her the strangest look—half smug, half resentful.

When the door shut Erik said, "Why didn't you come when you were called?"

"I didn't hear. I was sleeping," she said, longing for more sleep.

He looked as if he didn't believe her. He said, "I don't have time to go through the whole thing again. You know about Beta?"

She tried to remember something about a Beta, and shook her head.

"Signal Beta. An hour ago. My God," he said impatiently, "how could you miss it? Another alien transmission, an exact duplicate of the first one, except that the locus referents are different."

"What?" Hanna said, startled into wakefulness. Erik went on without slowing down.

"We're making the first Jump in that direction in four hours—sooner, if Navigation gets it worked out faster. You're staying behind. Shuttle Five's ready—should be ready by now. Get in it and take off. I want maximum distance between you and this ship when we Jump. I don't want you smeared all over the cosmos. Get moving."

"But—but—" A sense of time-run-out seized her. She could not remember why. She tried to pick out sensible questions from the mass of them that assailed her. "What about communications? I've never flown one of those shuttles—how can— When are you coming back for me? You're coming back, aren't you?"

"Of course we're coming back!" Everything she said irritated him. His anger had lost none of its edge. He said with plain restraint, "I don't have time for details. Communications has a station assigned to you. You can get all the information you need from them. You shouldn't have any trouble with the shuttle—if you're the hotshot pilot your dossier says you are."

She nodded. She wondered why she had never noticed that Erik's beautiful blue eyes were so small.

"But how long will I be out?" she said.

"I don't know. At least as long as it takes us to calculate

the parameters for a second Jump. You wanted to do this, dammit, and now you're doing it, so get started!"

She got up cautiously, mindful of her leaden feet. "I didn't want to do it," she said. "Commissioner Jameson wanted me to do it. Why are you taking off after them? They won't be there either."

"Maybe they will. That'd be the end of your theory, wouldn't it?"

"What's wrong with my theory? A theory," she said lucidly, "is just a theory."

"We were doing fine without your theories," he said.

"I don't understand you," she said helplessly.

"I thought D'neerans were supposed to be the best at understanding everybody. That's what all your damn theories are about."

She looked at him in silence for a minute, her skin prickling. She understood one thing at least, finally and unhappily: that her quiet exclusion from *Endeavor*'s small society had lasted only as long as she made it possible for the others to ignore her, and Erik to enjoy her. Now that she had opened her mouth she might face—if Erik were a bellwether—open hostility.

She said, "Never mind. I don't think I want to understand you."

She was at the door when he said, sounding pleased, "You didn't have any warning this was coming, did you?"

"No." She turned in the open door and leaned against its frame.

"Why not?"

"I don't know. Maybe they didn't try to touch us that way this time. Maybe they did and I didn't recognize it. Maybe I'm wrong about the whole thing."

"Maybe you are," he said.

He wasn't going to say anything else, so she left.

Andrella Murphy's home stood on the opposite side of the river from Polity Administration, to the north and past a curve in the river so that the administration complex was not visible. What Murphy could see, on a summer night, was a basin of light. The river was thick with bridges here, and the computer-controlled ground traffic poured across them like streams of fireflies. Light lay heavy on the gentle slopes beyond the river. Murphy's house sprawled across a hillside, and the brow of the hill cut off a view upriver to the ancient monuments of what had been the seat of a mighty government before the stars changed the world.

Murphy had gone to some expense to make sure metropolitan noise did not reach the house. On her candlelit terrace the only sounds were of summer insects and the occasional night breeze. Outside the candelight there was darkness, and then the precipice and the endless fall into light.

Most of Murphy's dinner guests had gone home. Her husband had swallowed a sober pill and gone to bed, and only three others were left. Muammed al-Nimeury of Co-op sat in a shadow and talked, ostensibly to Murphy; she rarely answered, however, because he was talking for the benefit of Henriette Guilbert. Henriette posed becomingly and did not answer at all. The story—no doubt true—was that Starr Jameson had warned her to look gorgeous and keep her mouth shut if she expected him to take her out in public. It was a fact (as Murphy had ascertained) that Henriette used intelligence boosters just to perform her duties for Admin's Central Records section. Whatever else she wanted out of life did not, presumably, require much intelligence. Murphy was not inclined to quarrel with her logic. Henriette was here with Jameson, after all, and having a remarkable effect on al-Nimeury. Murphy was willing to make allowances for Muammed. His wife was on Co-op, and Murphy supposed he was lonely.

Jameson had disappeared into the high-security communications module that was part of every commissioner's home. Murphy had not heard the call summoning him there. She was not concerned. If there were a Polity-wide emergency, she and al-Nimeury would have been wanted too. Most likely it had something to do with Heartworld's lively political infighting. But she wished Starr would finish and go home, and take Henriette with him; then Muammed would leave.

But when Jameson came back he dropped into his seat with every appearance of staying for a while. He looked very pleased with himself. Murphy sighed and said, "Well?"

"Henry," Jameson said.

"Yes?" said the woman, looking at him with great brown eyes.

"Go away. Go play with the Kits."

Henriette got up without resentment. An obliging puff of

wind pressed her gauzy gown to her body, and al-Nimeury grunted in appreciation.

"Where are they?" she said.

"Locked in the garden, I believe. I hope."

"All right," Henriette said. "But aren't they asleep?"

"They're nocturnal. They haven't bred all the original Cat out of them yet."

"They're working on it," Murphy murmured.

"Abominations," Jameson said in disgust. He watched Henriette cast about and set off more or less in the right direction. When she was out of earshot he said, "*Endeavor*'s finally got a Beta."

al-Nimeury made a rumbling noise in the shadows. Murphy said, "What does it say?"

"Same thing as before, except for the locus description. That's different. It'll pull them off in a new direction. The question, of course, is what to do."

"What do you mean?" Murphy frowned at him. "Shouldn't they just go there?"

"Should they?"

"Are you asking for advice?"

al-Nimeury said, "Want mine?"

Jameson looked thoughtfully toward the shadows and said, "I don't know."

"Drop it," al-Nimeury advised.

Murphy giggled. Jameson said equably, "The *Endeavor* Project is a reality, Muammed."

"Worse luck," al-Nimeury said. "It's not too late to stop it, though."

"It is," Jameson said. "The question is not whether or not to turn back, but how best to proceed."

He was looking at Murphy again. She said, "Well, then, of course you want to go where they want you to go. To do anything else would be to turn your back on them and fly away."

"Unless," Jameson said, "they're playing a game whose results accrue to their benefit, giving us nothing in return. Shall we go on playing it, Andrella?"

"Not at midnight," Murphy said.

Jameson ignored the hint. He said, "If there should be no one at the new location, we'll have to rethink our response."

Murphy smiled. "You'd already decided to send them on," she said.

"This time . . . There is a new sensor in operation."

Murphy knew Jameson well enough to pick up the faint irony in his voice. She said resignedly, "Tell me about it."

"The telepath," he said. "The D'neeran child. She barged into the strategy meeting today. Fleming was wild. The *Endeavor* is leaving her behind, Andrella, behind and all alone. We might have an advantage in the game that Species X does not suspect. She seems to believe she has sensed something frightening about them. I don't know how much credence to give it. She said perhaps she can come up with more, if she is alone."

"You sound," Murphy said, "as if you're putting her out to be a sort of gauge of what there might be to fear."

"She could be making it all up, of course," he said calmly.

"Probably," al-Nimeury said. He got up and came into the dim light, a square and solid man compacted of darkness. "You know what I think about the whole damn thing," he said to Jameson.

"Yes," Jameson said. "It's new, so it's inadvisable."

"You don't know what the hell's out there. You've got two hundred human beings out there with their throats wide open to anything that wants to cut 'em. I liked Katherine's proposal better, but no, you had to have it go out unarmed. Bring 'em home, Starr. Before it's too late."

Jameson said, " 'Here be dragons.' "

"What?"

"Look at the old Earthly seafaring maps, Muammed. That's what they used to write in the blank spaces."

"As I recall," Murphy said, "there were some dragons."

"Starr?" Henriette said from the edge of the terrace. She cradled a tank-nurtured Kit in her arms. It was soft and round and playful and innocent, and it would never mature sexually or grow into a cat. It purred loudly. Henriette said, "Can I have some of these?"

"I'll get you as many as you want," Jameson said, "provided you promise never, never, never to bring one to my house. It's time to go, Henry."

"Past time," Murphy said.

But at the last minute she held Jameson back with a hand

on his arm. His head was silhouetted against stars; she could barely see his face. "Is there really a danger?" she asked.

"You know the theory," he said. "Interstellar travel implies a level of technological achievement that makes it cheaper to manufacture wealth than to seek it through aggression. Likewise it implies a structure of rationality transcending aggression for ideological motives. Certainly F'thal has fit the theory perfectly."

"Then does it matter what the D'neeran girl thinks?"

He shrugged. "What do you think of Henriette?" he said.

"She's lovely. But—my dear Starr, what do you talk to her about?"

"Who talks? Now if you and I. . . ."

He did not finish the sentence but smiled at her, teasing. They had been friends for years.

"You know I wouldn't have you. Good night," she said.

She watched him leave with Henriette and went to bed, scooping up a comforting and undemanding Kit on the way.

The first thing Hanna discovered was not about aliens but about herself.

She missed *Endeavor*'s crew.

She was thousands of kilometers from the ship when it Jumped, and psychologically so separated from it that its vastly greater distance from her after the transit was of little importance. That was not a matter, as Jameson had put it, of proximity; it happened because she had begun detaching herself as soon as *Endeavor* released the shuttle she piloted. She had gone about *Endeavor* with a kind of low-grade awareness operating at all times, as naturally as sight and hearing, because that was the way she lived. But it could be shut off, as it was now. She would not use it again in any degree until she sought a specific entity.

The *Endeavor* made its Jump at oh-three-hundred Standard hours, which Hanna thought of vaguely as pre-dawn. By that time she had mastered the shuttle. It was a simple-minded machine, designed to ferry cargo or, as a lifeboat, provide life support and nothing more for twenty to fifty people for only a few days. It was bare of luxuries. It offered no entertainment. Its only sophisticated features were the antigravity plant which let it make planetary landings and provided Earth-normal gravity, and its Inspace communications facility.

Hanna found that Ludo Brown was assigned to monitor her. Just before the Jump she said, "Don't let the captain forget to set up relays if you go too far away."

Brown laughed at her. "He won't forget. If he does, Tamara won't."

"Are you going to come back here before the second Jump?"

"We don't know yet. It doesn't matter, does it? It wouldn't take long to get back."

Hanna knew a course could be retraced very quickly in deep space. *Endeavor,* having taken four months to come this far, could get home in a few days. Anyone from human space could reach them, now, as quickly—if there was anything worth coming out here for. But her new and unaccustomed isolation weighed on her heavily.

Brown checked with her again after the Jump, and then left her alone for an hour.

Without his voice there was no sound except the whisper of the shuttle's systems. There was nothing to look at but its no-nonsense gray fittings. The standardized color-coding of its displays shone without change when the lump of matter and energy that was *Endeavor* had vanished from its sensors.

Hanna sat in the pilot's module and looked about her nervously. There was no point in wasting time—indeed, the less she was out here the better she would like it.

She consulted the shuttle's handbook and discovered that she could not order it to turn off its lights; she had to douse them manually. She did so, and then had to turn them back on to find the switch for dimming the displays. She turned the lights off again.

She sat in the dark and looked at the stars and tried to relax.

She had been alone in deep space before. She had piloted a small freighter, by herself, all the way to Willow—partly because she wanted to see Willow and that was a cheap way to get there, and partly for the experience. The experience had been sheer joy. She had broken no new paths, but the currents of the space-time sea were deceptive, and navigating them had given her pleasure and excitement. Each Jump brought a new view of the universe. The solitude had been not fearful but wonderful. It made her think of her ancestors in humankind's dim morning, piloting organic cockleshells from continent to continent of the mother world in the days before it was mapped, navigating—as she did—by the stars. At times on that voyage she had felt her kinship with them so strongly that her individuality, her self, ceased to matter, and in her divided mind she saw herself only as human and undifferentiated from the species.

It was not a way of self-regarding that D'neera would ever foster. Her efforts to share it had been met with acceptance—but not understanding; and she had ceased to think of it. But she had not forgotten it.

Now she felt no pleasure. She was no far-flung outrider of a species of indomitable explorers, but a single scared being who wished only to retreat to the safety of the herd—for all that it was a herd of just such outriders.

She settled herself as comfortably as she could, and tried to clear her mind as Ling had taught her. This was the first step toward the satya trance of the Adept, wherein body and emotion alike disappeared and the universe took on new guises. But Hanna had not taken that path past its start.

Finally, tentatively, she let herself begin to drift through the field of consciousness that somehow was both inside and outside herself. It was closer kin to Inspace than realspace, its matrix less matter than life. Its essence was unknowable, and only its broadest contours had been sketched; but it was a medium real as air to Hanna and her kind, who used it without fear. Here in peace and solitude she might have touched Tam or Erik or even Iledra without effort, though they were caught in the flux and flow of other concerns and would not know her.

Hanna set the familiar aside, and quested for a shadow and an eye.

There was nothing. Nothing. Nothing.

A sound called her—real sound, made for the ears: Brown's voice.

"Mmff?" she said, emerging from shadow.

"*Endeavor* to Shuttle Five—"

"I'm here. Here," she said, forgetting the proper formula as she broke into the world of speech.

"How you doing?"

"All right. What time is it?"

"Oh-four-thirty. Why?"

"Nothing. That's all right."

She had turned out the lights an hour ago. She had not been asleep, only altogether focused on the ancient sense D'neera had brought to new flower. And telepathy, unconstrained by space, played tricks with time also.

"Anything to report?"

"Nothing."

"All right. I'm signing off for another hour."

"Ludo?"

"Yes?"

"If I don't answer right away, yell at me. I'm concentrating."

"Right."

Silence again.

She was reluctant to let herself go.

Why? It was utterly peaceful. She had sensed no threat. The shuttle's sensors showed nothing, absolutely nothing, near her.

She composed herself to try again. She was irritated with herself, and very tired. Perhaps she had been asleep after all; if she had not been, she would certainly fall asleep this time. But in the interval before sleep she would explore again, delicately, for the thing that might be nothing but the shadow of her own death-fear; and if that were all it had ever been, she would again find nothing.

There was nothing to report at five-thirty, at six-thirty, at seven-thirty.

"I have to get some sleep," she said then to Brown, meaning unbroken sleep.

It got her an interview with an exasperated Erik.

"You can't sleep," he said. "We'll be ready for another Jump by midday."

"How far away are they this time, anyway?" It had not occurred to her to ask before.

"No more than two or three light-weeks away. In clear open space. We can get there in a couple of days."

If, Hanna thought to herself, you drive Navigation like animals. And take unacceptable risks.

"I have to sleep, Erik. I was on boosters for days."

"Aren't you still?"

"I stopped them yesterday. I don't want to take them any more."

He started to swear at her, and stopped himself. The conversation was being recorded.

He said, "If you can't stay awake we might as well call it off. You're not getting anywhere."

There was no video transmission, but she imagined the look of satisfaction on his face. Her desire to rejoin *Endeavor* diminished.

"You could make the second Jump," she said. "How long would you have to be in place before the third?"

"The first approximation is five to seven hours. We're doing only essential observations. Are you suggesting that you stay where you are until then?"

"Why not?"

"We could use you in Navigation. And, uh, I know it must be very restful for you out there, but it's no light matter to maroon a crewman in unknown space."

Hanna smiled for the first time in days. It had not occurred to her to use the experiment to escape the rigors of Navigation. But now that Erik had brought it up, it sounded like a good idea.

"You want to give it enough time, don't you?" she said.

He was silent. He was imagining, she thought, what he would say if Jameson or Thermstrom suggested he had not been sufficiently conscientious.

"All right," he said finally. "But we're collecting you before the third Jump."

Hanna still was smiling when she went to sleep. It was very peaceful out here. There was more tranquility than she had known on *Endeavor* for a long time. Her fears were dissolving in it, and for a bonus she was getting, for a moment, a childish and satisfactory revenge.

She slept, and did not dream.

The change came even before the *Endeavor* made its second transit, but she did not recognize it at once.

She woke with so strong a sense of being watched that before she was fully awake she was looking over her shoulder into darkness.

There can't be anybody there, she thought, but her fingers seeking the light controls trembled with a purely primeval fear of what lurked in the dark.

The lights came on and there was nothing. Gray metal stared back at her, unmoving.

She was ashamed of herself. But she left her seat and looked into the shuttle's bare compartments. She thought of getting into a spacesuit and checking the cargo bay meter by meter, or pressurizing it so it would be accessible to her as long as she was out here.

"There are limits," she said to herself out loud. Nonetheless she examined the bay with video monitors. And then, cursing herself, the exterior of the shuttle. She was, of course, alone.

The exploration had showed her where survival rations were stored. She gnawed a whole-meal pellet, and then another, with the lights on full. She wondered just what the side effects of quitting booster dope were, and whether she ought to be taking something to compensate for them.

Ludo Brown's voice said loudly, "You awake?"

"I'm awake," she said, swallowing crumbs.

"We're about to Jump again."

"What time is it?"

"Fourteen hundred hours. Don't you have a chronometer?"

"I guess so. Somewhere. Why are you still on duty?"

"We all are, dear. Anything happening with you?"

She was not going to say: Yes, I've got scared of the dark.

"Nothing."

"You're more fortunate than the rest of us. It's a little trickier out here than we thought. Captain says to tell you you've got maybe twelve more hours. He says don't sleep anymore."

"Damn right I won't."

"What was that?"

"Never mind."

She was busy with Brown for a little while after the Jump, making sure her communication with *Endeavor* remained intact. Then the silence closed in again.

She was overfull, cramped, and restless. She prowled the stark control module. The sense of not-aloneness still was with her. If it represented an alien touch, surely she would have dreamed; this must be a product of something else, most likely the treacherous stimdope. There was no point in seeking further for aliens, because there were no aliens there. And she did not want to find them anyway.

But what if they were there?

She dropped into the pilot's seat and stared uncertainly at the oblong patch of space the port showed her. She had an unaccustomed sense of duty shirked.

She could hear herself say to Iledra: I was frightened, and so I stopped trying.

She pictured Iledra explaining that to Jameson, without whom she would not have been on the *Endeavor*. Without whom, for that matter—

Whose decision had it been to set aside official policy and tell D'neera's magistrates where to find the Nestorian attackers? Who had ordered the Interworld Fleet to stand by?

The same man, possibly, who had given her this precious chance; probably against all advice.

"I've got to do it," she said, and made a face at no one.

She turned out the lights again, and closed her eyes.

The aftermath of stimdope vibrated in her veins, but now she was watchful and alert. This time there was no possibility of sleep. She thought of seeking the shadow again, and on an impulse rejected the idea and concentrated instead on her own wariness. If she was really being watched, there must be a watcher.

Slowly, slowly, silence deepened. Here was the kernel of her watchfulness. She closed round it coldly. And here was a thread which she followed out, out, timelessly into a deeper void.

Into the silence fell a single whisper:

Wait. Wait for Us. . . .

Her concentration broke. She straightened, stiff and gasping. She was halfway across the module before she knew she was running away.

She turned and came back as fast, fumbled for the key that would call *Endeavor*, and stopped just before she touched it.

What the hell was she going to tell them, anyway? That her palms were damp, her heart thudding—and that was all? That she had tasted strangeness, and learned nothing?

She wiped her hands on her coveralls and sat down again. Blindly, urgently, because she had to do it, she tried to recapture her sense of the touch.

Its shape was too foreign to remember.

It fit nothing in her experience; she had not assimilated it; but it had left a trace.

She found herself hunched over as if in pain. Yet no part of her hurt.

The stars were mist against the black of in-between. She remembered nothing of the touch except a pattern of darkness and light. She closed her eyes to see it better and it coalesced into a picture: dark islands that rose from eternal waters.

She was sure of it, and sure also that it had no referent in water and earth. It did not mean the beings were island-dwellers. It had to do with time; time and waiting.

It was not enough. Not nearly enough.

She had to do it right from the beginning.

She composed herself to try again. The air was chilly against her wet skin. She did not want to close her eyes and shut out the starlight. She did it anyway, and was immobilized. She thought in circles round the act of will she had to perform, and could not undertake it.

Yet after a long time—when her breathing had eased and the sweat dried on her skin and her heartbeat dropped to a normal pace—something she almost recognized stirred within her.

It was not curiosity, nor duty. It was darker than either, seductive, unknown. Half in trance she reached for it, and flinched away.

She could not examine it closely. But she let it draw her imperceptibly outward.

There were no whispers. There was only, for eternity, the dark.

A spark of light appeared. It was born of a single photon, and expanded.

It was an eye: the eye of a dream.

Her body vanished. She hung before the eye in a place without form. It *knew* her: personally, individually, malignantly.

She could escape to her body, to the shuttle, to *Endeavor*. With all her will she forced herself to stay an instant, and reflected in the eye she saw: serene hearthfires burning trapped living flesh, a glittering detection device become a flying forked spear, the mad wriggle of a severed serpent which was herself, lost barren unlighted worlds tumbling anchorless, the watery lunge of a streamlined shape with a thousand teeth—

Straight at her.

She was pawing at the communications key, limp and choking in the dark. She never knew what she said to Ludo Brown, nor how long it took them to come for her. Later she remembered that she had not taken her eyes off the mass sensor till blessed *Endeavor* appeared; and that they did not believe her when she said it had changed once before.

CHAPTER V

"Take a look at that," Erik said. He pushed a display module at Hanna.

Hanna looked. The central data column, stripped of accessory notations, showed average mass readings over a period of some hours. There was a bulge toward the end of it.

"Is that from the shuttle?" she asked.

"Uh-huh."

The bulge had to be *Endeavor*. She lifted her hands helplessly and said, "So I dreamed it."

He came around the table and stood behind her. He reached over her shoulder and made an adjustment, and the figures flickered and changed.

"This is the last ten minutes," he said.

Now there were two bulges, the first much smaller than the second.

Hanna shivered suddenly. "So there was somebody there."

"There was. And you missed a chance of contact by yelling for help."

He was profoundly disgusted. Hanna opened her mouth to answer, and shut it again. There was nothing she could say. It was possible that he was right.

Erik turned away and went back to his place. The table in Briefing Room Two was littered with coffee mugs and reference printouts. Everyone who had anything to do with direct contact procedures had been in here in the last few hours, questioning Hanna. She had not been able to satisfy any of them.

Hanna said suddenly, "When did you get this breakdown?"

Erik shrugged. "A long time ago. Half an hour after you came on board, maybe."

"You let me go on thinking I must have imagined that reading?"

"What difference did it make?"

"It makes a lot of difference to me! I wondered if, if I couldn't trust my own eyes, what else could I trust?"

"Not much," he said. "You didn't get one goddam useful fact. Just a bunch of space-happy hallucinations. They were coming to talk to you and you panicked."

"You don't know they were coming to talk to me. They disappeared—" She looked at the mass readings again, to be sure. "They disappeared before you came into realspace. There," she said, pointing.

"I'm going by what you said yourself. You thought they were coming to you."

"Yes," she said, remembering the lunge of the hungry fish-thing and her mad obsession with the sensors until *Endeavor* came.

"That's the only thing you said that made any sense."

He stared past her. His mouth was set, but he was no longer particularly angry. Hanna had felt his anger die through the hours of debriefing, and it was a relief to her, although she knew the reason. Erik was convinced that he had won whatever battle he thought he was fighting. He thought her too incompetent to threaten his version of the way things ought to be. She had proven herself a failure, and proven him right. Nothing about her could engage his emotions very strongly now.

That was not true of Marte Koster, who had gotten more furious as time went on. Hanna said, "Did you tell Marte about this?"

"Sure."

"No wonder she was so mad."

Erik said indifferently, "You might as well get some rest."

After a minute Hanna got up. Her muscles ached. She was in fact very tired. She also felt, in some way she could not define, injured.

She said, "What are you going to do now?"

"I'm not sure yet. Plant an unmanned beacon and go on to the new locality, probably. Depends on what they say Earthside."

Hanna looked down at her hands. "I could go out again," she said.

"No. Nobody's going to try that again. Don't ask me why. Not my decision."

She felt a surge of relief—and on its heels, taking her by surprise, disappointment.

She started to leave without saying anything, and then turned back and said, "When do you want me back in Navigation?"

"You won't have to worry about Navigation anymore."

She said uncertainly, "What does that mean?"

"You're going home. Very quietly. Just as soon as I can get transport out here for you."

"But—but what about my research?"

He finally looked at her. He said, "You're wasting your time anyway. Who's going to take you seriously after the junk you came up with out there?"

"It wasn't junk! I don't know what it meant, but it was meaningful!"

"There's enough computer power working on it to run half the Fleet. If it meant anything we'll find out. Go to bed."

"Whose decision was it to get rid of me? I want to talk to him."

"It's mine. Don't waste your time talking. Get out of here. That's an order."

She got out.

Jameson did not speak of Hanna's adventure to anyone outside the *Endeavor* Project until the day after it happened, the last thing he wanted being to suggest that he was alarmed. He had been in his office in the early dawn, staring at the analysis of the girl's report while the mists rose off the gray river and the red sun, despite the early hour, promised a day of sweltering heat. The commissioners of the Polity met each morning, and he did not mention the *Endeavor* at all until the end of the meeting. He showed the analysis to his colleagues and was pleased when they looked at the masses of question marks, logical branchings and variant interpretations, and shook their heads—all except Katherine Petrov. Petrov was a very old woman, so old that A.S. no longer could give her the appearance of youth; but she was a very alert old woman. She looked around with bright eyes and said that the whole scenario was terrifying.

"Not really, Kate," Jameson said.

"How can you say that! Spears and cut-up snakes and burnt sacrifices! Do you know what it reminds me of? An evil myth system, the old planting sacrifices—I don't suppose this girl's a virgin, is she?"

Peter Struzik spluttered. Struzik represented Earth along with Petrov, under the old rules that gave the mother world two seats on the commission; but he was its president and did not vote, and could afford to find humor in situations that drove the others to frenzy. Petrov looked at him suspiciously and said, "What's funny now?"

"She's D'neeran," Struzik said. "Know the D'neeran definition of a virgin?" He leaned forward, grinning. "A kid too young to know which sex it is. Then it decides it doesn't matter anyway and goes after anything that moves."

Petrov snorted, but only to hide a snicker. Jameson disregarded the exchange and said, "That's just what I mean, Kate. You looked at this data and immediately patterned it in human terms. Lady Hanna is human too. The familiar elements you see are part of her background as well as yours. She did her own patterning here."

"Perhaps," Andrella Murphy remarked, "Species X was the origin of the myths."

She smiled pleasantly at Jameson. Murphy when bored was inclined to flights of fancy and outrageous speculation. Jameson wished he were a telepath himself, so that he could object to her in silence that he did not want any such ideas put into the others' heads.

He said, "Am I meant to take that seriously, Andrella?"

"I suppose not," she admitted. "But D'neera was cut off from us for so long—"

"Never completely," Jameson said, and Petrov said, unexpectedly supporting him, "That wouldn't matter. The continuity of human culture is so strong a few hundred years wouldn't matter. Not even a few thousand when you're talking about archetypes. The images that come down from before the dawn don't die. They're so embedded in all our cultures, they're nearly inborn."

Murphy looked rather sadly at the analysis and said, "So what looks like the source of a primal image . . ."

"Is only another image," Jameson said. "This is no literal rendering of the content of an alien mind. You're looking at Lady Hanna's creation."

"I wouldn't like to meet her on a dark night, then."

"Oh," Jameson said, "I don't suppose she's as bad as all that. It's not surprising the images she formed are frightening. She told me only hours before the contact that the quality of alienness, so to speak, frightens her. I think she would agree that she inevitably transformed the beings' thoughts in the act of perceiving them. It's impossible to disentangle a purely alien element from this combination."

al-Nimeury said, "What good is it, then?"

Jameson said regretfully, "Not much, I'm afraid. Not immediately. But it was communication, of a sort. It was governed by natural laws. After a few more such instances, perhaps we will begin to understand what those laws are, and form a theory that will make telepaths a useful addition to *Endeavor* in the future."

They were all beginning to look bored now. Struzik muttered, "This would make a pretty mess if the public got hold of it."

"Irrelevant, as long as Alpha and Beta remain secret."

al-Nimeury said suddenly, "I want to bring that up again. You came out to Co-op and talked the assemblymen into going along with this and nobody knows what's going on. Co-op's paying its share and they've got a right to know what happens—"

They all began talking at once, except for Murphy, who watched Jameson closely. Arthur Feng was not in the room but on Colony One. His head and shoulders seemed to hang in the air at the foot of the table; there was something wrong at his end, and through the apparition the wall of the room was visible. Jameson saw with satisfaction that something was wrong with the sound now too, and though the wraith's lips moved, nothing it said was audible.

Jameson let the others talk themselves into keeping the matter under seal. They subsided at last, more or less in agreement. Struzik said, "What if Beta comes to nothing and this is all the contact there is, Jamie? What will you do then?"

"I don't know," Jameson said. "Don't call me that, Peter. If Species X misses *Endeavor* again—and I think that may happen—I'll go out there to talk with Fleming and Koster."

Petrov said, "Why in heaven's name go all the way out there?"

"Review the troops, boost morale, that sort of thing."

Struzik said pettishly, "Couldn't you just do it by holo?"

"I'd be back in time for the budget hearings, Peter. Weren't you telling me only last week that personal contact is of utmost importance?"

"Is that new girl of yours going?"

"Maybe," he said with the trace of a smile.

"I thought so. You just want a few days off. I guarantee I'll make your life miserable. I'll call you a dozen times a day."

Jameson submitted to the teasing good-naturedly. He could afford to. He had set out to undercut the impact of Hanna ril-Koroth's report without entirely discounting her value, and succeeded. It was no small accomplishment in this group, and although they were predisposed to pay little attention to a D'neeran, he could not have done it so easily if Petrov had not, by chance, given him a custom-made opening.

At that, he did not think Andrella Murphy believed a word of it; she knew him too well.

Hanna made up her mind to risk smuggling out the data she wanted. She would record everything on a wafer the size of her thumbnail, and swallow it as she left; but so much of it was classified that she thought there was a good chance Erik would anticipate her, and she would be caught.

Therefore she worked frantically to salvage what she could from the wreck her venture on *Endeavor* had become. With no idea how long she would be on the ship, she plunged into its archives and worked with an energy that came not from stimulants but from desperation. She slept in snatches, fully clothed, and forgot to eat except when Tamara brought her food. The synthesis she had envisioned since one luminous moment when she fully understood the Hierarchus was tantalizingly close. An eyes-only report on F'thalian linguistics promised a foundation for describing a theory of separate but contiguous realities, and as she read it her notes on F'thalian thought, side-by-side with the Polity report, fell finally into place. The contradictions between true-human linguistic analysis and her perceptions were illusory; the two were complementary, paired but distinct outlines of the same structure, each lacking salient features. The reasons for omissions that had puzzled the analysts were clear, and so was the reason for F'thal's clear and baffling boredom with human beings. In the giddy swirl of F'thalian perception, interactions were substantial as material objects. Pan-F'thalian did not describe "things," only systems and an infinity of subsystems. F'thal had no word for "aliens" because humans were only a minor division of the great subsystems of life. There was nothing special about beings from other stars.

Hanna did not have to compare her memories of the Hierarchus with her experience on Shuttle Five to know that was not the attitude of Species X, though Tamara—her only contact with the life of *Endeavor* now—told her the aliens were invisible or absent from the second location they had selected. No dreams haunted Hanna. No one came near to ask what really had happened to her out there, and her report seemed to have sunk into silence and left no trace. But she thought of it anyway, the pain and the fear and the strangeness, whenever she lifted her tired eyes from her work or stretched out for a minimal nap; and she came to certain meager conclusions which she did not share with anyone—the persons around her having, it seemed, lost interest in anything she might tell them.

She worried a little about their insistence on ignorance, although in fact there was nothing she could add that would clarify her original impressions. She worried a little also when Tamara told her some two weeks after the incident that Starr Jameson was expected a few days hence, and that Hanna, presumably, would return to human space when he did. Hanna said acidly that the return trip should be entertaining; but she remembered with discomfort her sense of being in the man's debt. It occurred to her that the last year of her life, viewed from a certain perspective, bore in abstract the imprint of his hand. It was an unpleasant thought, and she kept it at a distance as her concentration centered more and more strongly, to the exclusion of all else, on her work. Undistracted now that she had no other duties, she saw solutions to puzzles that had seemed insoluble. She left the thicket of references and drew more heavily on her own experience of F'thal and Girritt, her own observations of the Primitives. The underlying structure of her thought crystallized and she wrote rapidly and confidently, sure of her ground. No doubt no one would read what she wrote, but it was truth. She was constructing a monument whose existence was testimony to the validity of its thesis, for it was founded on empirical data—but the data did not exist in true-human reality. She felt, when she thought of the grand futility of her effort, the exaltation she had felt when the *Clara* began moving toward its end, and she gave herself over to it. She did not forget Jameson, but the apprehension retreated to one small corner of her mind where she looked at it from time to time in a detached sort of way. In the long run, she thought, it did not matter. In the long run nothing mattered except what she was doing.

No one bothered to tell her when Jameson arrived, or that he wished to see her. The door sounded several times before she heard it through a daze that was half obsession, half exhaustion, and then she thought it was Tam.

"C'mon in," she said automatically, and not until he came to her side did she look up and see who it was.

Unprepared for the apparition, she only stared and said, "Oh."

She had to look up a long way to see his face. She recognized him at once, but familiarity with his image had not prepared her for his height, nor for the really shocking sense that he was in charge here—that he would be in charge wherever he was. Her experience with true-human authority was limited to Erik, and what she sensed in Jameson was not the same thing at all; and it held her silent and round-eyed.

Jameson looked from her face to the passage she was working on. He said without formality or introduction, "I've seen some of what you're doing. Captain Fleming pulled it out of the main data bank. I'd like to see the rest."

Hanna moved finally—to look past him and see what entourage he had brought. The door to her room had shut and no one else was there. Questions chased one another through her head. She opened her mouth to ask them and found herself too tired. It didn't matter. She did not think she could refuse his request even if there were reason to refuse. Weariness and shock made her movements uncertain. She pawed through a litter of printouts for a display module, plugged it into her terminal, and cued it for a current draft. When she turned to hand it to him she caught him eyeing her with something that might have been surprise.

She said, "Yes?" but he said only, "May I have the chair?"

"Oh. Yes. Of course."

She retreated to her bunk, which was as deep in annotated paper as the rest of the room. She had to move some of it before she could sit down, and under some of the scraps she found the remains of a sandwich. It occurred to her rather belatedly that Jameson probably was not used to such settings.

He spent a long time reading. Hanna set herself to watch him, but in the long unbroken silence she drifted irresistibly toward sleep. So much more work to do and she had to have some of those references, she could not emphatically criticize a structure of theory and double it in a new direction without references, lots of references, footnotes, oh Lord . . . Annual Report 2832, The Committee on Alien Relations, Starr Jameson, Commissioner-Heartworld, Chairman. The Coordinating Commission had not had much power five hundred years ago. Now, in theory, three of the five voting members could override the unanimous will of all the populations of the Polity. For a while. Until they were pulled and more amenable replacements appointed. And how did it work anyway? Why did she not know more about history? But on D'neera you could study what you wanted and she had never cared about history or art either, only fighting and aliens. And maybe gardening, sometimes, but the millefleurs got into everything. . . .

Hanna yawned and fell sound asleep.

His voice woke her. It was a very deep voice, and she liked it. The inappropriate thought woke her further and she sat up straight, shaking her head. He was not talking to her. He was speaking to someone on the ship's intercom, asking for coffee and spirits.

He turned to look at her directly and Hanna stiffened, suddenly wide awake and unsure of herself. His eyes were cold, and she felt herself being measured as no one had measured her before, not even Iledra. Jameson was a presence, utterly sure of his power and his right to judge her, and her response to this new thing was blank astonishment.

He said without ceremony, "How did you know this?"

"Know what?" she said stupidly. She was staring at him again. His face was too interesting to be ugly, with strong bones and unexpected hollows. She liked that, too.

He leveled a long forefinger at the wallscreen, which still

showed the passage she had been writing when he came in. It said:

"Most observers of Primitive B, citing winged-flight mass limitations as a curb on braincase development, have assumed this rudimentary culture will stagnate until environmental change forces it to evolutionary regression or extinction. However, the acknowledged complexity of B nestbuilding activity, until now wrongly attributed exclusively to instinct, illustrates the prevalence of logical operations in everyday life. For example, the pitch of the nests' woven-branch 'roofs' is determined not only by an explicit projection of expected severity of rainstorms in a given area, but also by individual preference for the fruit of certain vines which flourish best on more nearly vertical surfaces . . ."

Hanna gathered her scattered thoughts and said, "I 'heard' them. I was there when the flock I was studying was settling in for a nesting season. 'I think I will make it higher and there will be more to eat.' "

Jameson blinked. "That's rudimentary agriculture." he said.

"I was coming to that."

They regarded each other in silence for a moment. Then he said, "So you were frightened after all."

"What?" She thought she had misheard him.

"You were frightened when you undertook the experiment you yourself suggested. Why?"

"Why?" She shifted uneasily. This was not a question that had occurred to her. She drew up her knees and curled her arms around them protectively. She said, "It was what you said, I suppose. That they were strange."

"Was it? Was that the only reason?"

"Why—I don't know. I don't know. You said that yourself."

"I wasn't there. You were."

It was hard to look away from his cold gaze. Erik had looked at her like this sometimes, and only irritated her. Now a mountain might have been addressing her, compelling her to answer.

She was not used to finding true-humans impressive. Jameson must have thought she was frightened, because he said with a hint of exasperation, "I'm not going to eat you, you know. Just answer my questions as accurately as you can."

"Yes," she said after a minute, but she saw there was no

softening in his eyes. She looked at him very steadily, wondering what he was about.

He said, "I'm thoroughly familiar with your report. The imagery was all visual?"

"All. Yes."

"And frightening."

"Yes."

"It was anthropomorphic to an extreme degree. How much of it did you yourself create?"

Hanna had not asked herself that either. She pushed nervously at her hair and said, "I might have—I might have 'created,' as you call it, all of the images. But they were correlates of—of thoughts that weren't mine. That's how it works."

She could not keep away from his eyes very long. They were sometimes gray, sometimes green; she found them disconcerting.

He said, "Are you quite, quite sure of that?"

She was suddenly angry, for no reason. "Yes! Yes, I'm sure! I've had enough experience with F'thalians, with Girrians, to know that, that when something like that comes up it's a symbol for something that's really there!"

"And of what precisely are they symbols?"

She said unwillingly, "I pinned some of them down, as far as you can pin something like that down. They were impressions of—of a whole long stretch of time, and patience. And hunting."

"The spear?" he said quickly.

"Yes. But not hunting *with* it. It changed from something else, you know. It wasn't a real spear. It was all symbols I saw. It was—you read that I saw a snake?"

"I read that it was a living portion of a snake, and that you identified it with yourself."

"Yes. Well. It's not that they thought I was a snake, you see. It was a perception of me as . . . incomplete. Alive but divided."

"You did not say that in your report."

"I didn't understand it until later. That's all. Hunting and patience and that image of me. I haven't been able to think of anything else."

"I see," he said.

He leaned back in the chair and she jumped, the movement

taking her by surprise. He looked past her, frowning a little. She felt herself, for the moment, dismissed.

It struck her that of all the strange events of her life, strange as any was to have this man sitting in her tiny cabin, discussing a first contact in her terms.

Her terms. It came to her forcibly that she was being taken seriously after all: somewhere. You could not be taken much more seriously than this. But somebody had not wanted her to know it; somebody had not even wanted Erik to know it.

Jameson said presently, still looking at something else, "You still think they are telepaths."

"Yes. Oh, yes."

"You must have been as strange to them as they were to you. Might that account for the rather ominous nature of the images?"

"I suppose it might—no. Wait."

She bowed her head and stared at the floor. Textured matting. Jameson's elegant boot. She did not want to remember. She shut her eyes and called to memory the fabric of an instant, warp and woof, presence and absence interwoven. Surely the aliens had felt her surprise and apprehension; but she had felt no such thing from them.

More. More. The absence of surprise had been so complete as to be a tangible thing; but so embedded was it in the shape of the gestalt that she had not even identified it, until now, as an entity.

"They knew me," she said softly. "Like F'thalians who've met us before. They knew me for a human being."

Jameson said flatly, "That's impossible," but Hanna was caught in recollection. She drifted among images, examining them one by one and all at once for a connection that was not a connection.

"Lost," she said dreamily. "Lost and divided. Lost planets, that was it. Lost worlds, found again—"

Jameson said very sharply, "What was that?"

"Hmm?" She looked up, open and unguarded and pleased with herself. But Jameson leaned forward intently. Hanna's pleasure passed into alarm.

Jameson said urgently, "Are you certain of that?"

"Yes. Yes! Divided—lost worlds—lost worlds? Where have I heard that before?"

She put her hands to her head, which had begun to ache.

"Legend," he said. He looked at her with open curiosity.

She could not keep up with him. She said, "What legend?"

"The legend of the Lost Worlds, from the time of the Explosion. You know the history of the Explosion?"

"I only know the name, and that it was the, the great period of colonization."

"Umm-hmm." His eyes were still on her, but he was seeing something else again, something far away and long ago.

"It began seven hundred years ago," he said, and she tilted her head, caught in the deep quiet voice. "No one knows how many hundreds of millions of human beings left the Earth and its moon in the space of some three hundred years, nor how many vessels carried them. The ships that went officially to Colony One are accounted for; but there were many that were not official, and some that were desperate, and surely many did not reach their destination. The East threw its poor and dissenting away in the wastes of Co-op, till Co-op broke free. Its records never were good. . . . The private ventures were uncounted, ship after ship of men and women seeking better lives, freedom, riches, the fulfillment of dreams admirable or reprehensible. . . . It was the greatest fleet the human race has seen, and its full extent was never known. Some ships are known to have disappeared. How many others vanished? Often colonists were stripped of their goods and marooned—or simply killed. Some were found later, or their bones. Many were not. . . . You should know this. Everyone should know it."

Hanna found herself breathless. For a moment she had stood high above a tapestry of history, watching the sweep and scope of it. She wrenched herself into the present, shocked and resentful of the power that could so easily impose its vision. And she did not like being told what she should know.

She said, struggling for objectivity, "It's only a possibility. Though when you put it together with the—the quality of the images—"

She stopped short, not liking the implications. Jameson's face gave nothing away, but she knew he was thinking precisely the same thing.

In the sudden silence the door chattered at them. Hanna went to it, unthinking. She could not focus on the meaning of prior knowledge and the hunt. Her head was full of what she did know of the Explosion: Constanza Bassanio shaven-headed, pregnant and scarred, ransomed from death in a Lunar stockade just before the last ship left for the green promise of D'neera under Clara Mendoza's command. "Dreams admirable or reprehensible" . . . the outcasts' dream had only been to stay alive. . . .

A serving robot drifted through the door and wavered without orders to a landing at Jameson's feet. After a minute Hanna, compelled by courtesy, settled herself cross-legged beside it. She said reluctantly, "Coffee?"

"The coffee's for you." He leaned over and picked up a decanter and looked at the contents with distaste.

She thought of Heartworld and ancient wealth. She said, "I guess they couldn't find any Arrenswood whiskey."

"I certainly hope not. Not paid for with public funds. I'll have coffee after all, I think."

She went silently through the ritual of serving, obscurely astonished at the scene. Was Jameson thinking of Species X? His face told her nothing. She made no effort to probe his thought or feelings—he might, she thought, recognize the nearly palpable impact of telepathy for what it was—but she was wide open for anything that might escape him. Some true-humans, like Koster, were full-time explosions of emotion, natural broadcasters who made the air around them crackle.

But Jameson was as self-contained as any true-human she had ever met. There were not even any physical cues to help her guess what he was thinking. He did not fidget, he did not engage in nervous mannerisms, and every movement was precisely controlled.

Hanna, to her surprise, began to relax. His stillness was comforting, after the noisy activity of her own thoughts and the tension that accompanied all her days here. Jameson might have been alone, for all the attention he paid her now. But she could not doubt his intelligence or alertness; and she thought again of outriders and pioneers, and remembered a thing she had known but not examined—that Starr Jameson was the force behind the whole *Endeavor* Project, and the vessel and its crew and their work were the reflection of his will.

He said without prelude, very quietly, "You will not speak

of this conversation to anyone. Not even Captain Fleming or Dr. Koster."

She said with casual curiosity, "Why not?"

"Because everything you have said is unsubstantiated."

She was startled. "I thought you believed me!"

"The question of belief does not arise." He looked at her with, she thought, a trace of something new in the sea-colored eyes. Speculation?

She shook her head. He said, "Is it so difficult to promise silence?"

"Yes," she said. "As a matter of fact, yes. You can't keep secrets very long on D'neera even if you want to. People guess. Bits of data creep into overt content. The harder you try to keep a secret the quicker you give it away. I can't help it. You seem to know more about telepathy than most people. I thought you would know that."

"I do," he said. "That is why you are not going home."

"I'm not?" Hanna said, and was unprepared for the wave of desolation that poured over her. She must have projected some of it because Jameson made a sharp, half-protesting gesture. Hanna scarcely noticed, absorbed in the surprising knowledge that for all her anxiety to finish her work, deep inside she had heard, all along, a glad song: "Home . . . soon!" In the maze of Standard dating she had not lost sight of her native seasons. First snowfall was due in Koroth. The D'neeran year was longer than Earth's, and the seasons of Koroth were long and distinct. Soon fantasies of ice would rise in the city: palaces, statues, crystal vegetation, slides and labyrinths elaborated as winter darkened. In sunlight it was a city of flashing mirrors. The fires of Sunreturn . . . she could be home for Sunreturn. . . .

Jameson said something and she answered absently, "Yes?"

"I said: Have you thought of entering your work for a Goodhaven award?"

"Hmm?"

He said patiently, "The Goodhaven Academy's annual competition. You are familiar with it?"

"Yes. Of course." She came back reluctantly. "I've read a lot of Academy publications. They do good work, with F'thal at least. Not the kind of work I do."

"Then perhaps it's time you showed them something new."

"Me?" What he had said about the Academy's prestigious

award began to sink in. She sat back on her heels and stared at him. She said, "Wait a minute. They wouldn't give it to a D'neeran. Especially not me! I'm saying D'neerans can do exopsychology better than anybody else. And it's true. I've found out things, just by being a telepath, nobody ever found out before. But they won't want to hear that, Commissioner!"

He said inexorably, "You are creating a completely original work of great potential value. You should be finished with it by the deadline for the next competition. Are you afraid to try?"

If he meant to sting her with insult, it did not work. She was too absorbed in the new idea to become angry. She had never thought of submitting her work to the Academy. The scholarship structure of true-human society was so far outside her frame of reference that she might as well have thought of competing in a F'thalian courtship drama.

But what it could mean to be a member of the Academy! —not for herself alone, but as a means of making it easier for other D'neerans than it had been for her to gain access to data and persons and places—

She felt Jameson watching her very closely. She looked up and opened her mouth to protest that it was impossible. But he said, "I don't dispose of the prize, but I do have friends in the Academy. Your work would have to stand on its own merits; but if there is a question of injustice, I think I can see to it the award is fairly given."

Some seconds passed while she turned his words over, wondering what they meant. She really did not know at once. It was hard to follow him in her weariness. He had said nothing expected or predictable since walking into her room. If he was trying to keep her unbalanced, she was easy prey. She knew little of true-human networks of influence and dimly, trying to understand, she opened herself a little, a little, a very little more, and added it to the slightest intrusiveness, the barest touch of query, just to see what he meant—

She gaped at him.

He had taken from her burst of homesickness a conviction that she wanted to leave the *Endeavor*.

He had offered her a bribe to stay.

He knew instantly what she had done. She saw it in his face in the moment of engagement, and sensed—not anger nor guilt nor apprehension, but an intense curiosity so at odds with the circumstance that she was unbalanced even more.

She got up slowly. She could not think of anything to say, and stared down at him. Light glinted off a scattering of silver in his hair. The gray-green eyes were remote. No curiosity showed in them, nor anything else.

He said, surprising her again, "Aren't you angry?"

"Angry?" She was only bewildered.

"That is supposed to be the appropriate reaction."

"Is it?" She shook her head in confusion. "I only want to know why. Why is it so important that I not talk of this?"

"You needn't be concerned about that," he said.

"But I *am,*" she said stubbornly.

"It is important for you," he said. "Believe me, it is important for you."

A bare hint of threat hung between them. She might have heard it in his voice or sensed it elsewise. She said, thinking it through with great effort, "You mean because I won't get the prize if I break silence?"

"More than that."

It only confused her more. She shook her head again and said, "I don't know what you mean."

He folded his hands in his lap, an unexpectedly prim gesture. He said, "You're in an extremely ambivalent position, you know."

She looked at him helplessly. She did not have the slightest idea what he was talking about.

"You stand at a branching of the way for D'neera," he said, calmly as if he were commenting on the weather. "On the one hand this work of yours—what do you call it, by the way?"

"Uh—'Sentience,' " she said, startled into speech.

His face showed, for the first time, a flicker of amusement. "A little arrogant, don't you think? Never mind. It is brilliant. It is a foundation, certainly, for arguments in favor of a position I have held for some time—not a popular position: that D'neera is the ideal interface between the human race and alien intelligences. The *Endeavor* is funded for a mission of three Standard years. I don't intend to see the project end in three years' time. It will go on, and on, and on—through our lifetimes and into the future. This vessel will be joined by sister ships. Within our lifetimes, if we are fortunate, we will see contact with a thing that logically must exist on some scale—a super-network of star-traveling species. We might then begin to call ourselves citizens of the universe. . . . Have you ever thought of the part D'neera might play in such a renaissance? You might be our teachers, our translators, our first and most honored ambassadors. But it must begin now, my lady."

He paused, waiting perhaps for her to speak, but she could not utter a word.

He went on, "You are the beginning. An experiment; the first. Being first is a great responsibility, my lady. The arguments against your presence on this voyage were difficult to refute, and indeed you have fulfilled many persons' misgivings. I was told that D'neerans are erratic, promiscuous, unreliable and tinged with cowardice; over-emotional, stubborn, flouters of discipline and, of course, ridiculously communicative. . . . You cannot babble of Lost Worlds to anyone who will listen."

Hanna bit at her fingers and stared at him as if her eyes alone would pierce his skull. Intangible walls of promise and threat closed on her. There was something he was not saying, and everything he did say obscured it. She had guessed something she was not supposed to know, that her silence was important enough to make him offer her a precious gift unasked, and still he skirted the real "why." Another answer hung round his head like smoke. She listened for echoes of the unspoken.

She said slowly, "If I don't tell anybody about this, you and I will be the only ones who know, won't we?"

His face was empty and detached as a mask. He said, "The Coordinating Commission must know, of course. And key persons in the *Endeavor* Project."

"But," she said, answering echoes, "the project personnel report to you, don't they? So they don't matter. You didn't even mention Alien Relations. They won't know unless you tell them. And the commission—you can tell them what you think they ought to know. Any way you want to present it. You can shape how they think—"

She stopped, because he stood up. She had forgotten his height and she looked up, up, into eyes cold and dispassionate as the sea. She felt him put away the hope of deceiving her; he might have pushed away a useless object, but he said only, still calmly, "This is why you frighten us, my lady."

"Because you can't have secrets," she said breathlessly. "But you must have known!"

"In theory," he said thoughtfully. "In theory. I must say I was not prepared to test it myself. . . . I offer you a straightforward bargain, then. I am, as Lady Koroth knows, D'neera's only effective champion in true-human circles of power. This is not an easy thing to be, and I must have your cooperation. In this case I must have your silence. Without it—well. It is your world you risk. Not mine."

"But how can it be so important? Why? Why? Tell me that." Her voice was shaky. "Just tell me and—so I can decide! You would really turn against us? You would do that?"

He did not answer. Perhaps he would not do it. But he could; she felt the potential of his power, so intense and repugnant that she backed away from him involuntarily. She might have been running from rape, revolted. And then she knew that she had projected the sickening image, because she felt in the same instant his shocked disclaimer of any physical interest in her whatsoever.

She stood by her cluttered bunk, breathing hard. She had broken through his icy self-possession, anyway; they stared at each other in mutual outrage, and she knew he felt as violated as herself.

"You don't care," she said. "You don't care about D'neera at all! All that about a renaissance and what we can do—it's all for you, the project is all you! What are you doing? What are you using us for? What are you doing to me?"

She thought she heard him say: *After all, this is a terrible thing*—but he had not said it. He was angry enough now, furious with her. For a moment the sense of physical danger was so strong that she dared not disengage awareness out of fear for her very life.

The threat disappeared suddenly and completely. Hanna found herself in fighting stance, balanced and ready to move. She was ridiculous. She could not recover as quickly as he. Her muscles twitched. She thought: I went too far.

He stood before her silent and still. She felt the re-evaluation going on inside him, astonishing her again. She was dizzy.

She did not know anyone, D'neeran or true-human, who could move on so rapidly and coldly after what had passed.

Presently he said, "Would any D'neeran have done what you just did?"

"No—" She shook her head. The slight movement rocked her. She was close to her limit from strain and exhaustion.

"No? It's you, then? I might have known. . . ."

He pursued a tangential thought.

"What?" she said weakly, trying for the thousandth time to follow him with logic.

"Suicide maneuvers," he said as if she ought to have known. "You do believe in the direct approach, don't you?"

"Do I?" said poor Hanna. Her head thudded unmercifully.

"Umm-hmm . . ." His gaze turned inward. He said very softly, perhaps to himself, "What will you become when youth and luck and brilliance fail you?"

She almost knew what he meant. She did not want to know. She put up her hands and pushed it away. She said, "Just tell me why. Tell me why!"

He came back from wherever he had gone and regarded her, again, dispassionately. He said, "I will tell you this. The future should not be shaped by fear."

She was at such a peak of sensitivity that the tapestry-vision was tangible, obscuring him. Species X was a glowing point of change. Human destiny depended on a choice: advance or retreat.

She said shakily, "If, if they are too frightened of what I have found, they won't, they won't let *Endeavor* go on and there won't be any more *Endeavors*—"

The edges of her vision closed in, and she swayed. He stepped forward quickly and caught her arm. He looked down at her curiously and said, "That's it."

"But—but you could just have told me," she said.

After a minute, to her lasting amazement, he smiled. It was like a light breaking over his face.

"I never thought of that," he said.

Hanna did not hear him. Shadow lay on her sight and *Endeavor* writhed about her, insubstantial, thought not artifact. Dimly she saw it as seed for a new cycle of legend. The day of colonists lost and otherwise was over, having been but the foundation of a greater adventure. She looked at the hand that held her without seeing it, though it was a thing concrete and immovable among the shifting veils of time. Remembered islands soared above an alien sea. She muttered, "I understand now. I understand."

"I think you do. . . . Are you all right?"

"No," Hanna said honestly. She pulled her arm from his grasp and sat down with a thump. The *Endeavor* shivered and solidified. She looked up at Jameson resentfully. Meeting him, she thought, was like running head-on into a whirlwind. If you weren't careful it would take you just where it wanted, and you could not possibly ignore it.

He said, "You can do it, then? You will do it?"

"Stay quiet?" She hesitated. She did not know what she ought to do. Finally she said, cautiously, "For now. Because there's so little to go on. But not if I have—if I have what I think is proof they're hostile to all of us."

"I wouldn't ask that of you. You misunderstand—" Fluency failed him for the first time; she thought in surprise that she had touched him somehow. After a minute he said, "There is no going onward without danger. Not for an individual, and not for the human species. But I have responsibilities."

Hanna wished wearily that he thought plain speaking was one of them. Yet he spoke to her as to an equal.

She said, "You mean that I should trust you?"

He didn't say anything. She did not either. In the course of half an hour they had fallen into a strange and temporary intimacy; but she could not imagine trusting Jameson without direct access to his motives and intent.

He turned away without haste. He was going to leave without another word. She said impulsively, "Commissioner?"

"Hmm?" He looked around, almost smiling; he was very pleased about something.

"Do you trust *me*?"

"D'neeran sincerity is notorious," he said, amused.

"Well. Yes." Hanna pushed at her unkempt hair, tense and mistrustful. A hundred questions danced in her head. She picked one at random. "What if the aliens come back?"

"Do you think they are out here now?"

"No. No, I don't. But I don't think they're going to stop."

"No. We can't keep dancing to their measure, Lady Hanna."

"Meaning—?"

"The *Endeavor*'s voyage will proceed as originally planned. We will see how far the patience you detect extends."

The islands were momentous peaks; but the sea of time was infinite.

"A long way," she said.

"Then perhaps eventually we will have to do something else. Perhaps you will have to do something else."

"Me—?"

"You. You're a beginning, you know," he said, and was gone.

PART 2

CHAPTER VI

Hanna did not talk to Jameson again on that voyage, and the force of his presence and vision diminished.

Nothing happened to test her wobbly commitment. The *Endeavor* crept on, marking a trail through infinity, its progress even slower now because it paused before each Jump to announce a new destination.

No answer came. But the communications equipment sang again and again with the bugs now called, routinely, ambers. The working hypothesis was that they were overflow or feedback from Inspace communications between a ship outside sensor range and an unknown base that might be half the galaxy away; but their content was random, garbled, indecipherable.

There was a little space of hope when a series of robot probes were directed toward the star system that had served as a trigger, at least, for contact. The probes found a life-sustaining, pleasant planet, but it showed no sign of the work of hands or anything like them. Even Marte Koster finally gave up her dream of a super-civilization so energy-efficient as to be indetectable. There was no intelligent life here. Probably there never had been.

Hanna, immersed in "Sentience," ceased to think of Species X. It was background to a life settled into peace, even into contentment. She did her tasks in Navigation, and researched, and wrote, and watched "Sentience" grow under her hands. In her crystalline recollection of the aliens she knew, there was no space for those who insisted on remaining unknown. She felt sometimes a guilty relief at their silence. She did not know if her estimate of Jameson's responsibilities matched his own. If it did not, if events forced her to speak against his wish, he would—

She skipped away from the thought when it came, and also from the whisper that to know such a secret about such a man was power. But maybe not; who would believe her?

Endeavor went on its way, trailing a ghost.

She was slightly more respected after her lengthy interview with Jameson; not much more. Her mates regarded her as a sort of organic radio rig whose perceptions had been as valid, and as useless, as those of the ship's Inspace receptors. Hanna might quarrel with the generalization, but she could not correct it without breaking her promise to Jameson, and therefore let it pass. She never again had the conscious sense of an alien presence, and her nightmares did not return. Sometimes she thought on waking that she remembered dark and shapeless impressions, but they never came clear—not in her unassisted efforts to remember, and not with the help of Peng's skill in hypnosis nor even, with Hanna's reluctant consent, his pharmacopoeia, until she felt that she was becoming as saturated with brain-bending chemicals as the day's true-human fashion dictated.

The only result of these experiments was a greater liking between Hanna and Peng, and they became lovers for a while; until Hanna for no good reason grew bored, and drifted away.

She did not forget Jameson's prediction of what D'neera might become, and she finished "Sentience" with a daring and passionate plea that humankind make use of her people's abilities.

"Each sentient species," said the book which every day took on more life of its own, "exists perceptually, socially, and philosophically in a separate and entirely valid reality that in the last analysis is incomprehensible to us—unless we share their very thoughts. In our dealings with F'thal and Girritt and the two Primitive species we have only made analogs of Outside realities from bits and patches of our own. The models we use therefore are riddled with error and at best incomplete. They have worked, so far. Yet tomorrow or the next day we might meet beings whose comprehension of us, or ours of them, is essential to amity—or even to our survival, or theirs. Humanity would be wise to cultivate its telepathic cousins, who can reach into another being's heart, comprehend him from the inside, prevent dangerous errors of understanding and judgment, and ensure peace as we go on in search of the unimaginable—the same quest that shaped our ancestors, and has shaped us, and ultimately is the shape of humankind."

When she re-read the final phrases she recognized a voice that was not her own. She excised it from the text, but it was not so easy to get it out of her head.

When the work was done she applied for her release from the *Endeavor* Project, leaving to Iledra the task of submitting the book to true-human channels of distribution, and to the Goodhaven Academy. A flurry of messages passed between them. Iledra's were filled with uncharacteristic doubts; the refrain of Hanna's was an equally uncharacteristic "Be quiet and do as I say."

To Iledra's surprise, obstacles in important places evaporated. Hanna could not be surprised by anything of the sort—not since her discovery of an obscure sub-file during her research on Primitive A. It was entirely administrative and ought not to have been there, but there it was: documentation of her application for the visit, a handful of rejections bearing unknown names, and at the end a voice-recorded order to the functionary who had signed the final permit.

The order said: "Approve it." The speaker was listed by Admin's careful identicode system as SHJ.

Hanna wondered if she had been meant to find it.

Near the end of the Standard year she knew she would soon go home, because the *Endeavor* Project officially asked her for a recommendation on one or more D'neerans to succeed her.

She had few candidates to choose from. The D'neeran community of interest in exopsychology was small, and Hanna knew each member of it. She suggested Anja Daru of Sothred and Charl Zeig of Gnerin, and wrote to the two herself—and was informed by a Project Central missive that her correspondence could not be transmitted.

She understood why when she received yet another official communication, this one from Paul Rodrigues, whom she had heard of vaguely as some kind of confidential assistant to Starr Jameson. The recording showed a dark man impassive as Jameson himself. Rodrigues said, "It is requested that you do not communicate with your colleagues in any way before your departure from the project. Travel arrangements will ensure that you do not meet them aboard ship at the time of exchange. In the interest of maintaining—''

There was a pause. He was reading the last part from a note in his hand, and evidently had not looked at it before.

''In the interest of maintaining some pretense of scientific credibility, it is essential that Ms. Daru and Mr. Zeig should not be predisposed to duplicate your observations. This request is not subject to review.''

''Both of them?'' Hanna said in surprise to the oblivious Rodrigues. She stuck out her tongue at the image because she did not like Rodrigues' face, and played back the recording to appreciate the single sardonic sentence that had to be pure Jameson.

She complied with the order, however—if only because she could not think of a way to circumvent it.

Hanna left the *Endeavor* in January of ST 2836, having lived aboard the vessel a little more than ten months. Erik was guiltily relieved to see her go, and Tamara was regretful. Otherwise her departure drew little attention; she was only one of the first to leave in a cycle of personnel changes that would turn over a considerable portion of *Endeavor*'s crew in the second year of its voyage.

She came home to Koroth in mid-spring, ravenous for sweet open air and unpredictable winds. She went via a succession of spacecraft from the *Endeavor* to Earth orbit, from Earth orbit to D'neeran orbit, and from D'neeran orbit to Koroth's small spaceport. She walked from its tree-fenced expanse into Iledra's arms. It was morning, the starlight was golden, the very grasses rioted with blossoms, the trees were clouds of color, the windblown fountains were miracles, and her emotion collected a crowd. She came to the House in an aircar, like an invalid or an offworld dignitary, and some hours passed before she was composed enough for Iledra's remorseless debriefing.

All secrets were over now; but the passage of time and the aliens' silence had made them little, as (Hanna now guessed) Jameson had foreseen. The transmutation of human destiny had lost its impact in her thought, and in the bare outline of events that was all Hanna could provide, Iledra saw only opportunity. Bribery and threat at such a distance were harmless and abstract. Iledra was pleased that Jameson had reposed confidence in Hanna, and more pleased when Hanna made her understand the confidence had been forced, not given.

"You learned something of true-human diplomacy," Iledra said.

"Or expediency," Cosma suggested.

"Or corruption," Hanna muttered, thinking of Goodhaven, and the three women, dining privately in Cosma's quarters, regarded one another's versions of the truth and found no common ground, though each was so fully aware of the others' perspectives that it was impossible to decide the validity of one over another.

The discordance did not trouble them, accustomed as they were to the imperatives of a telepathic society. D'neera was a collection of anarchistic splinters whose more-or-less cooperative functioning depended always on a breathless balance. The ship of state, as represented by the lords and ladies of D'neera, tended to lurch wildly, though the goals it eventually reached had so far proved satisfactory. The lords and ladies were in fact harassed administrators, charged with maintaining an open oligarchy and subject to removal if they took their anachronistic titles too seriously. Iledra had once referred to her title as "rather tatty," which Hanna thought an accurate assessment. When she remembered her long conversation with Jameson she had an uneasy feeling that he knew just how accurate it was; that his careful formality might have been a reproach or a joke or a calculated effort to keep her off balance; that with no such grand title he was far more powerful on his world and in a larger society than she was anywhere, and called her "my lady" to remind her of the fact.

But when she said so Iledra answered, "Never mind. If he keeps to his promise one of us will at last be recognized for what our special gift can do. And what can his hopes do for us but good? You made a success of the *Endeavor* after all, H'ana."

"Or he made it one for me. . . . Or made it appear so. . . ."

Hanna pushed uneasily at her hair. She was thoroughly disoriented. She could not see the season of *Endeavor* in perspective from this leaf-brushed balcony. A night breeze touched her face softly, smelling of flowers. The crystal jars of luminescence that lit their meal could not compete with the stars; when she lifted her head she saw them blazing past the fragrant leaves. Had she really been there in that starry abyss? Yet this commonplace dinner at home was unreal too.

The other women thought tranquilly of transitions and adjustments. Hanna said, "You are missing a point."

"You are," Iledra said, smiling. "But I have not told you about Alien Relations."

"What about them?"

"I did not try to tell you before you came because I did not think the censor would let it pass. A representative of the committee has asked me to study the possibility of D'neera's enhancing and expanding its formal programs of study in exopsychology. I have already approached the university at D'vornan—"

"He would do that," said Hanna, thinking of something else.

"I beg your pardon?"

. . . *our teachers, our translators, our first and most honored ambassadors* . . .

"Nothing. Go on."

"There are difficulties, of course. The subject generally is not believed to warrant public support for full-time scholars. The Polity has offered some aid, but the university does not wish to accept assistance from true-humans. The first name mentioned was yours, of course—would you like to do that?"

"Me?" Hanna said, startled. "Teach? I don't think so."

"Good. We need you here. In any case, I hope the difficulty can be surmounted by inviting true-human instructors to D'neera, provided the course of study is integrated with the theories of 'Sentience,' and provided students manage field work with their own resources. They will have to make personal sacrifices to do so, but—that has always been our way. You did it."

"Yes," Hanna said, and sipped a delicate, tangy wine of southern Koroth. It was perhaps the wine that made her misgivings so disquieting, or perhaps she had suppressed them too long in the peaceful last months on *Endeavor*. "Sentience" had absorbed her utterly, and custom made the strange ordinary. Perhaps having stone underfoot made the difference now. Some of her reservations had to do with

Jameson and the Polity and all it represented; but the rest were rooted in incomprehensible silence.

Cosma heard the echo of silence and said in confusion, "The aliens?"

"The aliens. Don't forget them. . . . We talk of scholars and studies and, oh, hypothetical beings in some other time and some other place, but there are *these* aliens, the ones I could never see clearly, and they slipped away because—because—I don't know why, and I should—"

Her hand jerked on the tabletop, the Heir's Ring flashing. Iledra and Cosma thought together and disapprovingly that so long a time among true-humans must surely be injurious. But Hanna looked at her own brown hand and thought of more than that, of what she supposed might be called sacrifice, though she had never thought of doing anything besides what had to be done and endured: exile among strangers, the obsession with "Sentience," haunted *Endeavor*, Shuttle Five, the nightmares; before that, war; and before that, a youth divided among this House that had claimed her early, and Defense, and the travel and sunlit studies that had brought her to—this table and this night. It was not so long a time, but so full that for a moment she stood outside herself, and regarded with astonishment what she had become. If she felt more weary than her years should make her, who could blame her?

"I'm glad to be home," she said. "I don't want to leave again, Lee."

"You will change your mind," Iledra said placidly. "There is no need for you to go anywhere just yet. But if your strange creatures who follow the *Endeavor* should call, I think you will not be able to resist."

"I suppose you're right. . . ." She thought of shadows and strange images. She said, "I should have been able to see them. I should have. I should have."

Patience, said Iledra's thought, but Hanna shook her head and did not answer. Slow-moving rivers and webbed tapestries had their place, no doubt. But she could not quite consign the X beings to a current or a thread, and be sure they would comfortably accept it; not yet.

The New City finally was building, and Hanna went out to it and took up old duties. Spring swelled toward summer. She heard nothing of interest from *Endeavor*, not a word, and one bright morning after a night of rain, without pausing to examine her motives, she called Jameson. He told her readily that the second leg of *Endeavor*'s journey was beginning uneventfully as the first had ended.

It was then mid-morning in eastern Koroth, but early evening in southeastern Namerica. Jameson was at home, and Hanna had no way of knowing how unusual it was for him to take a call such as hers at such an hour. She had not bothered with security, and Jameson talked to her informally, so that behind him she could see a well-furnished dining room showing the remnants of a meal. In the background a tall woman briefly appeared and disappeared; not without taking a good look at Hanna's face.

"If anything happens," Hanna said, "will you let me know? If there's a direct contact I'd like to be involved."

"You might have stayed, you know," he said.

"To what end?" she said, feeling cross. Jameson's face on a video screen did not have the subduing effect of his presence. She would not let him quell her into self-doubt.

"Why, to be on the spot when something happens, of course."

"But maybe nothing is going to happen unless you make it happen. You said something about—" She fumbled, trying to remember. "About not dancing to their tune, or something like that. Well, they're not dancing to yours, either. It seems to be a stalemate. They're still following, aren't they? You'd let me know if there were any change?"

He regarded her thoughtfully. She wondered in exasperation if he ever said anything or did anything spontaneously. Finally he said, "This conversation is not secure. You are no longer officially connected with the Project, and you are residing in a culture where secrecy is unknown. I'm limited in what I can say."

"Then there *has* been a change!"

"Nothing substantive," he said delicately.

Damn true-humans and their secrets. She said, "And how do I go about finding out what this non-substantive development is?"

"You don't," he said calmly. "Not without rejoining the Project. Which I may ask you to do. Your tolerance for the routine drudgery of exploration seems very low, however.

When you had finished 'Sentience,' you wanted to leave the *Endeavor* at once."

Hanna decided she definitely did not like Jameson. Her hands, outside his range of vision, balled into fists. She said, "Do you know where I'm talking from?"

"No."

"Wait a minute." She pushed buttons, and panels slid open around her; a flood of noise poured in. She let him listen for a second before she shut it out again.

She said, "This is a construction site. There's a city going up here and I'm supposed to be in charge of it. Besides that I'm helping the university at D'vornan set up a program in alien studies. I've got responsibilities here. I'd rather be doing exopsychology than this, but I'd rather be doing this than creeping through space with nothing to think about but ambers."

"There is a little more to think about than that," he said maddeningly.

"But *what?*"

"We've changed the tune a little. We have had no success. There is a thing we might try. . . ." His face became remote, with the trick he had of looking at something that was not there as if he saw it plain. She was on the verge of speaking again when he came back to her and said, "I would rather not try it. If I decide to do so, you will know about it, my lady."

Hanna's hair was full of dust. In the summer heat she wore only the tiniest of briefs and a bandeau to support her breasts, and beside her lay heavy gauntlets she had just taken off. "My lady" had never seemed less appropriate.

She opened her mouth to ask another question, and decided it was futile. Instead she said, "Just keep me informed, will you?"

"I will," Jameson said, and Hanna closed the call with mixed feelings. He had not forgotten the importance of Species X any more than she had, and the knowledge nourished her in this self-absorbed world, where no one but Hanna cared about such things. But Jameson's restraint in the quiet elegance of his own milieu reminded her of how she must appear to him: mud-caked and mostly naked, savage product of a backward world.

"Bastard," she muttered, knowing it sprang from her own defensiveness; but she said it again for different reasons a little later, when she received his formal, written congratulations on her acquisition of the 2836 Goodhaven Award for her contribution to humanity's knowledge of alien species—a message notable chiefly for preceding the Academy's official notification by some hours.

Hanna had little use for remote supervision, and got muddier as the days went on, and darker from the sun, and more expert at soothing querulous engineers and sulky architects and overly fastidious construction crews. The fact that many of the New City personnel combined all three functions did not make her task easier. In the old city by the slow Earthly river, a hard winter began to give way to the thaw; it had been going on for some time beforc Starr Jameson noticed it, felt no pleasure in the prospect, and acknowledged with a shrug the deeper winter within himself.

He had not forgotten Hanna, whom he thought of rather grimly from time to time. He could hardly forget a person who had gone straight through a lifetime's carefully developed skills in defense at their first and only meeting, and taken a plain look at his heart. No less astounding was the ease with which she had accepted what she saw there. He wondered if she knew how rare she was. He did not think so; but he could not decide if such simplicity was an advantage or a danger for his purposes.

Hanna also was remembered on the *Endeavor*, where Anja Daru and Charl Zeig wished heartily that she were there, either with them or instead of them. Something was happening at last, and Anja and Charl did not like it.

"Locus referents. Finally," said Erik Fleming. He was a little pale, but showed no other sign of tension.

The man who had replaced Tamara as communications chief nodded. Translated to a visual display, the content of Signal Gamma showed a pair of carefully described stars, *Endeavor*'s relative position and, overlapping it, a point that pulsed with light. Ito Hirasawa had already ordered preliminary calculations of a course for the indicated point while the contact team was assembling.

"All right," Erik said to Hirasawa. "How long?"

"A day, maybe. One minim Jump and backtrack under conventional power."

"Close. So damn close . . ." He shook his head. "I never

thought it would work. Somebody at Central's got a brain. But why did it work? When nothing else did?"

Marte Koster said, "It seems clear they're not interested in making contact with this ship. As such."

"They lost interest in the drone, too. After a certain point. But here's Gamma." Erik looked down the room at Charl and Anja. They were much less trouble than Hanna had been. They had formed their own community of two, but they were polite and cooperative and deferred to Koster, which Hanna had not done. It said something for Hanna's impact, however, that they had been invited to this meeting from the start.

He said, "You two notice anything?"

They looked at each other briefly. Charl said, "I don't know."

"What do you mean by that?"

They looked at each other again. Charl said, "There was something. About the time they approached the drone. But I don't know what it was."

"Describe it," Erik said impatiently.

"I can't. It was just different."

"Different how?"

Outside Erik's perception Charl and Anja shared a conviction that might have translated to: I *knew* it would be this way!

"I don't have anything to compare it to," Charl said.

"Well, was it friendly? Hostile? What?"

"I don't know. It was just there." He added hastily, seeing Erik's mouth go tight, "I thought it was very strong. But I don't know what that means, actually. Strong compared to what? I don't know."

Erik stared at them hard and said, "Just let me know if you get anything else."

"All right," they said with relief, but when Erik let the contact team go they went back to Charl's room almost on tiptoe, like guilty children, and Anja said, "I think we should ask for permission to talk to H'ana."

"Then he'll want to know why. And we'll have to tell him. He didn't understand what *I* was trying to tell him. What's he going to say if you tell him you had a bad dream?"

They fell from Standard into proximity D'neeran, an intimate shorthand that relied heavily on telepathic exchange as a supplement to the spoken word.

"Well, but H'ana dreamed too, uneasily. I heard him trace her dreaming—"

"But of what? The chance of connection is so vanished-remote—"

"Oh, why isn't there more in the log! Why didn't she speak fully! Might there have been more?"

"Why tamper? This must be new, and of little sense—"

Anja hugged herself for comfort, until Charl hugged her. She said, "Terrifying. That eye!"

"Anja, they can't mean us hurt. What cause have they to pain us? H'ana says aliens are crazy until you join them. If you read a hunting predator it terrifies too, until—"

"That's it," Anja said suddenly.

"What?"

She looked at him with wide eyes. She said, "When I learned loving animals I went to shadowed wilderness in Garfield Province, the Mason Range Preserve, do you know it? Where the long-clawed wicas are, where foresters place them if they wander deadly through the valleys. And I read a wica patient-stalking a sorrowful pollitt foraging for her young. That's what it was like, the dream-eye."

"Like a wica?"

"Yes—no. In a way."

"Show me."

"I can't. It was dream, I can't recapture it, I remember what I felt but it's distant and I can't project."

"Maybe you're right. Maybe we should call H'ana."

"No!" Anja said vigorously, reversing herself. "I won't have Marte Koster laughing-hateful, the way she is when she talks about H'ana so solemnly and respectfully and thinks we don't know it's deceit. What's she got to laugh about anyway? *She* never got a Goodhaven."

They told no one of Anja's dream and did not attempt to call Hanna, and next day thought it would not matter; *Endeavor* got to its destination in double-quick time, but nobody was there.

The formal presentation of the Goodhaven Award was made on a cool evening that smelled of mud and water and the secretive growths of spring. Jameson sat in the small audience, one of the few invited guests attending the ceremony in person rather than by remotes, and congratulated himself.

He had not doubted, from his first reading of "Sentience," that Hanna deserved the award. He had not doubted either that it would take every bit of his influence to procure it for her. Since the announcement of the prize he had made a point of personally complimenting each member of the awards committee on his or her integrity and resistance to popular pressure—and in a few cases refrained from mentioning other forms of pressure which had left the persons in question facing a choice between evils. His conscience, however, was clear. He had no scruples about coercing people to act honorably, nor much inclination to question his own tactics.

Now he studied Hanna as she gave a courteous, diplomatic speech Lady Koroth had written for her. He barely recognized her, which troubled him, and he tried to account for it. She was smaller than he remembered; perhaps that was because her personality, tonight, was muted by good manners. Her voice was different, too, low and a little husky. She was less thin than he recalled, more relaxed, and decidedly unshabby in formal black. Altogether she had little resemblance to the tense, ill-groomed woman he had met on *Endeavor*. She was in fact very pleasant to look at, a dark flower that seemed to rise gracefully from a fanciful backdrop of stars. Jameson was surprised, but he went on looking.

"In closing," Hanna said, and he snapped out his bemusement. "I would like to say that 'Sentience' owes a great deal to Commissioner Starr Jameson, who gave me his support and encouragement—and, of course, his influence with the Academy."

Jameson felt the ground drop away under him. He was as angry as he had ever been in his life—and then knew no one but he had heard Hanna's last words, if they had been words. She gave him a smile that had a gleam of malice in it, and malice echoed in his head. Hanna remained the only source of his direct experience with telepathy, and he still could have done without it.

"When the final edition appears you'll see that the book—which has had no dedication until now—is dedicated to Commissioner Jameson. My very deepest thanks to all of you."

He stood with the others to applaud, and smiled at Hanna in a way she could not possibly interpret as gracious. He supposed the dedication of "Sentience," no less than that shocking stab in thought, was private revenge for his high-handedness. She would not let him forget the choices he had set before her on *Endeavor*, nor pretend she did not distrust them, and the dedication would be a subtle and permanent reminder of that ambiguous meeting. Her private grievances did not concern him, however. There would be public harmony; he was sure Lady Koroth, who had accompanied Hanna to Earth and stood composedly beside him, would see to that.

"My office," he murmured to Iledra as the applause began to die.

"Very well. As soon as I can detach H'ana."

"Did you have an opportunity before the presentation to speak to her of this meeting?"

"No," said Iledra, "but I will bring her."

He made a detour to the exit to avoid the Goodhaven Academy's ancient president, who was trying to catch his eye. His path gave him a momentary glimpse of Hanna; she was surrounded by a glittering restless crowd, Iledra bore down on her at speed, and Hanna alone was still, the focus of it all, the center of converging forces. An inexplicable surge of pity for her moved him. Her eyes fell on him and he wondered, meeting that cool blue gaze, dark as a summer sky at twilight, what reason there was for pity; he was in the process of making her career, and the future of her world.

When Jameson chose to make it so his office in the vast Polity Administration complex, like his home, seemed to have been lifted from another century. Nothing was synthetic; the glow of fine wood was everywhere, and the banks of electronic equipment he used could be hidden when he wished. They were hidden tonight, and Hanna, for the moment ignored, stood aside and watched Iledra, a forester's child and an expert woodworker herself, admire the woods of Heartworld.

Her eyes moved to Jameson and lingered there. She had been intensely aware of his presence all evening. Now she watched him lift an exquisitely carved head for Iledra's inspection, and saw with sudden clarity the strength of his hands and the controlled delicacy of his touch. A long-absent warmth possessed her.

So that was it. . . . She smiled at herself, acknowledging without self-consciousness an element that might have been in play in their meeting months before, though she had not recognized it then. Like him or not, he was a most excellent male animal. Her body spoke earnestly, approving a likely hunter on an ageless, age-old level. She looked at his shoulders and his movements with simple pleasure.

He had watched her tonight too with discomfiting intentness, but not, she thought, with desire. She had felt something else and more disturbing in the instant of feedback when her barb sank into his brain. Behind his surprise and anger, which she expected, and the dreamlike complexities of any intelligent mind, was something she had not recognized. Shadow and strength, she thought, unable to put more precise words to it; some great defeat, and poised against it an inflexible assertion.

Defeat by what? Assertion of what? She shook her head in confusion. Jameson saw the movement and looked at her curiously. He left Iledra to examine his collection of F'thalian artifacts and crossed the room to Hanna.

"You gave a very good speech," he said.

"A very bland speech."

"Precisely."

She shook her head again, smiling now, and looked past him to the edge of the room, which merged unwalled with the moonlit river. She said, "I thought power would be guarded better."

"The Polity is an administrative apparatus. It has no power; only influence."

"And I am a two-headed hornmaster of F'thal," Hanna answered, and looked up just in time to see him smile. The warmth of it was glorious; it made him another man; and she was still staring at him when he turned to her, saw her interest, and—was himself again.

He said abruptly, "I think we have found a way to induce explicit contact."

Hanna forgot immediately about everything but Species X. Iledra turned and came toward them quickly. Hanna said, "What is it? Have you done it?"

"We have not done it yet. It is a last resort."

"A last—why? What do you mean?"

He looked at her very somberly. He said, "You were

terrified after your single clear contact with Species X, were you not?''

''Yes. I was. So?''

''Look,'' he said.

He called up a projection of their sector of the Milky Way, *Endeavor*'s first voyage a thin green line threading among the stars, the present voyage—an extension of the first—in red. It hovered ghostly in the middle of the room. Hanna put her hand into it, watching the mist glow on her skin.

''*Endeavor*'s here?'' she said.

''Approximately. You see it has not gone far past the point where you left it. That is because we have been—experimenting.''

Hanna looked up quickly. ''Changing the tune?'' she asked.

''Yes. We tried inexplicable disappearances, without broadcasting prior information about where the *Endeavor* would go next. When the ship returned to its point of departure, Species X simply took up the chase again. We generated our own coordinates for rendezvous; they followed, and kept their distance. We tried varying the content of our base signal. There was no new response. Your compatriots on the *Endeavor* gave us nothing. Their perceptions were even more ambiguous than yours.''

''What were they?''

''Nothing to the point, believe me. Not to any point. But we have done something, finally, that has made them begin transmitting location signals again. So far we have not responded. I think it is time to do so. On their terms, as nearly as we can guess what those terms are.''

Hanna shoved her hands into the pockets of her short jacket and looked at him, wishing she dared try reading his thoughts. She felt Iledra's perception of her desire, and felt Lee's shock at the boldness and rudeness of the wish. But Iledra had not faced Jameson on the *Endeavor*, and won her way to a kernel of truth through layers of obscurity.

Hanna said, ''I think you'd better begin at the beginning.''

''Do you know what it is? I don't.'' The wintry amusement with which she was becoming familiar touched his face.

''I think,'' Hanna said cautiously, ''you can dispense with philosophy.''

''All right. I've told you about the experiments we tried—all but one. That one was more successful. You will remember that one thing, and one thing only, brought a reaction from the aliens while you were aboard *Endeavor*. That was your own approach to them, in isolation from the ship."

He paused, looking at her without expression. Hanna dug her hands in deeper. She thought she knew what was coming.

Jameson said, "I had them recreate that situation, in form though not in substance. The *Endeavor*'s engineering staff modified a shuttle for remote control. The *Endeavor* specified a location for rendezvous, took the shuttle there, and left it—just as you were left behind last year. A starship—to all appearances the same one that came to you—appeared at the proper location. It made a pass at the shuttle and disappeared. Shortly afterward the *Endeavor* began receiving locus references again. Now, it is clear, after so long a time, that the beings do not wish to contact the *Endeavor* itself. They were not interested in the unmanned vessel. I think they may wish to meet with a single representative of humankind, away from a vessel large enough, perhaps, to be threatening. I don't know if it matters who the representative is. But they—" He hesitated. "They know you, as it were."

Hanna had been very still. Now she moved suddenly, almost convulsively. She said, "I don't like it."

"Neither do I. I did not want to do this. I did not want to place any human being in so vulnerable a position. In a sense, of course, every person on the *Endeavor* is vulnerable. But I have not forgotten the intensity of your reaction to the earlier contact."

"Thank you very much," Hanna muttered.

"Hmm?"

"Nothing . . ."

She turned away from him and began to pace, flowing black trousers swirling about her legs. She said, "They veered off from your decoy. Why wouldn't they do it again?"

"They were telepaths. There is no doubt on that score; that is the one thing Zeig and Daru are sure of, without reference, incidentally, to your experience. I think they departed when they learned, telepathically, that the drone was not manned."

"Because it wasn't—" She froze where she stood. Iledra caught her thought and made a faint sound of protest and disbelief. Hanna turned slowly. She said to Jameson, "It wasn't the bait they wanted."

He looked at her without expression and said, "That is highly colored language."

"Is it? When I saw spears and carnivores?"

"Analogs," he said.

It was her own word. She could not repudiate it.

She moved restlessly to stare into the projection.

"What does Marte Koster think?"

"She does not know what to think," Jameson said, nearly at her ear. She had not heard him come near.

"Well, for once she and I agree on something."

She looked up at Jameson and said abruptly, "Send *Endeavor* on and ignore them."

"Why?"

"I can't give you a logical reason. They're manipulating us."

"I know."

"We shouldn't play the game without knowing the rules."

"We can't ignore them any longer."

"Why not?"

They spoke rapidly and quietly. They mght have been entirely alone. Iledra moved closer.

"*Endeavor* has been in space more than a year. I need results."

"Don't do it. Don't hurry."

He said savagely, "I don't have forever."

Hanna jumped, shocked. His will transfixed her—the implacable will that had created the *Endeavor* Project from nothing. No half-formed fear would dilute it. He would go meet the beings himself, if no one else would go.

She said, bewildered, "Forever for what?"

He looked at her without comprehension. She had to know. She put out a hand and touched his arm with a hesitance foreign to any D'neeran, to whom touch came naturally as breath. But it seemed a great liberty to take with Jameson. He did not shake her off, however. She said, "What are we looking for?"

For a minute she thought he would not answer. Then he said, "We are children, my lady."

"Children?"

"All the time of humankind is a second, a tiny fraction of eternity," he said, so softly that she tilted her head, close as she was, to hear. "It is nothing, my lady. Each of us is caught in our little millisecond of life, and we think that millisecond is everything. But all human history is nothing."

He hesitated, looking into her eyes with the first trace of doubt she had ever seen in him. Something reassured him. She felt him relax, almost in relief. He said quietly, "The *Endeavor* Project is a turning toward a future unimaginable as the improbable past. I am speaking of the far future. Not next year, but millennia to come. We forget the vastness of the universe. We think, skipping among a handful of stars, we have mastered it. We are children, playing on the edge of infinity. . . . One day, my lady, we will meet the adults."

It seemed to her clear, pure truth. She said in wonder, "And they will teach us—?"

"The unknowable?" he said. It was a question.

She asked with simple curiosity, "Are you mad?"

"I don't think so," he said as if he had thought of it before.

He had gone much farther than he intended. The moment of communication ended with a jolt in which Hanna felt his surprise at what he had said. He actually took a step backward.

He said abruptly, "I don't intend to order you into space on my authority alone. There will be some delay. But I think you can leave in a few days."

"But—"

Iledra overwhelmed her, thinking furious thoughts to an obstinate child. Jameson said, "You need not be entirely alone. You can take Zeig or Daru, or both of them. This time. Not the next time, perhaps—"

"Next time! I don't even want to go this time!"

"It is essential that a telepath greet them. You can make better guesses about them than any true-human."

"Of course," Iledra said, but Hanna could not let it pass.

"I don't know if I can!" She stopped in despair. Iledra's eyes were as cold as Jameson's. She went on stubbornly, "If they, if they didn't have a Change, if they evolved that way, they might be different, so different from us—We're still human. We're shaped by language. Telepathy's a function of the maturation of the nervous system. We learn to use it along with language. We've never got very far from the rest of you—whatever you might think," she added defiantly, but Jameson only nodded.

"The perfect interface," he said.

Soft-furred pollitts snugly burrowed, and downwind the eye of the hunter—

Iledra's hand closed on her arm.

Madness! Before the war you were not so. This fear lies in your own heart!

Hanna disengaged her arm easily; it was harder to free her thought. She said hopelessly, "We don't know enough about them," and saw Jameson's mouth set.

"You have the opportunity to learn more," he said.

"What they are doing does not make sense in any frame of reference we know."

"You," he said, and lifted a hand and leveled a long forefinger at her, arresting her. "You have just won an award for a work concerned largely with frames of reference—and with your own qualifications, as a D'neeran, to understand them. You have the opportunity to prove the assertions of 'Sentience'—that you can enter an alien's skin, obtain for us knowledge of his heart, and show him your own essence. Peace, you said, past any possibility of mistake, without conjecture, without deception, from the beginning. You have the opportunity to make a first contact. There has not been a first contact since Neil Girritt's two hundred and fifty years ago. No D'neeran has ever made such a contact. Shall I send Marte Koster instead?"

Iledra said empathically, "No!" The air pulsed with warning. Hanna needed no special sense to know what Iledra thought of: D'vornan's new course of study; a report, which Iledra would supervise personally, on the introduction of D'neerans into true-human mindhealing; a whole list of scarce-spoken hopes, a world's coming of age.

Hanna looked from Jameson to Iledra and turned away from them. She went back to the projection and stood beside it without looking at it. Hands in pockets, shoulders hunched, she felt Iledra's indignation that Hanna should even think of turning away from this opportunity. From Jameson she felt nothing, but exasperation showed in his face. He wanted her to see it, she thought. She had not missed his significant glance at the tiny jeweled symbol of the Goodhaven Academy sparkling on her shoulder. She was not through paying for it, nor for all those beginnings.

She took her hands from her pockets, and the Heir's Ring

sparkled too. She tugged at it and pulled it off. She said to Iledra, "Have you forgotten the inscription inside?"

Iledra remembered. She looked at Hanna coldly. It was the first time Hanna had felt anything of the kind from Iledra.

Hanna said, "I'll tell you what it is. 'The first duty of the D'neeran citizen is to the integrity of the self; for the welfare of the state depends on the well-being of the individual.'"

Iledra did not answer in word or thought. Hanna said, "Take it. Cosma can wear it for me. Just in case."

She felt a question form at last, and shut it out. "Take it," she repeated, and Iledra took the ring as if she might not give it back.

On balance, Hanna thought, Iledra was right, or right enough to leave no real choice. If there were a first contact, it had better not be Marte Koster who made it; better H'ana ril-Koroth of D'neera; better another stone laid to found Jameson's seductive vision.

"All right," Hanna said. "I'll go."

CHAPTER VII

The space ship was called *XS-12*. "X" meant Extraterrestrial, "S" meant Scout; Hanna never found out what the Twelve was for.

It was austere as Shuttle Five, and it was not big enough for three people.

When it had been in space six weeks Hanna looked out the ports in its nose and thought: It's just as well we hate each other. It gives us something to do.

(*"Why told you no one of your dreams?"*

"Why left you no record of yours?"

"I did, they kept it from you—"

"As you knew they would. Placid you ate the argument—"

"It was sense!"

"Now you doubt, too late—bitch, witch!")

The transmissions *XS-12* sent into space could be traced by an audible signal. Often they played it for hours. It had been on for hours now, high-pitched and faint and pulsing. Hanna could not bear it.

She said suddenly, "I want it off."

Charl did not look up from the game he played crosslegged on the floor. Bright chips shifted position in the air.

"Leave it on," he said.

"It's been on for hours!"

"I'm used to it."

They spoke in careful Standard, having rubbed so closely together for so long that the emotional burden of telepathy also was unbearable. Hanna said, "It's my turn to have what I want. Silence!"

Charl hesitated, acknowledging fairness in spite of himself. Hanna's hand crept inevitably toward the keypad that would silence the noise. A memory of the *Clara Mendoza* stabbed her, and she felt sick. Charl looked at her quickly and said, "All right."

"Thanks."

In resounding silence she headed for the cramped cubicle where she slept and which—the operations manual said—was supposed to give her privacy. In the narrow passage she bumped into a sleepy and disheveled Anja. Hanna squeezed past her.

Hanna's bunk made her bed on *Endeavor* look sybaritic. It would improve Erik to sleep here for a while. The single thin blanket did not even pretend to be fabric. It kept a sleeper comfortable, but it did nothing for the need to snuggle into substantial warmth in the night. Not that *XS-12* was cold; it was always the same and just right. It did not have *Endeavor*'s subtle diurnal and seasonal cues, and its scant drift through realspace allowed no shift in the positions of the stars. The souls aboard her might have been in hell, a hell of isolation and sameness that drove them to tear at each other because there was no other outlet for a tension that rose and fell irregularly and permitted them no action.

("I thought," said Jameson's voice—it was only his voice, and the transmission was not as clear as it should be—"that what you report is impossible. That telepathic contact without affect is a contradiction in terms."

"It is for us. I didn't believe Charl either, when he told me what he felt on Endeavor. *They're not us. They're different. I told you they could be different!"*

"They are interested in you, at least."

"Presumably. Who the hell knows?"

"And they've done nothing to harm you."

"But the dreams. I don't trust this change. Dammit, why didn't you let us talk before I came out here?"

"It wouldn't have mattered. They are analogs; for watchfulness and pursuit, perhaps."

"That's easy for you to say," Hanna said, but she liked hearing his voice. It was always calm and steady, and in each of their rare conversations it was a link to reason and the sanity of a busy larger world.

She said, "Jameson, I don't think I can take this much longer."

"Don't tell me that. The import of your presence surely—"

"Don't make a speech," she said quickly, and thought she heard the ghost of a chuckle.)

She was not scheduled to talk to Jameson for four days more. There would be nothing to occupy her thoughts and keep them from unanswerable questions except the laconic once-a-day contact with Project Central, and the prickly oft-broken truce with Anja and Charl, and the other thing. Which came when it would and was gone at once:

(*"To see what you are? To see that you are what you seem to be? I don't know. But you will stay there, harmless—"*

"Helpless!"

"Until I tell you otherwise. You need no help.")

So telepathic contact without affect was possible. There were no dreams of eyes or stalking warships. There were no affective images crafted deep in human bones. The touches were an assertion of existence: nothing more. They came at irregular intervals, not in sleep but to the waking mind, and no sensor on *XS-12* had ever registered a manifestation of matter to go along with them.

Hanna's tiny compartment was not soundproofed. She lay uncomfortably on her back and listened to Anja and Charl. The voices were faint, and she cocked an ear to the dreary round of the same words, same questions, same uncertain answers all of them had been saying and hearing for six weeks. It was Anja and Charl this time, but it might have been all three of them, or she and Anja, or she and Charl.

Anja said in her soft furry voice, "They might be super-beings, waiting to see if we are worthy."

"Or not telepaths at all. Could they be non-telepaths?"

"Impossible."

"Something altogether different, I mean. Made for another sense which we perceive dimly with the only one we have that can perceive them at all."

"But why wait? Why not contact us?"

"Fear perhaps . . ."

Hanna shut out the voices as best she could. They receded to a murmur. They could say nothing new. They had been through this again and again and again. The words were wearily unchanging like everything aboard *XS-12*. Hanna longed for the D'neeran summer, or even the spring left behind on Earth.

Hanna had gone out to *Endeavor* in *XS-12*, which did not

seem crowded with only a Fleet pilot aboard. Marte Koster met her with a certain sulky respect. Erik, however, greeted her with more than courtesy. It seemed she was now a person of some importance, a protégée of Starr Jameson and a member of the Goodhaven Academy. Hanna felt only indifference. She would not forget Erik but mostly, she thought, the memory would remind her that true-humans were not very sensible about love. She had never figured out what sharing Erik's bed had to do with following his orders, although the connection had seemed plain to him.

She forgot about him as soon as *Endeavor* was gone, leaving *XS-12* behind with one tremendous jump. Fleming had played the locus-reference game with Species X right up to the rendezvous with *XS-12*, though more slowly and carefully toward the end. Hanna, busy comparing notes with Anja, had not cared about the details. When *Endeavor* was gone the D'neerans turned on their own transmission—here-we-ARE here-we-ARE here-we-ARE—and sat back to wait. And wait, and wait. And the first fragile touch of contact had come almost at once, and again and again—and nothing else had happened, except that the mission had disintegrated into a series of subtle territorial squabbles.

We are acting altogether too much like true-humans, Hanna thought crossly. They insist on having privacy for the oddest things—arguing, making love, having babies—but they expect three people to put up with each other and stay sane in a space maybe big enough for one-point-five. I will never understand them. If something doesn't happen soon I'll go mad!

In six weeks none of her reservations had left her, though all the logical benefits of "something" happening were fully present to her mind, and her curiosity about Species X finally was grown ravenous.

She turned wearily—and jumped, all her attention arrested by an impersonal impact like a stutter in her skull, an instant of total absorption that suspended all other thought. It lasted half a second, perhaps: then it was over.

They were used to it, she and the other two.

She got up and went back to the control room. Anja and Charl were both on the floor now. The glowing chips formed a rotating pyramid.

Hanna said, "I had it again. Did you?"

They shook their heads without looking up. Sometimes two or all three of them felt the same touch, sometimes only one. Why? They could not guess.

Hanna keyed a note of the incident into the scout's memory. On Earth they had tried to deduce a pattern from this record, but there was no pattern.

Then she turned to the others and saw that Anja was entranced. She stared straight ahead, motionless, eyes wide. Hanna had seen this look before in the instant of contact, but this went on a second, three seconds, five—

She crossed silently to Charl and Anja and knelt on the floor. Charl, guiding a game piece with a fingertip, had seen nothing. Hanna hissed at him. He looked up and saw Anja.

"Anja! *Annie!*" He reached for her. Hanna caught at his arm.

"Don't. Shut up. Don't disturb her."

They waited. Hanna tried to glimpse Anja's awareness and found it closed. Yet there should have been a response to Hanna's touch, and there was none.

Anja sighed and shook herself and came back to them, and before anyone could speak the scout said: "Attention, please. I am receiving a radio transmission from an unidentified source analogous to communication identified as alien."

Before it was finished Hanna was at the compact control console, Anja and Charl scrambling behind her. Charl opened his mouth to give an order and Hanna said quickly, "No, wait. No radar. Nothing. Anja—"

"Nothing?"

Anja began, "Mental contact? If you two—"

"No! We've got to notify Central. Anja, what was—"

"Not Central! No. They don't want us to do that."

"What? Did they tell you that?"

"What?" Anja stared in confusion.

"Just then," Hanna said impatiently. "When you were—"

She stopped, because Anja was bewildered. She created a picture of Anja in trance and exhibited it.

"I don't remember that," Anja said.

"But you know they don't want us to call Central?"

The bewilderment deepened on Anja's face. "Something like that," she said.

"All right. We won't yet, then," Hanna said, and ignored an anxious sound from Charl.

There were two seats before the master controls. Hanna slipped into one of them and put her hands on the console as if to assure herself the scout would make no move of its own to change a precarious balance. She felt just as she had when Koster told her about Signal Alpha, so unprepared for this that she could not believe in what was happening. The aliens were unreal, a dream presence, hallucination. The message the computer showed her was the same old series of primes, so that it too had no more substance than a memory.

But it was a radio transmission; and creatures who moved among the stars used radio only across very short distances.

Charl half-thought, "H'ana, we must urgently act!"

She answered in the same way, "Patience. . . ."

He looked longingly at the sensor panel. Most of the time they drifted blind, and silent except for their beacon. Charl thought of mass sensors.

Hanna said, "No. Nothing. Wait passive as water. . . ."

(*"They have no prey that moves so," said an old echo in her thought*.)

Which was bait and which was hunter?

Her hands itched to shape the event. There was something she could do. The computer could tell her the direction of the radio signal and turn passive receptors that way. She keyed the main video screen, a black polygon tall as herself.

"Uselessness," she said. "Too-far. Computer. Begin passive-visual scan. Target's a spacecraft. Search: hypothesized alien mass. Highest magnification and full enhancement—"

"Oh!" they cried together, and saw for the first time with human eyes a thing made by Species X.

"Done," said the scout, but no one heard it. The image fell off the sides of the screen. It flickered as the computer fine-tuned it.

Fuzzy, sharp-angled, brown in color-compensation:

"Close upon us, crush us, time run out to run—!"

"Anja, shut up!" Hanna said strongly. She shook with the panic-reaction.

"She wounds thee, true-human changeling," Charl crooned, holding Anja.

Hanna gave them a look of disgust. Roly had thought her too good at things of this sort too. But someone had better be good.

She said steadily, "Back off, computer. Scale it down. Are they using radar on us? Yes? Scale down another step. Another. All right."

It was not so threatening when it fit into the borders of the screen. Anja and Charl peered at it anxiously.

"So close," they whispered. "How close? Too close!"

Charl looked out the nose as if he expected to see the ship there.

"It's 'behind' us," Hanna said absently. "You won't see anything, Charl. There ought to be more detail. Why isn't there any detail?"

"They come upon us from behind, then, stalking!"

"I don't think it *has* any details."

"H'ana, please!"

"Hmm? They're not that close, Charl. Computer: What's the naked-eye view?"

A secondary monitor came to life. It showed only stars against black velvet. Anja sighed. Hanna felt Charl relax.

"You see," she said.

She strained her eyes and cajoled the computer, but nothing changed except the object's apparent size. She thought of *N.S. Havock,* spiked and bristling with destructors. Now a brown box approached her. It had never been intended for atmospheric flight. No openings showed, nor any instrumentation.

She said, "Everything must be embedded in the skin. Or in a molecular film on the surface."

The others only looked at her. They had not been much in space.

"Or . . ."

The angles seemed not quite right angles. The faceted sides bulged softly.

". . . it's disguised, covered . . . enclosed. . . ."

XS-12 seemed warmer. Light and life drifted, contained.

"This wait destroys me. I must know them!" Anja said suddenly.

Hysteria was far away, but too close for Hanna's liking. She said, "Use Standard, Anja. They spoke to you. Do you remember now?"

"No," Anja said obstinately.

"Cease tormenting her, not-one-of-us!" Charl said, not in Standard.

"You did not have to come," Hanna said, falling back.

But what were they saying that she had not said to the true-humans?

This might be a peak in the sea of time, but time stretched on. The box moved toward them, but slowly. Anja, calmer, detached herself from Charl. With the quick D'neeran forgetfulness of conflict she said, "H'ana?"

"Yes?"

"When are they going to do something that tells us something about them?"

"I don't know." Hanna sat back. Her shoulders ached. More time had passed than she thought. She had been thinking the same question. She said, "I never thought I could see one of their spacecraft and not be able to guess something about them."

"They use right angles. The damn thing looks like a brick." Charl touched her shoulder. His anger was gone too.

"Not quite, but all I can think is they've deliberately designed something we can see without their giving anything away."

"The anthropomorphic fallacy," Anja said. "You've warned against that yourself."

"Yes, but if it's not that, you know what the only other thing is I can think? If this is just a typical spacecraft for them?"

"What?"

"They've all got galloping paranoia, and shut out *everything*."

"They're galloping closer," Anja said, and giggled. There was an edge to it, but not an edge of humor. She said, "In case you haven't noticed, it's partly off the screen again."

"Reduce magnification," Hanna said to the computer, and the box shrank with a jump.

Such optical tricks, Hanna thought, made the stately advance seem untrue. One could turn for ease to an illusion of distance.

They reduced magnification again and again. An hour passed, and a second hour. At intervals a data monitor showed them the radioed message was being repeated, but its content did not change. Nothing happened, except that the box came closer. Charl returned to his game. He moved pieces aimlessly and looked at them less often than at the image of X.

Anja sat beside Hanna, curiosity submerging her fear. And Hanna tried to touch the alien presence and felt: nothing. So slowly, so painfully accumulated, the bits of meaningless data. Did they know? Did they guess how little? Was it their intention? Surely.

Anja said into a long silence, "Collision course?"

"Maybe," Hanna said. She shook herself. "Ridiculous."

"But they must be awfully close."

"Yes. They must."

"Well?" Anja turned her head. Hanna felt Charl's attention too.

Do something something something something . . .

Their patience was giving way.

Slowly she reached out and silenced the unheard Inspace signal. Now it was inaudible to the aliens too.

"Wisdom?" Charl inquired, picking up Hanna's own doubt.

"They know our knowing of their closeness. Logic inevitable. Radio is for naught but closeness. Realtime makes it so."

"No purpose then in silence," Anja said.

They had fallen again into the use of more thought than speech. In Anja's vision time separated into segments discrete as beads. To act would change everything; for two civilizations. The moment of change was theirs to choose. She whispered, "Now, H'ana?"

"But their wish—" Dilatory, unwilling, Hanna hung back. "Silent and defenseless calls them—"

("*. . . their terms, as nearly as we can guess . . .*")

"*Our* terms," Anja said.

Hanna's hand moved, hesitating. Why not? Bomb them with detectors, slice into the alien box for knowing's sake. She could not quite touch the instruments to do it, nor order it done with her voice. Anja and Charl looked at her strangely.

She took a deep breath and said, "Computer. Full scan."

Numbers flickered and changed on *XS-12*. There were no strange shields, at least.

Charl said, "Fifty kilometers. Closing fast. I want a visual on that. Yes. That hotspot must be the reactor core."

He talked softly with Anja. Hanna paid no attention. She was dizzy, as if she had taken a step and fallen off a mountain. The ranks of numbers drew her. Close and closer: an approaching veil. Finally to be withdrawn? She would see through the mist at last.

"It's not featureless," Anja said. "You can see seams. Look, H'ana."

Hanna looked blindly and then with attention. She said, "It doesn't have any ports. Don't they like to look at the stars?"

"*I* don't like to look at the stars, except from solid ground," Anja said.

"But beings who choose space, like space. I mean, individual humans and individual F'thalians who come out here, we like to see where we're at. We—"

"Oh, look! Look!"

Openings appeared on the box's leading edge, black and bottomless. Hanna blinked at a burst of retrofire.

The scout said, "Decelerating."

There was another, shorter burst. *XS-12* said without interest, "The object will be at rest relative to ground zero in thirty-four minutes sixteen-point-oh-oh-four seconds."

Hanna looked at the box and thought she ought to be rejoicing. It was not a box. It was a space ship made by thinking creatures. She had trained for this for years.

She got up. Her stomach twisted but she said, "I'm going to suit up. This could be it."

Anja said nervously, "Shouldn't we try talking to them? From here?"

"You can try," Hanna said. "But *Endeavor*'s been trying for a year. To go out there alone—that's something new. . . ."

Her voice trailed away. She didn't want to do anything new. She saw in Anja's eyes the memory they shared of a dream. She said, "Nobody knows what they'll do. This is the only way to find out."

Anja said, "We're being foolish. There's nothing to be afraid of, is there?"

With one accord they looked at the naked-eye monitor. In the center starlight glinted briefly off something, still tiny, that had not been there before.

Charl muttered, "Paranoia. H'ana, we ought to make a preliminary report to Central. Now."

"We can't," Hanna said. She looked at Anja. "Not if they don't want us to. I was told—their terms. And it doesn't matter anyway. Central's a long way from here."

"Then let me record something for the black box," he

said, surprising her. For Charl was not a spacefarer. It was not routine for him to store information against his death at first sight of the unknown.

But Hanna said, "Do that."

She left them to watch the growing image. Near the lock reserved for spacewalks she dressed for vacuum. Logic told her she should not need to do it. In spite of their caution, the X beings had been the aggressors so far. Logic suggested they would rather come here than have her, an alien, penetrate their flying box. Yet she was certain that she would have to go to them, and that there would be no communication until she did. She did not know where her certainty came from. Intuition? But she did not believe in intuition. It was only logic in less visible form, the product of a structure based on details unconsciously noted. She knew they waited for her, in silence.

Anja said suddenly, "H'ana, something's happening out there."

Hanna waited, helmet in hands.

Anja said hesitantly, "There's an opening now. A new one. They're not going to shoot at us, are they? Wait. It's lit up now. I can't see inside."

Hanna said, "Step up the magnification."

"All right. Yes. It's just a little bare room. An air lock, I guess."

"What's the light like? How's it compare to Solar illumination?"

She heard Anja put the question to the scout.

"It is within Sol-normal parameters," the computer said.

"You heard?"

"I heard."

"It's at the kilometer mark, almost. Barely moving."

"Have you tried calling them?"

"We're still trying. There hasn't been an answer."

"Maybe that's it," Hanna said.

"What is?"

"An open door. An invitation."

"Weird way to do it."

"Direct, anyway."

But Hanna went on waiting for what seemed a long time. She thought that even if someday she forgot whatever happened next, she would never forget this chamber with its comfortless benches and rows of tool lockers. It did not seem connected with anything else, not even in time. Her suit's EV environment was not activated and she was hot. The niche from which it had come had a shiny door. She saw her reflection in it, barely. Her hair was pulled back and tightly bound for weightlessness. The oval of her face was clear, and the wide, too-wide blue eyes. Other details faded in distortions.

She thought there were times when you couldn't think much about what you were going to do. You had to just go and do it.

Finally she put her helmet on and fastened its seals.

"I might as well go out," she said. Her voice sounded too loud in the helmet.

"All right." Anja sounded scared again.

"Maybe you'd better program a panic button. Just in case."

"A what?" Charl said.

"Just tell the computer. It'll tell you how to set it up. What you want is to get the hell out of here the instant anything goes wrong. If you lose contact with me, for example."

She went into the air lock, listening carefully as they talked to the scout. They were doing it right. Locked away from ship's atmosphere, she watched ship and suit pressure gauges and presently, when their original readings were reversed, gave the outer hatch an exit command. The stars wheeled and her stomach gave way for a giddy instant as she left artificial gravity. She tumbled in a bowl of distant, shining glory. For the first time in her life the pleasure of this experience was shadowed by dread dark as the hulking scout. She stopped the slow spin, locked in star patterns for an upright referent, and started the drive unit on her back.

The guidance controls were at her waist. She touched them and drifted round the scout. The alien vessel and the glow signaling the open hatch were clearly visible. She moved toward them slowly. She thought of the enormity of what she was doing, making history, and chose not to think about that. She thought of Starr Jameson and said in a whisper he could not hear: "If you were out here you'd think twice about a renaissance."

"What?" Charl said.

"Nothing."

When she had gone about halfway she stopped. She said, "If I wait here do you think they'll come out?"

"No," Charl said promptly.

Anja said at the same time, "Yes."

"Well, let's see."

After a minute Anja said, "How long will you wait?"

"Well—why not an hour? Why not, long as we've waited on them?"

But the bravado grated on her own ears. She was ashamed of it. She started to move her hand to go on, and saw a shadow against the alien light.

She let out breath in a long, deep sigh, believing, at last, in a concrete reality.

She said, "See that?"

"I see it." Charl's voice was tense.

"Well?"

"What?"

"Dammit, bring the picture up and tell me what it is! It's dark out here!"

"Oh. It's got four limbs. And a head. I think. H'ana, that's all I can tell. It's in a spacesuit."

"Can you see its face?"

"No, the face plate's opaque."

She hesitated. Move and counter-move. Stopping had brought a response. She would stay where she was.

It was moving faster than she had been. She put a hand to her belt and touched controls that would boost contrast on the scene before her. The alien changed from a featureless shadow to a figure in a spacesuit. The suit differed only in detail from her own; given a little time, she would be able to figure out what everything on it was supposed to do. It was pressurized, and she could not guess at the body beneath it.

It came closer, and its helmet was subtly different in shape from her own—higher, wider, but shallower front to back, as if its head were oblong. Like her own it did not have a full face plate. There was only a darker band about two-thirds of the way up, presumably for it to see through.

Closer: Protruding from its garment at one side was something that might be a tool, or a weapon.

And closer: She could not see through the visor. The gloved hands had each three fingers and an opposable thumb.

In the last seconds it grew bigger, bigger, bigger than any human she had seen, like a figure of nightmare that would never cease growing—but it did.

It reached out and a four-fingered hand, huge, closed on her wrist. She must have made some sound because Anja said sharply, "H'ana, are you all right?"

"Yes. Can you see?"

"We can see. Why'd it do that?"

She swung round in vacuum and tried to see what it used for eyes, but the visor was dark to her.

Charl said, "Did you know you're moving away?"

She had not noticed. She looked ahead. The alien ship grew as she watched.

"Pretty fast," she said uneasily.

"Try to pull away."

"No. I have to go along," she said, but her throat was tight.

Anja said, her voice too high, "Are you brave or just stupid?"

Hanna did not know the answer. She was close enough to see details of the compartment beyond the open hatch. But there were no details to see; as Anja had said, it was bare.

"I'm going to try contacting it telepathically," she said, and without waiting for an answer reached out in thought as she had been doing since childhood, prepared for the rich, living texture of an intelligent mind.

There was nothing. It was not a machine; it was living, all right; but she could tell nothing else about it. She sensed none of its emotions, intentions or attitudes, not even its awareness of her presence. The impersonal connections she had felt on *XS-12* were shadows of this strength. She had never touched such a barrier, not even among the most powerful Adepts she had known.

She tried giving it an explicit message. She could not think in words to it; pseudo-verbal communication was possible only when there was a shared language. But visual-emotional-conceptual content could be shared across species, and what she said to it in this way was: *I am friendly–curious though afraid oh so afraid and wish to know you in rich sharing. Will you oh please commune?*

It did not respond in any way. They were nearly at the open hatch.

"It won't answer," she said.

"I don't like it." Charl sounded anxious. "They're too damn mysterious."

Anja said, ''You can't expect them to jump into our arms.''

''We're jumping into theirs.''

''H'ana is, anyway.''

Hanna said, ''Have you got that panic button set up?''

The air lock yawned in front of her. As if of its own will Hanna's free hand closed on the edge of the hatch. The being still held her right arm; her hesitation swung it around sharply. It caught at a handhold she could not see and edged into the cavity, and for a moment they hung facing each other.

Then it pulled her in, not with the gentle tug that would have been enough to break her light anchoring grip, but with a surge of effortless power that wrenched her shoulder and sent her crashing and rebounding from the opposite wall.

''H'ana?'' said a voice in her ear.

She gasped, ''Assume hostile—''

Gravity came on and she fell heavily on her behind with a jar she felt to the top of her skull.

There was an instant of tremendous noise in her helmet as everything on *XS-12* stopped working forever, and in her mind the silent screams of Charl and Anja as they died, and for an instant she was on the *Clara* again (shut them out, shut them *out!*), and made the screams stop and shrank into the silence. And looked up at the shape towering over her, too stupefied by that moment of death to understand, and thought without knowing why: I hope I die as quickly.

CHAPTER VIII

She came back to consciousness all at once in a breathless rush. There should not have been any consciousness; she was supposed to be dead. She had charged the alien to make it fire its handweapon, force it to kill her, because now there was no question of its hostility and she was afraid her mind would be open to it, all her knowledge of human science and defenses and government written out for it to see. The suicidal leap for its throat was the last thing she remembered, and she did not welcome this wakening.

Without opening her eyes or moving, she explored what her senses told her. She was spreadeagled on her back on a hard, smooth surface. Her wrists and ankles were tightly bound, and her clothing had been removed.

Sweat began to bead on her skin. This is impossible, she thought, and pushed against the bonds. They were metal; there was no play at all.

This cannot be happening to me. Can't be. Can't be.

She did not want to open her eyes. Through closed lids she saw bright light. It gave no heat and she was cold. Around her there was silence except for the subliminal hum of machines.

A voice of terrible power and clarity said to her thought: *Whowhat are you?*

She opened her eyes at last. She had never wanted less to do anything.

The alien stood near her, big as she remembered, half again her size. Its face was gray, and above that the skull was tufted with scales or coarse feathers. Two eyes were set very far apart in the flat face. Running nearly the length of the face and part-way to the top of the skull was a narrow strip of bony plating set a little out from the face, and under that a wide mouth that bulged outward, almost a muzzle. The skull was higher than a human's, but more rounded than the shape of the helmet had indicated. At the sides of the neck were organs that looked like gill slits, but they were armored with bone. A red tunic hid its upper body and arms. It also wore a garment something like a kilt; she could not see its legs.

She only stared at it, paralyzed with disbelief and unsureness and the beginning of a fear she did not recognize. Cold choices between life and death did not frighten her, and what else had there been to fear?

It said again, meaning the personal "you": *Whatwho are you?*

Her mind was blank in the face of the impossible. There was no emotional content in the thought at all, only the inquiry. D'neeran Adepts could do something like this, with rigorous concentration and discipline, but it was only a shadow of what this being did without effort. Yet there were overtones also of hard certainties, of things it thought it knew and echoes of other thoughts, and they were deadly.

It lifted a heavy four-fingered hand, and she saw that the fingers ended in thick curving claws. It laid the tips of the claws between her breasts and moved its hand, and there was a stinging as her skin tore. She trembled, but the slight pain roused her.

It said: *I am the Celebrant-Questioner and the triumph that dissolves you. Show me truth!*

Shaken, struggling to comprehend through fear and strangeness, she answered with an image: *I am Wildfire*.

Because that was how her own people sometimes thought of her when they spoke directly to her mind.

A rivulet of blood trickled her sweating skin. She said to the being, without trying to hide her fear because she could not: *What do you want with/from me?*

I will know the heart of our danger: the place/strengths/ safeguards of the beasts: their tools of death, their watchfulness: fulfillment and prediction all at once: the use and proper end of Wildfire. This is what I will have.

Hanna moved convulsively against her bonds, knowing at last and too late, an hour too late, a year too late, that this was what she had ignored, this was what she had been swayed from: the plain fact that the hunter's eye was no analog, but literally real. The end of courage and birth of fear had their reasons. She had not trusted herself or dead Anja enough. The being's thought made it plain it was interested only in military intelligence and—a horror she did not yet understand and therefore, in extremity, dismissed. It did not care about culture or history, art or philosophy or any of the other things *Endeavor* had gone into space to exchange. It did not care about her luminous vision of all the rich varieties of life. Her own senses had warned her, and she had turned away from them. She had failed, spectacularly and dangerously.

She thought in despair: *I cannot in rightfulness tell you those things. Peace follows me. My people will not harm you.*

But the strength of her own conviction was lost in fear, and the being knew that in this moment she would, if she could, harm it or kill it or anything else to escape.

It said: *You are not-People: clever treecubs come of old to ground awash in blood. You will show me what I ask, for I will hurt and force you.*

It meant raw pain, so clearly her body twisted of its own accord in anticipation. It would come if she spoke or did not speak, inevitable, but still she could not accept that and thought in familiar terms of interrogations. She did not know what to do. No one had ever taught her what to do. Human questioning could not be resisted; there were drugs to free a prisoner's tongue; there was no need for systematic pain and no one had ever spoken of it to her, except in whispered tales of forgotten hell-holes.

She whispered, "I cannot tell you anything," and it took the negative from her terrified thought.

It said confidently: *You will.*

It also heard her incredulous question—why pain?—and answered: *Will strength and spirit must end thus ending birth of the beast.*

What it meant had nothing to do with questions. But when she tried to see the meaning, it added: *Thought is chaos, drugged thought worse, lest shaped by will. You will shape it as I ask until will fails.*

I will not.

You will.

She licked her dry lips and thought: *You will kill me. You know not my physical being.*

We do know. We have met not-People, the treecubs, be-

fore. Not like you; not outward-bound in space; lost, their ancestors abandoned. How did this happen?

It showed her a handful of people, half-primitive, half-sophisticated, settled in mist yet adrift as an uncaptured moon. Distracted by wonder, she thought: *There is a story that when my ancestors began to go into space, for a time small groups went from star to star and of some all traces were lost; yet some survived. I did not think it true.*

It is true.

It turned away and she tried to understand. A Lost World was real. Myth was truth. Had been truth. She thought: the humans they *knew*. They are all dead.

Accumulated shock made an abyss and for a little while she fell through it. All the universe had changed in these few moments and there would never be a foothold again. She would not need footholds; the dead do not need them. When this thought crystallized into certainty she saw The Questioner had returned. It showed her and explained to her a picture in its thoughts. It said: *Do you know this instrument?*

I know. I know in shame. I know.

She had not seen a neural stimulator that looked like this before, a square of silvery fabric, but she knew its principle. Her experience of it had not been pain, and the being added that knowledge to its store.

It looked away from her. It said: *My companion is the Questioner's Assistant.*

Hanna turned her head and saw the other one coming toward her with the shining cloth. It thought of triumphs and transformations. The questions it would ask were secondary. Hanna did not understand and did not care. Her mouth was dry. The neural stimulator could cause excruciating pain, and although it did not damage tissue directly, the indirect effects were frightful. Convulsions of agony, she had heard, could tear muscles, break bones.

There would not be time to think about this or decide what to do if there was anything left to do. Endure, said the deep voice of instinct. It was hard to hear past the clamoring crowd of things she did not want to give up. Protect, it said. Endure.

The Questioner said: *Show me the space of your Home.*

The image was strange and shadowed and wrapped in on itself, but Hanna understood. She said: *I will not tell you.*

The Questioner's Assistant stood over her for a long moment, perhaps reviewing its knowledge of human anatomy. Then it leaned over and carefully molded the gauze over her belly.

The Questioner thought to a hidden control, and she screamed.

Tonight Henriette had worn a pale golden gown that glowed where it touched her skin. It lay near her now on the thick soft carpet, still shining a little with its own light. Henriette, chin propped on hands, looked up at Jameson in a way he knew well.

"Now?" she said, and he smiled at her from his chair.

"In a little while," he said.

"It's almost four in the morning. I have to go home and start working in a few hours. You just mean you're still too high."

"Possibly. Possibly."

But it was only that he had no inclination to move for any reason. Moments when the universe was orderly and forgiving of pleasure were rare, and he was balanced now between pleasure past and pleasure future. Henriette, who was now future, would be present. Soon. Whenever he wished. . . .

The Imagos in his blood was living up to its name. Nothing had disturbed his weekend on the waters of the rich and wind-chopped bay, and its blinding blue and gold still framed Henriette's long graceful body. When he closed his eyes the bowl of scarlet roses at his elbow drifted before him, and everything was heavy with their scent. In a few days he would go home to Heartworld, his first visit in several months. The great Siberian tigers flourished there under greenleaf skies, not knowing and not caring by how narrow a margin they had escaped extinction. He thought he saw Henriette's gown stir and become sunlight dappling pale fur. He felt the shaft of a spear in his hand, and forgot for a moment that he was no longer young enough or foolish enough to hunt tigers with the spear only.

He got up with a sigh and pulled Henriette to her feet and against him. Her hands moved on his back, and he felt a tremor begin in her thighs almost at once. It was one of the things he liked about Henriette.

In his ear Rodrigues's voice said clearly, "Priority one,"

and followed it up with a series of tones guaranteed to wake him if he were half-dead.

He cursed the transmitter implant violently. Henriette said, "Oh, no!"

"House! Tell Rodrigues to shut up!" The noise stopped. He said, "Be a good girl and get some clothes on, and bring me the Imagos antidote, would you?"

Tucked away behind an elegant bronzewood door was a private communications center. He disliked using it; it was a cold reminder that chaos was no respecter of his working hours. It would not open for anyone but him, and required palm, voice and retinal identification. He gave it a slap, a curse and a glare; there were certain liberties one could take with machines. Inside the lights were too bright, and a sharp reflection from somewhere shaped itself into a spearpoint before his eyes.

He said, "All right, Paul," and blinked to focus the other man's face.

Rodrigues said without preamble, "Anja Daru and Charl Zeig are dead. *XS-12* is out of contact." His face changed briefly to something else and back again. Jameson ignored it.

"What happened? Oh—"

Henriette was back. She injected the Imagos antidote with practiced fingers. She's used to this, he thought.

"Out," he said, and made sure the door locked behind her.

Rodrigues said, "Apparently Zeig and Daru died about two hours ago. I tried raising *XS-12* myself, no luck. I got General Steinmetz out of bed and he's got Fleet Communications trying."

"How did you find out about it?"

"Lady Koroth. D'neerans know when somebody they're close to dies, you know. She got a call from Daru's current, uh, spouse? He'd already been in touch with some of her other relations and they all thought she was gone. Lady Koroth then talked with Zeig's mother—same thing was going on in his circle. It took her awhile to get to me. Central didn't know what to do and passed her on to Martinson first, and he put her through to me."

Jameson's head was clearing. He let the blue-and-gold go without regret. He said, "Has there been any alarm from *XS-12*?"

Rodrigues shook his head. "They checked in Sunday morning as usual—twenty-two hours ago now. Nothing to report. No contact since."

"Have you still got Lady Koroth holding?"

"Yes. I thought you'd want to talk to her."

"I do. Get back to Steinmetz and see if he's having any luck. If he's not, get on to the commission. Let me talk to Lady Koroth."

It was midday at Koroth. Iledra, who must have been jolted hard by the news, appeared calm, but the younger woman at her shoulder looked anxious. Cosma ril-Koroth: Jameson remembered she was likely to be Iledra's heir if anything happened to Hanna.

He bit back the obvious question and said instead, "Rodrigues has filled me in. Did he tell you he's been trying to reach *XS-12*?"

"No, he didn't. We have not tried. It would go through Central, and be stopped. He has had no answer?"

"We're still working on it. Tell me what happened."

It was only a more detailed account of what Rodrigues had told him. She recited it with precision, filling in names, times, circumstances, but she moved restlessly as she did so and once Cosma touched her hand. When she finished he said finally, "You have no reason to think Lady Hanna also is dead?"

"None. I would know; so would her parents and cousins. I've spoken with them, too."

Jameson found it hard to picture Hanna with a family. She had grown up with her mother, he remembered, but likely had been close to her father; such relationships were common on D'neera. "Cousins" could be siblings or half-siblings or entirely unrelated people with whom one had intimate ties; D'neerans often did not distinguish among the categories.

He said, "Would you know if she were injured? Unable to respond to us, for example?"

"Probably not. It's nearly always clear and unmistakable when someone you love ceases to exist, no matter where they are. You seldom know of any trauma short of that, unless they're close at hand. It sometimes happens; not often."

"All right." The antidote had taken full effect now. He did not have to think about what to do next. "Unless we get some word from her in the next few minutes I'm going to get a search underway."

"There is already a D'neeran ship on the way. Estimated time of arrival is seventy-two hours."

Jameson blinked, taken by surprise. She was not supposed to know *XS-12*'s location. He remembered Hanna's insistence on finding it out. She must have passed it on before she left Earth, probably without even thinking of security. It could not be undone, however. He said, dismissing it, "We'll have something there sooner. Can you keep this quiet until we know more?"

"No."

There was no point in arguing about it. He could exert little influence on D'neeran public information policy. But it meant the news would be known on other human worlds in a few hours, and he would have to deal with that problem sooner than he would have liked.

He closed the call and paused, thinking. Hanna had not known, and Lady Koroth could not know, that *XS-12* had not been entirely unsupported. Sadam Aziz Khan in the Fleet warship *Mao Tse-Tung* was hours away. Clearly the communications blackout no longer was necessary. Better check with Steinmetz and get the *Mao* moving.

It was fruitless to consider what this disaster would mean to him personally. If *XS-12* had only blown up by itself it would not be so bad. If the aliens had something to do with it it would be the worst crisis for humanity since the plague years of the twenty-fourth century. And there would have to be a scapegoat, and he would be it. He would be lucky to end up an assistant to some village mayor in the wilderness; very lucky.

It was going to be a bad Monday.

The Questioner's Assistant shoved a nipple against her mouth, but it was still too short a time since the last red bout of pain, and the water dribbled unnoticed onto the tabletop, already slick with her body fluids. She could not scream any longer and her right arm, broken in some massive convulsion, hurt all the time now. Her body twitched and jerked uncontrollably even when they were not doing anything to her.

Her mind began to work a little again in a slow daze. She licked a drop of water from her lips with painful concentration. Her vision cleared for a moment and beyond the scarlet shape of The Questioner she saw others like him. They were not even trying to block out her pain; they were drawn to it, hungered for it, ate it, absorbed it. Always outside her own agony she felt their gluttonous satisfaction, and sometimes, dimly, savage flashes of joy and ancient victory.

When she could think—less often now—she knew it was impossible. Everyone knew it was impossible. She had accepted unquestioning the common wisdom that star-traveling aliens could not do things like this, that xenophobes do not take to the stars, that compassion and intelligence are inextricably linked. No telepath would know her suffering without sharing it, nor disbelieve her assurance of harmless intent. She had said so in "Sentience." She did not think she would live to write a retraction.

The Questioner saw her limbs quiet, and felt the fog clear from her thought. He said (she knew now it was "he"): *Where in misted stars do the unPeople lair?*

The thought was a glimpse of bloody fangs, and she shook her head weakly. A hank of sweat-soaked hair clung to her cheek.

We are not beasts, but People like yourselves.

With what arms would the not-People kill us?

It was utterly and absolutely impossible to avoid telling him something. Her perception of each question carried a partial answer within itself. The common barriers of her kind, which were all she knew, were nothing to The Questioner. She did not even have the privilege of thinking of the meaning of her death; there was nothing safe to think of for distraction.

Therefore she counted; did sums, remembered logarithms, cherished listings of the elements; that was all they would get, unless pain broke her. This death was slow and hard and worse than anything she had ever imagined, but she thought it could be endured. She was stubborn, adamant. Such qualities had given her trouble in life; they would serve her well in dying. The core of her was strong and inviolate. As long as it stayed so, she could keep silence. And no matter what they dripped into her veins to keep her alive, sometime she would die.

The Questioner said: *This tool has other uses.*

She knew that. She remembered them very well, from one riotous trip to Valentine that had left her shaken and unsure and forced to the conclusion that D'neeran sexual mores, notoriously flexible, had their own rigorous limits for her.

She thought the being was going to try bribing her with pleasure, since pain so far had failed. It made her angry; but that would not work, either.

When she understood its intent, however, she wanted to scream again, and could not.

The commissioners of the Polity rarely all met together in the flesh; for once all of them were here. Andrella Murphy had been a little distance from Earth when Rodrigues called her, going home to Willow, and was breathless from a last-minute rush to Admin. Not only the six of them knew what was going on. After Lady Koroth's announcement some hours before, everyone knew.

Struzik gave Murphy time to settle in a chair before he called the meeting to order. Murphy's single glance at Jameson was anxious; the others were nervous or resentful, angry or triumphant. He knew that all of them, even Murphy, had already taken steps to dissociate themselves as thoroughly as possible from the *Endeavor* Project. The groundwork would be laid—had been laid for months, no doubt—and all the subtle machinery would begin working as soon as they had a little more information. They would have it in a minute now, and he would be left to face the storm alone. He had never expected anything else, and had accepted the risk from the beginning.

"I think," Struzik said, "Starr has a new report for us."

From long habit Jameson spoke calmly, his face betraying nothing.

"I spoke a few minutes ago to Aziz Khan on the *Mao,*" he said. "I'm sorry to say he had a worst-case confirmation. *XS-12* has been destroyed by enemy action."

He looked past them to the end of his career, and waited for the frozen silence to end.

al-Nimeury leaned forward and said, "What weapons?"

"Simple lasers, Aziz Khan said."

"Why? If these aliens have Inspace capability, why not anti-gravity derivatives?"

Jameson resisted an impulse to inquire how he was supposed to guess why aliens used one weapon and not another. He said, "Aggies are very destructive. It may be they wanted to preserve the vessel for study. Aziz Khan said there's very little debris, not nearly enough to account for *XS-12*'s full mass."

Murphy said, "Is there any trace of them?"

"No. You know how easy it is to disappear using Inspace. They know too, evidently."

Katherine Petrov had not been listening. She said, "They've taken it away, then?"

"It appears so."

"Then they've got everything. . . ."

Her old hands hovered anxiously. Jameson said, "Maybe not, Kate. They might have made a mistake. Aziz Khan says the nature of the debris indicates central control took a direct hit. Main data storage almost certainly was destroyed, and the backup may have been damaged."

"Why?" said Murphy. "It doesn't make sense. Why waste the computer?"

"The theory is that their prime target was a human prisoner. It's likely that Lady Hanna, as the logical contact, was the first to come into their hands. It would not make sense to us, but when I notified Lady Koroth—" His eyes were on Murphy, but he found he was seeing Iledra's face, with its barely hidden pain. "Lady Koroth said if they are indeed telepaths they may find it easier and less time-consuming to interrogate a prisoner than to analyze human language and mathematics and hardware."

"You're sure Lady Hanna's alive, then?" Murphy looked worried but far from hysterical—and not nearly so thunderously angry as al-Nimeury.

"Quite sure."

Arthur Feng said, "How much does she know?"

"Too much," Jameson said wearily, thinking of that intent young face. "She has detailed knowledge of D'neeran defense capabilities. She's state-of-the-art where Polity defenses are concerned, although she's never been in a position to know the details."

Petrov said, "We'll have to assume she tells them. And that they're hostile."

Jameson said nothing. According to "Sentience," a defensive posture to a newly encountered intelligent species was inappropriate when a telepath made the contact. But according to "Sentience," not to mention humankind's cherished beliefs about intelligence, such a species would not, as its first act of contact, destroy a human space vessel.

Struzik murmured, "It'll have to be max security."

A storm of voices broke out. Jameson listened without comment. Probably it should be max security. He would speak with Damon Taylor, president of his own world's general council and the man responsible for Jameson's presence on the commission, but he thought "maximum security" would be Taylor's first words. It was expensive, it was frightening, it interfered with commerce and lawful travel and it was of questionable value, given the nature of Inspace transit, but probably it should be max security. Until they found out what was going on. If they ever found out what was going on.

"But—" Feng's voice rose above the babble. "Three conventions next month in Foresight alone. Foresight alone! And anyway they don't have the computer data. And Lady Hanna might not tell them anything."

al-Nimeury growled, "I do *not* want to count on that."

There was an overtone in his voice Jameson recognized, something more than the bruise to pride the *Endeavor* Project had been. al-Nimeury simply disliked D'neera, and violently distrusted D'neerans. It was only an extreme form of a widespread prejudice; Coopers had made themselves into a human unity and combined a checkered assortment of settlers into a human whole against great odds. They were hard on outsiders.

Maximum security was the only realistic choice. It would take days to implement; there was no time to waste; even in this room, which was supposed to hold humanity's coolest heads, there was a shadow of fear. Jameson cast his vote without a word, knowing it might be his last.

When they got up to leave, Struzik nodded to Jameson, who recognized the signal to wait until the others were gone. But Struzik, who gently pried whenever he had the chance, only wanted to gossip, and Jameson was in no mood for gossip.

"You know everything I know," he said.

"I know. Still . . ." Struzik hesitated. "We've never had to do this before."

"No."

"Dust off the contingency plans. . . . We never really expected hostile aliens."

"Somebody did," Jameson pointed out. "That's why the plans are there."

"But I never thought we'd have to use them."

Jameson shrugged. "You take your chances," he said.

"*Your* chance. Your idea."

Jameson waited, watching his oldest Earth-born friend.

Struzik said, "How much did you know?"

"Nothing," Jameson said, understanding the question perfectly.

"Tell me the truth, Jamie. You thought she might be right all along, didn't you? Being scared of them as she was?"

Jameson did not answer. Struzik said. "This puts you in a spot, doesn't it?"

"You might say that." Jameson had made mistakes before, but he could not recall another that had endangered the whole human species. In a day or so the pack would be in full cry. It would be folly to dispense with his experience in a time of crisis, but he did not know if Taylor would be able to avoid it.

Struzik began, "All the fuss about *Endeavor* in the first place—"

"Seems to have been justified."

Jameson started out the door. Behind him Struzik said, not without sympathy, "You really put your foot in it this time, Jamie."

"Don't call me that," Jameson said automatically, but his heart was not in it.

Hanna found humiliation could do things simple pain could not. The boundary in her mind between rape and the pleasures of love had been clear; that made it worse. Rape was a true-human crime which she had heard of but never met, and she had faced the possibility of the start of war with Nestor with a certain equanimity. If it happened she would endure it, and when there was a chance—even if years passed before the chance came—she would kill the man who did it. The principle was as clear to her as anything in her life, her mastery of this part of herself indisputable and a foundation of her existence. In this matter there were no gray areas.

What happened to her now was different, and beyond enduring. Bad enough, insane enough, to have the paths of pleasure charted by some monstrous being unmoved as the tool it used; but each time, at the end, to want what it promised! The instrument was forbidden everywhere except Valentine; her own experience had shown her why; it took away your humanity. The body had its own imperatives, and no matter how she set her will the moment would come when she gave in to them, and her will would be broken. And when she wept in shame and self-hatred the pain would come again, and it would be harder to resist that too.

Stop. Stop. Oh please, I beg, oh please.

I will not. Thus were beasts destroyed before you time-ago; in this and other ways: We learned.

Abject I crawl, I beg, implore, I will do anything save speak!

That too. How not? Ask when. There is no escape. Of all agonies that is the worst: no ending nor escape.

Pain merged with pleasure, she got them mixed up, the creature was as close as her self, the bond was irresistible. Yet she resisted.

Answer, if thou lovest me. A single flame. The heavens thus. Knowest thou this benchmark?

I know. . . .

And this? No? Then this?

No! I will not.

You will.

The universe contracted to Hanna and The Questioner. She resisted, surrendered, forgot she was human, remembered. The past died in the evil present. The little certainty that was left her blurred and dissolved; but The Questioner was certain. In an unguarded moment he let her see his sureness that he hammered at a fracture point, that she would split cleanly as a crystal, and he would not let her shatter into dust.

On Tuesday night Jameson went home and immediately broke an ampoule of a high-powered tranquilizing drug under his nose. After a minute he did it with another and the world slowed around him, and the muscles of his back and legs reluctantly, lingeringly relaxed.

He was leaning against the wall of his study, his breath clouding its shining surface, when the room said, "Ms. Guilbert is calling."

"Just give me audio in here . . . Henriette?"

"Hello. You told me to call you today."

"Did I?"

"Umm-hmm."

He shook his head, a gesture she could not see.

"I'm sorry, Henry. I haven't had any sleep for a couple of days and I don't know when I'll be able to get free."

"I thought that was probably—Starr?"

"Yes?"

"Can I ask you a question?"

He smiled in spite of his weariness. "You know the rules about answers."

"You'll either tell me the truth, not answer, or lie to me."

"That's right." He had laid the rule down solemnly early on, and Henriette rarely asked about the commission.

"Are you worried?"

"No," he lied.

After a pause she said. "They're saying President Taylor is going to recall you."

"Who's saying that?" (Besides half the Heartworld council and sometimes Taylor too, he thought.)

"It's on all the newsbeams. They're saying—well. Somebody said you're a megalomaniac and you shoved the *Endeavor* Project through, knowing how dangerous it was."

She sounded uncertain. Very likely she believed it. Damned if he was going to defend himself to Henriette; she had never listened to a word of his public statements before she met him, and rarely did so now.

"Cut your losses, Henry."

"What?"

"Never mind. Henry, my appointment will not be revoked. A minority faction in the council will try to pass a resolution demanding my resignation. They won't have nearly enough votes. That'll be the end of it. It happens all the time, Henry, in one form or another."

"All right." She sounded dissatisfied. A village mayor's assistant would not suit her.

"I must go now. I'll call you as soon as I can."

He went to his bedroom, thinking the last thing he wanted right now was Henriette beside him in the big bed. No, not quite the last thing; he could do without partisan politics just now too.

He barely had time to get his clothes off before the dope put him to sleep.

Not crystal
but steel.
It is stronger
than Lost Ones
and beasts.
There is more to protect.
Much more. Worlds and
weapons unsuspected
it has shown us.
Not enough! It
cannot die
will not die.
Not yet.

The promise and the threat were nothing to Hanna, nor had she the clarity of mind to wonder what could follow. She could not move. When she was sick from time to time they turned her like a slab of meat so she would not choke to death; she could not and would not have done it by herself. Her mind also had retreated. For some time she had not felt anything; blessedly detached, for a little while she wandered the golden hills of her home. Once it was night, the moonless star-clouded night of D'neera. It seemed that at some time she had wanted to soar into the bright cloud, borne by her own wonder and curiosity. That could not be right. The stars were too terrible. Her mother said, H'ana, when will you be home? Soon, darling, she answered.

And where is this place? someone asked in her dream.

Here, you see, not far from the gentle sea.

And if I wish to go there from another star how may I find it?

Dutifully she began to think of astrogation. And remembered in a surge of terror what asked the question.

They are stronger than
stronger than
We. Pierce its heart.
No! Lost We
lost the vessel
knew not Our aim
and Our goal and
destroyed it

unknowing; now
nothing
useless
metal
twisted
unspeaking.
Wildfire is all.

They did not bother to hide their thoughts. Hanna understood none of it. Their new agitation only threatened her precarious peace. An ocean's slow pulsebeat rocked her.

This was not the
purpose of the
purpose of the Rite.
Time is changed We
are changed. They too.
And they. The
old records the
Lost Ones the
Students knew the
key
which is death
which is madness
We will try.

A new and powerful voice said: *One star may be all that We need; its Home, whence it returns: first known, last to fade in the end-of-self. We will try.*

We will try.

They were specialists in their way. They knew what mutilation did to the human spirit and made a ruin of her breasts. They knew what disfigurement did to identity, and destroyed her face. They knew what sudden blindness did to courage, and put out her eyes. They knew about humans and their children, and did things in her belly that made her pass out again, but not for long, because they never let her stay unconscious for long.

Wednesday night Jameson called the *Endeavor*. There was no choice. It was too vulnerable, too tempting a target, sailing space with its computers chuckling to themselves and blithely inviting the aliens to come say hello. So he was told, anyway, and reluctantly he believed this much at least: now was not the time to expound on the philosophical arguments in favor of alien contact.

Another name for the *Endeavor* Project was current in certain circles. It was "Jameson's Folly."

Erik Fleming asked to be reassigned to the hopeless search for *XS-12* and Hanna. Jameson had no direct authority in the matter, but he still bore his precarious title and his hint to Fleming's Fleet superiors would go a long way. He said he would see what he could do.

When he was done with Fleming he poured a drink and stood at the edge of his office for a while, looking out at the river as Hanna had done not long ago. Once he had thought of pitching her into that same river, if she did not stop turning his well-ordered staff upside down.

He did not think he would see Hanna again, and in memory, memory of a time so separated from the desperate now that it might have been a distant past, she came before his eyes with her odd blend of adamant and innocence. He had thought: she needs only a little shaping to be a precious tool; a little patience with compromise, some skill in the way things work. Now he thought: she did not want to go. And did not even think about the courage that took her out there. And neither did I.

He had spent his life in public service. He was responsible for humanity first, then Heartworld. If he were to accept responsibility for every individual who came into his work the burden would crush him. He could not afford to forget the fact, and now he was reminded of the reasons he had learned it in the first place. He had begun to like Hanna ril-Koroth; and he had personally sent her to her death.

You know this configuration. I see that you do. And from here to your Home?

She was quite mad. When she thought of something they wanted they cut off another bit of her. That was her reward. Sometimes it was the other way around. It seemed proper and gratifying. When it was finished there would be nothing left of her. An orderly and needful procedure.

In a moment of vague anxiety she asked, it's all right, isn't it, Iledra? Yes, Iledra answered.

This being is your Leader? But there are others. What are you?

I am nothing. Nothing does not live, therefore I do not live, therefore kill me.

We will not. Show me the Homes again in your thought. Not that one. The others. The others!

I have no eyes, no hands, therefore no thought.

Have you learned any more?
No. No. No. Too late.
We must know.
Cannot know.
At the last. . . .
Was it true? Its Home a mote
defenseless. The rest
beyond power. It is true. There is
more than We thought.
Then We must
We cannot
Yet I will.
Experiment only
new as the new-things
as Treecubs
as Renders
as old
but We are equipped and
supplied for the
bending the
shaping insertion
command
I will try.
We will try.

Iledra sat up in bed and called "H'ana?" but there was no answer. Dawn showed at her windows. It was night in Namerica, she could talk to Jameson if she wished, but what was there to tell him? Hanna was still alive. Iledra could not explain the shock that had waked her. She was not even sure it was real; perhaps she had been dreaming about Hanna, and only her own anxiety had roused her.

She lay down again and pulled the feather-stuffed quilt over her shoulders.

* * *

Four days later the mayday from *XS-12* reached the *Mao Tse-Tung* and the D'neeran light cruiser *Voltaire*, which haunted space where the scout had disappeared. It carried position referents which were arrogantly clear. The *Voltaire* had no chance in the race that followed. The *Mao* plunged through uncharted space much faster than was safe, and in a steaming empty place with an atmosphere that could just be breathed, Aziz Khan found the wreck of *XS-12*, the pieces of Charl Zeig and Anja Daru, and something he did not at once recognize as H'ana ril-Koroth, which still barely lived.

CHAPTER IX

It wasn't really dark. There were flashes of light, pinwheels, silent explosions of brightness, firework forms pursuing one another, a mad dance against the blackness.

Hanna watched them for a while. It did not seem to matter that she was blind.

Nothing hurt. She did not know why that was so important.

She felt nothing: nothing at all. If that was the alternative, fine.

Iledra said: *Beloved H'ana-daughter. Attend to me.*

Her mourning filled the darkness. Hanna felt tearful. Iledra was lost to her, it was only her own sad desire that spoke.

H'ana daughter, I am here.

Here? What is here?

The bright images gave way to a room where men and women clustered round a shrouded figure, half-machine, that lay unfeeling and unmoving.

That is you.

No. That is not me.

But it was not important.

"She is aware of me," said Iledra's voice through deep water.

"Ask her," said another voice she ought to know.

She felt Iledra's reluctance, but slowly an image formed, the details changing, shifting: a little space ship as Iledra imagined it, two persons whom she recognized.

"She does not want to think about it," Iledra said.

"She must. She will not for us. She must for you."

Think. Remember.

No. Oh, no.

But it was not so much a protest against thinking about

what had happened, as against the thing itself. She was not sure what that was, but it was bad.

Think. It is important, H'ana-daughter.

The keystone so. Tomorrow rain. We rest by speaking pools, enclosed. . . .

Remember. It is important to me.

Her awareness leapt, and for an instant she knew she was alive.

Iledra?

I am here. Tell me.

"Tell her," said the voice she ought to know, "to think it to you in words. I want the clearest report possible."

"She's too weak. It will have to be images."

In the silence Hanna's mind murmured along pleasant, harmless paths.

"All right, then," the voice said presently, "Describe them as well as you can."

Show me the aliens. Show me what happened.

The urgency and sorrow seemed distant. It was, perhaps, safe to approach them; memory too, perhaps. She did so cautiously, for Iledra. Who would not push her to terror and then recoil from it as others (others?) had done. She fell through a kaleidoscope of the New City, Koroth, Earthly glitter, black space, and thought very clearly: *The signal.*

And then?

A picture: Anja and Charl at her shoulders, not knowing the last hours of their lives had come; the tension, apprehension, fumbling at a mystery.

And then? And then? And then?

It was not so hard to make the images, as long as she remembered it had all happened to somebody else. Not to her. Never to her.

A quick intake of breath, involuntary. "So they destroyed it without reason or warning."

Iledra's voice. "None."

The pain! I cannot, I cannot, no! No! No!

There were quick, half-sensed flurries of movement that she knew only through Iledra's perceptions.

"This is what happened each time—"

"All right. Yes. I can block it and go on."

"Not so much," said still another voice, a woman's voice.

Hanna's mind soared suddenly into the air above southern

Koroth. Here was the little town where her mother taught the neighbors' children, and orange blossoms were heavy on the air. The summer sun late in the evening cast long shadows from every hillock, and the heat was thick as water. I can feel that, she thought, and reached for a shadow. She thought she knew how it would feel between her fingers.

She had no fingers.

The voice said close by, "What did you tell them?"

D'neera. D'neera. I told them only of D'neera. They asked where my People are.

"D'neera," said Iledra's voice, sounding sad. "Yes. The center of her universe is D'neera. She is not only human; she is D'neeran."

"Did she not tell them about the Polity?"

"Not much, I think. It is not clear. They guessed there was more. But it was too late then. Their only dangerous knowledge is of D'neera. I do not know how they made her tell them even that."

"You see what they did."

"It would be enough."

"For anyone."

"Yes."

The third, strange voice said, "Enough. Enough for today. No more."

"One moment." Something came near. Close to her ear the familiar voice said, "Hanna. I'm sorry."

Sorry? she wanted to say. But she could not speak, and the question still rang in her mind when they put her to sleep again.

"Horrible," said Iledra. She noticed, with detachment, that her hands were shaking.

"Horrible," Jameson agreed. He stood before her still holding the glass of wine she had refused. She had no comforting illusion that today's ordeal was over. She needed a clear head.

She breathed deeply, trying to compose herself. For a brief space, here in Jameson's private office, the world was quiet. The wall to the river was shut, although she could see through it. The water was gray and restless under black clouds, the horizon a sick glare of light. She saw lightning, but no thunder was audible here. In another room close by, Cosma was exchanging stares with Paul Rodrigues and with an assortment of military and intelligence men whose questions could not wait. Iledra did not know if they would permit her to leave Earth. She could not and would not promise to keep her new knowledge to herself; to do so would be a rejection of principle amounting to treason. And the true-humans would want to control what she had taken for them from Hanna. They would filter it, edit it, shape it and tell a hundred societies what was good for them to know. A D'neeran could not stand for it; but she did not see how they could keep her here without producing as much trouble as the truth would create.

Jameson moved away from her, looked at the glass in his hand as if he wondered where it had come from, and drank the wine himself. Iledra thought he would go to his desk, an enormous thing studded and surrounded with devices for spanning human space. The ambience the room had had on her last visit was lost in the glitter of tools for communication and information retrieval, and the array had the secondary function of subtly intimidating anyone who faced Jameson when he took his place at its center.

But he stopped short of it and looked aimlessly about the room, and Iledra's attention sharpened. She read signs that Jameson was very tired and had been taking stimulants for several days, but that should not produce this absence of mind.

He looked around, gauging her recovery from the hour just past. He said as if it were inconsequential, "Why did they send her back?"

"Why did—?"

"They send her back. You must have wondered."

Iledra said unwillingly, "Yes. But I have been too worried about her to give it thought."

"It was not altruism." He came back to stand before her, and she got up as if some subtle alarm had sounded. The conversational tone did not deceive her.

"You think it is important?"

"Obviously. They went to no little trouble to keep her alive. She must have been near death when they stopped—from shock, pain, loss of blood. They nursed her through the shock, sealed her wounds, and provided her with a fair substitute for human plasma. Enough to keep her alive for a day or two; enough to save her until Aziz Khan got to her. Why?"

"She said nothing of it. I don't know." At the moment Iledra did not care. "Can she be healed?"

"I think so. The medical people think so. They've seen worse."

"Worse!"

He said dispassionately, "Accident victims. She was mutilated with surgical precision, and all her vital organs are intact. Accidents are not so careful."

Iledra had never liked Jameson much. Now she loathed him from the heart.

"I want to take her home."

"D'neera does not have the facilities to care for her."

"As soon as she is well enough."

"It will be months."

Iledra was a tall woman, and did not have to look up very far to meet Jameson's eyes. She said flatly, "You would not let her go anyway."

"The point's irrelevant. She must stay here for her own sake."

"You would not have let me near her if you had not needed me. If any of you had been able to communicate with her without being unmanned by her fear, you would not have let me see her. If the *Voltaire* had not been there when the alarm came, would you have told me, even, that you had found her? I think not."

She was right about all of it. He would not say so; but she heard it anyway.

He said quietly, "It's pointless to exacerbate public fear. It must be known of course that she has been found, but not everyone needs to know exactly what was done to her. I do not want to deal with a panic."

"I think you already have one," Iledra said. She had come to Earth very speedily, but she was no pilot and had spent her days and nights in gathering all the information she could. She knew knots and eddies of the credulous already wanted to run—if only they knew where to run to. Soldiers everywhere watched the void for traces of an invader, and an innocent merchantman approaching Colony One had been blown to bits. All the commissioners' seats were in jeopardy, along with the bodies that had appointed them. And someone,

someone not unimportant, had suggested Jameson be tried for unspecified crimes against humanity.

But he said, "There is no panic yet. But it is not wise to provide fuel for one. There are disjunctions enough in every society, and more will come. You cannot be unaware of what is happening here. Security measures already are affecting our economies. Earth's old proposal for tightening inter-system controls is on the verge of approval. It will take lifetimes to complete, it will drain off more resources than we can afford and restrict our descendants' freedom of movement to an intolerable degree. I thought the idea was discredited years ago; yet the mood of Heartworld governments is such that if it comes to a vote I will have to acquiesce. Power is shifting on every human world, including yours. For you, if I read the currents correctly, it is taking the form of a return to isolationism. I do not like a new thing I hear from D'neera—that a movement is gaining strength to build up your own defenses, and dispense with Polity protection. What will your people do when they learn that we have just learned—that your world is the aliens' prime target?"

Iledra said softly, "Don't try that with me."

"I beg your pardon?" He looked genuinely surprised.

"Don't try to frighten me. You lie. The prime target is the Polity. D'neera is no threat to them. They are interested in D'neera only as a means of getting to you. H'ana did not tell them enough."

Irritation crossed his face; she thought she was not supposed to see it. He said, "When the attack comes their reasons will not matter. You couldn't fight off Nestor without the Fleet. You can't do without us now. I hope you can convince your fellow magistrates of that."

"I am not likely to have much success. The outcry against me has been great. You are right at least about shifting power. I may not be the Lady of Koroth much longer."

"And the call will come at any moment telling me I am no longer the commissioner for Heartworld. But we still have our responsibilities, Lady Koroth. Neither of us to one world only; both of us to the human species. I will not try to force you to keep silence about Hanna's condition or anything else you have learned. But I will ask you to use all the influence you have to ensure D'neera's cooperation. I will ask you to make D'neera see where its duty lies."

"Duty!" she said, and turned away from him. She was on the edge of tears, as she had been since her first sight of Hanna; it had been a great shock, in spite of Jameson's warning beforehand. She had made Hanna see where *her* duty lay, and would regret that success forever.

There would be no attempt to detain her here, for she had made her own prison. Her efforts to insinuate D'neera into true-human society had ensnared her, and all ways out were closed. It would not be her part now to shape a world's course; the aliens glimpsed as forms of horror in Hanna's tormented memory would shape them all. Jameson would let her go free so that she could bend or frighten the Houses to docility—meaning that she would smooth the way for a Polity military presence that would come whether it was wanted or not. Her part was to play the go-between; to discourage resistance and make palatable the truth that the Polity would descend on D'neera not for D'neera's protection, but for its own.

She looked back at him and said, because she had no choice and it did not matter what she said, "I will do what I can."

He nodded slightly. It was not much of a tribute to what she promised. He said, "There was no indication of their motives in returning her?"

The repetition annoyed her. "None."

"Perhaps we will find out in time," he said too casually.

Iledra thought of the useless hulk that had been Hanna and clasped her hands together. They would question Hanna as remorselessly as the aliens had, and she could not prevent it. She could not even say that they were wrong. Where Hanna and the aliens were concerned, no information was trivial.

She said, "There is one thing."

"Yes?"

"Probably it does not matter—"

"What is it?"

She said slowly, "There seemed a difference in H'ana."

"What sort of difference?" His tone was unchanged; but she knew that every sense he possessed was concentrated on her answer.

"I don't—I hardly know. Images and, oh, turns of thought, the equivalent of phrasing, perhaps. . . ."

She was unsure of what she was trying to describe, and the

impact of her contact with Hanna was fading. She knew the contours and tastes of Hanna's personality as well as her own, or she would never have seen the subtle difference; and it might after all be only part of the memory of fear and pain, or the greater disjunction of trauma and drugs. The first would leave greater or lesser traces in Hanna, as tragedy always did, but much of it, and the immediate effects of her physical condition, would dissipate.

She looked up and saw that Jameson still waited for her to go on. She shook her head. "It's not important," she said.

"Are you sure?"

She hesitated, but the impression dimmed as she considered it. It had been difficult to induce and hold Hanna to concentration, and dream fragments had kept intruding.

"I'm sure," she said.

"All right. Are you ready to talk to the others?"

She looked once toward the river, as if she could escape to it, but rain obscured it now, silently. "Yes," she said.

They went to the door together. Just before they got there he said abruptly, "I was glad to hear about her eyes."

She trusted him too little to think he meant it, but she said, "I'll have them sent in a week or two. We were going to do away with the bank. None of our defense people have needed their spares for years."

"It was good news you have them. The plan was for a stock transplant."

"I know." Iledra's own eyes filled with tears. She said, "I would hate to think of H'ana with someone else's eyes. Her own are so lovely."

Jameson looked down at her and said to her surprise, "Yes. They were very lovely."

The door opened, and the questions began at once.

Chaos. Dream sweetly.
?
Not this Home. Circled
!
unfearing
not mine! not me!
we rest
oh help me oh help
unheard. Dream. Forget.

The next wakings were less painful, and even more dream-like. Some she would remember, some she would not. Part of her mind began to store information. They were fixing her, re-growing much of her, patching together the rest. Her own eyes, grown on D'neera and banked there when she joined Defense, were available; that was good. Her flesh responded eagerly to regeneration, the speed was something built in at the time of the Change; that was not so good, not when there were so many different things to juggle. She could not move or feel anything. They explained to her once that so many delicate processes were going on in healing her that it was best she stay away, stay asleep, and let them go about the business of repairing the envelope that held Hanna ril-Koroth.

Presently they tried waking her to full self-awareness, and in the first burst of memory she was frantic to flee, and could not move nor even cry out. Her panic blasted a hundred people. They knocked her out to stop the nightmare-silent screaming and, reluctantly, since Iledra had gone home, asked D'neera to send a telepath to aid them.

Dale Tharan came without protest, approved by the Polity precisely because he was an outspoken advocate of giving it anything it wanted and taking in return all D'neera could get. But he did not like Hanna, and when he had eased her into reality as he was supposed to do, he told her she had not done him or herself or D'neera any favor by failing to hold out against the aliens. *And hideous now. A limbless lump,* he added, but even Tharan was not proof against Hanna's first clear sight, through his eyes, of what the aliens had made of her. They made her sleep again, and next time they woke her Tharan, with considerable dedication, painted her portrait as she had been and would be again. It was not much to hold on to, but it was something.

Jameson had the interrogation sessions linked with his office. He listened while he went about his business, and when he was with other people he had the transmission routed to the implant in his ear, which was supposed to be used only for matters of extreme urgency and when he had shut himself off from the world by every other means.

The data extracted from Hanna were, then, twice disembodied. She could hear, but she could not speak. The questions therefore were asked by the men whose business it was to ask them, but the answers were filtered first through Tharan, and then through the complex electronics that fed Tharan's voice into Jameson's ear. What he heard might have been messages shouted by Hanna across a river, the meaning twisted, distorted, blown away by distance and the wind. Those about him were often disconcerted. He wore a wrist communicator, as was his habit, but ordinarily he was courteous about its use. Now he would interrupt anyone or anything to raise it to his lips and snarl, "Ask her—"

Ask her anything. How many? On their ship? On their world? How many planets? What weaponry?—until they had to give up questions, because Hanna would get confused, and think aliens not humans questioned her, and send Tharan with a spinning head stumbling away, unmanned, as Iledra had said, by her fear.

What she said of the Lost World jolted Jameson. He had not really believed in it until now, thinking it a bare possibility; but it was real; and the spectacle of a human population tortured, manipulated, subjected to experiment and killed, was appalling. Humans had almost stopped doing such things to each other—a hopeful sign for the future, he had always thought. Now there was the prospect of its starting all over again with an aggressor to whom economic sanctions and human opinion meant exactly nothing.

He seized on what the sacrificed colonists could do for him, however, without permitting himself compunctions about using a ghoul's opportunity. The information came early enough to save him for a time, because it was immediately clear that Species X had been searching for humanity for a long time. Jameson said publicly and privately to anyone who would listen, playing the idea for all it was worth, that it was fortunate the first contacts had been with *Endeavor* and *XS-12* so that humankind had some warning. It was not enough to get back all the ground he had lost, but Heartworld did not replace him and he was still in control.

Except—control was an illusion. Maybe he had known it from the moment Rodrigues's voice called him from the illusions of his last hours with Henriette. If he had not known it he found out one night when he took an enormous dose of Imagos, hoping to lose grim reality in the blurred edges of beauty for a little while. But the coals in his fireplace were Hanna's charred eyesockets, bone showed through his own unsteady hand, and he could not get the antidote into his bloodstream fast enough for comfort. Nothing like it had ever happened to him before. He sat sweating in a room cool enough to need a fire and acknowledged something he had pretended not to know: the dreams that had given birth to *Endeavor* were finished. There would be no brave leap into the future; only torturous courses dictated by need. Past and future had come seeking *him,* and he was as helpless as Lady Koroth.

Another purpose?

Another. Old old. Incomplete. They did not finish.

Finish what?

I don't know. An ending. More than death. More than me. They stopped. And still another.

Purpose? What?

I don't know. I don't know!

"Tharan," said an audible voice. It must have said his name several times before it penetrated his dialogue with Hanna.

He got up, shaking off Hanna's frantic grab for contact. To stay sane himself he had to harden himself against her clutching terror. If she had been anyone else, if she had been here for any other reason, they would have let her sleep through the months of helplessness and enforced paralysis. They could not, and she sometimes skirted the raw edge of panic. Tharan kept trying to tell her she was safe now. She kept forgetting.

Stanislaw Morisz had called him. Morisz beckoned and Tharan went out the door with him. There was nobody in the corridor. This was a very busy medical center, but they'd sealed off a whole floor for Hanna.

Morisz said, "I read yesterday's transcript. There was nothing. Nothing definite."

Tharan said patiently, "Telepathic communication is not a one-to-one correspondence with fact."

Morisz only looked at him. Tharan knew Morisz was impatient and beginning to get angry. Hanna should be a mine of information and she was not, and the true-humans did not understand why. Tharan was not surprised. He had come to Earth prepared to explain the uses and limitations of telepathy. Now he settled himself against the wall in the corridor outside Hanna's room and began to lecture.

He said, "Every bit of information exchanged is surrounded

by a network of associated concepts, memories, emotions. It can be very precise if you have a language in common, and fairly precise even without that if there's a shared cultural matrix. If you don't have either of those things, you have what H'ana was writing about in 'Sentience'—very broad, global concepts with a high degree of subjectivity. She's trying to put into words—or sometimes I am—things that were images, symbols, very fuzzy when you try to objectify them. To put it another way, she knows a great deal about the aliens, but it's not the kind of knowledge you want. You'll notice all they got out of her was hard-science information. Stellar configurations are a shared objective reference, so she could show them where D'neera is. But they were the ones doing the questioning, not her. And where the 'soft' side is concerned, how they think, how they live, that kind of thing—as I said, she has a lot of information, but there's no program to plug it into. So it doesn't make sense to her or to me and it's not going to make sense to you."

When he stopped he saw Morisz's mouth twitch. Morisz said, "There's some objective data, though. The Lost World, for instance."

"Sure—because there was something in her cultural matrix to connect it to. But it's very general. No detail."

Morisz pondered. He said, "I don't understand what she means. That they were doing something besides questioning her."

"I know. I don't either. Neither does she. It's very vague. Maybe religious but not really, she says, and then somehow divorced from its original context. They ripped her up for a reason, but she doesn't know what it was."

"You have to get more."

Morisz looked tired. Tharan said sympathetically, "Jameson on your back?"

Morisz did not answer. He didn't have to. Jameson kept turning up at odd moments, straight and stiff and staring at the remnants of Hanna with an inhuman lack of queasiness. The man had a strong stomach and maybe, Tharan thought, some things going on inside him a mindhealer could hardly resist. But he wanted Hanna sucked dry anyway.

After a minute Morisz said, "We're wasting time."

"Yes," Tharan said, and set about calming himself for the return to Hanna. What he was doing was hard. Everything he got for Morisz was filtered through layers of blind pure animal pain.

Tharan thought it was a good thing they had him. They'd have gotten nothing by themselves.

After a while it seemed to Jameson that he had been hearing Dale Tharan's voice all his life.

They found out what the aliens looked like and made pictures, and Hanna looked through Tharan's eyes and agreed (with what pain Tharan did not say) that the pictures were accurate. They found out what the outside of the alien spacecraft looked like, which told them nothing, and what an alien torture chamber looked like, which told them less. They found out you could make a neural stimulator from something that looked like living fabric and set about trying to do so, hoping if they succeeded they could work backward to some bit of knowledge about the aliens. They searched for records of the Lost World, but there were none; that was why it was lost. They tried to figure out how an alien stungun worked. They analyzed blood samples taken from Hanna on the *Mao*, and came up with something unexpected.

"Psychoactive drugs?" said Jameson, who saw every report anyone made on Hanna. His eyes hurt constantly and he seldom slept. The first narrow escape from being recalled to Heartworld might be over, but only his intimate knowledge of the situation here kept certain key councilmen in line.

"Yeah. Funny thing is, she doesn't remember any effects." Morisz's eyes were red too.

"Can you tell when she got them?"

"Late in the process. Very late."

"Before or after her memories gave out?"

"Impossible to say. The best guess is it was after she lost consciousness more or less permanently."

"There would have been no point at that stage."

"There's no point to any of it. Why do they think we're some kind of goddamn tigers? What could a bunch of ragged-ass colonists do to make them think that?"

"Whatever the reason, she ought to have been able to show them otherwise."

"What?"

" 'Sentience.' Section Six."

"Oh," said Morisz. "That."

And then?
The right response.
But then
Exactly the right response.
Then
One of us two of us three of us defenseless
Then
Vulnerable.
But later?
No later not ever.
There was later.
No later. No.

"What's that for?" Jameson said.

"What—oh. The screen. I don't know. We started using it at the beginning. I forget why." Morisz was so used to having a barrier before the module holding Hanna that he had stopped noticing it.

"Get rid of it."

"Right."

But when it was gone Morisz remembered why it had been there. This outer room was large enough to seem uncrowded in spite of its masses of equipment, for even minor regeneration was not a simple task, and Hanna was not a minor project. Now, however, it was crowded with people, and with the screen gone they had to look at Hanna. Eight weeks into the regeneration process she was, if anything, a more repulsive sight than she had been at the start. The medical people liked to see what was happening, though their eyes were not as good as their instrumentation, and sometimes they forgot to cover up the tangle of flesh and tubes and wires with decent sheeting. They had not forgotten this time, but the contours of the figure centered in its zero-*g* bubble were horribly suggestive. But at least, Morisz thought, she has a face again. The only recognizable thing about Hanna when he saw her first had been the straight pretty nose. The aliens had not wanted to obstruct respiration.

The scene taking shape was Jameson's idea. He seemed not to believe Hanna had told Tharan everything, though the questioning went on for hours each day, and insisted on trying one more thing. Tharan, just outside the chamber where Hanna lay, was already in tenuous rapport with her;

she was more heavily sedated than usual, and the effect showed in Tharan's face as a vague slackness. Neuro- and psychopharmacologists were in place, and a physiogeneralist stared over their shoulders at a mix-monitor panel. A Fleet liaison specialist and one of Morisz's assistants ignored each other from adjacent seats. There was nothing more to wait for. Morisz was about to witness—in a sense, even, to direct—something he had heard of but never seen: a mindhealer-Adept of D'neera undertaking a telepathic deep probe.

He said to Tharan, "You know what you're looking for."

"Something . . . hidden . . ." Tharan's voice trailed off. It would be difficult for him to maintain a double awareness—inward to Hanna, outward to the others—but it could be done. He would not attempt to speak to them unless he got what he was after.

"Anything new. Anything at all. You've been over most of it so often you should notice anything different. But don't waste time on the stuff we know. Get down to the end and concentrate on that."

Tharan did not answer. His eyes glazed as the contact deepened. Hanna, Morisz knew, had not wanted to do this, but Tharan had appealed to her sense of duty—and, Morisz suspected, her guilt.

He glanced over his shoulder. "Everybody ready?" he asked, but not until he saw Jameson's bare nod did he say to Tharan, "All right. Go ahead."

Minutes trickled by. Morisz watched Tharan, but he was motionless as Hanna. He would be living through her experiences now, not just turning them into words for Intelligence but guiding her attention to details unconsciously noted. If he could he would damp the emotional strain, holding her to detailed objectivity. Morisz had expected signs of strain, but there were none. Time passed, men shifted position and coughed, someone spoke. Morisz wondered why he had ever thought a deep mindprobe would be a dramatic thing—

Blackblackblackno

"No!" Morisz whispered, and wiped sudden sweat from his face. The sensation had been one of falling, as if he had been on the edge of sleep and jerked back just in time from an endless black pit, wide awake. He looked sidelong at Jameson and saw a hand slowly withdrawn from an instinctive grab for support. He felt a flicker of satisfaction that

Jameson was not immune to *this* at least, and then was ashamed.

He whispered to Jameson, "Tharan lost it."

"Mmm-hmm."

Morisz glanced uneasily at the pharmacologists. He had been there for Hanna's first waking, and knew first-hand what happened when a half-mad telepath lost control. Tharan was supposed to be able to focus and channel her awareness, centering it on himself and reinforcing the inhibitions against random projection that Hanna had internalized in childhood and practiced all her life. If he failed, the pharmacologists would take over. But even they were using negative alerts, so a circuit would close and Hanna would sleep if they made any move without warning. That first time their colleagues had nearly killed her when all they wanted to do was shut her up.

Tharan was quite still, his hand resting on the thin plastic film that provided a visual cue for the force field containing Hanna. Sometimes he went inside with her, but not today; she could not be touched indiscriminately, and in the deep probe the urge to do so would be strong.

The tension had grown with that fragment of Hanna's memory, and Morisz muttered to distract himself, "He's getting attached to her in spite of himself, isn't he."

"Yes." Jameson just breathed the word.

"Says she knows what a mess she made of it."

"Mmm-hmm."

Morisz was not an imaginative man, but he remembered Tharan's confidence and was chilled. What would it do to you, he wondered, to lie paralyzed and blind and anesthetized for weeks, remembering how you got that way, reflecting on your failure, living with the conviction of the man who was your only link to life that you had endangered everything you knew?

mistake mistake mistake stupid mess D'neerans look what how'd we get here goddamn

Words, even seemingly in Hanna's voice. Jameson turned his head and said, "She's getting that from one of us." There was ice in his voice.

"Not me," Morisz said a little nervously. He looked around and saw the Fleet major gone red-faced and too stiff, unused to his private thoughts becoming public property.

lovest me thy father mother brother lover here fullsharing lest cold night

Tharan shifted abruptly. Morisz was on his feet. No words that time, not until he created them, and not in Hanna's voice but silent strangeness, a jolt of madness.

Jameson said quietly, "Nothing new."

"What?"

"Think about Tharan's reports. That's what he's been describing all along."

"Oh. . . ." Morisz sat down slowly. The men behind them whispered to each other. "She was identifying with them."

"Sometimes," Jameson said, but he was leaning forward now and watching the two D'neerans closely, as if he could force his way into Hanna's brain himself.

But Tharan, after a while, straightened and shook his head. "That's all," he said. The words were a little slurred.

Jameson continued to stare at him. Tharan put his head in his hands. When he looked up his face was more alert; he had broken the rapport.

"There isn't any more," he said. "I told you there wasn't."

Jameson got up and went to stand beside him, looking through the transparency at Hanna. Morisz followed, uneasy. In the weeks since Hanna's return Jameson had become more reserved than ever. It had never been easy to guess what he was thinking; now it was impossible. He seemed to be turning to stone, perpetually preoccupied with something no one else perceived. But whatever it was focused the force of his personality instead of subduing it, so that when he spoke it was like a glimpse of flame, and Morisz sometimes thought that one day Jameson would explode.

Tharan stood up and Jameson said, "There is more."

"There isn't. It just ends."

"They hadn't finished with her. You know what was in her bloodstream: psychotropic drugs. You know what they would do. It must have been done *after* what you have shown us."

"It ends," Tharan repeated.

"Memory does not vanish. The organism records everything. On the cellular, the chemical, the molecular levels, if nowhere else. If you are as competent as you say, you could retrieve her primal memories of gestation. Why not this?"

"I can't retrieve something unless there was enough consciousness to organize the experience in the first place. There wasn't. They dissolved her ego."

"She perceived it as dissolution. That does not mean it was dissolved."

Tharan said blankly, "That's exactly what it means."

"I don't intend to argue semantics. Is there any possibility she is deliberately blocking you?"

"No," Tharan said positively.

"Could there be a block imposed by another?"

"No."

"How do you know?"

Tharan said angrily, "I'm a D'neeran, a telepath, an Adept, and a mindhealer. Don't try to tell me I don't know."

"You are either incompetent or a liar," Jameson said, and turned away and started for the door. The ghoulish little tableau was broken. Tharan took a fast step after Jameson.

Sweet winds, summerfruit, soft-plumed love eternal thy warm waters unbroken.

In a great rush of wellbeing Morisz saw a hand slip from its place. The circuit closed; he drifted for an instant toward sleep, and it was over. Hanna was entirely unconscious. Tharan stood still, looking toward her, and the others were between him and Jameson, babbling questions.

"Later," Jameson said. "Stan."

It was an order, and Morisz ducked between the others and followed Jameson into the corridor.

"What," he began, but Jameson shook his head, and they went through half the building, a long walk, in silence. Hospital personnel stared at them with covert or open curiosity, but Jameson paid no attention. Behind them trotted a man from Administration internal security. Two days ago someone had planted a homemade firebomb at Jameson's door; it was primitive but dangerous, and Jameson had reluctantly accepted this minimum of personal protection.

Outdoors the August sun burned hot. Jameson stopped on a deserted flight of stairs, waved the bodyguard away, and said, "They expect to permit her mobility in about three months."

"Yeah. She'll be able to talk then. Maybe we can get more."

"I doubt it. But from the moment she moves a finger I want her watched. With spyeyes. Without her knowledge. I want every room in this center in which she spends time wired for sight and sound, and I want you to form a team to study the record, every minute of every twenty-four hours of it, and report to me."

"Report what?" Morisz said in frustration.

"I don't know."

Morisz thought: He is going right over the edge. Right here. Right now.

"Starr . . ." It came out more plaintively than he intended. "It's a dead end. You can't get anything better than what Tharan did. Go right into her head and pull it out—what the hell can I do that's any better?"

"Then send the tapes to me and I'll study them myself."

Morisz could not refuse the direct request. There was his personal liking for Jameson, for one thing; for another, there were implications for the future. He did not want Jameson telling anyone he was uncooperative in a matter of such weight, and certainly he could not defend himself by accusing a commissioner of unreasonable caution.

"I'll do it," he said. "But it's a dead end, all the same."

"Think so?" Jameson started down the staircase. The sunlight dimmed. The sullen air promised rain.

He said, "They don't leave dead ends. Every time it's looked that way they've set us up for something. Remember that, Stan. It's nearly the only thing we know about them."

"Yes," Morisz said, "but they've already set up D'neera. What else could they want?"

"Just watch her," Jameson said.

CHAPTER X

The water was always warm and clear, and drew her irresistibly. She forgot sometimes to push against it, floating in a timeless sea, and the physical therapist who took her to the pool each day would call, "Hanna! Hanna! You've rested long enough." And she would make a dreamy effort, forgetting the purpose was to make her stronger, filled with wonder at the play of muscle and the sensations of water against her skin. It was strange to inhabit a body. She remembered inhabiting one familiarly, but she could not get used to it again. Parts of it surely were gone? Movement unbalanced her; food was distasteful and she spilled it; her face glimpsed in a mirror with clear blue eyes surprised her.

They had made her body whole by slight degrees, and would do the same with her mind. Living in the unworld of brain barred from body was painful, so she had been unconscious for five months, except for the sessions with Tharan. The exceptions might have been her undoing, for she opened her new eyes to memories of The Questioner, repeated daily and ingrained past forgetting, and very little else. Tharan had not been a reassuring companion. His head was filled with images of fleets on the move, chaos at home and his anxiety to return, mistrust of the men around him and violent dislike of Starr Jameson. That was Tharan's version of events, or all of it Hanna saw, anyway. Her final waking, therefore, was to unrelieved bleakness. To ease her transition to physical life she was given drugs that softened without changing the prospect. It was always at a distance from her, and so was grief—for herself, for D'neera, for Anja and Charl, for something else; but what? It was too distant to see. It was there in dreams she could not remember, a loss and an emptiness that would never be filled. Tharan was gone, and there was no one to uncover her dreams.

So faithfully had she been cared for that after a week she could walk. She could not walk very rapidly or very far, but she could walk. She came out of the hydrotherapy pavilion one day, moving hesitantly and wearily away from the water's support, and found Jameson waiting for her.

She thought he must have come to see someone else, but that made no sense. He was here for her, then. Barely clothed and wet through, she forgot the chill of dry air while she searched memory for the proper thing to say. Ordinary courtesies no longer came automatically, and never sounded right when she remembered them.

He said, "Hello, Hanna," providing the clue she needed.

"Hello," she said in relief, but fragments from Tharan came together without warning: the ruin of the *Endeavor* Project, the near-ruin of this man's career, the ragged end of his visions, devastation of his life, and had it not sprung from her? She had never given a thought to what he risked in trusting her. Now, when she saw the size of the gamble, it seemed to Hanna in her distress that he must have come here to accuse her. She might have panicked, except that he appeared utterly unchanged. As it was, she looked at him piteously.

He said, startled, "Are you all right?" and took her arm, which had seemed very far from his intention.

"All right," she said faintly.

"I can come back later, if you wish."

"No," said Hanna, so unused to having power to postpone the unpleasant that she did not really understand the option.

He went with her to her room, and she leaned on his arm most of the way. Seeing him had jolted her from her fog—and she wondered with new clarity how much of it was self-created, not chemically induced. But the question sank in her painful anxiety for his welfare, and she was not clearheaded enough to think such anxiety might be ludicrous while his strength literally held her up.

Her room was comfortingly dim. She sank onto the bed with a sigh, telling herself she must not fall asleep just yet. The light flared, and she blinked. She had forgotten that her preference for semi-darkness was not shared by everyone.

Jameson came to stand before her, tall and solid and

wrapped in the old stillness. He watched her intently, not trying to disguise it. There were deeper lines than she remembered at the corners of the gray-green eyes, and his gaze was colder than she had ever seen it. She felt a twinge of unreasoned fear of something besides reproach.

She could not think of anything to say. After a while he said, "How are you feeling, Hanna?"

His eyes and tone were so at odds with the concern in the conventional question that she did not understand immediately, as if it were necessary to translate what he said from one language to another. "I'm—well. I'm feeling better. Time," she said, pushing at her hair. It was cropped close, a silken cap, and felt strange to her hand.

"Intelligence is rather anxious to get at you without the intermediary. Think you'll be strong enough to talk to them soon?"

"Soon. I think—soon." But Ward, her chief physician, spoke of that or something like it at least twice a day. He must know the answer. She hardly heard the next trivial questions, answering by rote. He had to have the answers already. He did not care what she said. He was not listening; only looking. He had come here only and specifically to look at her.

He took a step toward her and without warning, swept by fear, she shrank away from him, fighting an impulse to run. She could not run. She was too weak.

"Hanna?" he said, but she could not answer, huddled in on herself and shivering.

After a minute he sat down beside her. There was a tangled coverlet on the bed, and to her astonishment he picked it up and draped it about her shoulders. It was the first gesture of kindness she had known in many months; the men and women who cared for her were not unkind, but busy and impersonal. She began to cry, the acid tears tickling her nose incongruously, and to her further astonishment felt his hand on her back. The simple act of compassion overwhelmed her and she turned to him blindly, reaching out, expecting nothing. Very slowly, he put his arm around her.

"Forgive me," she whispered.

He shook his head, but the movement came from some sharp conflict within himself.

"Please," Hanna said urgently.

"There is nothing to forgive," he said as if against his will.

"What I did. . . ." Tears blurred her eyes. The shameful memory smothered her.

"You did all you could. . . ." He spoke slowly, reluctantly, but his arm tightened around her. She responded to it, not to his words, and laid her head on his shoulder without thinking, knowing he would not mind; he only thought he ought to mind it. He was a point of wholeness in a sadly tattered universe, and she clung to him, needing wholeness too desperately to care if he wished to be clung to or not.

He bent his head and she moved a little, holding her breath with a sense that time and space had slipped and left them, the two of them, miraculously alone and secret. He said close to her ear, very softly, "I wish it had not been you. But I'm glad it was you."

She said on a long breath, "Why. . . ."

"You did not speak. It was not you. They destroyed you."

"Everyone blames me. . . ."

"They are wrong. Who could have done better?"

"Anyone. You—"

"Not I." He touched her hair, a delicate gesture of comfort. "If anyone tells you he would have done better, he lies."

She turned her head a little, almost secretively, as if he would not notice that his lips now touched her cheek. Her skin seemed to have been dead, and suddenly was alive. She whispered, "But I told them—"

"Not enough. Not enough for their purposes. . . ."

She was passionately grateful. He had strength enough for both of them. She was safe with him. *Safe*: from doubt, from guilt, from memory. She had never needed anyone before, nor anything so badly. She would tell him so.

Then he remembered something he had forgotten, and she felt it fall between them like a knife. He drew away from her with a movement so abrupt it was nearly violent. Time resumed. She actually cried out, bereft. The act was so deliberate and implacable that he might as well have gotten up and walked out, and she wept, uncomprehending.

He waited without moving or touching her until her sobs eased. Presently she straightened, sighing, and wiped at her wet cheeks. Jameson turned his head, but he did not speak at once and his face was unreadable. A last sob choked her. He said—it might have been another man talking— "Do you remember the probe Tharan did?"

She nodded, hardly hearing.

"What happened after he broke the rapport?"

"After?" Confused by his contradictions, still shaken to the bone, she tried to remember. It had been so long ago. It was mixed up with all the interrogations before it and after it, and besides she had been sedated, which was not customary. The healer was supposed to be strong enough to share your full awareness of whatever made you seek him out. But Tharan had not come to her as a healer, and nothing about that probe had been customary.

"I fell asleep," she said. "Or passed out. I don't remember which."

"I mean before that, but after Tharan broke the contact."

She shook her head. "I don't remember anything. Did something happen?"

He said after a moment's silence, looking directly into her eyes, "No. I thought perhaps something had occurred to you afterward. But if there was nothing. . . ."

"No," she said uneasily.

He stood up, remote as ever, preparing to leave. She said quickly, "Commissioner?"

"Yes?"

There was a question she had asked no one because she was afraid of how they would look at her. But whatever he felt, it was not, at least, contempt.

"Why has there been no attack on D'neera?"

For an instant she saw exhaustion in his face, and pain so great it shocked her into silence. He said something she did not absorb; said good-bye, and she nodded numbly; left her staring after him. If she had ever thought him impenetrably armored, the minutes just past would have shattered that illusion. But this was different; she had with her question gone straight for a nerve, all unknowing, and seen something she was not supposed to see. Why, when it was a question everybody must be asking?

She could not think of a reason, but she stopped wondering about it because she was preoccupied with something else. She had finally remembered his reply, and also the inflection he gave it. It was a non-answer, but why had he said it that way? She could not get it out of her mind, and it worried her till other shadows hid it: "*You* ask me that?"

She saw Melanie Ward every day, and also Larssen, the physical therapist. When she asked them when she could leave they gave her no answer. She did not belong here. This was a Joachim Beyle Center, an acute care facility specializing in regenerative techniques. There were half a dozen of them on Earth, half the total in human space, and this one was within sight of the Polity administration complex. Hanna's small room had no window, but when she was strong enough she walked round and round the Beyle Center, scuffling through dry leaves over carved stone, and looking at Admin's distant spire with the stylized star at its tip. Somewhere in those buildings were Jameson's rooms, where she had been an honored guest. She wished he would come see her again, but he did not. She wished the medics would let her go, but they would not, though now she was as whole as she would ever be and needed only outpatient care. "Wait," they said, and tested her over and over, and days and then weeks went by.

"It is autumn here too," said Iledra. "We are together in that for once. Strange places you've been, H'ana-ril."

She paused, waiting. It was a minute before Hanna stirred. She was a faraway face to Iledra. Her eyes were dead. Iledra looked at her more closely. Fear seized her that Jameson had been wrong and Hanna would never be well again.

But the blue eyes shifted, came to focus, and were Hanna's: sad, but intelligent and alive.

She said, "Hello, Lee. This is a surprise."

It was the second time she had said it. Iledra said, "Are you all right, H'ana-ril?"

"Yes," Hanna said. Fleeting surprise touched her face. "I'm getting stronger," she said.

"Good. I expected to hear from you, and I did not, so. . . ."

"Oh," Hanna said. Her eyes shone with quick tears. She turned her head away so Iledra could not see her face. She said, "I couldn't bring myself to— There was so much I didn't understand from Tharan, and I've read . . . I've read about the, the, the . . . tree . . . tree—"

She stopped, fumbling. Iledra said, puzzled, "The what?"

Hanna now seemed utterly confused. Iledra watched her with amazement and alarm. Hanna said at last, triumphantly, "*Things*."

Iledra closed her eyes for a moment and thought: Her mind is broken. But Hanna went on sanely enough, "The soldiers of the Polity. Half the fleet's in the system, isn't it? They say there've been—disturbances—"

Tears glittered on her cheeks.

Iledra put down her mug of honeyed juice. It was the last of the season, and she would not take a meal outdoors again this year. The rainbow glimmer of fading falseoaks surrounded her, and fine nurturing dust powdered her hair and shoulders with a million subtle jewel-flashes; but the wind was rising, and one more stormy night would scatter the last of the tree-borne light. Had Hanna been thinking of falseoaks? But the connection was obscure.

Iledra said slowly, "There are disturbances everywhere. The Fleet strategy is to stop an invasion here, but it is not popular. I have secured the communication here. Are you secure?"

It did not occur to her that the question represented a marked change in her own attitudes. It did not occur to Hanna either, apparently. Hanna only shook her head and said with an effort at a smile, "None more secure. I tried to call Cassie and they wouldn't even let that go through."

"Indeed. I'll tell her I've spoken with you. I said there are disturbances everywhere. The governments of the Polity worlds bicker and shout. They think we have too many ships, men, guns, sentinels, and the commission leaves them too little. You know the administrators of WestCon have fallen on Co-op? And the governors of Montana on Heartworld, though all Montanans are mad in any case. Even Lancaster's parliament has been overturned. I thought Lancaster forever asleep. I suppose you've heard of these things, but. . . ."

Her voice trailed away, because Hanna was not listening. Rather, she listened to something else. She turned her head and stared into a room so dark Iledra could see nothing in it. In reflected light from the video screen her eyes were a stranger's, and slitted.

"H'ana," Iledra said softly, but there was no response.

After a minute she went on. She spoke steadily and conversationally. Chill wind clutched her hair and trickled down her neck.

"You know all that, I'm sure. But probably you have not heard of Colony One's proposal to evacuate all D'neera and destroy the Houses and the cities, so if the aliens come there would be nothing, and the Fleet if it loses here could retreat to worlds the aliens cannot find. They might even have done it, H'ana—but they could not think how to resettle all of us."

"Yes," Hanna said. "That's right. All at once. I hadn't heard." She turned back to Iledra, looking only wistful. She said, "What did Jameson say?"

"Nothing," Iledra said. "Not a word. He knew it must come to nothing. And he is in no position to protect us."

"No," Hanna said. "I wish I could see him. But I haven't. Tell me more."

But her face was so sad that Iledra hesitated. She thought now that Hanna's deficiencies might be neither physical nor intellectual, that something else perhaps had broken, and she could say nothing that would not bring further pain. Hanna could not know all the tumult the forced marriage of true-humans and D'neerans had brought, because true-humans now controlled most of D'neera's channels of communication, and chose what to suppress. All the old prejudices had flared again, strong as in the years of isolation. Polity soldiers no longer were permitted to visit the surface of D'neera for rest and recreation; there had been rapes, batteries, thefts, finally a full-scale riot. Most Polity societies closed their doors to D'neerans for, they said, the outsiders' own protection. This meant D'neerans who wished to evacuate voluntarily—and there were many—could not do so. They stayed at home with everyone else, watching a hostile sky whose harborage of the true-human fleet seemed more threatening, for now at least, than hypothetical aliens of unknown power.

And it was Hanna's doing. And to know all that she had brought about would not help her.

Iledra said, "I will tell you more another time. Are you comfortable, H'ana?"

"Yes," Hanna said doubtfully.

"But unhappy. . . ."

"I can't," said Hanna, lines creasing her forehead, "seem to think. They don't—want to talk to me. They're not allowed to, I think. The people here. I only ever see a few. And men from Intelligence. I go to, to where they tell me. The pool. The gymnasium. Nobody's there." Something like horror came into her eyes. She repeated, "Nobody's ever there. I can't, can't think to anybody. They don't like it. There's nobody to talk to. I'm living in a box. I'm not living—"

She stopped suddenly. Her eyes were dim again. Iledra waited. After a minute Hanna said clearly, "It's all right here. I'll come home when I can."

Iledra said, "Are you quite sure you're all right?"

"Yes. Yes."

"Not, perhaps, a little—confused?"

"Confused?" Hanna said. "Why, no." And now she only looked, in fact, tired.

Afterward Iledra called Jameson, but when she said she wanted to talk about Hanna, he would not speak with her.

She did feel odd. Fuzzy. Maybe even a little confused. She spent many hours in the pool, comforted by water. Melanie Ward talked of womb-returns and said she could not do it forever. But in the pool she could keep her eyes closed, and she did not like looking at things. Objects and bodies and faces had taken to having periods of unintelligibility, as if she had lost the patterns of what they were supposed to look like. Speech sometimes was mere noise, meaningless and almost painful. She was possessed by a lethargy of mind and body that seized her anywhere, at any time, so that she stopped what she was doing and neither moved nor thought until someone spoke to her or something else happened to rouse her. The commonplaces of technology were sporadically, unnervingly beyond her grasp; not that she did not understand principles, but that she could not remember which knob or lever or button did what, and she had to stop and think how her bath or the terminal in her room worked. She was glad her meals were brought to her so she did not have to cope with their preparation, though it meant always eating alone, when she bothered to eat.

She did not want to tell anyone about these things, but exhaustion drove her finally to tell Ward that sleep did not rest her. She woke in the mornings tired as if she had not been to bed at all, and seemed always on the edge of remembering an evil dream. She thought it out with some difficulty, and decided the transition drugs must be responsible. But when she put the question to Ward, Ward said she was no longer being doped.

"But every day they give me—"

"Immune boosters, because your resistance is down. Nutrients, because"—a hint of reproach—"you don't eat properly."

"I don't understand," Hanna said. She made a vague pass at her hair, missing by some distance. "Can I have something, then? To help me with the dreams? To help me rest?"

"No," Ward said, and made an explanation to which Hanna did not attend. The truth was that she was afraid of sleep. She was afraid she would die in the night. There were mornings when her first thought on waking was that she *had* died, and somehow revived with the dawn. She felt as well an urgent need for sleep, no matter how much she got, and the conflict between fear and desire was painful. She did not want to tell Ward about it, because she also was afraid to confess that she was afraid. The Questioner had exposed too many unsuspected weaknesses. Hanna would not herself expose more.

"Tell me," Ward said invitingly, "about your dreams."

"I don't remember them," Hanna said truthfully.

After that the I&S men who came to her every day wanted to hear about her dreams too, but she could not satisfy them.

In December the first snows came.

Hanna got worse. She felt more and more as if she lived in a box that shut her off from the rest of the world. At first she thought the difficult, complete suppression of telepathy was the source of her isolation, but it did not explain everything. Her body, once strong and athletic, was unreliable. Her muscles twitched, she walked into walls, dropped things, fell sometimes. She had headaches and her eyes felt so tired she thought something was wrong with them, but Ward said otherwise. Ward did, however, tell the Intelligence agents to stop hounding her. They stopped; less for her health's sake, Hanna thought, than because there obviously was nothing more she could tell them.

The relief from that pressure did not halt the decline of her mind, however. She cast about in desperation for release, and a longing came upon her to go home. It seemed that if she were on D'neera she could be well; that the universe would look right, smell right, fit her comfortably. Even the passage through space drew her, even anything that was not here, where nothing but water was right.

Still they would not let her go, and they would not tell her why, and when she thought of tapping their minds to find out why, she was afraid. Because they seemed so strange to her: almost alien, in fact.

Early each morning Morisz went over the previous day's and night's reports on Hanna ril-Koroth. They were lavishly illustrated, because she was watched as closely as even Jameson could wish, though Morisz still thought it a waste of time and resources.

This morning, however, the report was accompanied by a nightside operative. Morisz canceled an appointment and had her brought in at once. She said, "This might not be important, but you did say to report anything unusual."

"I meant it. Let me see it."

He waited while she searched the night's record for what she wanted. His office looked inland from the river, and in the weak winter sun he picked out the bulk of the Beyle Center with its fringe of parkland and snow-dusted trees. What was Hanna up to now? Whatever it was, if Wills thought it important enough to show him, it had better be passed on to Jameson.

Wills said, watching the timeline, "Most of it was ordinary. She went to bed early, got up after a while, and started studying. A text on Terrestrial evolution this time. Toward morning she went back to bed, but this time she got up again, and she didn't seem to be in fugue. I think she'll say she remembers this if she's asked."

"I think she remembers all of it," he said.

"Well, it's just an opinion, but I don't think she knows how much she's up. Otherwise why would she complain about being tired? Here it is."

They leaned forward simultaneously. The room from which the image came had been dark, but the picture was enhanced to full visibility. Hanna's room at the Beyle Center was, by the center's standards, highly decorated. The patterned walls with their ornaments of crystal and metal made it almost certain Hanna would not find the near-microscopic spyeyes by accident. The furnishings were spare, but Ward had had rich fabrics brought in, and pretty objects that when activated moved or spoke or projected rippling color. The object was to provide Hanna with plenty of positive sensory stimulation; but she seemed not to notice her surroundings, and did not play with the enchanting toys.

She was in bed, just beginning to stir, in the picture Morisz saw. She sat up, pushing away the sheets with a quick motion. She wore a white gown that fell from her throat to her feet and covered her arms as well. Until recently she had slept naked, but the habit had changed overnight and, it seemed, permanently. She stayed away from mirrors, too; Ward said she had contracted a revulsion to the sight of her own body; a reaction finally, she thought, to its mutilation.

Hanna swung her legs over the side of the bed and sat up straight. Her face was slack with weariness. She tilted her head as if listening for something. Her eyes moved, searching.

After a minute she got up. She moved to the middle of the room, so unsteadily Morisz thought she might fall. She looked around her and began to move again. She looked into the tiny bath cubicle, opened the door of the room and looked out into the hallway. She slid open the panel of the room's small storage module and pawed through her sparse collection of clothing. Morisz realized to his astonishment that she was trying to find something.

He said to Wills—in a whisper, as if Hanna could hear, although what he saw had happened hours ago— "I wonder if she's caught on to the spyeyes?"

"She's looking in the wrong places. She'd be looking in the room itself."

Presently Hanna gave up the search. She went back to her bed and sat down slowly, dejection in the lines of her body. Still she looked about the room. It seemed to Morisz that she almost sniffed the air. She stopped that too and was still. Her lips parted and she said in a whisper, faint and sibilant but clear: "Come out! Come out where I can see you!"

And listened painfully for a reply. And heard none. And lay down again and began to weep, her face pressed into a pillow.

Wills froze the record and said, "That's all. She cried till she went back to sleep."

Morisz scowled at the sad little picture. He said, "What was she looking for, anyway? If not the spyeyes?"

"She's a telepath," Wills said. "She *says* she's not exercising the faculty, but I understand they can't always help it. If she senses she's being watched, she might be looking for something without knowing exactly what she's looking for."

"That's right," Morisz said, not happily. "So don't ask her about this incident. Next time she'd be looking for spyeyes, because she'd *know* she's being watched."

He told Wills to include the scene in Jameson's précis and got rid of her. He thought about calling Jameson, and decided against it. Starr was on his way to Heartworld, where Taylor had just succeeded—barely—in quashing a demand for hearings on Jameson's fitness for his position. "I seem to be making a career out of smoothing feathers," he had said to Morisz just before he left. It was something he would not have said a year before, but they were by way of becoming friends, and the strain of the last months was having an effect. The very term he had used was proof that Jameson, with his fine sense of discrimination for a phrase, was not himself; nothing native to Heartworld wore feathers.

Morisz decided this last bit of nonsense could wait until Jameson got back.

There seemed always to be someone looking over her shoulder. She heard sometimes a breath at her back, and turned to find no one. Some of her clumsiness came from starts at footsteps close behind her, but always when she looked there was nothing. They asked her occasionally what she did in the night. The question made no sense; she only slept; she sensed they did not believe her, but she never asked what they meant by the question. Because she was afraid—afraid of what she might hear, afraid she might be doing something dreadful in the dark, afraid The Questioner had kept some of her sanity and she would never get it back.

One day in desperation, thinking if she did not challenge her intellect she soon would have none left, she tried to catch up with developments in her field. The first extract the index showed her was a critique of "Sentience" that suggested all its conclusions—all her years of work—were suspect because her predictions about the uses of telepathy at first contact were flatly wrong. It was cross-referenced to an item that informed her she had been, during the months of unconsciousness, stripped of her Goodhaven Award.

She stared at the text for some time, feeling nothing at all and wondering why there were tears in her eyes. No one had considered the matter important enough to tell her about it. She supposed it was not, then, important. The Academy's little ornament was somewhere in the wreckage of *XS-12*, or lost or destroyed or, fittingly, in alien hands.

"But it *was* important," she whispered despite the constriction in her throat; and she was reaching for the key that would erase the screen when Jameson's name caught her eye. His part in getting her the prize had been suspected.

Finally alert, filled with real anxiety, she searched for more information. There was no more; there had been only that one hint of it. But there was plenty of other information on the last six months of Jameson's life, and Hanna read into the night, fighting sleep.

Tharan had thought with some triumph of Jameson's crisis, but he had provided no details. Now Hanna learned that at one point only a single vote in Heartworld's general council had saved Damon Taylor from having to demand Jameson's resignation. Taylor insisted doggedly that Jameson was the best man to have in the commissioner's seat now, and as long as law permitted him to keep Jameson there he would do it. There had been talk of impeaching Taylor; it had come to nothing, but certainly he would be gone after general elections two years hence, along with a number of other councilman.

The revelation that Species X had known what it was looking for did not make Jameson better liked on his own world or any other. He had always been too liberal a commissioner for many Heartworlders' tastes, and controversial from his first day in that position. The *Endeavor* Project had not been popular at home; now the worst pessimists' fears were realized, and they did not let anyone forget it. There was another side to the early-warning argument Jameson and Taylor had used. It was this: the aliens might have searched for hundreds of years without success if it had not been for the *Endeavor*. On other worlds, and for the same reasons, Jameson was called everything from incompetent to insane. Muammed al-Nimeury criticized him publicly, and the other commissioners tolerated this breach of official etiquette. No one—not even Andrella Murphy, who was said to be his friend and possibly his lover—defended him.

There were images from an earlier life Hanna had not wondered about before: Jameson leaving a theater with an exquisite, dark-eyed woman on his arm; Murphy whispering in his ear at a hearing on interworld law, saying something that produced the kind of radiant, open smile Hanna had seen only twice; Jameson shaking hands with some Co-op dignitary at a glittering formal gathering, poised and inscrutable. His private life was very private indeed, but some of it had surfaced recently, not through the efforts of his friends. Hanna tried to tally the rumors of dissipation with the austerity of his usual manner and with her own glimpses past his self-control, but she could not make them fit together.

The present was easier to understand. Now he was always alone, except for a bodyguard or, sometimes, a grim-looking Rodrigues at his shoulder. She guessed his world was divided into two kinds of people—those who sought to bring him down, and those who were waiting to see if the others would succeed. What she did not understand was why he tolerated it; why he did not go home to comfortable obscurity; why he endured the weariness she had seen, when all his hopes must be ended and there was nothing left but duty.

But that is precisely what it is, she thought when she lay down at last. That is what I did: endured all I could, without hope, because it was my duty. He knew it. That was why he could forgive.

The thought comforted her, and she clung to it down the sickening slide into sleep.

But the dreams were worse that night, in the morning they were closer, and soon the days were nightmares too.

snow too deep and where the whitesky seeking prey? Lost, all lost and fallen. Death and loneness, waste of white.

"Hanna," Ward said, raising her voice.

Hanna lifted her head slowly. Ward's face *dark as deeprock* was attentive.

"Hanna?"

"Sorry. . . ." Hanna rubbed her face. Her hands had shrunk. The fine planes of her face felt deformed.

"Melanie," she said in panic.

"What is it?"

"Nothing." She licked her lips. They felt almost like her lips.

Ward stared at her, and finally dropped her eyes to the surface of her desk. The characters and diagrams on it changed as she keyed in, one at a time, the morning's test results. Hanna stood up and Ward said, "Where are you going?"

"Look out," Hanna mumbled.

"What?"

"To look out. The window."

"Oh," Ward said, and returned to her study.

Polished metal round the window showed Hanna her face. It looked wrong. She put a hand to her throat and stared blindly at snow, waiting for the fit to pass. This morning was the worst yet; but it had been getting worse for days. She was horribly afraid. She put her forehead against the warm transparent window, trying to remember if Ward had stopped recording before the onset of this last break in reality.

She jumped as Ward said, "You're all right. A couple of anomalies, nothing outside chance. I'll see you again tomorrow."

Hanna did not move. She said to the window, "Melanie, when can I go home?"

"Not just yet. You've been a very sick girl."

"You just said I'm all right. Why can't I go home, Melanie?"

There was a small sigh behind her. Ward said, "Hanna, you know you can't."

Hanna drew a fingertip across the window's surface. She said, "I'm a prisoner."

"You're not a prisoner. You go wherever you please here, you can go outside, you can go into the city if you want to."

"And risk being recognized and—never mind. That's not what I mean. I want to go *home*. To D'neera."

Ward said more gently than before, "Not just yet."

Hanna turned around. Surely Melanie would notice something was wrong with her face; but nobody ever did. So there was nothing wrong with it. So she was going mad.

"Melanie. I don't need you anymore. I need a mindhealer." It took some effort to keep her voice steady.

"Why," said Ward, looking up at her through dark lashes, "do you say that?"

Hanna did not answer. After a minute Ward said, "We could get Tharan back."

"No." Hanna's hands were quivering. She put them behind her back. "Melanie, what's your rank?"

"My—?"

"You're not on the staff here. Somebody told me. You're with Fleet."

"Yes. Well."

She looked disconcerted, almost guilty. Hanna did not know why it was supposed to be a secret and did not care. "Can you let me go?"

Ward shook her head.

"Who, then? Morisz?"

Ward hesitated, but decided, perhaps, she would save herself trouble by answering.

"I suppose he'd have to approve. But ultimately the decision would be Commissioner Jameson's, I think."

"Can you arrange for me to see him? I can't," said Hanna, desolate, "call him myself."

There was another hesitation. But Ward said at last, "I'll try. He's on Heartworld, though."

"When he gets back. As soon as he gets back."

"I'll try," Ward said.

On the way to her room Hanna had a moment of sheer terror when a spasm took her right arm and bent it at the elbow. She stumbled against the wall to stop it, to hide it. She got to the room, to the bed, and crouched on it for some time, biting at her hands.

She did not remember the beginning of her fear. Perhaps it had begun with The Questioner, who now visibly pursued her in her dreams. Sometimes in the morning she could not make herself look in a mirror, convinced she would see raw meat with bone showing through. Her body was more strange to her, not less. It made movements of its own accord, and caused her to stumble, shaking her with alarm out of all proportion to the event. She felt an urgent need to hide these incidents and did so, telling herself confusedly Melanie would never pronounce her well if she did not. There were times when she found herself in the pool when it seemed she had been in her room the moment before, or vice versa; times when she was staring at the face of someone who had not been there a second ago and who was waiting for her answer to some question. She did not tell Ward about any of these things, and she was afraid.

Fear had grown on her so gradually she was not aware of its progress, but now when she looked in mirrors she saw that her face, which had always reflected her thoughts because she had no talent for duplicity, had become a mask to hide the fear. Even that was a relief, though it was not always her own ruined face she was afraid of seeing. It was something else—someone else, she thought once—and she did not know what. But each day the fear was greater, and she moved in a haze where she examined each word and hid even her treacherous body's rebellion from unseen watchers.

And now this: reality distorted, familiar shapes shifted, images drifting through her tangled brain that came from nowhere she knew. Had the Questioner been less guarded than she thought? Had she absorbed memory, knowledge, an alien essence, despite his powers? She had told Intelligence otherwise, and they tested her when she said it and knew it was the truth. Truth at the time; perhaps not now; but what might surface now did not matter. She could not face questioning again. If her brain still held treasures of knowledge she would tell Iledra, and Iledra would tell Morisz from the shelter of D'neera. If they suspected it now they would not let her go. And she had to go. Had to go.

At length she dragged herself off the bed and called Iledra. It took a long time for the call to go through. There was action at Morisz's offices, no doubt: flurries, discussions, but approval in the end, because Iledra answered. The quiet, familiar room behind her pulled at Hanna's heart.

Hanna passed a shaky hand across her mouth. "Lee," she said, knowing others listened, "I want to come home."

But Iledra said reluctantly that home might be no haven. Hanna made her say it plainly: many D'neerans blamed Hanna for their distress. Hanna had wondered uneasily about the possibility, but that did nothing to lessen the hurt of hearing it.

"How bad is it?" she said.

There had never been much room for evasion in their friendship. Iledra said, "H'ana, I do not know what place there is for you here."

"Well. . . ." Hanna stirred anxiously. "Defense needs people, doesn't it? I'm trained."

"H'ana-ril, I think you had better consider resigning from Defense."

"Now? When there's going to be a war?"

"I do not think," the older woman said sadly, "you will be given any responsibility even if there is a war."

Hanna thought of everything she had learned and done for Defense, the years spent learning spacecraft, weapons principles, unarmed combat, the honor after Nestor, everything, all of it: all gone.

"What about D'vornan? The university?"

"The program has been closed," Iledra said, her face blank.

"Oh. . . . But the House—there must be more work? And not enough people?"

Iledra looked away for a minute. Hanna said in dread, "Lee?"

When Iledra turned back there were tears in her eyes. She said, "Lord Gnerin has suggested to me that you resign from this House, and that I name Cosma my successor. There has been no formal motion . . . yet. If it comes to that they will all be against you."

Hanna looked at her hand, numb. The Heir's Ring had come to Earth with Hanna's eyes. The frosty blue stone was not ostentatious; the Ladies of Koroth could be flamboyant enough when they chose, but they took their responsibilities seriously, and that was what the understated ring said. No one had ever given her a greater honor than Iledra had in selecting her to someday head Koroth. She did not think she would do it as well as Iledra, or Penelope before her, but she had always thought she would do her best.

She said, "What do you want me to do, Lee?"

"I will not—" Iledra stopped and drew a deep breath. "I will not attempt to dictate your course. They cannot force you to resign, or force me to repudiate you."

"But what do you *want*?"

"I want, I want things to be as they were before. And they can't be. They won't ever be. I will not alter my choice. I will not ask you to resign. But as matters stand now you would be entirely ineffective at Koroth."

Her face twisted, but Hanna could not spare a thought for her pain; her own was too great. She said stiffly, "I will send the ring back for Cosma."

"No. Bring it. Come home."

"But the House would not be home anymore."

"It will always be your home. It will be—it will be hard. But where else are you to go?"

"Nowhere," Hanna said. "I have nowhere to go, except to you."

After that conversation she understood at last the full extent of her loneliness. The haze of fear deepened, and she was unhappier than she had ever been in her life. In desperation she reached out to the only person here who had seemed really friendly to her, and invited her therapist to her bed.

Larssen was pleased; he had kept intimate watch on her body for weeks, after all. He was also kind and affectionate and not unskilled, but Hanna felt nothing. She hardly knew he touched her; all sensation seemed to leave her skin, it was like the hide of some alien animal, no part of her at all. Her thoughts blanked again, and she came back to awareness huddled in a cold ball on her bed, weeping bitterly.

"No use," she said from somewhere in space. "No use. Go away. Please."

Larssen was unoffended. He knew the details of what had been done to her; he said it was only to be expected. He made sure she would be all right alone, accepted her apology, and left.

Hanna lay alone in the darkness with an emptiness in her and around her she had never known before. All the rich years had led to this, they were all poured out now, streaming away as such years did at the moment of death. Her work, her pride, her place in her world, even her physical being were come to nothing. She felt nothing but the pervasive fear. She had nothing left but Iledra. She was not sure that would be enough; she was not sure she could ever be filled again. But there was nothing else to try.

Starr Jameson would return to Earth in a few days. She would ask him if she could go home.

CHAPTER XI

"That's it," Jameson said.

The holograph image that seemed to stand in the center of his office moved slowly.

"See the hesitation? Now watch this."

The image kept moving. The figure tried another step, lurched awkwardly, and fell in slow motion. It was Hanna. Her face was curiously expressionless, even when one elbow hit the floor with a surely painful impact.

Stanislaw Morisz said doubtfully, "I see what you mean. It's not much to go on."

"Not by itself, no. But taken as part of a pattern, beginning with that set-up rescue. . . ."

He waited while Morisz thought it over. His theory was far-fetched and he had broached it to few persons besides Morisz. He was not prepared to be laughed at unless it was necessary.

"All right," Morisz said finally. He leaned back in his chair. The winter day was nearly over, and behind him the river was black except for its edging of ice. "Maybe there's something to it after all. How'd you spot this?"

"I've been looking for . . . oddities. Anomalies in her behavior, besides the obvious ones. I checked this as a matter of course; it happened to pay off."

"My people should have caught it."

That was true, but Jameson said, "She's very good. It's hard to be sure even when you know what you're looking for. But I've watched hours of these things. Days. If you run an incident like this against a kinetic model, there's no doubt she's faking the falls to hide the other thing."

Hanna's insubstantial figure lay before them in a grotesque sprawl. Morisz stared at it, and Jameson, moved by some obscure impulse, touched a switch and said "Endit." The image vanished. Not that it matters, he thought. She hasn't had a moment's privacy in weeks, and after all this is only a picture.

"If she's supposed to do something—think she's supposed to do something? Sabotage? Spying? If you're right—" Morisz caught himself up short. He looked faintly embarrassed by his own half-belief. He said, "We'd better find out what it is, first. Conditioning, programming—we can do things like that too, you know. Shouldn't be hard to figure it out."

"She doesn't remember what they did."

Morisz answered with emphasis, "She *says* she doesn't remember."

"Tharan would have known."

"You weren't too sure about him yourself."

"I think he reported honestly what he saw. I think he did not see all there was. And of course there is still the possibility Ward suggested—that it's some sort of hysterical reaction, delayed shock or something of that nature, she's disguising for reasons of her own. Afraid to admit it to Ward for fear of losing even more autonomy—"

"Doesn't explain the nights."

"No. If I'm right she may know—as she says—only that she is tired in the mornings."

"But the rest of it. . . ."

"She knows she is somehow out of control, of course, and she has spoken of it to no one. And I think Ward is wrong."

"Well, then?"

Jameson said, "There is only one expert on the aliens, on what happened to Hanna, and on Hanna's state of mind. I intend to ask her."

"Sure. And a lot of good that'll do if she doesn't remember, or she's hiding everything she can from us, or both."

"One can always ask. She's under a hell of a strain, Stan. She's frightened. It shows, when she thinks no one's watching. A direct confrontation might be enough to get a start, at least."

"So what happens if it doesn't produce anything?"

"I'll try to get her to agree to another deep probe. Maybe duplicate the drugs the aliens gave her—"

"You wouldn't let us do that before," Morisz said resentfully. "What happened to 'intolerable' and 'inhumane'?"

Jameson said, "They got lost somewhere between expediency and desperation,'' and Morisz eyed him doubtfully, not sure if he was joking or not.

''We should have done it a long time ago,'' Morisz said. ''Six months since they dumped her in our laps. Six months lost, six months without a sign of them when we could have been getting somewhere.''

''Not lost,'' Jameson said. ''Perhaps if we'd done it at the beginning we'd never have seen what we're seeing now. I did not and do not think creating an artificial psychosis will accomplish anything except her further torment. I still hope it won't be necessary.''

''And if it is, and she doesn't agree?''

''We do it anyway. We can take her into official custody as an intelligence source. You don't need to remind me how gently she's been treated so far. We do not have to keep doing that. There is no way for her to stop us from doing anything we want to do.''

It took a greater effort than he expected to say that quite coldly, but Morisz noticed nothing and said only, ''You're sure of this, aren't you.''

''I'm sure the implications are so important we have to assume I'm right.''

Morisz was thinking ahead. He said, ''If we have to go that far, how do we justify it to D'neera?''

''We won't have to. D'neera is united in nothing, and less than ever now. There will be no protest; except from Lady Koroth, of course, but she'll be alone. No one else on D'neera is likely to give a damn. Hanna is not exactly popular there.''

''The old story.'' Morisz chuckled, but without humor. ''After Nestor she couldn't do anything wrong. Now she can't do anything right. Yeah.'' He got up, stretching. He seemed a little larger than he had when he entered the room. There was a plain course before him, a thing to do. He said, ''I'll get started on it right away.''

''No,'' Jameson said. He sounded peculiar even to himself; Morisz glanced at him in surprise. He said, ''I'd like to give it a try myself.''

''You?'' Morisz said, looking at him too closely. ''What for?''

Jameson said slowly, ''She knows me. Not well, perhaps, but she respects me and I think trusts me as much as she trusts anyone here. She regards I&S as a threat. The analyses of the direct interrogation sessions made that plain. I should like to see how she responds."

"It's irregular," Morisz said disapprovingly. Jameson folded his hands and waited. Finally Morisz said, reluctantly but with no rank to pull, "It makes sense, though."

"Quite," Jameson said, and was shocked at his own relief. The reason he had given Morisz was sound enough, but he had not admitted even to himself, until now, the other reason: that his intervention might, just might, mean that Hanna could be spared some quantity of pain.

Morisz said, "When are you going to do it?"

"I don't know. Soon. Why?"

"I'll have to have somebody on the scene."

Jameson shook his head sharply but Morisz said, "He can stay out of sight. I don't—I beg your pardon, but you have to consider appearances. I don't mean to imply anything about anybody, but—we don't want anybody thinking this is some secret kind of—"

He was talking himself into a corner. Jameson almost smiled. He said, "You mean if Struzik or al-Nimeury were doing this without an I&S representative at hand, I'd bite your head off. I see. You're right, of course."

Morisz relaxed visibly. He said, "Anyway, it wouldn't hurt to have help there. If the worst-case scenario is true she might get violent."

This was a possibility that had not occurred to Jameson. Whatever his suspicions, he thought of Hanna now as so fragile that a look might break her. Yet the chance existed, and he had finally managed to get rid of his bodyguard, an appendage Heartworld considered a weakness—though the threat of assassination was real enough even now. The tradition of personal courage was strong in his culture, and he wondered what would be said about his accepting assistance with a woman still frail from illness. But Hanna was trained in personal combat and he was not, and he had not struck a man since early youth.

"All right," he said finally. "I might as well do it immediately. She's been asking to see me, in any case. I think I'll ask her to come to my house tonight. It might be as well to get her out of the medical atmosphere."

"Soft light and flowers," Morisz murmured.

"What?"

"I've seen the same reports you have. She's lonely. Vulnerable, maybe."

Jameson said frigidly, "That was not what I had in mind."

"Of course not." Morisz looked abashed. "Sorry. Larssen was after her again the other day, by the way."

"What do you mean?"

"Said he wanted to try again. I hear she was in tears by the time she got rid of him. I'm surprised she didn't just break his arm."

"She would have, at one time." Jameson had not seen the record of Hanna's earlier encounter with Larssen and had told Morisz to destroy it. He knew one or two of the Beyle Center's directors very well; now he made up his mind to see to it Larssen lost his job. Surprised by his own anger, he hardly noticed Morisz getting up until he looked up absently, hearing the man speak again.

"What did you say?"

"I said, I just can't believe it. It's fantastic."

"I know. That's what the others said. But you are becoming convinced, aren't you?"

"Let's say," Morisz said cautiously, "the evidence is suggestive. It would explain a lot. Are you just going to come out and ask her about it?"

"Why not? It would simplify things considerably if she admitted I could be right. And when she knows we've found out her evasions, what would she have to lose?"

"More than you think, maybe. The last man who sold Polity secrets—remember Harrison? He's still living on Nestor like a king."

"I don't think she's done that. Tharan would have picked it up."

"Not necessarily. It's no crazier than what you're suggesting. If that really was an artificial block Tharan ran into, who knows what they can do? Maybe they bought her and taught her to hide it. Maybe Koroth isn't enough for her. Maybe they promised her she'd be a queen. Keep it in mind. You can't leave out the possibility."

"No," Jameson said, but he did not mean what Morisz thought he meant. The slight, shivering woman who had shown him her agony at failing had not been bought by anyone; but he would not let Morisz see his certainty.

The evasion left him uneasy, and he was still uneasy when he left his office some time later. He had not spoken to Hanna, only left a message for her at the Beyle Center, but he did not doubt she would come. The interview would be recorded, and one of Morisz's men would be within earshot.

It was dark on the concourse before the administration complex, and a bitter wind was rising, laced with snow. Jameson suddenly remembered he had not arranged transport for Hanna. He had personally vetoed letting her have access to a credit network, which in effect made her a prisoner under the guise of making her a guest. That meant she would have to be on foot, and he thought of her walking five kilometers on legs that did not always obey her, and winced.

"This won't do," he said into the wind, but it was no use. It was too late. His detachment where Hanna was concerned was a poor illusion at best. He could not afford to hide the fact from himself; he doubted his success in hiding it from Morisz; and there was little hope of hiding it from Hanna, who from the beginning had ignored the face he presented to the world.

He had begun by pitying her, an easy thing to do. The wreck Aziz Khan found, considered as a human being, was pitiable enough. Considered as the author of "Sentience," the lively sharp-edged presence that once was Hanna, it had the impact of profound tragedy, a random discontinuity that mocked human effort to read meaning into the universe. Jameson knew very early that Hanna could be made whole physically. When he learned also that enough of her mind survived to answer questions, that should have been the end of it. It had not been the end; and in the months past, increasingly troubled, he had sought to find out why.

It had nothing to do with her beauty, as he half-suspected at first. It was true that as he watched the ruin of her face take its old shape under the physicians' hands, he understood at last why on each meeting he had the sense of seeing her for the first time. She was lovely, a fact he had ignored as best he could, and one which was the more piquant because she was entirely without artifice or seductiveness, unaware of her own impact and seeming not to care. But it was not that that affected him. Desirable women were everywhere, and all his adult life he had taken for granted the attraction his status and wealth exerted. He had been immunized to beauty more years past than he cared to remember.

Nor was it Hanna's personality that drew him, the antithesis of his own. Impolitic, honest, direct, she had ambushed him more than once into responses he did not want to make; it was a warning clear as a spoken word, and he had intended to heed it. He could have done so easily; could have put the attraction aside, ignored the flattery of her half-sensed interest, regarded her as valuable in her way, useful, nothing more—

Until now. Until her destruction; until it was likely (said Melanie Ward, citing the long-term effects of torture) she would not be the same woman again.

He had gone to the Beyle Center often when she could not see him, nor know in any way he was there. He felt no revulsion at her rebirth. Instead it seemed he watched a metamorphosis; that her steel-framed chrysalis was midwife to something new and, perhaps, rare. For what had she been before, after all? A girl becoming woman; a bright child who had never been hurt, defined and circumscribed by qualities he had named at their first meeting. What would she do, now that youth and luck and brilliance had failed her all at once? —not through the slow pressures of time, the series of defeats that forced men and women into courses they did not choose, but with a single blow that tore her loose from every anchor she had known and left her harborless. It disturbed him that she had so accurately, in their brief meeting, perceived that he might allow her to turn to him, and her willingness to do so disturbed him even more. She had been kept deliberately—not maliciously, but coldly—from everything and everyone who could give her comfort; and in his occasional, erratic impulses to provide it, Jameson recognized the uncertainty of his own balance, which he had once thought so secure.

The cold truth was that he faced the ending of his own life, as he defined it and had chosen to live it. It was not only that there would be no more *Endeavors*. What was left was perilously fragile. His associates were slow to forgive mistakes, and his prestige had not recovered from the blow the aliens dealt it. He had never walked such a tightrope. If he fell now there would be—nothing. Only the broad fields of Arrenswood, the life of a country gentleman in which he would dwindle and waste and grow old too soon. The miracles that gave men twice the lifespan they deserved were capricious, and unkind to him. There would not be time enough to wait for Heartworld to forget, not time enough to forge his career a second time. There would not even be another Henriette, because his pride, next time, would revolt. Hanna might recover from what had been done to her, in spite of Ward's opinion. Jameson might not.

For weeks now he had watched Hanna move against the backdrop of such thoughts. She did not know he watched her; she did not know he saw her uncertainty, and later her fear and despair. He knew her intimately, without her knowledge and against her will, and it seemed to him the aliens had created no crueler disjunctions than those that faced both of them now. For despite his intense familiarity with every terror that touched Hanna's face, she still held a final secret; and though his wish was to let her seek shelter, necessity demanded that he take from her the last hope of it.

It was a pleasant house, set among trees that were bare and frosted now; in summer it would be heavily shaded. It was faced with some wood Hanna did not recognize in the gathering darkness and looked old, old, like something from a more primitive culture than Earth's. Even through the leafless trees she could see no other buildings, privacy unheard-of in the heart of a Terrestrial city. She remembered the house belonged to Starr Jameson, not to Heartworld. He must have wanted this solitude very badly, she thought, to spend what it must have cost him when there were no guarantees he would last even this long on the commission.

She went slowly up the long hill before the house, stumbling once. The spasms that racked her when she was alone had mercifully spared her during her long walk, but her coat was light and its thermal control had failed, and she was frozen and exhausted. He has to let me go, she thought. I can't take much more of this; it gets worse every day; but D'neera was a blur in her mind and all that was clear was the space she must traverse to get there, the freedom of the void. That would be safe.

She touched the front door's beveled glass curiously, and jumped when the house spoke to her. Mr. Jameson was not yet home, it said. She was expected, however; would she come in? She did so, grateful for the warmth, and followed directions to a softly lighted room that was sleekly paneled and breathed subtle woodsmells. The furniture was big and comfortable and there was a working fireplace. A faint tang of smoke hung in the air.

The house did not speak to her again. She took off her coat and sat down uneasily; something shifted a little with her presence and fell softly in the fireplace. The silence was profound, and for all the need she felt to be alert it seeped into her, and her mind drifted. This happened often now, and she floated on drowsy waves of images that had to do with Earth or D'neera or places she had never visited, half-formed glimpses of worlds she did not know. An occasional gust of fear shook her, but most of the time she was too tired to be afraid. If I do not get to a mindhealer soon there will be nothing left of me, she thought, and terror woke her; the thought was too reminiscent of The Questioner.

In that moment Jameson came in, and stopped abruptly when he saw her, staring at her face.

"My dear girl," he said, "are you all right?"

"I was just dozing," she mumbled.

He said, "You told Ward you wanted to see the mind-healers."

She looked up quickly. "Yes," she said.

"Why? What's wrong?"

"Nothing," she said, lying hopelessly. "I just—it was the trauma. That's all."

A long time went by. Finally he said, "No."

"No?" She turned back to him anxiously. "You won't let me?"

"That's not what I mean." He paused then said, "Hanna, you must tell me a little more. Just a little more."

His voice and eyes said: I am your friend. She believed him. She longed to tell him. She whispered, dizzy with gratitude, "I'm going insane."

"Why do you think that?"

He spoke gently, leaning forward a little, and her lips parted but she could not speak. If she told him they would try to fix her here. And she had to leave. Had to.

She looked away, hardly breathing, knowing he waited for an answer. But she could not think what to say, and after a minute he said, "I know about some of it."

"You know?" said Hanna, but a voice said in her head in great alarm: *No. No. No.*

Jameson for a moment receded. He said, barely heard through a wall of mist, "Some of it."

She shook her head. "No. What?"

When had she become so inarticulate? Oh help me, she thought, but she could not say it. He went on quietly, "The muscle spasms. The movements you can't control and try to disguise with falls. The blackouts. The night-walking. The conversations you don't remember. What else?"

"How could you know!" she said incredulously. Her mind went blank. A single tremor shook her. She was an empty vessel filling slowly, inexorably, with fear.

When she could move again she looked down at her hands, afraid to meet his eyes.

"What else?" he said softly.

"It's been you. Watching me."

"Yes."

"Why?" she whispered.

He did not answer at once, but presently he leaned forward and took her hands. It seemed an invasion, and she shuddered.

He said gently, "Don't be afraid, Hanna. No one wants to hurt you. But there are answers we must have. Too much is unexplained. What did the aliens hope to accomplish by giving you back to us? What did they do to you with their drugs? When Tharan probed you he could not retrieve some memories that must be there—why? What does it have to do with what's happening to you now? Tell me what you think. Somewhere you must have the answers. You are the woman who wrote 'Sentience'—"

She shook her head violently. "A failure," she said.

"No. A brilliant work. In essence accurate, I think; flawed perhaps in detail, because you did not take into account some things that—well, that no one could imagine. Not a failure. . . . You are quite capable of reading the pattern, reading your own behavior. Do you read it as I do? Think."

She did not know what he was talking about. She said in confusion, "I can't—I can't—"

"Think, Hanna. Do it. This is your last chance."

"My last chance!"

She looked up at him in terror. His hands were warm and there was sympathy in his face, but what he said might have come from the man who had come to her on *Endeavor*, offering cold alternatives and enforcing them with threats.

She tried to pull away but he held her hands tightly and she had no strength.

He said, "You cannot convince me nothing strange is going on. You cannot convince me you are not hiding something. At best, hiding; perhaps deliberately lying. And I am not alone in thinking so, Hanna. Stanislaw Morisz believes I am right. I have talked to General Steinmetz, I have talked to Peter Struzik, I have talked to Andrella Murphy. When I say this is your last chance, I mean it is your last chance to cooperate voluntarily. Trust me, Hanna. Tell me the truth and nothing will happen to you. I promise you will not be harmed."

She tried to think and could not, and felt nothing but unreasoning panic. She did not know where it came from. It seemed part of her mind was screaming before a long-expected danger, but she could not tell what it was.

He said, "The night-walking—"

She said through the panic, "What are you talking about!"

He said, "Do you really not know why you are never rested?"

"No. No. I don't know what you mean." It was hard to speak because, she thought dimly, she was going to faint. She spoke only because to speak, to comment on the unknown, was a human habit. Her thoughts were surface-level and sprang from no foundation of logic; under the superficial web there was blackness.

He said slowly, "You don't go very far. Only to the terminal in your room. And all night you study mathematics, history, military science, other things, astrogation—always, every night, astrogation. You have known for years the approximate route from D'neera to Earth, yet in the last weeks you have studied it carefully. Why have you done this, Hanna?"

"I don't know—I don't believe it—" She moved restlessly, helplessly. There was a great pressure behind her eyes and she thought vaguely of Ward, she ought to tell Melanie about that, maybe something had broken loose.

"I believe you, I think." He let go of her hands at last and looked at her strangely. He said, "You are exhibiting classic symptoms of a dual personality, you know."

She rubbed her hands over her face. She did not understand what he was saying. But something connected and she said, half a question, "The mindhealers?"

"No. I wish it were so simple. The evidence suggests you're under some kind of control, Hanna. From outside—"

"That is impossible," she said clearly, and then heard herself say, "I am not. That is not true."

He and the room seemed to have become very small, as if she were a great distance away. She saw that he shook his head.

"Who knows what's possible for the aliens? Powerful telepaths, evolved not engineered telepaths—you said once that you are too human to guess what that might mean. Until we know, we cannot let you go."

She stood up suddenly. It was not she who moved and she swayed, seeking balance in a moment of darkness. Her eyes cleared and she saw Jameson on his feet, his eyes wide with alarm. She stretched her hands out blindly.

"Help me," she said.

He said quickly, "Yes. All right."

"I remember," Hanna said, and watched her hands lift, and in a last wholly human moment wanted to tell him what she remembered: the drugs, the dissolution, the whisper in what was left of her mind, the overpowering presence of the creature who was their Leader, desperate, bending over her as if her ruined body would accommodate him.

I remember, she started to say again, but instead she backed away from him for more fighting room and Leader spoke, directly to Jameson's mind, and said: *I will kill you now.*

She sprang straight for his throat. The edge of her hand nearly broke his forearm, thrown up just in time to save his life. Her foot smashed into his groin and he went down in agony with a strangled animal sound. Through the roar in his ears he heard running feet, Visharta, Morisz's man, he would be too late, she was fast and skilled, one more blow—

There was no other blow. He managed to unfold himself. Visharta stood over Hanna, the snout of an armed laser handgun pointing at her head. She lay face down and limp, dead or unconscious. Visharta began to talk into a communicator on his wrist.

"Stop that," Jameson said. "Shut up. Not on an open channel."

"But Mr. Morisz—"

"I'll talk to him myself. Tell him to wait."

He eased painfully to a sitting position. It hurt to breathe too deeply and he was weak and nauseated. He said, "Is she dead?"

"Nossir. I didn't touch her. Found her like this."

Hanna suddenly rolled over in a single convulsive surge. Her eyes were open and unfocused. Visharta shifted his aim.

Jameson said, "Is that all you've got?"

"I've got a stungun, sir."

"Then get it out, for God's sake. She's no good dead."

Hanna's eyes focused on Jameson. Visharta said behind her, "Don't move." She swiveled to look at him and when she turned back to Jameson he saw she was breathing unevenly, gasping, eyes wide, an animal in the extremity of panic. She tried to say something and nothing came out. Her hands made erratic movements that went nowhere.

Flight reflex, Jameson thought dispassionately. Dangerous as hell.

He got slowly to his feet. The pain was bearable now and he could ignore it, with some effort.

"Back off," he said to Visharta.

"Nossir," the man said stolidly. "My orders were to protect you."

Jameson went slowly across the little space that separated him from Hanna and dropped to one knee in front of her. He was not interested in arguing with Visharta and would chance getting stunned. He looked into Hanna's terrified face and saw that it was, at least, her face. Perhaps he had only imagined that half-formed distortion.

He said, "Hanna?"

She still gulped for air in irregular sobs, but the convulsive efforts to move had settled into tremors. She nodded in jerks: Yes. I am Hanna.

"What is it?"

"One of, one of them." Her voice was thick. She took another breath. "Inside me. Alive."

"Impossible."

She shook her head and reached for him in the gesture she had not finished before. After a second, unwillingly, he put his hands on her shoulders and drew her closer to him.

"What does it want?" he said in her ear.

"It wants to go back," she whispered. "It came to find out what I didn't tell it. It knows now. It wants to go back."

"Back where?"

"I don't know. Where it came from."

"How did—never mind."

He patted her back absently, holding her close and looking past her at nothing. This was worse than even he had thought. She said, still against his shoulder, "It's gone now. Hiding. Inside me."

"But it can come out whenever it wants? Control you? Do what it wants?"

"No, not—" She lifted her head a little and let it fall back. Her breath was warm through his shirt and her voice was calmer. "Not whatever it wants. It wanted to kill you. I stopped it."

"But who's in control?" he said, and discovered with profound shock that he was rubbing the back of her neck. The skin was silken under his fingertips.

"I don't know. I don't know. I knew it wanted to kill you and I stopped it. I don't know how."

"Can you feel it inside you now?"

"Yes, like—" She fumbled for words. "Like carrying a stone around inside me."

"A physical entity?" he said, incredulous.

"No. No, I don't think so. It's been there all along. I didn't know what it was."

"Can you communicate with it? Try," he said, and deliberately held her more closely, reassurance against panic.

Another tremor went through her and she said, "It doesn't want to. I can't make it. It said so. It's afraid—"

She lifted her head and he saw the fear was gone from her face; there was only a look of wonder.

"It said so," she repeated. "It's gone again now."

He felt her curiosity, so strong it left no room for fear. She met his eyes, inviting him to share it. He could not afford the luxury. He said, "It only comes out when it wants to?"

"I guess—yes."

"You can't get at it unless it wants you to."

"No. I don't think so."

"Well," he said, "that settles that."

He touched her hair once, regretfully, and let her go and got up. She looked up, startled.

"What are you going to do?" she said.

"Call Morisz. Get the experts started on you."

"What do you mean? What are they going to do?"

"I don't know." All his aches had started up again. He said tiredly, "Maybe we can get to it if we duplicate the drugs. That must have had something to do with it."

"But—wait." She stood up too, a little unsteadily. Her eyes were anxious again. "What do you mean? What they gave me?"

"Yes. If—"

"Oh, no. Please. I remember. I remember what it was like."

"If it is the only way—"

"No!" She was frightened again. She came a step closer and looked up into his face. "They said that too," she said. "The only way. It's like dying. It's worse than dying. It was the worst, the worst of all. You can't. You can't do that to me."

He said with finality, "I'm sorry. I have twenty billion human beings to think of."

Her hands closed on his shirt. "No," she said. "No. Please." Horror blasted him, and a silent, powerful plea for help. She had trusted him, still trusted him, wanted to trust him. The flood of mental intimacy revolted him. He got hold of her hands and nodded to Visharta, and the contact ended, leaving him empty. Visharta drew her away.

Jameson said thickly, "Arrest her. The assassination attempt, for now. Maybe espionage, I don't know—"

"But I didn't! I didn't know!"

"It doesn't matter," he said, and turned his back on her outstretched hands and walked away. His footsteps were loud on the polished floors and he thought he heard her call to him. He did not look back.

He went on through the house to his private communications module and plowed through the identification routine, moving stiffly. He thought she still begged him, distantly; but it was only the aftershock of that assault on his emotions. He cursed all telepaths, Hanna above all.

Morisz was waiting for his call and said, "I'll send more men over."

Jameson thought of Hanna being taken away by a squad of armed men. He said, "That won't be necessary. The less disturbance, the better. Visharta can put her under light stun."

"I'll be waiting at the complex," Morisz said, and signed off.

Jameson leaned back wearily. The light in this little room was too bright, as always. He hurt in places where Hanna had not hit him, and he was more shaken than he had thought. He had done his duty—and he thought flatly that it might have been more difficult if he had not been fueled by fear and revulsion and pain.

It was time to put out of his mind forever the vision of Hanna as the fragile survivor of shipwreck, because she was not going to survive this one. The charges they would hold her on were a joke, but they would serve to keep her while they studied her, poked her, probed her, drugged her, took her apart to the bone to find the real prisoner, the alien spy.

She knew it, too. The look of betrayal on her face was clear in his memory. I have no choice, he thought, but the deep blue eyes accused him and he thought: Perhaps when this is over I should resign. I do not think I could do this again.

He would have to face her sooner or later. It might as well be now. I will tell Visharta to stun her, he thought, and went slowly back to the room where he had left them.

He had waited too long. The utter silence told him before he stepped through the door that something was wrong, and as he did so he felt the cold draft from another door open somewhere to the winter.

Visharta lay on his back near the fireplace, alive but unconscious and looking peaceful as a baby. His weapons were gone, and so was Hanna.

CHAPTER XII

Murderer!
You too
I stopped you
too soon but you wanted
to kill—stop it! Stop!

Her skull seemed full of voices. They would shatter it. And all of them were right. She could not murder humans but she had to. If she had to escape.

Drifted snow sucked at her. She floundered, going nowhere, and sank to her knees. The pressure in her head was everywhere, it was going to burst. But she hadn't killed Visharta, though the thing inside her urged it. Calculated tears, eyes swimming, body lax, a fake collapse, he came to see if her heart still beat and then—

All hers. The plan and calculation were all hers. And the restraint, above all, at the end.

She was not going mad. She wasn't insane. Relief swept over her, all her own and so great she cried out aloud in gratitude. Alien-seeming reality, body, thoughts, dreams—they were all *his*. The presence that haunted her had been not the watchers but *him*. Now that she knew he was there he could be resisted. Her present danger seemed almost insignificant.

She stumbled to her feet with difficulty, possessed by an urge to run. Hers? Leader's? Both.

Leader gabbled in soundless terror. She tried to think where to run to.

Hopeless. Nowhere to go.

Another wave of panic nearly blacked her out. She swayed where she stood and screamed at him.

Stop it! Stop! I have to think!

The terror eased but she was shaking, gulping for air. It was easier to start these things than stop them and Leader, feeding on her terrors, feeding her his, for days, for weeks, was near breaking.

An oblong of light showed a hundred meters away: Jameson's front door opening. Trees and shrubs showed against reflected light with the vividness of hallucination, black and knife-edged. Her first flight had carried her halfway down the long hill before the house, and her footprints were clear in the dim snow-light shimmer. She cowered at the end of them.

"Hanna!" Jameson was silhouetted against the light, a target-practice cutout. Her hand tightened on the stungun.

"Hanna! Come back! You can't get away!"

Kill!

"Not him!" she said violently, but her hand jumped. The stungun dropped to the snow and she was holding the deadly laser. She cried out to Jameson: *Get back!*

His shocked comprehension mixed with Leader's rage.

Fire! What he will do to both of us!
I will not harm him! I will not!

The pressure suddenly was gone, given up, relinquished. He'd given her body back to her. She shivered on her side in the snow, half-buried. She struggled to her feet. Snow resisted her, heavy as sand. There was a hot trickle of blood down one ice-slashed leg. The door was closed and there was no sign of Jameson.

She was vulnerable, visible, her trail a pointing finger. Animal running. Easy to find. She would use the laser on herself before she let them have her and burn out her brain, she would burn it out herself, her own way, let them reconstruct her body but they could not reconstruct—

Snow stung her and glittered in the wind. The Questioner's Assistant came toward her with the shining veil, a palpable figure, companion forever. She cried out in horror and fell again.

Go on, or it goes on forever. You will live in dissolution every instant of your life—

Not that either. She would not give herself to the humans; but not to the aliens either.

She grasped the laser and tried to turn it on herself and—could not. It twisted in her alien hand.

She retched, racked with convulsions. A merciless eye impaled her and ice chips flayed her hands. She could not face the fear again, fear of helplessness and pain without end, not that, never again, and he controlled it, recreating it at will. If there were grounds she could fight him on there were some where she could not. He would not die, and all the force of his refusal went into The Questioner's promise.

I run, then—

She could move. She gathered her battered body and ran. For what good it would do. Toward the house.

Not back!

He tried to turn her flight and she staggered.

It must be this way! Nothing behind but the river, and Enforcers—

She made him see her caught between the river and well-armed men, and he wrested the image from her. It took substance and the Enforcers were a ravening horde, more savage than sentient. The laser flared and cut them down, food and sustenance. Leader thought with satisfaction: *Succulent.*

The vision faded. She caught at a substantial wall to keep from falling, tasting foulness. This succubus that fed on pain was part of her, loathsome. She would never escape it.

Escape. Escape. Run!

No, she thought, grasping at slippery wood. They will follow.

In a disconnected moment of clarity she saw that she had stumbled to the back of the house and was leaning against a bay built into it. It had no windows and was surely a hangar for an air-land car. There were few private permits for flight over Terra's dense-packed cities, but Jameson would have one of them. Leader suddenly was silent.

Footprints. I could fly—for a while—till they find me.

It would open only to Jameson's personal code, perhaps only to his voice. Unless she cut her way in.

She fumbled for the laser. At maximum destruct it cut an entry in seconds. There should have been alarms. She heard none. Heartworld and its dangerous mores. Oh, stupid man, brave man, to go unprotected on Earth!

Leader agreed: *Stupid,* and she felt his contempt.

There was no time to explain what it meant; that life bounded by fear was no life. Instead she said: *Smart enough to spot you! If you want to escape, shut up!*

She used the laser on the aircar too, listening for the hum of aircars or groundcars, the efficient machinery of a city used to crime. Nothing. Metal smoked and glowed in the darkness and the car said querulously, "This unit has sustained considerable damage to—"

"Shut up. Shut up." She wrenched the wrecked door open, burning her hand, and slipped into the pilot's place. The stench of burning plastics faded and the smell of fine leather engulfed her. The enclosure was haven. She or Leader was sick with relief. She pawed at what she hoped was the right switch and all the displays came on. Her eyes flickered over them.

"Can you fly?" she asked the computer controls.

"Yes. Hours to maintenance—"

"Never mind. Open the door and give me manual control."

The exit door peeled open with maddening slowness and the car said "Ready," and she whipped it out so fast it complained again. The controls were standard, thank God. A meter off the ground she careened wildly to avoid a tree and the car said severely, "Is the operator qualified for this vehicle?"

"Yes, yes, yes!"

She went up in a hurry and her stomach lurched. She looked over her shoulder and saw the house fall away, a child's toy, impotent. The dark snow, the darker sky, were empty of pursuit. Ahead of her were low hills and then dense city lights. She made for the hills at top speed. They would be shelter, but not for long; her eyes caught a monitor that showed moving blips of Enforcement activity, heading this way. Trust Jameson to have this little feature. She muttered, "Thank you, Commissioner," and for a wild instant longed to go back. She meant more to him than danger, and what damage would this do him?

No. No. Do not think of that!

A shadow showed behind the protest. Reptilian beauty, unbreakable bond: she knew what it was and in a wild leap of hope reached for it savagely, it might be a weapon powerful as The Questioner was for him.

But the agony of loss was her own. She was alien and

human male and female all at once, Leader's bondmate, was that what she'd glimpsed? And, oh dear God, Jameson—

The car dipped. She broke free, gasping. Leader withdrew as violently as she, revolted. Human sex was a maze of dark tunnels that fed into each other endlessly. He wanted no part of it. He longed passionately for the simplicities of his Home.

Home, yes. Rounded towers in the dawn, the young splashing in pebbled pools, scarlet plumage warm at fullsun—this is not my home!

Leader said: *It is mine.*

The car hovered, bereft of guidance, and she passed her hands over her face, her human face. Home, safety, a refuge against the night; her own thought had sparked Leader's, was that how it worked? The arms of his bondmate were gentle. She left to wake the hearth before dawn. He was not whole without her. They were a single living animal, and neither would ever bond with another. They were that way because, because—

She reached for it, almost understanding the imprinted bond for life, so foreign to human instict.

The sky lit up behind her. They were there, searching for her. She would go back. To Jameson, who could not hurt her—

Leader thought with contempt: *He will. He will. You are not Us but separate. Duty compels him.*

The Questioner bent over her and the tattered mote of Hanna-then hung screaming in an abyss of nothing. Hanna-now whimpered, lost. The humans would make her endure that again, and forever.

Leader said: *Space. Safety. Freedom.*

She caught at it—some of it—space; time to think, time to fight, time to get herself back. Jameson would destroy her. A man with responsibilities.

She growled to the car, "Outport. Top speed," and sprawled with the burst of power, teetering in the broken doorway. The car tilted and spilled her safely to its other side. It began to remonstrate.

Her mind cleared. A public outport would do her no good at all.

Something she had read tugged at her memory. She cut into the safety lecture. "Does Commissioner Jameson have private Inspace transport?"

"Yes. The *Heartworld II,* a Class D yacht, based at Nordholm Field—"

"Take me there," she said, shocked by sudden hope. "It's not a military port, is it?"

The car veered and nearly threw her out again. It said, sounding cross, "The field is maintained by the Nordholm Society as a service to its members."

Nordholm Society. The name meant nothing. Lights and water flashed beneath her. The car showed no Enforcers pursuing her. But by this time they would know the car was gone. It was now locked into local airspace control and could be located and stopped in minutes, maybe seconds. How far was there left to go?

The car decelerated gently, cruising in over a black ribbon of water to hover over metal shadows in the darkness. Above them on a hill there were lights. The reference connected. Nordholm Society: a private club; elegance and service for the rich and powerful. Tight security?

"Which is Commissioner Jameson's vessel? Put me down next to it."

"It is not his vessel. It is the property of Heartworld—"

Hurry!

"—and if we descend without the proper signal, Enforcement will be notified," the car said.

"Do you know the signal?"

"No. Air-surface vehicles are prohibited—"

"Land anyway. Down. Now!"

The alarm began before it reached the ground, a deafening burst of noise, and light flooded the field. What else would there be? She jumped the last meter to the ground, slipped on ice and nearly fell, wrenching her knee. The car shouted at her but she could not hear what it said over the clamor. The yacht towered over her, two hundred meters long and streamlined for atmosphere. The sun-and-crossed-spears of Heartworld gleamed on its bow. She scrambled along its side, slipping, until she faced the main hatch. She fired at it, hands numbing with cold as metal flared, waiting for the end, anything, sleepygas jets, supersonics to drill into her skull. There was nothing. Serves you arrogant bastards right, she said to all Heartworlders collectively and individually, and the hatch burst open and she sprang in. She touched a switch and the inner lock opened instantly, disarmed by the pressure outside.

She heard an angry yell and turned, firing blindly at the voice; a man, private security probably, ducked, and the inner lock shut behind her. Its design was familiar. She knew how to disable it and used the laser to do so; they would have to burn it open, and private security forces could not carry lasers.

She shouted orders as she ran for the flight deck, still waiting for the end. But the ship responded as if it were keyed to her voice. Bulkheads opened for her, slid shut behind her; lights flashed around her; in her feet she felt the purr of a thinking machine coming to life. She could not stop now. Her own fear and Leader's propelled her, she had to get away, get to space, think or plunge into a star.

Leader said: *Why so easy? When the not-People steal?*

She understood.

Because on Heartworld you die for such theft.

Die? Die!!?

Adjustment. Brainsoup alterations. Death, more or less.

The flight deck was an elegant statement in black and white; this was a luxury machine. An enormous window in its nose showed more men running toward her, and then the white hull of an Enforcement vessel landing directly before her. She ignored it, her eyes on the master controls. Their simplicity stopped her; she was a defense pilot. Even if she knew what to do it would take too long to get power and they would shoot their way in. And it would be over. She sank into the pilot's seat, giddy with relief. She would let them stop her, Jameson deserved that—

Leader wailed without sound, and a communications signal spoke urgently.

"Shut up," she said automatically, and the beeping stopped but Leader did not.

Do something, do something, there, there!

The urgency was her own; she forgot about stopping. She touched something without knowing what it was and the yacht said crisply, "Conventional power at seventy-five percent and building. Takeoff checklist commencing."

"Seventy-five?"

Jameson must have to move quickly at times.

Her hand twitched on a lever, an unwilled weight. The yacht said, "Inspace checklist commencing. Conventional power eighty percent and building."

"No!" she cried out loud.

Leader said: *Remember*.

Ship and Earth and she vanished and died; a split second later, wringing wet, she was staring at numbers, levers, winking panels, bright displays. The drug, she thought. The thing they thought of as human undeath. She could not bear it again. The humans did not even know how to make it, they would have to experiment. Endless dying without death, time stopped, all she was shredded and lost in the void. Jameson watching it all, cold sea-mist eyes in the cold howling winds.

"Conventional power ninety percent and building. Takeoff checklist completed. All systems go. Is itemization required?"

Dust clogged her mouth. Leader said: *Tell it no*.

She said with difficulty, "No."

"Ninety-five percent."

The heart of a star, fiery ending—

"At power."

She said like a sleepwalker, "Commence countdown." Reflected warning lights blinked red on the Enforcement ship's hull. It stood sharply against floodlights, there was light everywhere, then it jumped as if kicked and spun away. Men would be running, getting clear. She hoped. She hoped no brave fool would charge into the wrecked airlock and try to cut his way in as she had.

"Minus five and counting."

The flight panel wavered, steadied, and suddenly was comprehensible. She reached for atmospheric guidance. *Heartworld II* would take off faster than it ever had before.

"Two . . . one . . . liftoff," it said, and shot up and out through an invisible ceiling just as the Enforcers decided to fire, and power flared under her and disabled God knew what.

She went straight up, ignoring atmospheric drag until the yacht screamed in protest: too much, too much! It was not made for takeoffs like this. Gravity compensation wavered and for a moment extra weight crushed her. The yacht skittered to one side, bucking and trying not to crash. A display for local airspace said: RED ALERT. The city was paralyzed now, everything in the air dropping fast. Except this vessel which was exempted anyway, and those of the Enforcers. She let the computer take over for a second, two seconds, three: her path stabilized into a long glide oblique through atmosphere. She changed the angle, more acute now, and lights flashed but the stresses were tolerable. An override circuit blinked in and a voice began talking about its authority to order her to turn back. She located the speaker, aimed the laser, and fired. The voice stopped.

"Go," she said to *Heartworld II*, which was already going as fast as it could. It was a match for the Enforcers, who would have only atmospheric capability. She could not remember what the law enforcement agencies of Earth had to meet this contingency, a private Inspace vessel stolen and on the run. Probably nothing. Probably this did not happen very often, possibly never. She was doing the unthinkable, but something would meet her from Fleet orbital stations and treat her like an alien enemy. They would fire rather than let her get away.

She said to *Heartworld II*, "I want to Jump the nanosecond you can do it."

She did not know what Earth's limits were for Jumping. Beyond Lunar orbit? The spacetime disruption of a Jump was a disaster for anything nearby and the yacht would be programmed for all the legal limits and inhibited from Jumping inside them. She could not outrun Fleet vessels. If the limit were not close she could not make it.

"Destination?" said *Heartworld II*, and she saw the sky was black, the stars bright; already she was well out of atmosphere.

"What are you programmed for? And how many Jumps?"

"Heartworld in thirty."

"Do Jump One and then program for a random Jump."

"Fifteen seconds to One. A random Jump is inadvisable. The probability of failure is unacceptably high."

"Do it, God damn you! And show me Earth, naked eye."

It was more distant than she had thought. A spear of pure blue stabbed her eyes from a sea in its bulge of light.

"Radar visual—"

Half a dozen vessels after her. She ought to be dead already. But automatic defenses were set for enemies coming in, not going out.

"Countdown, please."

"Seven . . . six . . ."

They were closing. There was nothing she could do. Private transport would not have weapons-evasion systems. And evasion would not help her; this was a race.

"Five . . . four . . . three . . ."

A backview monitor showed a flare of light. Someone had fired something.

"Two . . ."

If they killed her now at least she would not have to worry about what to do next.

"One . . ."

Leader said: *Thou art mine.*

"Transit," said *Heartworld II.*

The stars changed, and Leader was free.

It occurred to Jameson once that nature might have reversed herself and established permanent night, or that by some magic he had been transported to the endless ice and darkness of a polar winter. From his rooms at Polity Admin he saw floodlit river-ice melding into blackness and nothing else for longer, surely, than was possible in this zone of Earth. Nor was there order or normalcy inside the walls of Admin. There was one face or another or many at a time and he had to talk to all of them and they blurred together. There was the intricate dance of politics and defense and personalities and bureaucracies, an unceasing storm of words, the rigorous logic of attack and defense exercised by men who still were in irrational shock at the occult-seeming power of their enemy.

The Fleet, rather early in the night, had issued a directive that none of its personnel were to allow themselves to be taken alive by the aliens. Certain other things had been accomplished also, more to the immediate point. Fleet vessels were leaving D'neera and streaming back to the Polity worlds, for now an attack could come at any point. They left behind a contingent of some two hundred Polity troops who descended upon Koroth and quietly took over. No one was hurt, but the soldiers were armed and alert, and no one who was at the House left it, and no one came in. Their commander did not bother with diplomacy, and the word "occupation" was used freely. In the unlikely event that Hanna managed to come undetected to the city, she would not be able to shelter in her home. There was a scant possibility, Jameson thought, that she would go there, and the troops were ordered not to harm her if she did.

"Because," he said to Peter Struzik some hours after the occupation began, "if she goes home it will mean she has some measure of control. That is not where the alien wants to go. And, of course, if it's at all possible she must be taken alive."

Struzik appeared to be standing in Jameson's office, but he was in his own suite. It was only a few hundred meters away, but Struzik was lazy. There was a petulant look on his face. He said, however, "You've been right so far. I suppose you're right about that."

Jameson held his tongue. Not the least of his concerns this night had been making it clear to the commission, to his own government, and to Fleet how right he had been; how wrong, by extension, others had been. He had gone after Morisz with a savagery that surprised even him. Somebody would have to pay for the events of this night, and Jameson did not intend for it to be himself. The unfortunate Morisz, responsible for Visharta's stupidity, was handy. A long and honorable career was about to end in disgrace. Jameson, without vindictiveness, motivated by pure self-preservation, would make sure of it.

Struzik said, "Anyway, it's done. One down."

He meant one point in the plan he and Jameson and the others had hammered out in the hours since Hanna's escape. So far they had met no serious opposition; not because any of them were loved, especially not now, but because they had a formidable weapon in reserve. They had not formally declared a state of emergency. If they did their power in the Polity worlds would be frightening. They would have the power in theory, at least; no past commission had ever invoked emergency rights, and who knew what the reaction would be in practice? Not even Jameson wanted to find out—though it might be something to be one-sixth of a god.

His office was very quiet. There seemed to be a great deal of noise in his head, however. Some of it was left over from the frantic activity of the past hours, but some of it was the echo of Hanna's pleas. He said, to shut it out, "Let's have a quick review, Peter."

"All right," Struzik said discontentedly. He began ticking items off on his fingers. "Defense. Saturation of the Polity.

Steinmetz is still working out the details. The non-Polity worlds are getting the idea something's wrong. Nothing's leaked from here or D'neera yet, as far as I know, but they're starting to get worried. Their reps'll have to be briefed pretty thoroughly and pretty soon. Search. Steinmetz wants a dozen vessels searching *Endeavor*'s route—''

''Nonsense.'' Jameson did not pound his desk. He would save that for Steinmetz.

''If we don't search,'' Struzik said reasonably, ''how are we going to explain not trying?''

''We've got to give the appearance of trying, but I see no reason to waste more than one or two ships on a hopeless task. I dislike tying up even one.''

Struzik had liked the idea of a search from the beginning. He said, ''Well, it *is* a clear interface between us and them.''

''An interface many light-years long, where Hanna may be lost effectively as a single drop of water in the sea. There is an infinite volume of space in any direction from it, which Species X may have explored though we have not.''

''The rendezvous must be a pretty recognizable point—''

''There are thousands of easily recognizable points. Peter, it is a truism of space flight that an interstellar vessel is simply invisible unless it wishes to be found. In effect, it's just not there. And suppose there is no rendezvous? Suppose she goes straight to their homeworld? No, Peter. I'll talk to Steinmetz.''

Struzik gave up. ''Public information. Are we ready?''

''Nowhere near it.'' Jameson looked away from Struzik. A gray day at last grew over the gray ice. Plenty of expert propagandists had been working hard all night, but he did not think they would concoct anything that would soothe the public. Hanna's possession and escape could not be kept secret, not with D'neera involved. The prospect of warfare would be terrifying enough to a population largely free of it for centuries. The revelation of what Species X could do—what they had done with Hanna—would rouse the latent xenophobia of a whole species. Plans for martial law were being updated everywhere.

''Koroth,'' Struzik said, and Jameson looked back at him quickly, waiting for news. But Struzik only said, ''Still no physical resistance. They're talking our people's ears off, though. Lady Koroth's hopping mad.''

"I can imagine."

"Why won't you talk to her?"

"I am the wrong person to talk to Lady Koroth."

"She thinks you're the right person. As you know," Struzik said pointedly, "she has talked to *me*. And to Andrella. And to Muammed and Katherine. At length."

"Not Arthur?"

"Not Arthur. But she really, *really* wants to talk to you."

"I'm sure she does." On a panel out of Struzik's sight, a light had been blinking all night. Lady Koroth was waiting. If he pressed a key and said "Fourteen" she would be there.

"What else, Peter?"

"That's it, for now."

"All right. We meet in an hour. I'll talk to you then."

Struzik vanished. Jameson looked at the winking light. Other, more productive, lights were flashing too. He wondered what Lady Koroth had ever expected; wondered if she had thought she could move D'neera into the tumultuous mainstream of human history without paying for it. The price, it was true, seemed high.

He also wondered what she wanted so badly to say to him. He knew Andrella Murphy had told her of Hanna's escape; did she want to speak to him of Koroth? Or of Hanna?

He discovered then that his reluctance to face her was rooted in the latter possibility; and with the thought he touched the key and said "Fourteen," and a video screen came to life and floated into position before him.

He did not see Iledra at once. He saw a shadowed room, a burst of light near the video pickup, more light farther away, a window open to white daylight. It was late afternoon there; snowing, somone had said. The shadows were a tunnel between the two lights and in it, suddenly, Iledra appeared. She came closer quickly. The nearer light fell on her face, and he saw it was cold as the snowlight.

She came as close as she possibly could, as if a handsbreadth mattered in the light-years between them. Her eyes were swollen, and her sleek fair hair was disarranged for the first time in Jameson's experience. He recognized instantly that Struzik was wrong, or the reports he quoted stale. There was more than anger here.

She said without preamble, voice hard, jaw hard, "I want you to tell me about H'ana."

For a moment he had felt kinship with her, which had something to do with Hanna, but it was gone. He said, "There is nothing to say you have not already heard. I know Tharan has told you of all the questions she answered, and those she did not answer. This is the final answer. This somehow was the reason for what was done to her, the one thing she could not remember. They made her over in their image."

"You saw her. You spoke to her. I do not believe she could be controlled as completely as I am told."

"Believe it," he said. "If you'd seen her face when she attacked me—"

"You don't know her." The woman actually clenched her teeth. "She is strong. Strong!"

He took a deep breath, for once disconcerted. He wondered fleetingly if Iledra had passed some endpoint of sanity. He said, "The alien persona, entity, whatever it is—it's very strong too."

Iledra seemed not to have heard. "Why did she run from you?"

"It was *not* she," he said emphatically. "It was the alien. I suppose its intention, when its work was done, was to get away from Earth as quickly as possible. Perhaps it was anxious to get to D'neera or just into space, where escape would be easier. But it found out I suspected its existence and knew I would not let it go. It had to escape then, or never."

She stared at him, the gray eyes so sharp he wondered if she heard him thinking. He said, watching her face, "Lady Koroth, you said I don't know her. I think now she is a stranger to you too. When you spoke to her last, was she herself? You know she was not. She was fighting something she did not understand. She did not know she was fighting; but she sensed she was losing."

Iledra looked at him with abhorrence. She said, "You are coming out of this very well."

"Yes?" he said, taken aback.

"I think in the end the consensus will be that you are brilliant. That no one took you seriously enough, and the only man who did gave you an incompetent for backup."

"Very true," said Jameson, who had spent a good portion of the past hours encouraging just that point of view.

"I think you are mad. Mad to keep power. I think you would do anything to get your way."

"You are entitled to your opinion," he said quietly.

She made a sound in her throat that was almost a growl. She said, "I once thought to find in you an ally. I have found instead a creature that cares for nothing except its own ends. I forgot the lessons of my ancestors, who came here renouncing your ways. We are not experienced with the hidden motive, we D'neerans. We do not always love one another, but each of us knows what another is about. I don't have the habit of disbelief. When you spoke of your hopes to me and to H'ana, I believed you. I gave her to you for your ill-fated Project with some thought of the unity of man. I was a fool to trust you or any true-human."

He should not be taking this from her or anyone, a personal attack that was at best a distorted reflection of reality. It was advisable to measure her enmity now, rather than wait for more drastic proof; but he had had enough. He was reaching for the key that would end it when she said, "You destroyed her. There is no difference between you and the aliens."

He should not answer at all. But he said as if compelled, "She made her own choices."

She said venomously, "Choices! Her choices have been those you gave her, or drove her to. Ruin and suffering and the waste of a life precious to me as my own—she was lost, and she wanted to come home. She only wanted to come home!"

He saw the anguish behind her fury, and understood. No one had to tell her some of Hanna's choices had been made by her Lady. He said, because it would be easier for Iledra if she could believe it, "She was not herself even when she told you that. The woman you knew as Hanna may no longer have a real existence."

"You can't mean that! When I am told she might have killed you, and refrained—"

"But she is gone," he said. "If she comes to you I will admit she has some measure of control, or if she returns here—"

"Returns! She would never go back to you. She was escaping from you!"

"The alien—"

"There is more to it than that," Iledra said. Her eyes glittered.

"No," he said, impassive from long habit.

"I think you are lying."

He said deliberately, "She struggled and lost. The path she made in the short time she was on foot looked as if she had been fighting a physical entity. I'm sorry. But those are the facts and you must accept them."

"I don't believe you. I saw her heart before she went away. It was turning toward you. She would have turned to you in her pain. What did you do?"

He cut her off, with finality. "Nothing."

"She was running from you. *She*, not the alien."

"No. Good-bye, Lady Koroth."

He closed the call without ceremony and was still for some time, staring into space. The guess was too close for his liking. Iledra could not know of his promise to Hanna that she would be safe, and her pleas when she knew he lied. Iledra could not know he had taken Hanna in his arms and comforted her—and then put her away. Several people knew of that intimate little scene, to his profound discomfort, but none of them would have described it to Lady Koroth, not even Andrella.

And if someone did, what did it matter? His only mistake, he was told, lay in having been too kind. He should have had Visharta knock her out as she clung to him.

Oh, hell, he thought. If I had it to do over again that's the only thing I would change. Otherwise I'd do the same damn thing. There was nothing else to do.

He reached for the key that would call Rodrigues so he could get on with his job: Steinmetz next, another commission meeting, another attempt to get heedless F'thal to understand the danger. But he paused at a last thought of Hanna, words Iledra had used: the waste.

For an instant he saw clearly the woman Hanna had been becoming. Wonder had outweighed her fear, until she saw a new danger in him. She had had a chance to kill him after that, and warned him instead, with passionate concern. And then made a clean, straight escape, with that thing in her head and the hounds close behind her.

The waste, he thought. The waste.

After a while his hand descended, and Rodrigues said, "Yes, sir?"

"Steinmetz," he said, and leaned back to wait, thinking rigorously of organization.

CHAPTER XIII

The planes of reality were all discrete, white emptiness cut by darkness, so sharp-edged Leader thought it would all fly apart at any moment. The split was intrinsic in the universe. He knew it, all the People knew it, and bridged it all-together. Now there was nothing to contain it but himself and this alien and memory unsupported by the binding We. Though empty, she functioned, an automaton operating by animal compulsion, automatic and implacable as the universe. She did not even see that reality was unstuck.

Her thoughts cut him, and he was entirely exposed to them now and sometimes, even, thought them. Revulsion and hatred washed over him; in denial of his existence she would drown him. Scalding blasts of negation threatened him. Hating in return was salvation: so the Student-Celebrants whispered long ago: *HATE AFFIRM. AFFIRM. AFFIRM.*

Stronger than captive or paradigm she had also her Home at her back close at hand and around her a Render's artifacts

they made none we stopped them in time

and now that her enemy was visible she faced him powerfully and he was alone, save for her. Save for her who

would Us
kill, I would kill
the Students were
bloody were beastly were cruel were
right. You
kill. You kill!

She made the random transit over the yacht's repeated warnings. The arcs of thought were not all hers. She followed them one by one. Danger danger danger too dangerous a game suicidal (but if it were not sometimes necessary all ships would prohibit it utterly. The instructor shook his solemn head. They should; there is no reason for it ever to be necessary. You ought to be with me now, Umberto.)

Artifact of beasts THAT IS NOT MY THOUGHT I WILL NOT THINK IT.

The random Jump would save her from pursuit; the computer that ordered it would itself need time to determine where it was. There is Sol. *Firsthome of water.* NOT MY THOUGHT.

In the strange starfield she tried to think, but the alien bubble burst in her head and she swam in its shards. *Heartworld II* trembled around her, its planes and angles quivered with immanence, poised, changing to something else. It too would shake apart and dissolve in non-being. There was no color in the universe. It was a white fog cut by shadows from dead space, being and unbeing clearly distinguished. She fell through its cracks to the Students' arms, experienced in pain and in murder . . .

clearly remembered dimly foreseen

and murder I will—!

She shook her head violently over and over until it ached. The pain made a handle and she hung on it. The disjunctions were Leader's reality, not hers. Or his perception of hers, shaped by living millennia; their weight crushed her. She ought to have a soul and she had nothing—

"Stop it!" she cried out loud, and buried her face in her hands. The skin of her face grew hot, grew coarse, and she moaned from her own deep fear.

Home, Nearhome, warm sea of thought gently turning

gentle sea indigo amethyst white spires of Home

"Home," she whispered, and slowly, painfully, straightened. Her thoughts cleared. She could go home. Iledra would protect her, help her dig out this monster and never, ever hurt her.

She said to *Heartworld II,* too quick for Leader, "Set course for D'neera."

"Working," it said, and all her muscles convulsed in his blast of fury.

He did not know how to speak. He was not made for it, and even using her he could not do it. Wildfire was constructed to find aural equivalents for thought and written symbol, and he was not. Nor was she exquisitely alive to currents in the atmospheric sea, so that even commanding her consciousness he was robbed of a potent sense and irreparably numbed. But he used parts of her well.

He held her paralyzed in horror and moved one hand to cancel the course she had just set. Fear and rage rained on him like blows. The hand jerked; toward her head; as if she could plunge it into her skull and tear him out in handfuls of dripping brainmatter. But he held steadfast to the hand. It was a soft and disgusting paw, nearly black against the white of this living, thinking room. Yet she was very light compared to many of the Treecubs, who ran a spectrum that confused him.

Their machines could be run without speech. He had learned how to do that in the long nights, driving her weary body so that in the end he knew more than she did, drawing fierce and invisible on her knowledge, for survival and escape depended on it. She understood the workings of this vessel only because he had showed her and forced her to see because she had not wanted to see and not wanted to know because: because of the other one. Whose eyes had picked him out.

Now the other hand, set to dancing over a keyboard whose logic was mathematical. He understood that, too.

Yes. More much more much closer his goal than he had hoped. Yes. Yes!

She said in despair, to no one but inevitably to Leader: *He was right.*

??

to keep me there. No choice

??

the future on his shoulders

I have too.

Heartworld II said, "The first portion of this course requires intensive calculation due exclusively to randomization. The remainder is known. The probability is ninety-five percent that no more than sixty transits will be required to reach subject terminus. The probability is 90.233 percent that the journey will require less than 144 hours."

Hanna stared at the course display. Its rainbow colors were incomprehensible, and then coalesced into something she could understand. It was almost a course for D'neera. Almost.

Points beyond.

He hid nothing. He could not. Numbers, only numbers. But their meaning to him and to her differed so that she could not grasp fact at once and worked it out painfully.

D'neera must be the rendezvous but it could not be but it had to be. Because the crew of the First (Sentinel) (Watchman) (Watchsetter) knew it and (from Hanna's own thought) could find their way there. Not there. Not quite there. To a star as such things went nearby. She knew D'neera's space intimately. Training cruises.

This was a triple, one a red giant that shone rust-bright over Koroth. They called it the Dragon's Eye.

A course once established in human space was logged centrally. The Polity ran the library and withheld some things, no doubt. D'neera participated in the give-and-take. The crisscross of safe courses in its little sphere of exploration was standard navigational programming, not much used but there it was. And there they waited, at the Dragon's Eye.

Luck, she said to him, *luck, you could not know the course would be here.*

Near is near enough, he said: *I am an Explorer: I would have found the way. This is a gift of time.*

She said: *I will not let you do this.*

You will.

His confidence was too much like that of The Questioner, who had been right after all. She shrank away from it, watching him use her hands. She was not connected with them. He was busy and occupied and she might have leapt upon him but did not, seizing instead on the moment to think. He was too busy to prevent her. She looked at the alien thoughts her brain somehow thought. But that could not be. He could not be a physical entity! He could not!

Watchsetter/Sentinel/Explorer at the Dragon's Eye. Red light—but no light penetrated. They were sealed in and would not/could not go out. She thought experimentally of old pleasures, whirling stars in free fall, the mind-wrenching glory of solitary consciousness lost in all of creation. Her body trembled. The ghost of The Questioner whispered in her brain.

Do not think of that!

Thou fearest the void?

Do not think of it!

There is much then thou fearest of space?

Much. Yet We came for thee. And dissolved thee.

She twisted away from the memory that was nearly upon her. She thought in despair: *You have won from the beginning.*

Since the dawn. I/We must. It is harder. You are stronger.

Stronger than?

Stronger than a furred and evil darkness. She did not understand. She did not feel strong. But it was true, because he could not deceive her.

He added: *A desperate chance.*

I?

You. Desperate. Theory. Process catalyst experiment who knew you would bend to Our use? You have. You are used.

A thousand memories rippled in his thought. They were his/not his; they were old. The living dead jostled her in them. What had they altered and dissolved? Before Hanna, before the colonists? Something not-People but other-than-beast.

She was close to it. He wavered and weakened *alone with a Render-thing!*

The memories invested her with strength beyond her own. She understood this suddenly and drew on all of it and unseated him with one great heave. Reality rocked and was hers again, her body was hers again, her mind was entirely clear. The hands Leader had used were hers, and she concentrated on remembering them earth-stained in a garden, caressing a lover, competent, dangerous: her hands, not scaled and clawed. She could speak.

"Are we still on course for D'neera?"

"No," said *Heartworld II*.

"Cancel the program. Calculate a course for D'neera—no—can—"

She was not speaking aloud any longer, and her hands were gray again.

So strong, too strong!

That was both of them, possessing one another's fear. There was a resonance effect; it grew stronger with each loop, and each time it swung round and struck them they were weaker. He had not expected this. It had not been so with the Lost Ones. Who would think that one alone—?

He scrambled for balance and pounded her with memories of subjection and the alien limbs jerked. The stars twitched through her eyes and he thought they had Jumped. No. Not yet. But she had gotten the command out before he stopped her, and the course was direct for her Home. To make it work he had to reconstruct reality, rejecting hers, but that was her strength and his weakness. She could make a universe in solitude. He could not, nor could he master fear alone: not without the architect the People together were, not without the dampers, baffles, comfort of a billion living brains.

She thought triumphantly: *I can!*

And concentrated on the humming metal around her, building a universe on it and on its master, reconstructing reality from memory and a seed. The weight of millennia would not shape her. She herself was enough. She thought she could see Starr Jameson here, one eye on the readouts, the other on—what? Some theory of governance, perhaps, here in space, free for a little while from the clash of cultures, translating in the ambiguous pathways of thought (and his more ambiguous than most) abstract to concrete, principle to power. The largesse of solitude—

The first Explorer to go alone into space saw craft and cosmos dissolve, and opened a hatchway and stepped into unbeing. After that no one went alone. Solitude could not be borne. They had not known it. How should they have known it, never having felt it? Yet space was necessary. They had to go, to find what inhabited the stars, for fear that Renders did, having won the conflict otherwhere. As indeed they had, it seemed, everywhere.

Now Leader impossibly lived with one. If it were really Leader he could not have endured it a single day. But he was not real. Not real, and not alone. He lived in close company with Wildfire, who was fascinated—

—and let *Heartworld II* slip away, forgetting to be afraid. What could he mean, real and not real? The People were just out of reach, but she saw what they made, a tangible network real as a magnetic field around their Home. A collective dream, impossible for one alone to maintain—

She understood too late that fear was as much defense as defeat. Leader was not afraid either now, and his strength was terrible. Something like the power of The Questioner seized her arm and she wiped out the program for D'neera and rose, trembling. They were not going anywhere now. The compulsion to reprogram was powerfully her own, and she resisted it. Leader was not in control, but neither was she. She stepped away from the console and her reluctant knees gave way and she fell against the equipment and then, squirming, to the floor. She did not feel her cuts re-opening, but there was blood on the polished white floor. She lay with her face against its coldness and when she tried to get up could not. This time it was not Leader's doing, however. The weeks of exhaustion, the mad flight, the final struggle, were too much.

She begged *Let me rest* and images of peace descended: melodies of falling water, harmonies for the skin, she moved almost to meet it, almost felt the plangent drops.

Leader was arrested. This fragile flesh would serve neither of them much longer. Leader knew it, and did nothing to her now, and was gone: almost gone.

She rested and tried again, and this time pulled herself to her feet. She did not know how much time had passed, nor how long it had been since she ate or slept. Earth and D'neera were dim memories. The struggle within her filled time and space, and time was an all-consuming now.

She went painfully through the stalemated ship, a step at a time. The living quarters were luxurious and the food service area well equipped, but there was nothing to eat. She went on vaguely, feeling Leader at the back of her mind, waiting balefully for something but saying nothing.

Without conscious thought she found her way to the emergency stores. Nutrient tablets, which would keep her alive. Why? She swallowed two, compelled. She explored further, her knees shaking. Medical supplies. No stimulants. She would have to sleep, and was afraid to do it. That was what Leader was waiting for. Awake, she could keep some command of herself; asleep, her body would be Leader's to use as he pleased, voice and hands and all that was necessary to take her where she did not wish to go.

Another door opened and she looked at a room which burst upon her with the immediate and present sense of a human personality. In the deepest heart of space, centered in humankind's most sophisticated machine, he would have wood. It smiled warmly from walls and she tripped on the hand-pieced carpeting. The great bed drew her. The richly worked counterpane came from the looms of Arrenswood. It looked warm, though the colors danced before her eyes. She lifted it with a trembling hand and slid beneath it, leaving smears of blood. She apologized silently to Jameson and let her head fall with relief. Peace, stability: you could defeat him, but you could not break him.

Do not think of that! said Leader, and threatened her with a memory of The Questioner but it was weak and far away because Leader lived in this body too and its exhaustion was his too. *I cannot help it,* Hanna answered, human, female, and felt him drift away. She closed her eyes, comforted. Perhaps he would let her sleep for a while; this was his body too.

When Wildfire slept it was like being at Home, in some ways at least. The undercurrents of dream, the fragments of thought, were alien; but in a way it was a warm sea in which one knew one was not alone; not, in fact, one. The daemons that peopled her brain were a company, a shared reality her waking mind excised from existence, and he could almost forget it was her creation alone, and let himself almost believe it was woven of threads of We, changed but real.

The relief was so great that he wanted to dream with her, but there were other things to be done. He opened her eyes and heard her groan. He hoped she would dream of quiet things, pods and vessels, rooms and structures and houses, as she often did; but sometimes they were open to the wind, ragged, tottering, threatening to go dark and populated by monsters. And Leader was the monster.

Or was it Wildfire herself? Did she see herself as he saw her, as a Render, padding from forest to city? Although Renders were forever extinct; even if here there were worlds of them; even if—

She could smell the millefleurs, and they thought to her. Iledra did not; she only spoke. There was a split in her mind and one side spoke, but the other screamed without words. Here was Leader, an endless succession of Leaders blending into one another back, back to the beginning, outlines blurred and overlapping. She tried to fit into the spectrum and rebounded, reeling at Leader's revulsion. For an instant she saw herself through his eyes. She knew it was herself although her fangs dripped blood and she hissed, scarlet eyes speaking murder. The skies blurred in pain. Beast almost-other she writhed under knives. Their enemy was no-thing; they gathered it in, and harvested her. *YES. YES. YES.* Voluptuous agony; she was ash, assimilated.

He felt the pain of exhaustion in the alien limbs, and the dizziness was physiological. He stumbled against a wall and she nearly woke, but this time it was easy to make her tormented mind stay asleep, because she did not much want to wake up or even, perhaps, live.

The thought gave him pause; he let the fragile frame sag and thought about it. She was wired for self-destruction, in the months past he had seen it running like a silver thread through her thoughts, buried deep but shining sometimes clear and purposeful. She had come to them with it, bringing it like a gift and a readiness, a thing that must ease what they did. It was there long-before in the filament of consciousness the time they almost had her. And afterward: leaping gladly for Bladetree in order to die. And before: something to do with a human war, and were they all like this?

And now it was irreversible. For The Questioner knew intimately the original purpose of the rite, and taught it to her well, though present need called forth a different end.

She dreamed of Renders, and there was no one to soothe her. He was glad enough to stay out of this dream.

He had to feel his way through the vessel, putting one foot in front of another, steadying himself with her hands on the walls. Each touch sensed through alien cells was a shock. He had to let the body rest. But first there were tasks to perform, and he found the laser where she had dropped it and ejected it into space. She would try to damage herself, to die and escape that way, and he could not let her to do it.

Then he set course again, and afterward let her head rest on the main control console, wishing he were still hidden from her. Everything had been easier when she did not know he was there, lurking behind her conscious thought, her fear masking his, acting when she slept, night after night matching her knowledge to written symbol . . . it was so much easier to hide. So much easier. And he might have done it longer and avoided this, except that in the end he could not hide his presence from one dangerous man.

Waking was difficult. It was the most difficult thing she had ever done in her life, because she was drowning. Her lungs were full of amniotic fluid and she fought to be born.

Leader was growing stronger.

I can't wake, I can't, I can't, and I will die.

A hand reached for her, a real hand, human, strong, and pulled her to the surface of consciousness. A shell cracked, and she was born. But when she looked for the hand it was gone. The controls of *Heartworld II* surrounded her, and no one was here except the two of her.

She tried to speak and felt Leader come alert, and ducked out of his awareness. She felt him searching for her, puzzled and alarmed.

She wondered: *How did I do that?*

It was midnight at the Center, and her fingers moved in the familiar sequence that would link her room to the library network. She struggled to interpret the Standard symbols she had been reading all her life. Sometimes they shivered into alien notation, and then she could understand. Her telepathic sense had never been this keen and she was on guard, and would not have heard the footstep but felt the intention. And turned off the display and slipped into bed, and someone came in.

Half her self disappeared. She almost felt a pop, and then forgot. She opened her eyes to a room no longer strange and reassured the attendant, and that was how it was done.

If he can go from hiding to control, can I?

She looked through his/her eyes and saw their course was toward a red point in nothingness where the alien ship waited, crewed by her torturers. And came out of hiding and took him by surprise, felt him unbalanced and falling, said "Cancel course!" before he could react, and felt his rage.

Her strength was terrible. He panted, or she did. They would careen back and forth forever, a pendulum till death overtook them, unless he could secure control. He needed a weapon; not one of matter, for this was his flesh too. But. But.

She moved. He went along, perforce. What weapon was safe to use? What had he used that she had not learned to take and use against him?

One thing. Only one thing.

She felt his intention and hunted for the laser. Maybe this time he could not turn her hand.

It came to her that she had done nothing with these aliens but try to die.

A forgotten reader lay in the lounge. It came to life when she picked it up. Philosophy: elegant abstractions danced before her eyes. She shook her head at them, feeling like a savage. In her universe abstraction had no meaning.

The ship is dying, she said. *Most of us are gone. We can let them take us prisoner. Or fly into final chaos, and take them with us.*

She could not find the laser. She supposed Leader had hidden it with her hands while she slept. There was nothing left to do but dive into a star. She should have gone for Sol at once, while Leader still was shaken. She would try it now. She turned back to the flight deck.

He was weary, weary as she. He had not believed the will to die could be so strong. The Questioner in truth bore a share of the blame. Bladetree, son of Celebrants a thousand generations old, had gotten his first name for a reason. Their voices were fainter to Leader. Bladetree lived *then* in the ancient rite. The aim of *now* was different.

But she feared The Questioner, lyrically though she had responded. The last weapon had worked well so far. He did not like using it, for the trauma made her briefly useless and was torment to him too, but it would stop her long enough.

The Questioner had conditioned her thoroughly. If he must, he would use her living memory again.

She opened her mouth to tell *Heartworld II* what to do and nothing happened. Leader, forewarned, prevented it.

She moved her hands with nightmare slowness, as if many gravities crushed her. But they moved toward an input terminal.

Damn you, thought Leader, and stopped, shocked. He had thought in words.

The universe narrowed to a keyboard. Her hand wavered;

pain assaulted her, top of head to tip of toe. "The body," said a voice from the past, "forgets pain." She thought, *no it doesn't, you fool.* She did not remember falling, but she looked up from the floor to the terminal she could not reach.

She made another effort and The Questioner was there, and her vision halved as one eyesocket became charred bone. Pain consumed her intention, and she screamed. She tried to move and it happened again. Tried to move and it happened again.

Leader watched in a certain suspense as the small hand crowded with too many fingers jerked and fell back. Her heartbeat shook him and then she was gone and he lay panting on the floor. When he got up the limbs moved easily, though they hurt and were very tired. She was gone.

He set course once more, one last time. She was gone and it was easier to hold up the universe, now that he was not fighting hers. A little at a time, at least; these controls were all that mattered. He could do it in this body that was used to its brain's commands, used to living solitary. He could do it a little longer. If he were true-Leader he could not have done it at all. But he was Leader-in-her-thoughts, and drew on alien resources.

He thought: *She is the best they have. And she is not good enough.*

His/her body needed rest, and so did he. He gave himself a vivid suggestion and went to sleep.

The skin she thought flayed from her face was still there, and both her eyes.

Leader slept.

She said to Starr Jameson, "I am not strong enough."

He was standing in the corridor, looking at her with friendliness.

"Suicide maneuvers," he said. "What will you do when youth and luck and brilliance fail you?"

"Fail," Hanna said. "Again."

"You are on your feet and he sleeps."

"Only," she explained, "if I don't change course. Or try to kill myself. Or—" She considered. "Yes. Or if I try to communicate with anyone. Then he'll wake. And do that again."

"Well," Jameson said, "think of something else. Suicide

maneuvers indeed! D'you think I'd be where I am today with those tactics?"

She said doubtfully, "What do you suggest?"

"Oh, something more oblique. Keep 'em guessing till the time comes, then go for the throat. That's called diplomacy. It's how you stay on top."

"Ah," Hanna said with satisfaction. "I see. But you hated doing it to me, didn't you?"

He said, "You're very pretty, but quite mad, you know."

"But you are a rock," she said, "and I have no place to stand."

He disappeared and she cried out, "Come back!"

But the misty walls sharpened and clarified and she was indisputably alone, and not even a footfall echoed in the corridor.

Leader half-woke at the echo of her soundless plea. It broke through the shadows that hid her, and the poignance of her loneliness made him think of Sunrise. He wished her heartily not to move; their muscles longed for rest. She subsided, falling into denser shadow. The intentions to which he had sensitized himself were absent; otherwise her thoughts were hidden with the trick she had learned from him; but they were on course and alive and would continue so. He was safe. He went back to sleep.

Ignored, forgotten, Hanna went to the yacht's galley, seeking her last hope. *Heartworld II* was big, far larger than a shuttle. One might sometimes use it to take colleagues in the exercise of power from place to place, and entertain them on the voyage. And feed them. And, if they were from certain cultures, give them meat. Which needed to be carved. In the ancient and most basic way: with a gleaming razor-edged knife.

She thrust the knife into her belt.

Leader would not let her die, but she was a Render. Renders killed.

CHAPTER XIV

Darkness. Sough of breath, heartbeat's drumbeat. Paralysis. Like the months when—I can bear it. . . . Where is she? Hiding not hiding how can she? Only We. They cannot but I am mad he is mad they are mad I am mad. In space a few are mad alone he is mad so he is doubly mad. And I prisoner passenger my body possessed by definition mad.

Do not notice the knife. I cannot find her. Eternities of love and bonds that do not break. I will believe that I will taste her, if not I then other-I the same but not I cannot bear. Such loss. All lost.

If he is mad he cannot be permitted but if I am mad I must not but I am mad and logic fails so

you do not
remember
the knife.

The first Watchsetter is alone in space. Its defenses are thick. Its deflectors overmatch all the creature Wildfire showed Us, all she knows. No stones will pierce this shield.

The First Watchsetter is alone and: *A different color from Our skins, she thought. What difference? What colors did she see what We do not?*

The First Watchsetter is alone and the gemstone light of a cooling sun illumes it the color of her blood. At Our backs, ice. A globe of rock and ice and frozen gas; no life here; no life, ever. Before Us the bloody giant dances, doubly escorted.

We have been here so long.

so long
so long

no Watchsetters before Us have been out so long, and echoes of Home are faint and far and

probably unreal

the chronometer says nothing that means anything and realtime is etched in Our bones too long

too long

too long!

for five of the People five only.

I am Leader, he thinks. He must do this often, daily, ritually, all of Us must. For all of Us begin to forget, for five are not enough.

Here, Leader. At Home, ah! At Home!

At Home he is Hearthkeeper's Fulfillment; as she is his.

Five is the least-shape. Five cohere; with difficulty

We are exceptional

selected

trained

brutally

Explorers

Watchsetters

We

only five!

It would be better with twenty. With twenty it would be better. But so few can survive sundering. So few are so exceptional. There are not enough for liberality. We cannot spare three crews to augment one.

Thus will Renders rending space defeat Us in massed attack. Space is Home to them. They traverse it confidently, leaping through stars, unminding the void save in awe. Not horror.

Wildfire spins through stars, escaping.

Our craft is not the same physical entity as the First Watchsetter. It is blind to the horrible void which We only dare see through instruments, it is filled with memories, it is propelled by the promise of Homecoming; it has these things in common with the First Watchsetter, but also with the others. It is First because its crew traces an unbroken line to the First. The Apprentice of the first voyage of the First Watchsetter rose to Leader of a later voyage, and the Apprentice of that crew in time succeeded him, and so it went in everendless cycle through the years.

And all of Us are here.

It is an honored calling, Leader thinks, *though in memory something else. Once*
We flew in joy
in fascination
not by need
not in fear.
In common memory the forays share in the pleasure of creation, darkness and abrasion making one current of a complexity whose rewards were/are worth seeking but
it is all darkness now.

Here or there a world of beauty begs Us to stay. We cannot stay. We never stay. Wonders wait even in ice. They wait forever for Our return.

For this is the function of a Watchsetter and so has it been for a hand's-hundred years.

The Leader of the First Watchsetter Long-Ago remembering:

I was boy Apprentice lately tapped into the then/now of the First Watchsetter. Truly first for me; my first voyage. Left I Weaver at her loom. Left the mountain Nearhome, falling water. The Ordeal nearly broke me. Alone they said a little while. It seemed forever. Later the bond formed, one by one.

Then-Leader took Us dizzily through darkness. Mountain memories filled my eyes. Apprentice only, their good aid and hands. Knowing I will one day be Leader.

Weaving shuttle woven night. Ship the primal birth-sac. Air sweet-scented. Not mountain air. Long between stars. Not here: no globe cool enough. Not here: none warm enough. Here? No. None alive. They seek life, the Treecubs, leaf-lovers.

Barren rock. The universe is made of barren rock.

Always We were on the edge. Everywhere We went was new.

Rock.

We came on the edge to a brilliant star, beacon-lit. Its companion was shadow beside it. A shoal of planets, swarming. Some were near-stars, ripe with sullen heat. The rest were rock. Save for one, very-far-out, born by chance in the narrow rainbow strip where ice liquefies, gases volatize, the thick rich broth is jolted, transcends rock, and lives.

By chance.

Thick and rich and dark leaf-analogs coated rock. We went unwilling, questing, afraid. We breathed the air. The wealth of that air! The glory of its light! Objects peered from leaftops, bright-eyed. Treecubs, it may be. It may be that in some distant now they come to ground, grow savage, learn to leap into the dark.

The Treecubs were not here. Not yet.

We set the telltales carefully in caverns. The caverns shone with Our light like stars. I took their waters in my hand and tasted water pure as my Weaver's eyes. The telltales are skeins of energy, no more. Deep within this world is heat to feed them. We left them in darkness to wait. Sooner or later the Treecubs will come. Somewhere not-in-caverns they will call to their kind through Nospace. And the telltales will urgently fling forth warning; and dissolve.

We went to mountains, for my sake, which was Our sake. Air pure as my Weaver's hands.

It was not Home.

Afterward we set the relays, carefully. Which also will dissolve, once used, and used for nothing else. When they come here We will know.

It took a year to place the relays. I went Home then to Weaver. Not long. I left. Again. Again. At last I learned to be Leader, but Weaver died. Thereafter, soon, I too.

And this is what it means to be a Watchsetter. And this is why We honor Us.

This is not much of a brain, thought pseudo-Leader, and recognized the thin high note of hysteria. His. Not hers. But the sardonic despairing humor was not his.

She was, she must be, gone. He found no trace of her consciousness when he searched. She lived however in her cells and bones. The too-fragile hands were competent if he did not think about them. When he thought, they dropped things and trembled. When he was undecisive they flew to the soft heavy hair whose texture made his skin shiver. *Her* skin. The trim and rakish spacecraft was alive with noise. Her hearing was acute. The People barely heard at all. Sound cascaded on the alien ears. And was labeled, identified, and put away. Not by him. By, then, the residue of her that lived in flesh. It taught him when to eat. It taught him, shuddering with revulsion, how to care for the alien organism. Thin slick skin. It slept more than he.

He thought, washing it, I hid from this. From the intimate secret needs of her body I shielded myself, revolted.

He had succeeded in the first-aim, the People's need. But did he own her body, or did it own him?

Leader, pseudo-Leader, Leader-in-her-thoughts stood helpless in her body in the command chamber of an artifact of Renders. Black-and-white soothed his eyes. Dizzy rainbow colors elsewhere. The color perception was finer than his, widely ranging, delicately discriminating. They did not have true-sight at all, most of them. Only Wildfire and her kind.

An uproar of sound jolted through him. Only a chime, her body said placidly, undisturbed. The ship announced another Jump in tones he did not comprehend. It made the Jump. By itself. He saw no change; he had opaqued the port so he would not have to see the great emptiness. The ship had the name of a planet.

The government of reason and logic. The rational use of power. They do not favor eccentricity, but old money buys the right. Few in numbers, highly stable, formidably strong. The balance of real and ideal. Hidden warmth and loneliness—

He had the information. But all mixed up with it were her opinions, her prejudices, and also the drawing-near to one man of that place.

Too much like the People's bonding.

Too different and distorted.

Do not think of that.

Serene numbers announced to him the journey's end was near. He had done nothing but show the craft where to go. It bore him majestically across great depths. He was distant from the process. It was not like the First Watchsetter, demanding intimate involvement of brain and hands. Her body accepted it, unquestioning.

Was she still here in some way?

The unperceived does not exist, said an Explorer of long-ago.

You here! Leader said. The body shuddered with relief.

His living, long-dead mentor answered: *I am here.*

I thought you left behind with Us—

All of Us are here, Explorer said.

But there was a note of uncertainty.

Pseudo-Leader sat abruptly on the floor. The knees were weak.

Feel, he said. He meant the lightness, lack of weight, fragility; hair lightly brushing the slender neck; thin fabric over soft skin. The sensitive breast-pads, pointing forward, made him cautious. Naked feet; he couldn't bear her boots. He said, *You know well the invisible has real existence!*

A matter of instruments, said Explorer. His meaning was obscure.

The floor felt very cold to Leader's flesh. He said, *I cannot find the answer to my question.*

Explorer said: *Questions answer one another.*

That is no answer. Is she here?

I was present at such an answer, Explorer said.

Show me, Leader urged. Although he was not sure the question—is she here? —was the question he ought to ask.

Explorer said, *I wandered in the days before Watchsetters, the days of joy, though the question shadowed Us even then, having shadowed Us since eyes turned from forest to stars.*

The question was answered/not answered in a place of dull red rock. The star was red, like that We seek; the light was red; all things were red in the light. A planet's spectrum showed as We approached a Home like Ours. It was the first. Life was rare and precious in the slow early days; microscopic, mindless; lichens at best. Mosses answer no questions. Here was more.

We came to ground eagerly through ruddy cloud. Descended on savannah, crushing copper shrubs. The things that ran away were thin and black as wiry sticks. Six limbs they had and ran like rippling water with queer grace.

They were pitiless though terrified, bestial, disconnected, lacking true-sight, separate from Us and from each other. They were Render-things, though they had not a Render's spark or skill; not yet. Thus was the question answered.

And We said: now We know. Life bends elsewhere toward Renders not Us. But We said: now comes another question. Are there some who are Our equals in thought and in skill?

The answer came not in my time.

Leader said, *It shaped mine.*

The alien body twitched. He thought someone peered over his shoulder. He thought miserably: *So was it with her when I hid. But is it the body remembering?*

You know not who you are, remarked Explorer.

I am Leader. Leader. Leader!

The instrument is the brain. Recall the purpose of the Rite, Explorer urged.

Leader struggled to fix his thought. For Explorer always

since infancy had been his guide to objectivity and cold reason.

He said in obedience, *The objects of the Rite were two. First, dissolution; and second, identity with Us.*

It has not changed, Explorer said.

I never loved the agonies of the Rite, Leader confessed.

You did, Explorer said. He was afraid.

He was gone.

I did? Leader said. But no one answered.

Wetness blurred his Render's eyes.

Renders fought with tooth and claw, savage, wielding stones. Later they bound the stones to wood. They fought the water-People ages long, broke the living eggs, devoured the young. Different, separate, hardly seeming native to this world, though they were: the People tried to claim them.

Symbolic, remarked Explorer, and vanished again.

Leader thought in a kind of frenzy, *That is not a concept of Ours!*

He huddled on a square of polished black, half or less than half himself. If she were here, surely he could find her. Her brain the instrument was limited, however. It bound his powers and defined him. If she was here she suffered the same limitations; therefore she could not hide; therefore she must be dissolved as the Renders in the claiming of the Rite had been dissolved (but all of them died), as the Lost Ones had been dissolved (but all of them died).

They had not let her die. What happened when a Render survived the Rite? Was that the true question?

Heartworld II said, "ETA three hours," but Leader did not understand it.

Time is slipped, blended, schizophrenic. Hanna admires her former self. A lizard owns her pretty hands. She thinks few names for anything; exists in the infant's timeless wordless universe of light and dark. She has been his parasite forever. He is faulty and disorganized, wherein lies her hope, if hope it is. She does not think of hope. She thinks of blood, a deep contented song. Iledra would not know her for herself. She does not know herself. She is only *here*.

It is the end of the day's last sad watch. True-Leader rises. Ship's midnight is full around him. We think of the task We fulfill: always. We think of the avatar-of-Leader, distant. Triumphant?

The leads that enter Leader's brain differ little from those of the past. His thoughts are those of the First Watchsetter. He thinks of power and distance, orbit and momentum; the gravitational complex like heavy stones that can be grasped in the hand, smooth and round and water-worn. In their polish shine the eyes of Sunrise. In his braincase, in Our skulls, are sockets drilled and shaped ubiquitous as eyes. We are the First Watchsetter. The ship is We. It thinks Our thoughts. Unlike Treecubs enslaving metal. We knew long-before. That:

Renders
their machines
are separate
primitive
stones bound to wood
inorganic

as their homes as their hearths as their hearts—

It is time.

Thy task, says Leader to Steersman. Steersman sunk in recorded memories of Home and bondmate and sweet clean skies stands dutiful. We say to him: *We know the call.*

Thy task, Leader says, *thy watch.*

Steersman sorrowing says: *Grim task,* and the hearts of Our companions, some waking, some asleep, answer Us:

grimly answering
need We are
desperate,. ends
it now ends
with new hope
or despair—

Hope withers, Leader thinks, looking round in dimness at the sturdy unfailing machines bright with winking lights.

(Unfailing . . . but . . . somewhere a failing craft drifts smoke-filled death-filled to deliberate oblivion. Bursts of dying hamper the tampering hands crazy-wiring wreckage into motion. Still she goes on. not Ours! not Ours!)

Hope dies as days pass and We weaken long-absent from Home. The lattice of existence fades; its structure blurs. We move wraithlike through a ghostly ship, and the endless emptiness of outside weighs on Us through its walls.

Empty of hope
in the new
the untried
Hope!

he thinks, and seeks to turn the current of Our being. Leader truly, one of the great who appear in deep need; but it has been so long, so long, that even he can bend Us only to least-change, and Bladetree the Guard who was Questioner, answers: *The only hope,* and We are turned:

only hope
it may be, though
desperate, and
brave, but
is not desperation
always hope?

We acknowledge the truth of the equation, but Leader withdraws in sudden impatience. We let him go. For this too is the mark of the great, to retreat and consider and gather strength for Us all. And We have not strength to comfort one another's moods. And his sometimes might weaken not aid Us; for he is first-source of an experiment whose outcome will be hope, or not. It will work, or it will not.

And everything has been experiment since a long-placed telltale, a Watchsetter long-ago's shade, registered the Treecub transmission and stalking began. The less-than-People are coming, sailing toward Home, and their message comes before them, coruscating: *We are intelligent carbon-based oxygen-burning bipedal intelligent intelligent intelligent. . . .*

Steersman comes through the muraled corridors. We look at them through Steersman's eyes, and regard the darkened command chamber along with Leader. The walls once showed Us comforts of Our Nearhomes; but their seeming life depends on shared belief; and now there is not energy enough among Us to make them real, and they are arbitrary and meaningless lines that sink and waver, and darkness slowly overcomes them.

All is quiet, Leader says, and Steersman acknowledges, entering: *All is quiet,* and We echo in Our thoughts,

quiet . . .
quiet . . .
quiet . . .

Leader gives over to Steersman the traditional sidearm of the one on watch, its weight cold and heavy in Our hands. It is a relic of Renders, the transfer a custom spontaneously risen at the start of Watchsetting. Not that the Treecubs are prey to such weapons, with all their means of killing from afar; but the ritual commands Us to vigilance.

Relieved of weight and duty, Leader paces through the ship. We feel Ourselves together a pale shadow of Home in boundlessness, dying caricature of a Nearhome. *We are doing well,* he thinks, *for so few so long in emptiness. But We have been out too long, We starve for Home, We are stretched thin and tenuous and Our functioning declines. How much longer should We wait?*

He comes to the place of rushing water and strips off his clothing, thinking sadly of the waters of his Nearhome and Sunrise sporting there. Three other of Our living companions are bonded too, and find no comfort but in one another's pain. There is no comfort but memory. Only those who endured before Us teach Us how to bear assault on the unassailable, loss of that We cannot lose and live, disjunction that ends and reduces Us to ash.

For an instant he sees Sunrise in the stones that surround him. We take alarm and warn him, as We always do. But not immediately; We are not so quick as before; and will the day come when We cannot? He will not look at the glimmering stone. Blossoms and fireferns hang over him in damp thick air, and he floats in warm stillness. We miss the pleasant pooldarter, the little animal that lived in this place, but in a mutual excess of revulsion We killed it and threw its body into vacuum; its timorous isolated animal thoughts reminded Us too vividly of Wildfire, who—

Is not what We wanted. Is not what We expected. Does not yield as she ought to yield. Forces Us to final measures and a new one, thus herself designing fate. Is something new—

The worry of it weakens Us, then and now. Weakens

Home too perhaps, but no, he struggles to discriminate in thought between We and We. Five here alone so long however wrong We seem now must have been right, the consensus of the People: right in stalking, enticements, patience to wait for a few alone, plans changed by the differences perceived but not understood in Wildfire and later two others. Why was there no memory of Wildfire's kind? So We could not watch as closely as We planned, because her kind perceives an eye. But We said take one and torment her and quickly she will show all We need for a crippling blow, their skills not Ours but We have had time to make them Ours and so We will save Ourselves.

But even faced with certainty, Wildfire does not believe it.

The final choice to which she forces Us is right, We say. Perhaps it were better to chance the one world, Wildfire's Home. . . .

Folly, Leader thinks, repeating the arguments that swayed Us to consensus. Her homeworld is not what We seek. In the changing years the species is spread and increased. There is no longer one homeworld. Wildfire has hers; but there are those others shining half-sensed in her ill-shielded thought like the light of a mighty fire seen through water, blurred and trembling. All that power to fall upon Us . . . and she edged toward death, and what is to be done must be done before she thus escapes. And maybe she is dead anyway. Maybe the Treecubs cannot repair her, despite her faith.

Bladetree says implacably, *or they repaired her and the plan did not work,* and Flametender stabs Us with fear from his sleep: *and if it did not*

work then, Steersman says,

and Apprentice echoes: *what then?*

Start again but

they are gone there is

only her Home which

is folly, Leader says, and

Sudden shock takes Us, driving all else from Our thoughts:

He is coming! Now! At last! Steersman cries, We sway waking and sleeping in his alarm, and the patterned lights that warn him are bright in Our eyes as lightning striking long-expected

here at last!
too late—
too soon . . .

Excitement sweeps through Us in storm waves, gathering momentum and rebounding one to another and gaining strength. Fear and apprehension not joy nor sureness; it takes too long to damp it; five are not enough, We are gone too long. Our rigorous training cannot hold—yet it does. Leader splashes from the pool and across mossy rocks, trembling, and the sleepers wake, trembling.

Identify. Identify. Identify!

He sees through Steersman's eyes the keyboard We use, hands wavering in shock. He says: *We will have no intelligible answer. There is no translation program. We must wait for the arbitrary code.*

Steersman's embarrassment washes over Us.

I forgot. . . .

Leader pulls on his scarlet uniform and runs through the First Watchsetter, shedding droplets of water. Bladetree comes eagerly, Flametender in alarm, Apprentice uncertainly. But Flametender thinks: *It worked!*

Relief is a long-unknown softness. Steersman says: *I was afraid. Wildfire was strong,* but Bladetree who was Questioner says: *Not at the end.*

And it is true that at the end she is not strong; seems, even, to understand something of the essence of harvest, and properly yields her pain; but still she denies Us. She is a shapeless lump of flesh, intelligence suspended, docile, surrendering to Our claim; but also mad, nearly mindless, leaving unanswered questions We did not ask soon enough. She evades us though captive and helpless, and in the long distracting ecstasy of her dying, slips away.

Therefore a semblance of Leader has gone with her, and now returns.

Touch me, begged pseudo-Leader, yearning for his People, and Hanna crouched in darkness and watched him, brooding.

He paid her no attention. For a while he had searched for her and then given up, wishing her silenced forever.

She was not silenced but hiding. She had had some practice in enduring isolated consciousness without mobility. Her long recovery on Earth had taught her something about it. Then she had clung to Dale Tharan's thoughts, inimical as they were, as to a lifeline. Now she was an observer of Leader-in-her-thoughts, though she hid from him.

Touch me, he begged, and they did, and Hanna flickered and was blinded by his/their burst of joy, and then went on detaching herself, observant and purposeful.

Home, Home, nearly Home and no longer alone—

Hanna was a mote, an atom, a spider death-still with its legs curled and balled, but they made a web of living threads intricately loomed and she sorted them out. The steersman, the apprentice, the flametender who was the engine master, the one who had been The Questioner. And Leader; but there were two Leaders. One of them was mad, a parody, a crippled thing. That was Leader-in-her-thoughts.

I am Home, Home, I have returned, he rejoiced, but the other said: *That is not I!* and all of them, true-Leader, pseudo-Leader, Hanna too, froze in consternation.

It was I
it is We
but not I
it is thou!
I am thou
at least We—

Ripples of confusion surged around her. There was a beacon now, however, and *Heartworld II* made for it. It was close, very close, and They were altogether present.

Hanna floated in her unworld and studied them. She heard their thoughts as speech, although they could not speak. The web was raveled and bedraggled with their discomfort. If she had been able to smile, she would have smiled. The germ of an idea, born from her struggle with Leader-in-her-thoughts and fed by his memories, was practicable. One's fear or distress affected them all. To control it they needed time, and this handful of long-sundered wanderers was susceptible to disruption and slow in control, like those who had found the colonists, the Lost Ones.

She knew how to do much that pseudo-Leader had done to her. She knew perhaps how to do more: she knew how to be alone: her human brain made it a condition of existence. And she had a Render's single-minded savagery, and bound to it true-sight and all that implied and more than that implied for she was something new and knew it, and they did not; and all their suspicion, being vague and tenuous, fell short of the truth.

It could work.

She darted through their communion like a hidden fish, listening.

I/not-I do you not see?
it cannot be
you but think it
is that is
madness
danger
chaos
if madness I must
die you must
die I must
die, but not
into silence!

Stark fear; not of death but something more; an obliteration. Hanna did not understand it, and ignored it. She was not part of the web. She could ignore it.

Die, she thought with satisfaction. Into silence or not, you will die; not I.

I cannot look on my own madness!
But it is not ignoble its
will is set to duty though
it suffers; it has been
long alone and
in pain

True-Leader said suddenly: *Where is Wildfire? Where is she?*

Hanna retreated in alarm into a deeper blankness. But Leader-in-her-thoughts said: *I do not know. She is gone into silence.*

There came a burst of triumph that battered them. Hanna watched with interest their reeling.

It was truth! cried an ancient Celebrant,
truth! echoed Bladetree
truth! all of them said and Hanna sickly, savagely, closed out the memory of the Rite, the Rite that had claimed her, or nearly.

In the triumph and the glory of victory spanning eons pseudo-Leader said: *Open the docking bay that I may enter.*

And true-Leader moiled the ebb and flow of radiance piercing it with fear: *That is I and not I!*

She is gone into
silence you
said so—
The Persona itself is changed!

She would have held her breath, if she controlled breath to hold, for she felt him near her.

They fell back, doubt swirling among them. But Steersman said: *Docking begins. I have opened the bay.*

Heartworld II, shining in red light, moved forward. They said:

We do not understand
why We fear why
it is thou
it is We
but not-thou?

On a level that was not hearing she heard them muttering, uneasy and straining. The Celebrant and Celebrants were gone. But they had really/not really been there and were there. True-Leader reached for her, stretching and pulling their strength to break free. Or break through.

But Leader-in-her-thoughts was Leader too, and they paused to hear him, and he said: *I do not think there is aught to fear, for We have claimed her.*

Only Bladetree stirred uneasily, remembering personal hatred. Hanna felt his movements clearly as those of her own body as Leader-in-her-thoughts made it rise. He/she wore the knife. He did not know it. She hid it from him though it lay at his very hand, and laughter bubbled deep within all that was still Hanna. She thought with pure joy of what she was going to do to Bladetree, if she had half a chance.

Bladetree said, *You are strong,* and fear lurked in their thought.

Yes, Hanna thought, but only to herself. As you will see.

I am Leader. I am strong. I have been long alone, save for Wildfire.

Steersman said: *Docking is complete. I pressurize the bay.*

The space filled with air that she and they could breathe. Pseudo-Leader waited, barely restraining himself, eager to run to their arms. A secondary hatch opened at last (the primary having been destroyed; he had not forgotten that) and he leapt from it lightly in his new body. Hanna looked with savage alien eyes on the alien ship. Pseudo-Leader climbed stairs, with some unsureness; the risers were made for longer legs than Hanna's.

True-Leader said suddenly: *Save for Wildfire. She colors this change.*

Their attention shifted from pseudo-Leader. He passed through wavering passages whose bare-sketched living images leered distorted and the face of Sunrise transformed by stony fear made him stumble and—was forgotten. Did not exist. Had not happened.

He laughed. He did not know where the laughter came from.

True-Leader said: *In the work of the Students there was only negation of the Treecub, and identity. I do not understand this change.*

Pseudo-Leader walked on. Hanna waited in shock. He was too close to truth; what if they regained the balance of their unity, and pursued Leader's doubt with all its force?

But the command chamber of the First Watchsetter approached and surrounded her, and the moment of danger passed when they saw her, and forgot fear in common wonder.

Hanna watched it, and waited for her moment.

Deep in Our thought, Leader's thought, not-his thought, since Steersman's alarm, was this body. Surely We knew it would be she. Yet We are unprepared, for its thought is Ours. And its wholeness is wonder, because We remember a mutilated carcass, and memory sickens Us. Nothing could have made Us believe it would live a day past Our disposal of it; nothing but her conviction, until she passed beyond hope of life, that she could be repaired; and despite Our conviction We think now We had not believed.

Their skill in killing We believed, for that was Our long-present fear. But how can Renders be so skilled in healing? How can their biological science so far surpass Ours?

She looks as she looked when first she came into Bladetree's hands, small and smooth and fragile and unharmed. But the destruction had been so great that now We think:

Keep them
keep some
to heal Us
they can heal
even death!

It stands before Us and it is cruel as the junction of two universes. The color of its eyes is impossible. We did not see that before. How can such a small thing be so dangerous? But it bears a Render's spirit or would if it were not displaced by Ours:

We must know these things, it says,

these things! We answer in awe, and are distracted: drift helpless and suspended in a vision of knowledge and techniques past all Our experience. Machines move and hum, glistening; fluid bathes unfeeling limbs and the transparent air glows with energy; the Treecubs move around Us, shaping Us; cells dutifully reform remembered patterns: the tiny flame of life, almost extinguished, swells and grows steady.

And before it is time, before We are ready, he says/We say/it says from the alien flesh: *I will show you what We have learned.*

There is an edge of anxiety and uncertainty in the thought and We do not see its source. We mill restless and wary in the chamber, the heart of the First Watchsetter. It seems there are not five of Us but six of Us, seven of Us, not seven! The air is faintly acrid with Our odor. What does this mean? A life-support flaw?

A Student long-ago remembers and all of Us remember: *The disjunction of alien senses,* and We did not experience this before because then Wildfire's terror filled her and suppressed all else.

So this is right; but true-Leader says, *It is wrong*.

The alien that is We looks at Us with impossible eyes and says: *You will not have to bear me long. When this is done you must kill me. How can I look on Sunrise through these eyes?*

We tremble with many-edged grief for Hearthkeeper of Leader's Nearhome who is to true-Leader Sunrise, to pseudo-Leader Sunrise too, beautiful and unfailing as the dawn. His other self's loss is Leader's own. He is gone from Sunrise too long, and in this moment his longing is doubled, rebounding from pseudo-Leader and gaining strength each moment from each of Us:

Not sundered forever! he thinks despairing,

but the other weeps, *forever,*

and the chamber shatters and the air trembles and Sunrise appears but to each she is his own and longing overcomes Us; for Our bonding is endless and unchanging as the stars, and the unPeople's lack of it marks them beasts.

I did not mean to remember her!

Do not think of that!

We rock, are steadied, slowly make the vision fade. So slowly! Our weakness is greater, Our danger more each day. There can be no more storms of emotion. The bonds on which Our functioning depends cannot survive many more.

The alien body slumps in shared sorrow and apprehension. It says: *We must finish quickly.*

Clearly it is right; its very presence disrupts Us.

In Our acknowledgment of its reasoning it crosses to Steersman's place. He moves aside and awkwardly it takes his seat. Wrongness nibbles at the edges of the aftermath of grief, but We cannot bring Our selves near it. The alien looks at an input bank and its confusion tugs and jerks at Us, distracting. It says apologetically: *I cannot translate quickly from their terms. And this is not made for these hands.*

At last the stunted paws (pretty hands) ill-made and fumbling move (in lost grace) and symbols stand before Our blurred eyes. We crowd together and all of Us long-ago crowd closer too, watching Our hope (or destruction) Our fear; it is clear fear was right. The locus references are clear, starbeacons ineradicable. There will be no escape for the Treecubs, who can no longer hide from a hidden enemy and must wait for Our blow to fall.

Here is one world, their birthplace, bursting with life. In alien memory it glitters with snow.

Here a second, long-settled and nearly as strong and its name is the graceful soft name of a tree.

What have We to do with sounding names?

Lights glow with acknowledgment from Home. The vigil there is ending, the data pouring into the Generals' hands—

The alien hands falter. Wrongness gathers in corners like smoke.

We have no such function—

We do but We do not. Something like it, since the Students' time; but not this; not quite. The new concept is pseudo-Leader's

contamination, Bladetree says, and all of Us fall back in alarm.

The alien says through Our great uneasiness: *I will show you how to translate the data in the human vessel—*

Human? What is Human?

—a clear course program for these worlds—

Its vision dazzles Us with wrongness—

—while We sought them their power increased. Five Homes rich and powerful are their heart and the heart of danger—

Five! We are frozen, the fear, the power, corruption, wrongness, aloneness resonating together. The fragile balance rocks. True-Leader struggles to anchor it: *Five but not that of the Wildfire-thing—*

And the alien says: *She might have been someone's Sunrise.*

Sunrise among Us again is created from his/its/Our longing and caught in tumbling currents of grief and fear the alien throws back its alien head as at a mortal blow

I did not think of her! It was not I!

Do not, do not!

When I am dead—

Stop, stop!

you must tell her I loved her even in this form—

The thought hurt them physically and sliced them in two. True-Leader, wrenched apart, existing twice, relinquished Sunrise to himself. He stumbled desperate toward the alien, reaching out, and the others reached for him, overcome with sorrow and altogether unbalanced with this last blow.

But pseudo-Leader's thought impossibly winked out, and the alien rose and reached for them too.

In that instant they understood the wrongness, the thing hovering behind this changed Leader, and the understanding was too late; the alien moved convulsively; something glittered in its hand; true-Leader's agony flared in his knowledge of certain death, and the knife ripped through flesh and membrane and all of them felt it, impaled and transfixed by horror. The alien was among them free and strong as rushing water, and Steersman stumbled toward the creature, fumbling at his belt, but he failed in the chaos of Leader's dying, and he also died. Then all of them were blinded, and it caught the weapon from Steersman as he fell, and killed Flametender and wounded Bladetree, and sprang for Bladetree with the knife while Apprentice sought to flee and could only crawl.

A weapon, Apprentice thought, *I must get a weapon lest it escape*.

But he could not, prisoned by the weakness of his kind and reeling in the dissolution of other minds dying without solace, the unbearable disruption of the last worst horror. And it took its time with Bladetree and Apprentice writhed with his agony, and Leader screamed both alive and dead and reality began to die about Apprentice. The corridors were a marsh in which he sank and drowned in hate. He clutched for support but there was none, the universe was ending, and he did not even know Hanna had come for him when she shot him in the back and he too died.

CHAPTER XV

A word drifted through the dark, half-transparent air, drawn out into many syllables and at first meaningless. Hanna saw clearly that it was a material and perhaps living thing.

It flared against the darkness; shortened, wavered, crystallized; settled into solid reality, and vanished.

Just before it disappeared it spoke. It said: "Blood."

When it was gone time was uniformly gray and blank. Not even memory marked it.

Presently she saw that time was the gray flooring of the corridor, centimeters from her eyes; saw blood on it; saw that some was subtly lighter than the rest, and remembered.

The lighter patch was *her* blood.

She lay unmoving and watched a pageant of fantastic deaths behind her eyes.

Thus have you wrought. . . .

Dreary droning voice from nowhere. Her own thought.

Presently she considered turning her head. To do it, or not to do it, was a most profound question.

At last, because her right arm hurt horribly, she moved. Her cheek was sticky and stung as it pulled loose from the floor. Her flesh was insubstantial, but it responded to her will.

Only yours only yours only yours! cried the voice, and she shuddered and cringed from it.

Leader was dead. In her mind there was a whimpering where he had been. But he was dead. The whimpering did not stop.

Presently another word appeared. "Up," it said. She clung to it, used it for support, climbed it slowly, and was sitting. It disappeared.

Apprentice's torn corpse lay near her. There was a gaping

hole in his back; Steersman had been carrying a projectile weapon. The custom was associated with a past shadowed by Renders, which responded unpredictably to any defense save having big holes blown in them.

"No. No," Hanna muttered. That bit of knowledge could not come from *anywhere*. They were all dead.

She stretched consciousness cautiously. The effort cost an almost physical pain. Nothing living met her. She reached inward and was empty, like this spacecraft, like the universe.

She preferred it to the frenzy of their dying, which had gone on for some time even when their bodies were certifiably dead and past reviving even with human techniques. It ought not to have been so much like the *Clara*. These things were not human. But the blackness was the same, and the wailing ghosts. She had thrown herself on the floor in shattering hysterics and clawed at her ears to shut them out. Her throat was raw from screaming. None of it did any good at all, and in the madness she had nearly died too.

Now it was finished, and to what end? Sunrise would wait forever, a whole Nearhome subject to her grief. That was all.

Hanna sat on the cold floor and looked inside her right forearm, which was on fire. It was clear true-Leader or Steersman had turned the knife back on her somehow, though she did not remember it. The wound was ugly, but it had missed the big veins and nearly stopped bleeding. Her whole arm hurt and was stiff, but she could use it.

Use it, she thought, for. . . .

And quailed. She did not want to use it for anything. She wanted to lie down again and go to sleep, rejecting thought and purpose.

The whimpering went on and on and grew into a howl of pure and untainted despair. For a moment, in slow confusion, she looked at Apprentice's body; but he would never speak in thought again.

Leader still lived in her mind. He did not want her to stop. He did not want to die a second time.

Tears of weariness came to her eyes. Even dead he was not dead. There still was no escape.

She lifted a hand to her hair, but the pain in her arm was so great she let it drop.

Over the mourning came unbidden a memory of Leader's creation. He was a creature of drugs and suggestion, with true-Leader's power behind them, constructed in the chasms of an ego violently disorganized by pain.

So precariously founded he might, she thought, be vulnerable. Perhaps he could be destroyed. Perhaps the mindhealers could do it.

The thought compelled her to rise. She began to stumble through darkness, supporting herself against the wall with her uninjured arm.

and the oldest blackness and the falling years mourn us lost riches parts lost from the whole—

Be quiet, she said in despair, *oh, quiet!* and quiet descended.

She had no goal but clumsy motion. She was at one place or another with no recollection of getting there, as if movement required such effort there was nothing left for the perceiving of it. But presently she was in a docking bay, looking at *Heartworld II* through a fog of pain. The hatch from which Something had emerged was open. She went through it and in time found herself by a disordered bed. It was big enough for a big man, or one of the People. She was lost in it.

She fell on it. She felt the automatic pulse of thought from pseudo-Leader, she would sleep and he could regain control—and then her conviction and then his that he could not. He was herself.

She slipped into blackness, too tired to be grateful for the peace.

When she woke Leader was still there. If he had not been she might never have thought again, but as it was she said to him, *Go away, you are not real.*

I am, I am, I am, he wept, so clearly she heard the words.

Tears covered her face. Which was odd, she thought, because the People do not have tears.

She sat up. It was nearly as difficult as the first time. Weariness past enduring enwrapped her.

I am real, Leader insisted, and Hanna fell back again, helpless. Dark and warmth and wetness surrounded her. The medium she breathed was joy. She struggled to escape a clutching memory, not hers. "No," she said, but he would not be denied, and *Heartworld II* changed to:

A chamber hewn from rock richly carved in celebration. Lifetender's task was nearly done. She tapped an embrittled shell with a silver hammer, and tiny claws appeared at a crack, tiny fingers reached for the world. They fastened on the fingers of Leader and Sunrise, sealing a communion begun while the little one was an embryo. They bathed together in running water and all the community was a song around them. In other Nearhomes, and in other times, the same ritual simultaneously was being performed or had been performed or would be performed. He danced in the water, stretching his baby limbs *as swiftly as I,* said a long-dead swimmer, and now in this place he was Swift.

The vision faded. Hanna saw the rich woods of Heartworld again.

He is my son not yours, Leader said. *I am real. This happened to me!*

She turned slowly, unable to move quickly. Crumpled fabrics rubbed at her face and woke pain in her wounded arm. A trace of a familiar scent—imagined, perhaps—brought Jameson before her.

When she thought of him she got up slowly, swaying, feeling curiously light. She felt an edge of panic at the smallness of the room—no, at the absence of those other eyes, other dimensions, other perspectives which her two eyes alone could not see.

She thought of the hearthstone of Leader's Nearhome, a brilliant mosaic that made one pattern from many. She thought of the sculptures made to be seen by many eyes at once, at which Flametender had excelled.

"No," she said, pushing knowledge away, but it would not stay away. They were so vulnerable, so fragile for all their strength, subject to one another's pain so that a hurt to one robbed all of competence and a community's strength wasted exponentially. And through Leader she had come to see this weak place, and she had gone for it with all a Render's savagery.

I do not want to think like them! she thought, and thought: *. . . telepathic cousins, who can reach into another being's very thoughts, comprehend him from the inside, ensure peace as we go on. . . .*

She had written the words in another life, when she was herself and Leader, though she did not know it, stalked her. Echoes of dashed hopes, confidence unfounded—what would

Jameson say when she told him she had thought about nothing but killing? About what she had done to Bladetree?

That she had done all she could, perhaps. And then he would forgive her. Perhaps.

"Fraud, fraud, fraud!" someone said. It was her voice.

"But I had to. I had to," she said; and thought there were other things she had to do.

She moved slowly to the flight deck, seeing nothing, stumbling with exhaustion. Exhaustion would never leave her. She had to go on in spite of it. She had to get back to Jameson and tell him she had won.

But nothing lived on the First Watchsetter to signal the docking bay open. She could not leave it yet.

She shrank from facing the bloody work of her hands. But she must do it or never leave; and unwilling, unthinking, she stepped from *Heartworld II* into a ghost ship where nothing lived but herself. Nothing could; she had heard the end of their last fading thoughts.

The route to the First Watchsetter's command chamber was as familiar as if she had walked it a thousand times, though the stairways were hard to climb. The corridors were dim and their walls altogether blank. The murals were keyed to living brains, and had died with them. She felt that she had spent weeks, months, years maybe, in this ship. The command chamber would have been homelike as her rooms at Koroth, except for the evidence of carnage. A burst of grief, hers or Leader's, brought her to her knees among the crumpled bodies. She could not look at the tatters of Bladetree. True-Leader's face was twisted in death, and she knelt in his dried blood.

Fraud, fraud, Render!

"No," she said, "Oh, no. How can you call me that? After what you did to me?"

Renders, he said, *buried their dead. Not Ours.*

"I can't do anything! They're too big, they're too heavy, how could I move them?"

And what did it matter to the dead?

And truly death for Us, said Leader, *far from Home and transition and life in We, though you might for me—*

She did not know what he was trying to tell her. He could not force it upon her. He was less strong than before. He had lived through his own death, but in the passage he had lost the greater part of substance. And what he tried to tell her was so strange there was no place for it in her reality.

She tried to get up, and her hand fell on something that yielded. It was Steersman. She rose then in one quick movement, driven by horror.

It was hard working in the dimness with the silent shapes around her. Leader tried to withhold his knowledge, but he could not, no more than she could reject it. There were more lights here than on a human ship, or there seemed to be more in the half-night the People preferred; all of it spun sometimes before Hanna's eyes, and once she thought it looked like nothing so much as a tinseled habitat seen from outside, a glittering explosion of life in the depths the People hated. She did what she had to do manually; her scalp itched; she was using backups, there was nothing wrong with the front-end system, she ought to plug the ship into her brain and *think* the First Watchsetter's instructions.

You do this very well, my friends dead at your feet, Leader said bitterly when she was done.

Her skin rippled. Almost she heard Roly long-before.

"I will pay for it," she said, not at once sure what she meant. But with the words a thing she had not thought of for two human years came with perfect clarity into focus.

Dorista had stopped her hand in time, but not her heart, which had gone on to touch the bit of metal that ended a universe, Hanna's universe. Some of her had stayed in the night, detached. Easy prey for the First Watchsetter, drawn to its dark promise . . . easy prey for Leader, who had only to expand a cleavage already there. . . .

We do it better, he said.

She shivered, fighting the rush of her own memories which he pressed upon her.

Truly the body's death is ending for you, Leader said. *Not for Us*.

She had a hard brief vision of herself and her kind as a parody, an incomplete obscenity, as if an animal with thumbs grafted to clumsy paws were to think itself thereby human. She felt herself pulled and distracted at the sight, and then saw that his intention was to distract her. Something was happening, and he wished her attention withdrawn from it.

He could not do it. She had hidden a knife from him, and now he could hide nothing. New lights flashed on a communications panel, pulsing urgently. She read them without effort, but it was a moment before their import burst on her.

COME IN. COME IN. DO YOU READ? WHAT IS WRONG? DO YOU READ? WHAT IS WRONG? WE ARE COMING. WE COME.

She stared at the message, transfixed. It could not be true! But the denial was founded on what she wanted, not on what was, and she stumbled finally to the lights and peered at them, and then tapped a hesitant code on a panel shaped for other hands. A strip of paper, or something like it, unreeled from a slit. She tore it off and squinted in the shadow. The characters on it were sometimes intelligible, sometimes not. When they were intelligible they also said: *WE COME.*

They were coming because her/Leader's information had been fed Home as she gave it, by prearranged program, and the transmission had been interrupted without warning or explanation. There had been no answer to their increasingly urgent inquiries, so they were coming.

She remembered, then, and thought: No. Oh, no. An endless time spent watching Leader-in-her-thoughts and holding to her purpose, and all for nothing. They were coming, and they knew where Earth was, and Willow. True-Leader was dead, but he had beaten her. Tampering with them, unsettling them, unbalancing them, waiting for the moment to attack their disarray, she had hardly noticed what pseudo-Leader told them. She had not seen its importance. They were coming, and it was all over. She might as well have told The Questioner.

She rubbed her face in confusion, bits of dried blood peeling off unnoticed, and looked at the mocking lights. She thought of using Leader's sidearm on herself, for what could she take home now except the acknowledgment of this second and greater failure? But pseudo-Leader stormed at her, *I will not die twice!*

She thought of waiting for them to come after all. Leader liked that. But there was still a great deal they would want to know, and she was not so lost as to tell them. There would be another Questioner to rend her.

"Not in my body you don't," said Leader, shocked.

It was her voice again. What, oh no, what was happening to her? She ought to be terrified—but she was past terror. Her capacity for fear was used up at last.

She would go. She could not stay. But she could not face Jameson, either; but she had to, to tell him Earth and Willow were uncovered.

Best to move the Watchsetter first, if she could, so the People could not find it and she could bring humans back to it. If she could do it. If one person could move it.

"No," said Leader, impatient with her stupidity. "One person alone in space cannot do anything. Why build spacecraft for the impossible?"

"All right," Hanna said.

She half-turned to flee, then turned back, weak with the importance of a new thought. The Watchsetter was a treasure for humans. She could not give it to them, but she could take with her the most important thing. It would skew the odds, at least. It might do more; might permit such destruction of the People's threat as to leave them harmless to humans forever. She might have failed utterly in what Jameson had expected of her in an innocent time long-before; but she thought he would settle for victory.

She dropped into the watchman's place and entered a half-remembered code.

"No!" Leader howled. She saw her hands change to hairy paws, but Leader was weaker and her fingers barely faltered. She shook her head to keep coarse ghostly hair from her eyes.

"Render!" Leader hissed, but she went on. No madness or illusion could stop her now. She had strength still for one last hope. If the Watchsetter dissolved around her she would go on until her body failed.

More paper fell from the printer's slot. She did not try to decipher the heading in the bare illumination, but she knew she had made no mistake. She had in her human hands the clear route to Leader's Home, a mathematical map of safe channels through space that would permit humankind to go from this point to Home at wartime speed. If she got *Heartworld II* away the People would have no equivalent for human space. A location was one thing; the course program embedded in this substance was another.

She thrust the parchment into her shirt and went back to *Heartworld II* with memories of the People coming in waves, buffeting her. Voices shouted in her head. They were not all Leader's.

I was Student of animals only, Historian of Renders, pre-

pared against the day. It came. They called Us, desperate Explorers having found Our dread. I went through space, a thing I had not dreamed. And hated it. The severing!

She veered from her course at the Student's power, fell against a wall and saw it flicker; a mural came briefly to life.

Found carnage in a star's light, Renders penned, Explorers dead or dissipated terrorized. The grasses were golden, like some of Home

A scarlet-suited Student reached from the wall. Hanna avoided his grasp; he disappeared.

Knew at once what they were what We feared had feared and fear: Renders without question, for they killed Us: Renders grown to master metal, worse: Renders of a distant star

She stumbled into a room she had not seen before. The chairs looked comfortable, though too large. The ceiling was hung with gems that would dance in moving air; but no air moved.

Prisoned them and questioned, but they knew naught. Called on a sky-born Render to crush Us, but it came not. Some said it was not. Hate scalded Us. We remembered Renders' hate. And its extinguishing.

The room shrank. There was no way out. "Let me out!" Hanna gasped, but the walls closed in remorselessly. The glittering stones were the People's eyes.

Remembered the Rite of Renders' days. We used it applied it to flatten to claim them, defuse and defang them. They crawled, begged, yielded, and died. One by one

Hanna chewed her fingers, crawling. Illusion! The door was where she had left it. She climbed to her feet and trudged toward it and through it, head down.

dissolved them and changed them and learned alteration the source and the secret and thou final fruit

The pseudo-familiar corridors dilated and expanded with her breath. She was a Student, and saw a helpless Treecub vanish in agony; was a colonist racked into insanity.

learned We the change that might aid times-to-come

She got through a last portal and *Heartworld II* was there. All the beings stored in Leader flung history at her. Here were memories of a thousand Nearhomes still walled against long-extinct Renders, here was the Last Hunt which had spanned two hundred years, here were ancestral deaths remembered by survivors whose loss was more final than humans could know. More: burning brands defending misty seacaves, naked hunters hunted by the essence of evil, an archetype ages old that was a living presence still.

She walked into *Heartworld II* and to its flight deck, wobbling but upright, and still bombarded. Human fittings welcomed her. The computer's human-seeming speech soothed her.

"We are leaving," Hanna said to *Heartworld II*.

"Destination?" it inquired without anxiety.

"D'neera," she said, suddenly remembering it was a day or less away. "D'neera. Oh, dear God. D'neera."

Listen, Leader said.

"Shut up."

She let *Heartworld II* do most of the work—that was what it was made for and carried on with it a dialogue in which her part was more crystalline and uninflected than the yacht's. Leader brooded at the back of her thought, contemplating going as a prisoner to D'neera. He said, "You are now alien there as I."

"I am human," she said, opposing his doubt. To be human was to be Hanna, and she would not be Leader. Or the other thing, "which you are," Leader said. "No," Hanna said.

Nonetheless (the docking bay opened slowly on darkness, and *Heartworld II* meshed fields with the First Watchsetter, pushed against substance and non-substance, and lifted) it was true. The day when humans became Renders was not ended. The People had met therefore were meeting therefore would meet a handful of humans stranded on a hostile world, and had seen Renders and were seeing them and would see them. Hanna did not understand how this could be, but there was no question (*Heartworld II* floated gently into space, and frost glittered in pale starlight where it had been) that was what the People saw. No question they would see it again and forever "because you *are*" Leader said, complexes of Render instinct, and barren of the living omnipresent communication through time as well as space that made up this thing she must call the People, or their soul.

No Jump had ever been so welcome as the one that left the First Watchsetter behind.

* * *

Why were there no stimulants on this ship?

Clouds drifted erratically and at intervals into her vision. Her reading on Earth had hinted at glorious devastating drugs in high places. There was a guarded link to Jameson. Imagos, Fantasee, Reomla, Dite's Dream—why not the common ordinary boosters everyone used? Why couldn't he have left her some?

You will be Home soon, Leader said, *and will rest. Or not. Not I. Not you, while I am with you. They will not permit!*

Hanna muttered through her weariness, "Iledra will."

He believed it. He shared her faith in Iledra; he could not do otherwise.

He said, *Close to Home closing destruction of mine—*

"Close," she agreed hazily; got up to keep herself awake; saw facing her a map of human space.

The map was an automatic display, an entertainment, a pretty pattern, a reduction of space to the dimensions of the mind. She wondered what it was doing here in a place that belonged to Jameson. He was not a man to diminish the reality of night and rock.

But other people came here too: Heartworld's councilmen, perhaps, or guests of its governments from other worlds. They would come to watch a pilot, maybe Jameson himself, manipulate the controls that flung them through space-time. Here it was, anyway. She regarded it with somber fascination. Schematic and out of scale it showed everything, a child's-eye view of the universe, where the stars humanity called its own twinkled merrily, connected by thin diamond-bright lines that showed common courses, relay networks—

She was near such a network. Within one? Yes!

(Kiri grinned at a face from Control, unflappable, unquenchable. "A tricky maneuver with minim data. Bassanio in command. Not bad!"

"I don't remember this group being reported ready to up-phase—"

"It was safe enough. Anyway I couldn't stop 'em."

The face said furiously, "Damn you, Kiri, one of these days you're going to lose a whole pod!"

Kiri, laughing, closed D'neera out. The training vessel Star of Gnerin *was too filled with delight for gravity-chained faces to distress it.*

"We know better, don't we?" she said, smiling at Hanna.

"I wish there were no relays—they'd never know what we do!" Hanna agreed, happy and triumphant. She was sixteen, carefree, and immortal. . . .)

"D'neera," she said to *Heartworld II*. "Call D'neera, the House of Koroth, I want to talk to Lady Koroth."

No! Leader said with violence. He needed time; D'neera was too close.

Heartworld II made its busy calculations, located a target, and spoke. Its identicode preceded its message. This was so routine that Hanna gave it no thought, nor the probability that through all of human space the code was flagged and tagged—

"Stand by for holographic transmission," *Heartworld II* said tranquilly.

—and diverted to—

A uniformed Fleet commander who stood before her larger than life and with no warning, so that she jumped, thinking in confusion that she had blacked out and they had boarded and this was a flesh-and-blood giant and really here.

He said politely, "I am asked by Lady Koroth to tell you that she invites you to return home."

They stared at each other. It seemed a long time since Hanna had looked on human being. She found her voice and said, "Where is Lady Koroth?"

He had to think about that a minute. She saw that he looked weary. A patch on his shoulder said his name was Tso.

He said, "She is nearby."

"I want to talk to her."

"That is impossible," he said, still courteously.

"Why is it impossible?" she said, already knowing the reason as if the knowledge had leaped from the brain of the invisible Lady Koroth to hers. There had been Fleet troops in plenty on D'neera for months. The magistrates now were only figureheads. Compromise was over. It was no longer possible for Iledra to speak for herself. Hanna's dream of going home had been folly from the start. And all Iledra's other hopes. They would not even let her speak to Hanna. They must be afraid of what she would say. And what could that be but a warning to Hanna *not* to come?

Tso shifted tactics. "Nothing will happen to you," he said. "We are under the strictest orders, from the highest possible sources, not to hurt you."

Hanna said, "If Iledra tells me it's safe to come home I'll come. Not otherwise. I want to talk to Commissioner Jameson too."

"Of course," Tso said. "Immediately. It will take only a few minutes to patch through to Earth."

He turned away and issued orders to, from Hanna's vantage, a wall of *Heartworld II*. When he turned back Hanna had had a little time to think. Tso's official face was as blank as Jameson's at its best, but his eyes flickered. Hanna was thin and blood-stained and disheveled. Fleet would not be much impressed, nor whatever watcher of Morisz's they called in—and I&S certainly would be called in. What would they say to Jameson before she spoke to him, before he even saw her image for himself?

"I still want to talk to Iledra," she said, "or Cosma," but Tso did not answer. He said casually, "How long will it take for you to come here?"

"A long time," Hanna said as casually. She drifted without haste toward the communications panel of *Heartworld II*, skirting the insubstantial giant. The obliging yacht, without orders to the contrary, was projecting her semblance to D'neera. Somewhere—even, no doubt, in her House itself—her image walked ghostly through familiar space.

She cut off the communication with a movement of her hand. When she looked around, Tso was not there.

Leader had what he wanted, but she jerked at his wave of—pity? Pity! For her!

He said in what seemed a whisper, "Not to be able to go Home . . . !"

"You can't either. . . ."

She fell wearily into the pilot's seat. Another Jump was imminent. She would not feel safe until it was over. They would pinpoint her location through the relays, and come here. She was not even sure *Heartworld II*'s course could not be remote-sabotaged. The dense-written course program for Leader's Home lay between her breasts, folded and crumpled. She could not go home; she must put the course into Jameson's hands. Why? She thought confusedly that it would be more sensible and safer to put it into Iledra's. But they guarded Iledra against her coming. To get to Iledra she would have to throw herself against a wall of them. They would take the precious thing from her and send it through safe channels to Jameson; and to the commanders and Intelligence and the rest of the commissioners. She would never see Jameson face to face again. If he permitted her to speak to him she would be a prisoner, powerless and subdued and far away from his presence. Half the security force of the Polity would be listening, and his public persona would concede what it must to all the other eyes and ears.

But Hanna had nothing to do with his public persona. She had never had much to do with it. Every contact she had had with him had come down quickly to essential truth. So she must get to him and see him alone, and tell her story to him and only to him; and maybe by then she would know what, after all, was essential truth.

Five days to Earth, said an ETA display. How long had she been gone? It might have been weeks or months, for all her prisoned time-sense could tell. In five days she would be able to think of being free from the People forever.

The chime she had been waiting for sounded. She was safe again, for a little while. She sighed and rose, thinking of the paper that would give humans mastery, and her duty to take it to them.

She looked out the port at the stars and the universe split at ill-made seams, and she fell through nothing, gasping, and then it was over. She had been looking through Leader's eyes; but he was not real.

He said insistently, "I am."

She looked again at the enormous port, the window on nothingness that frightened him so. Her eyes picked out a constellation that by chance resembled the Bowman, the tip of his shaft an ancient mariner's reference. But Bowman circled in Leader's sky, not hers.

She sat down, shaking. Her hands looked strange and were covered with dry blood. She was filled with longing to bathe in a golden pool where sapphire flowers mused and Swift played on sun-warmed stones, diving sleek into the shallows, rehearsing old courses of sea-born life.

She buried her face in her filthy hands. After all, it was only her own human wish to cleanse herself of blood; but it was transfigured.

"Yes," Leader whispered, and she felt something like a song begin. It was no music *she* had ever known; it was music by analogy only. And she did not know, huddled in this black-edged whiteness that was foreign to her in its very human-ness, why he sang.

He saw something she did not.

"Changeling," one of them said.

"Not me," Hanna said. She understood only dimly what it was she denied. She thought, desperately, not of D'neera but of Earth, birthplace of the species humankind. She concentrated desperately on Jameson, quintessentially male, reminding her that she was female; embodiment of human power, reminding her that she deserved a human fate. For all else seemed slipping away.

"We are both changed," said one of them.

She felt relief like soft rain to nourish her, but it was not her relief. Yet it was comforting. Leader-in-her-thoughts curled round her like smoke.

"Changeling, hybrid, two-in-one," he crooned with her voice.

Hanna got up again, and could not take a step. Leader did nothing to stop her; it was only that there was nowhere to go. This time it did not occur to her to say he was not real. She never thought of it again.

Instead she said, "I don't want that. I don't want it. I don't want it."

"No," Leader admitted, "but you begin to see."

"I see," said Hanna desperately, stubbornly, "that *you* are changed. *He* saw it." She meant true-Leader.

"And you," said Leader-in-her-thoughts.

"But I don't want to be changed!"

"But you are," he said. He seemed and sounded like a man come to safety through a tempest. Hanna felt his feelings clearly enough; but she did not know if they were hers also. They might be, if she let them. Because suddenly she had none of her own, none at all. Everything else seemed to have run out of her along with fear.

She took one aimless step and then some more. She faced a polished black panel and stopped because there was no particular reason to turn around and go in another direction. Her reflection was a dim shadow of herself, and she did not like looking at it. She called for darkness and slid into a heap at the panel's foot. All the lights went out, and all the black and white edges smoothed into grayness under starlight.

She said almost conversationally, "Look, I can't take any more. I just can't."

"There is not much more," Leader remarked.

" 'Not much more.' What does that mean?"

"Why," Leader said, "I am prisoned in death. But if we come to my Home I will be freed."

She understood only in part. She shook her head. "They'd kill me when they were done," she said.

"But when you are finished with me in the presence of your People, they will obliterate me, who am already dead!"

"I'm sorry," Hanna said, meaning it, "but I won." She did not have to explain to him the significance of her mastery of this tired but functional human body.

"Fraud!" he said to her again, and lashed her this time with a memory of her own from an age ago on *Endeavor*, when she had in her arrogance criticized true-human limitations and proffered herself as the ultimate link to strange minds.

"You do not wish to learn anything," said Leader, a disappointed pedant.

"I am too tired to learn," Hanna said.

"It is easier to be a Render," Leader said bitterly.

She answered wearily, "What else can I do? If I choose your way I betray my own people and make my death certain."

"But you do not know what my way is," he said. "And even if it were only what you think, how is it worse than your way?"

The air before Hanna thickened and blurred, and in it she saw Sunrise burning, the silver groves of her Nearhome gone up in flames, Swift bewildered and deranged and his mother's death consuming him. "You rob him of my springtimes," Leader said. A child who was both Leader and Swift reached for the delicate, sweet-smelling tendrils of a young tree which blackened and melted along with the child, and with it melted also a million recollections and history known through living minds treasured since the first thought net formed in a primeval sea.

She wanted to tell Leader there was nothing she could do about it, but he was gone, hidden, sulking in a corner of her consciousness. The knowledge he had tried to thrust upon her lay between them, uncomprehended. Because she would not comprehend, or maybe could not; she was not structured to comprehend it. She spoke instead what seemed a truth she could understand: "It's got to be one or the other. The advantage depends on me, don't you see? They know where we are but not how to program all the way. Now I know where you are—"

She paused, dubious. We and they and you seemed remarkably interchangeable.

But Leader did not answer. He only sulked—and grieved.

Hanna stayed where she was for a long time. Most of the time her eyes were fixed remotely on space. Twice *Heartworld II* said a Jump was coming and ran aloud through chains of equations; twice a chime sounded, and what Hanna saw changed. Each change took precisely one chronon. Or perhaps it did not. She wanted to touch a human presence and reached out for Jameson, for Iledra, for anyone, and could not sense the existence of a single living entity. She was not an Adept, and she was very far from anything human. She was alone with Leader, and he had discovered something that might be her conscience, and jabbed at it unmercifully.

The fourth Jump showed her, very small and distant, a glowing nebula. Stars were being born in its heart. Life would come from them in their turn. By which time humans and the People too would have vanished, or gone on to "a future unimaginable as the improbable past. . . ."

She heard Jameson's deep voice say the words. She almost saw the room beside the flowing river where he had spoken them. She moved finally. She was cold and cramped. She did not like the way her thoughts kept going back to him, and to her own blighted promise.

She got up and went cautiously through *Heartworld II* to the living quarters. Nothing looked quite right or entirely wrong. She took off her clothes and dropped them into a cleaning bin—she thought that was what it was; once she had known, but now she was not sure. Drawing a bath was less difficult, but when she slid into the water she cupped a little in her hands and touched her forehead to it. In memory, of course, of the First Home.

After that she bathed very quickly, and left the water as soon as she could. She was afraid that it would dissolve her.

She wandered naked through *Heartworld II* and thought about Leader. She had not thought about him before. You could not call it thought, that first battle for control. Nor had she thought about him during the days? weeks? as a passenger in her own body. Then she had only studied every detail of *his* thought as if he were under a microscope, so she could use it all for ambush. But Leader-in-her-thoughts, pseudo-Leader, changed Leader, had declined to die. He remained explorer, watchsetter, father, bondmate, an intelligent being steeped in a rich culture which resembled nothing humans had ever encountered before; a culture organically founded, more strangely structured than F'thal's, as limited as Girritt's but transcending its limitations.

On the flight deck she leaned across the unused pilot's console, looked again at the bright nebula, heard a chime, and was suspended in a dense field of stars. The starclouds shone for her, great drifts flung across the velvet of night, the jewels of creation promising gifts of life. A memory stirred: the old pull of curiosity beyond bearing, the seductive whisper born of desire saying she could deal with whatever she encountered.

With my body a weapon and fire in my hand and the great fleet pouring death from alien skies. . . .

She saw herself and Leader, People and Renders, humans and bestial aliens, locked in a dance of hate.

She thought of the very first steps, which had determined the form of the dance.

She had thought, when she wrote "Sentience," that the meaning of her life was the pursuit of understanding.

She had pursued nothing. She had only fallen into the pattern of the dance, not acting but reacting, seeking escape, even into death.

Leader whispered, "Full sentience is the power to choose the harder path."

She turned her head sharply, as if he stood beside her.

"What can you know of it," she said, "when you see us as nothing but beasts?"

"I know what I have learned from you," he said. He meant "Sentience," as if he had read it, and she saw, shocked, that he had. He had read it within her; read it in her cells and brain and the perspectives she brought to all that he saw through her eyes, whether she was consciously aware of them or not; and he accused her now of denying all she was.

"But I didn't know about you then," she said. "I didn't know it could mean this!"

"But what if—?" he said, and he meant: What if someone stepped outside the dance? What if there were a hybrid, changeling, two-in-one, someone who could think simultaneously in two realities and show each to the other without the fear that was the heart of the dance?

If one could do it without being insane to the eyes of both, or be reassuringly the same and yet different. If one could do it. If she could do it. She and Leader—

"Yes," he said; for it was his thought she thought.

"But how?"

"I don't know," he admitted.

She sought within his reality for a key. His memories lay complete behind her thought, a secret known to no other human being. His knowledge was hers to use as she chose, freely. Death and transition and life-in-We—

"Saved safely in thee—"

But transmuted—

She said, "I think I know." She put a hand against the thick transparent barrier that kept out the cold of space. The hand trembled.

He said after a little while, "Have you the courage?"

"I don't know. Oh, I don't know!"

He said slowly, "You must know more."

"More," she said, seeing what he meant and dreading it.

"You must *be* more."

She rubbed her bare skin, shivering, clinging to her humanity.

"I will be utterly mad," she said.

"No more than I," he answered ruefully. That was true already, in any case. Neither ruefulness nor any other form of humor was part of the People.

"All right," Hanna said, and bowed her head. Choosing. But no gratification accompanied the choice; she was compelled rather by the shadow of what she had been—which would mean nothing and be nothing if she did not make this choice. And she only knew that she had chosen when:

Smoke rose beyond marsh grasses that obscured her view. Something screamed barely audible in agony; barely audible though its throat was bursting because another battle was joined; on one side the cloud of which the thing was both part and (to the People) whole; and locked with it, wrestling with it and seeking to consume it, the People, savage and new, near foundering.

The grasses rippled past her, traveling. Or she moved, though without body or volition. She was coming near the Celebrant, on whom their power was focused. She could not see him past the ragged band that circled fire and stone and sacrifice.

"Not sacrifice." Leader stood beside her in the wholeness of his prime, uniformed. Scarlet blinded her in the sunlight of the People's beginnings.

"Then what?"

Through the kin-group, through the fiery circle to the stone where lay the Render, screams diminished in extremity to choking sounds. She saw herself. Her flesh convulsed. She cried out in anguish and:

". . . not sacrifice," Leader was saying. "That is a human concept. This is other."

She lifted her head from the floor of *Heartworld II*.

"I cannot," she said. "It's *him*," meaning Bladetree.

"It is all of Us," Leader said. "We are not human."

She lay on ice. Her skin shrank from it.

"I will try," she said, though it was impossible, and at once the common memory seized her again, vivid as if this ancient day from the morning of the world were yesterday.

She stood beside a fair deep pool, freshwater, tree-shrouded. The sea was far away, though ever-present in the soul; the People had spread far in great migrations. They had well-made weapons of stone and wore glossy furs. Before her stretched on massive stone was a Render. Its fangs gleamed; but its eyes were intelligent, its thought aware and utterly filled with hate.

It was less alien to her than were the People.

Celebrant lifted the stone knife and Hanna's hand rose with it. A ring of fire surrounded them. She would use fire too.

"No," she said. "No!"

Taken one by one and costly beyond measure for they kill Us easily and overpower Us. Leaving no-time for transition. Quicker increase, many mates. Meat-eaters even as We and We are their prey. We are no match. Therefore We must believe and shape. . . .

The thing thrashed, crying out, lost. Hanna saw herself, The knife slipped from her hands.

Honor thee who taketh pain transmute to joy create their end. Lest coming-time sees Renders only weaponed, powerful, dominant, Our vanishing all the ages of Our selves

The mountain stream spoke icily. Fire and stone. Fishers and farmers gathered for the Rite. Precious stones gleamed on her breast. She wielded knife and fire with scaly hands. The implacable bestial will flared, faded, and was malleable.

This is true. Is real. We change the real, make truth. They dwindle, yet We kill few. Yet they dwindle, unsubstantiated by past years past lives directed by a Rite that

Seawind blew strongly on her sea-colored skin, and tore at her rich garments. A city gleamed beyond the dunes. The creature's pain was ecstasy.

Vanish and dissolve! she cried, all cried, and it was nothing, strength and self obliterated and with it all its kind. Reduced to protoplasm, mind gone, will gone, it was ripe for harvesting. They took it in, its nothingness.

So are they nothing, harmless, impotent, and blown and tattered on the wind and threat no more, and We have made them so

Once more for an instant she was Hanna. She lay in darkness in *Heartworld II* and a human mind sought to understand, and could not, because: under the knife and her hard bloody hands a sentient species expired, driven to death by the People's will. And nothing else.

CHAPTER XVI

Dreamdust is a transparent powder with potent effects on the human nervous system. It produces, inevitably, sleep, but it is taken because it guarantees pleasant dreams, shaped by the dreamer's desires and providing whatever gratification he does not get in waking life. It is a product of Co-op, where the first, mostly unwilling settlers used it and thus, according to one view, survived the years of privation with some sanity intact; or, according to another view, failed to achieve any lasting thing until it was outlawed. Now it is used for the alleviation of chronic nightmare, and in expert hands for the guidance of dreams to modify personality without brainsoup intervention. But it also is used—not legally, since it is addictive—for its own sake. Most users dream of the erotic, and after many nights with ideal mates no longer form real relationships. But some use the powder to evoke tranquility, though that too is dangerous unless they are sufficiently strong-willed to refrain from comparing night to day.

Starr Jameson, lately not much interested in eroticism, spent his nights dreaming of sun-warmed seas or, sometimes, Arrenswood; of broad empty sweeps of water or forest or grain, warmed by the light of unspecified suns. In these dreams he did not have the insistent transmitter implanted in his ear, and was relieved of responsibility and twenty years younger; all of which only made each day's waking reality a more potent shock.

The part of his mind that guided dreams was puzzled, then apprehensive, then alarmed when it got out of control. The sweep of radiant water faded, its coolness vanished from his skin, and he was in the dark. Hanna ril-Koroth was back, a nightmare shape crouched on his bed with a hand twined hard in his hair. Something icy nicked at his throat. She said, *Wake up. Now! And don't move, or you die.*

The not-quite-words were frantic. He mumbled, "Not me, Hanna," and started to move, and nearly lost a handful of hair.

She said out loud, "Damn you, I'm real. You're not dreaming. Wake up!"

He thought she was Iledra's pale hand reaching for him, vengeful, and then that she might be real after all; but it was hard to tell with the Dreamdust coursing through him. He opened his eyes and saw a blacker figure melding with the darkness.

He said with difficulty, "Turn on the lights."

She gave the command and in the burst of light moved convulsively, shoving a knee hard into his stomach. It hurt. He lay very still. She was real, all right, and so was the knife against his neck. He blinked until her face came into focus against black draperies, pale and familiar; but she was changed and haggard.

She said, "I've g-got something you want. We, I, want something. From you."

He stared into her eyes and their blue mixed with his dreams and he fell into a summer evening's sky, a new dream stirring. Knife, fist and knee evaporated. He lifted a heavy, tentative hand that brushed her hip.

"Stop it!" Her voice was high-pitched and impatient. Her face blurred, but not before he saw it was a stranger's. She said in a stranger's voice, "What's, what the hell's wrong with you?"

"Dreamdust?" he said, but it did not come out right and she said, "What?"

He said more clearly, "Dreamdust."

She said, "Oh, hell." The hand in his hair relaxed and she drew back. The knife left his throat, but it trailed across his chest and the point stopped between two lower ribs. If she drove it in it would not kill him at once, but he could be entirely disabled.

He had to get the fog out of his brain, which told him even now, earnestly, that he was alone with a woman who had a knife, and grievances, and maybe an alien army at her back. He wanted the Dreamdust antidote. He made her understand,

and felt a suspicious probe for the truth of what he said. In his helplessness it was a violation.

"Get it," she said, but she kept the knife where it was while he reached for the panel that hid the antidote. Dreamdust is physically disabling, and his hand wavered. Ordinary people could burn out all the brain cells they wished without having to worry about instant recovery. Jameson kept antidotes for everything at hand, because he did not have that common luxury. He resented it.

He had trouble with the phial and after a minute, wordlessly, she took it from him, letting go of the knife to do so. It lay close by his hand, but he was so foggy he had no chance of making a grab for it without risking death, and both of them knew it. She opened the phial and held it out to him. The bitter liquid trickled down his throat, and he saw her take up the knife again before he put his head back and waited for his thoughts to clear. He closed his eyes and felt her weight shift. Her hands, knife and all, rested intimately on his knee.

Presently he said, "I hoped you would come back."

"What?"

"The house let you in, didn't it?"

She was silent for a moment. Then she said hesitantly, as if precision were costly, "I thought, I thought you'd forgotten to, to tell it not to. After I was here before. I didn't, I didn't know how I, I was going to get in. But it knew me and it. . . ."

Her voice trailed away. In the dark behind his eyelids he pictured her creeping through the silent house, fumbling through unknown rooms in search of him, waiting each second for discovery.

"I didn't forget. I wanted to make it easy. You might have come for shelter when I wasn't here," he said, and felt her reach for the truth again. This was why D'neerans did not lie; there was no point to it. But he was telling the truth.

He opened his eyes and saw her clearly for the first time. She looked terrible as his dream had made her: thin, hollow-eyed, the pale brown skin bloodless and sallow, her body stiff with tension. Her clothes were torn and hung on her loosely.

She said, "Was there, was, was there an alarm?"

"What kind of alarm?"

"To Morisz. Or somebody. Because you have to listen to me."

"There was no alarm from here," he said. "I don't know what you might have done getting this far," and irritably, at another stab in thought, "I wish you would stop doing that. Do you think I would lie to you?"

Yes! said her thought resoundingly.

"All right. All right. May I get dressed?"

She hesitated a moment and said, "All right. But move very slowly."

He pushed away the coverlet and saw her eyes widen, taking in the heavy muscles of his chest and arms. She backed away from him. The knife fell to her knees and she was holding some kind of archaic gun. She said, "I don't forget you hunt tigers. This would stop one. I got it from the, the, the aliens."

He barely kept still. "From—you have been with them?"

She nodded. He looked at the chunk of metal she held. Her thumb hovered near a stud whose function was unclear, but the hole in the end was pointed toward him.

"I believe you," he said, and eased out of bed very slowly indeed.

He slept nude, but it did not occur to him to be self-conscious. He dressed slowly, giving himself time to think. Leaving himself open to Hanna's return had been a hopeless gesture. It was inconceivable that she should get this far, even supposing she wanted to come to him. And she ought to have been headed for D'neera, if anywhere in human space. "Rational but uncooperative," Tso had said. Lady Koroth, witnessing that interview but kept from interfering, had been less temperate; she had used words like "hunted" and "driven." They might both be right, Jameson thought, watching Hanna as closely as she watched him. Her sleeves were rolled up and an angry red wound showed on one forearm. Tso had reported it, with a note: Combat, query? The fast-healing D'neeran flesh had closed over it already, but scantily and unevenly, and the skin around it was dark and unhealthy. She held the heavy alien weapon awkwardly, using both hands; but the muzzle did not waver.

When he was finished he said in a carefully even tone, "Why don't you put that down, Hanna? You know I was half-expecting you and you know there has been no alarm. I'm willing to talk to you, but that thing makes me nervous. What does it do, anyway?"

She looked at him with round eyes and said, "Are you—are you going to call for, for help? Don't lie," she added.

He did not think she would like the truth, and answered reluctantly, "I won't tell anyone yet that you're here. Sooner or later I will have to. Not immediately."

After a minute she nodded. She looked down at the weapon and turned and pointed it at a shrouded window. Her fingers moved and there was a loud click. Nothing else happened.

She said in mild surprise, "Oh. must be out of power or something."

She let it fall on the bed and with it, as if it were an afterthought, the knife.

"I didn't want to hurt you anyway," she said.

Tension Jameson had not been aware of left him. He went to her and picked up both weapons and took them to a far corner of the room, where he locked them in a cabinet that until now had held nothing more dangerous than a lady's forgotten jewels. Hanna did not object. When he came back and stood before her, she looked at him quite trustfully, almost smiling, as if she were glad to see him. He did not smile back. He said, "You know what I want from you. Tell me what you want from me."

"What," she said rather vaguely, and just as he began to speak again, "do you want from me?"

He said, puzzled by the disjointure of her speech, "I want full cooperation. I can promise you nothing, except that you will not be pilloried unnecessarily."

"It's all right." The smile disappeared, and she was solemn. "I won't fight anymore. I won't run again. Just listen to me before you talk to anybody else. That's all I ask."

"I will do that."

"Really?"

"Really."

Her face lit up with gratitude. He was not above encouraging it, and he sat down beside her and took her hand. But relief, in truth, made him weak. She had seen the aliens and been in a fight, but she had escaped, with God knew what knowledge of them.

"How did you get away?" he said.

She was very still for a minute. Then slowly, slowly, she reached into her shirt. She pulled out a long tangled strip of a paper-like substance, edged with incomprehensible script. She held it close to her breast, looking at nothing.

"What is that?" he said, but she did not move or answer and was still as death, so that he looked at her carefully, trying to gauge her sanity and stability. He saw the marks of privation, exhaustion, and the poorly healing injury that must keep her in constant pain. But he did not see fear or madness or any sign of alien control.

"Hanna," he said softly, and touched her face. She shuddered and moved.

"It's the course program for their home," she said.

He stared at her, disbelieving, and reached for it. She twitched it away uncertainly.

"But you have to listen to me," she said.

"I'm listening. How did you get it?"

"I don't want to talk about it," she said clearly.

He said carefully. "I wish you did not have to talk about it. But you must. And you must give me that program. You understand why, don't you?"

"Yes, but—oh, he doesn't want me to! He can't bear it!"

Jameson made a patient, noncommittal noise. He did not have the slightest idea what she was talking about.

"Will they see the ship? And come for me?" She looked up with sudden anxiety, and he was uneasy. She had displayed half a dozen moods in ten minutes. He had always thought her volatile, but now she seemed a feather on the wind, immediately responsive to whatever was going on inside her.

"Where is the ship?" he said.

"In the hills." She nodded vaguely in the wrong direction.

"If they find it I won't let them take you away until you've said what you have to say. How did you get past orbital surveillance?"

She said with perfect clarity, "Hung around until I found something coming down that had about my mass. Fell in behind it and faked a duplicate of its ID. Followed it down and then split off when I thought it was safe. I was hoping they'd think I was a freak echo. I guess they did."

Heartworld II was not too large for Airspace Control to treat as just another traffic blip. If it had gotten so low without being identified, it was unlikely that anyone suspected Hanna was there. The technique was clever and daring, and he was impressed. He made a mental note to make certain no one else got away with it.

She did not elaborate, but turned to him and laid a hand on his shoulder and smiled, and then looked at the hand as if confused. She seemed lost inside herself, and after a little while he said, using the D'neeran form of her name, "H'ana? What is wrong?"

She looked up, blinked, and was there again. She said, "It would take—" She started counting on her fingers. She got up to four and started over again. She said, "It would take five days to retrace my route and eight more to . . . to . . . to Home."

"Home? D'neera?"

"Home," she said impatiently. "That's what they call it. I mean, they don't call it anything, but that's how they think of it. Not their, their, towns? Not that. Groupings. More personal homes. Hearths. They change. There's no spoken language at all. No fixed names for things or people. Except writing of course and that's numbers. It's just what they agree on at any given time. But Home is always Home. And they are—*now* there should be some of them—I can't tell you about that." She gave him a sideways glance, almost sly. "We'd kill each other. They know where you are, I mean where Earth is. And Willow. I couldn't prevent them from finding out—"

"Hanna!" His hand closed painfully on her arm. "What did you tell them?"

"I didn't. I didn't tell them anything. Oh, stop!" she cried in distress. "You said you'd listen!"

"There is no time to listen if you told them that!"

"But there is. Please! They had time to chart the way to D'neera before, but it's no different than that was. It will take them months to work out the course here!"

"Are you telling me the truth?"

I am telling you the truth, she thought painfully. He could not disbelieve her. He let go of her slowly. The fear and anger she had roused would take longer to subside. The marks of his fingers showed on her arm, but she did not try to rub them away. He eyed the paper she still held out of his reach and said, "You'd better begin at the beginning."

"There isn't one," she said. "It's a closed system."

He had the vivid impression that a tired child was speaking

from a dream, and wondered if he would be able to get any sense out of her at all.

But she said, "Wait. I'll try. Listen. I'm not myself. Not anymore." She looked at him intently to see if he understood, but he did not.

"I wanted to understand them. The People. Do I sound insane? I am thinking now in some ways like one of them. And they are very different from us. But I think I understand. I think maybe, maybe there is a way to make them understand. I think maybe I can stop it."

"Are you sure?" he said, too roughly because the sudden hope was painful.

"I can't be sure," she said, almost whispering. "It's only a chance. They might kill me. Or question me again. If I can break the loop—I don't know if I can. I am human and alien and cannot be either. I must stay detached, outside the dance. Let me try."

She laid her good hand against his cheek. Her face was luminous, and his skin prickled at an eerie thought that much of what had been Hanna was burned away, leaving a wraith that might, if she were right, prove stronger than armies. It came to him then with a certainty whose source he did not know that the Hanna he had known was gone.

Hanna said, "I'm still here. For a while."

Don't read my mind, he wanted to say, and shook his head instead. He said gently, "You must tell me more."

"It will take a long time."

"You'll have time. As much as you need."

He took her to the room she had left many days before, put her in a deep chair, and gave her a drink loaded with nutrients. When he lit the fire she leaned toward the first flames as if their warmth drew her, and a little, a very little, of the tension went out of her face. The silence of deep night was close around them, and they might have been the only two people on Earth.

Then he sat down near her and said, "Tell me, Hanna," and she told him.

It was not yet morning when she finished, but his muscles ached from long stillness when he moved. He felt then a curious detachment, as if a potent drug still worked in his blood and customary realities were in abeyance, and he was a spectator at events that took no notice of him save to demand his acknowledgment. Hanna seemed sometimes an essence of otherness, a creature come from new dimensions, as if the impossibilities of Inspace had come to life. An alien being spoke with her lips, paradoxical: grieved or aggressive, fearful or stately by turns. "I cannot explain!" it cried, or Hanna cried, at times; and then they would bear him, willing or not, to other times on another world, and it seemed a massive alien held out its hands to his fire.

But sometimes it was only Hanna, though (he thought again) not the Hanna humans had known. He kept to himself a new conviction, born of the story she told and the ways she used to tell it, that neither he nor Hanna nor any D'neeran had properly estimated the power of telepathy—nor the cost to one who used it to its fullest. For even when Hanna spoke in her own voice she was new—or damaged. There was little straight-line logic to what she said, and he stopped her again and again, mystified by statements from a separate universe of discourse, making her show him the foundations of a reality more strange than any she had guessed at in writing "Sentience." And always she did as he asked her, painfully sometimes when memory shook her, but dutifully and doggedly, until he began to feel he was kin to The Questioner and Lady Koroth was right after all, and all his dreams had come to in the end was the torment of a woman who would not fight him.

Because he did not think there was any defiance left in Hanna. She had given him her weapons, and in the spaces between her words he heard her clear intention not to take them up again. With every separate sentence she put herself more firmly in his hands, offering herself for his use this last time. Her trust was terrible; and yet he saw, as he had seen from the day he betrayed it, that it was not new. It had always been there, from their first meeting: her conviction that he would choose rightly for the future, a faith as strong as his in his own vision. Perhaps she was not even conscious of it. It seemed part of an implicit, unspoken communication that had gone on under the surface of their words and actions each time they met.

He wished he could uncover and deal with that alone. He was tired, and he wished he did not have to listen so hard to what she was saying. He had had enough of strain and threats and sleeplessness, of aliens and work. He had spent half a lifetime gaining the responsibility of choosing for mankind, and now he wished he did not have it. The face of mankind was not as close as Hanna's face, and all that she said and showed him led in one direction only: to sending her away again. Yet that was what she wished him to do, and the bitterest ending of all was that, though she did not know it, he might no longer have the power to do it.

Silence lay between them when she was done; he broke it at last, inadequately. "I never dreamed of anything like that."

"Nor did I. But that was the point of 'Sentience,' was it not? That each species shapes its own reality . . . but I didn't mean it quite so literally. And is shaped by it, you know. Is shaped by it. . . ."

She seemed to drift away. Jameson stood up, a little stiffly, and went at last to get a drink for himself.

"Run through the reaction model again," he said. "Simple fear! I don't believe it!"

"The dynamics aren't simple."

"Quite obviously. Tell me again. I want to make sure I understand."

"All right." Toward the end she had been talking more easily, as if human speech came more readily with practice. Now she said quite normally, "It starts with what the People are, full telepaths. I don't know just where in their evolution the ability showed up. It seems there are other animals on their homeworld with a form of it, even plants somehow, but in the People it reached a peak of mutual consciousness that's nearly a group mind, and shaped them and their history and their culture all together. And the past is alive. Very seldom does anyone just die, just end, as we do. That's the worst thing that can happen to them. . . ."

Her voice faltered, and he saw grief in her face. She said, "It happened to the ones I killed. Because of me. They were so far from Home, it happened so fast, there was no chance for the living to absorb them."

"I don't know what that means," he said.

"Why," she said, as if it were very simple, "the experience of generations is transmitted directly, not in words or pictures, but what it was to *live* it. They *are* those who came before."

"But they have individual identities as well—"

"Clearly, yet they can't exist apart from one another. Space travel is painful for them. Dangerous. They're a space-time collectivity, and individual identity depends on it. And its most important manifestation, where we're concerned, is that life for them is Us or not-Us. No exceptions. No borderlines. There are the People, and there is everything else. And everything else is harmless, or prey, or predator, and because they are so self-identified, they lack the ability to identify with anything else. They make analogs from their own reality to ours, just as we do with other things, but they are even more limited than we are in the sources they have to choose from."

She looked at him uncertainly, and he said with some relief, "I think I do understand that. It's a blind spot, like Girritt's limitations in technology."

"Yes. And what makes it worse, what makes it more dangerous for us, is that the deaths of not-Us beings are gratifying to them. It had to be that way, you see. Because you cannot subsist without killing other life forms. They even sense something—I'm not sure what—from plants. And you can't eat something if you experience its death as your own, can you? I think they have entirely different receptors for each other and for not-Us beings, and the perception of the death of prey or predator is something we don't have any words for at all. I could call it a kind of pleasure, but that's not fair. It makes them sound like sadists, and they're not, not really. You like the taste of meat, don't you? But you don't think that makes you a killer because the meat has to be slaughtered. Well, they don't kill or torment for pleasure; it's a by-product, so to speak. But it's there, and at the same time, among themselves, they've had no experience of war or conflict, nor compromise nor accommodation either. Because to kill another is to kill oneself. And everything else—"

She hesitated, and he said, "Is harmless or predator or prey. Yes? And which are we?"

"Predators," she said promptly. "And that's where the next element comes into play. There are dangerous animals on their homeworld. They are not specifically dangerous now, of course, because for many centuries the People have had a weapons technology that deals with them easily. But the most dangerous of all for many ages, the archetype of the beast, a sort of primate as it happened, was very close kin to us. Not literally, of course, but in the structure of its instinct and behavior it was much more like us than we are like the People. It was non-telepathic, and growing sentient. And it was—it was them or the People. There was only one that was going to be the dominant species, and take the niche humans got here. And so they—they—" She stumbled. "*Made* them die. With ritual death as the focus. They made the . . . the disappearing, the dissolution they wanted, real."

Jameson did not understand this any better than he had the first time she said it. He let it go by. He said, "But they were wiped out long ago."

"Yes, oh, yes. But they still live in the ancestral memory which is this generation's memory. And the People have not left their evolutionary response to danger behind any more than we have. You know what that response is more intimately than most of us, I think. You don't hunt tigers with disruptors; you use a spear. And I saw you have scars?"

Her easy tone caught him off guard. Tiger-traces were a mark of honor, women of his own culture found them exciting, others sometimes were revolted and could not understand why he kept them; but to Hanna they were just there. He pulled himself back to the matter at hand and nodded. "I was lucky. I made a mistake once, long ago, and lived to remember it."

"Were you thinking of trying to reason with the tiger at the time?"

"What do you think? Of course not. There are only two things to do with tigers—stay out of their way, or kill them."

"Well," said Hanna, looking at him with some distaste, and he lifted a placating hand.

"No, don't," he said. "I'm quite fond of tigers, actually. You'd be surprised how much I know about them. But we are talking about instinct, are we not? And instinct has no middle ground."

"Yes," said Hanna, "and that is where the circle closes, and the model is what happened to the human colony they found, and not only what happened to the colony but what happened to the People because of it. Just as things happened to them because of those others. Although they don't know that, I think. *He* doesn't think so."

Jameson waited, but Hanna, eyes unfocused, was silent;

inwardly arguing a point, perhaps. He said encouragingly, "But they couldn't make the colonists just disappear."

"Oh," she said from her dream, "it took centuries with the others. And the People had the upper hand technologically, of course. But not at first. And that was how they got it. Or at least they believe that's how they got it. By willing it."

"But it is objectively true?"

"Starr," she said with finality, "it is objectively true for them."

She had never used his first name before. It startled him. He said unwillingly, "Then I suppose it doesn't make any difference," and gave it up.

He stood near her and stared into the fire. Soon he would have to decide what to do about this, the parts he understood and the parts he did not understand. If his decision, any longer, would prevail. His judgment still would make a difference, he thought, but it did not carry the weight it used to have. Hanna did not know that.

She said suddenly, "It's quiet here." He looked around and saw that she had leaned back into her chair, eyes closed. She seemed to have drifted into sudden sleep. He had put her in that seat, which he did not use himself, deliberately. Its comfort came from more than seductive fabrics and soft cushions; it also emitted a subtle mélange of subliminal commands to relax and feel safe. He found it useful for semi-official guests, especially adversaries. He had not used it the night of Hanna's escape because there was a witness then. Now he looked at her curled and softened in it, trusting, vulnerable, and thought: *I wish I had not done this. I wish her safety were real. . . .*

She was so weary, and her bone-deep tiredness woke echoes in him. Better for both of them if he were to put off decision and take her gently to his bed, warm her in the cold dawn, watch over her and give her a space of peace. It was not sensible to think of her as fragile: not with the knife so near that bed, not with her tale of blood. But she declined to be sensible about him; she insisted on speaking to parts of him he had successfully forgotten, almost; he supposed it gave him the same right.

She lifted her head and smiled at him as if in answer. He

sighed and sat down on the arm of her chair. He said, "You haven't told me everything."

She looked disappointed, then guarded. It was characteristically human, but it was not Hanna. "No?" she said.

"No. You haven't told me just how you propose to—to stop the dance, I think you said."

"I can't explain it," Hanna said. She looked away from him.

"That is not easy to believe. After all you've managed to explain tonight."

"I mean I won't. You won't understand."

"If you won't tell me," he began, and stopped. He could not threaten her or press her one more time. He could not.

But he had to.

He said, "If you won't tell me I can't let you do it."

She stared into a corner. The room's one clear concession to the present gleamed there, a pattern of abstractions that appeared and disappeared because in certain aspects it was not real, and was created anew on each appearance. He did not know if she saw it or not. She said, "If it doesn't work, things won't be worse than they are. I've already told them everything important that I can."

"So you think you might fail. They might try to get more from you. The same way they did before? You would risk that?"

"I don't know what they would do. I told you."

"I wish you would tell me what you think you can do."

After a minute she said, "Even if it does work, I don't know what's going to happen to *me*."

He looked down at the top of her dark head and saw that a twist of wire salvaged from *Heartworld II* held back her hair. It seemed infinitely pathetic. He reached for it, and Hanna sat very still while he unwound it. Her hair drifted across her shoulders. He brushed it aside and thought of kissing the nape of her neck.

He thought: If I coax her she will tell me. I could use the affection I have not earned.

No. No.

Hanna said suddenly, "It's the hybridization. I'm *him*. You've talked to him. He is the . . . the . . . the key. To change them."

"All right. But how?"

"I'm already one of them. The perspective is unique, something they've never had or even imagined. But I really can't explain any better than that. You will just have to trust me," she said with finality, and looked up at last into his eyes.

"I suppose I must," he said. But even as he said it he thought: She is lying. And then: But Hanna does not lie. She does not know how to lie. It is the truth.

And then he could not put off decision any longer, because the implant in his ear erupted at such volume he clapped a hand to his head, cursing.

"Come in," said someone, not Rodrigues. "Jameson, are you there? Come in immediately."

Hanna looked at him as if he were a madman. He roared an order to his house that shut off the transmission in mid-word. "And find out who the hell that is and put them through in here," he said, because he did not want to bother with the security module.

"What is it?" Hanna said.

"I think," he began, but Stanislaw Morisz's voice filled the room.

"Jameson, are you there?"

"I'm here. What the hell's going on?"

"Are you all right? *Heartworld II*'s down near your location—"

"I know. I know. Lady Hanna is here. It's all right, Stan. Everything's under control."

Morisz said too casually, "Mind if I come see for myself?"

"No. Come on, if you have to make sure. How many people know about this, Stan?"

"Uh, a civil patrol that spotted it and went in for a closer look. Enforcement personnel. How long's she been there?"

"Not long." Jameson glanced at Hanna. She looked frightened. He said, "This is most-stringent-restricted, Stan. As of now. Get Enforcement out of it."

There was a silence before Morisz said, "Who have you notified?"

"Nobody, yet."

"There are regulations. Enforcement is already in."

"You can hold them." If you will, he added, but not out loud. "What about I&S?"

"Some of my people are alerted. Naturally."

"Some of your people? What have you got, a task force around the house?"

"I can't discuss that. Under these conditions."

"Then come see me," Jameson said, and waited for an answer. There was none.

Hanna said, "What does this mean?"

"It means we're running out of time," Jameson said. He leaned back, a hand on Hanna's shoulder. He thought of the ripple the news must make as it spread in erratic circles; the play of action and reaction, responsibilities real and fancied, the stir among those for whom Hanna's coming—or capture—might be turned into advantage. Morisz could control it for a while—if he would. Once Jameson could have counted on him to do it. Not now.

Hanna said, "Why not?"

"Are you reading my mind all the time?" He looked at her curiously.

"Not all the time. A lot. I have to," she said apologetically. "You don't say what you think. Why won't he help you?"

Jameson said slowly, "I did something that—in the end made no difference anyway. Sentiment for Stanislaw's resignation was rather strong after you . . . left us. He wouldn't resign, but he is . . . temporarily acting in a subordinate capacity. Pending outcome of an investigation into the qualifications of operatives who joined I&S during his tenure as director. He is back where he was thirty years ago—regional duty officer on the nightside."

Hanna regarded him with utter lack of comprehension. She said, "Are they going to come get me?"

"I don't know. I hope not. But the truth is—" He thought of softening it; but Hanna would know if he tried. He said, "The truth is you are wanted more intensely than any fugitive within my memory. From Enforcement's vantage alone you have broken so many laws that local and Fleet jurisdictions might argue for years over who will try you first. And I&S wants you, and I want you, and all the commissioners. Morisz is a conscientious man. Under the best of circumstances he would not keep silent very long. And these are not the best. Don't say anything when he comes, Hanna. Don't mention that course program. You'd better give it to me."

She had put it back into her shirt when they came into the room. Now she gave it to him, still warm from its place against her skin. Her face was grave, but there was no hesitation; perhaps she saw the nightmare vision he had formed of Morisz taking her away over Jameson's protests. He took it, hurrying, to the security module no one but he could enter. When he came back to Hanna she was on the hearthrug, hugging her knees. Soothing the doubting alien? He said, "You have not told me exactly what you want from me."

"I only need one thing," she said without looking around.

Jameson's ears were pricked for the sound of Morisz's arrival. He said, "What's that?"

"Authority to act on behalf of the Polity."

He stood behind her and looked down with bleak amusement. "You came to me for that?"

She glanced up uncertainly, not understanding. She said, "I must be certain any promises I make them will be carried out. If I had gone there on my own, you see, they would have known. They would have known I spoke for no one but myself and they would not have understood or accepted it. I must have your word."

"Mine alone would not do in any case. You need formal authorization."

"Can you get it for me?" She looked anxious now; sensing, at last, that something was wrong.

He said, "I don't suppose you connected with a newsbeam on your way back."

"I had other things to think about," she said stiffly.

"I'm sure you did. If you had you might have heard—"

"Mr. Morisz is here," said the house, and Jameson said, "Let him in."

Now there was no time left at all. He had not exaggerated the passion with which so many people, so many agencies, wanted Hanna. If he waited for a meeting of the full commission there would be nothing but trouble. The formal motion of which he had spoken would never be approved if the commissioners consulted their home worlds. al-Nimeury would be hopeless in any case, and the paranoid Petrov too. Endless time would be wasted in objections and obstacles, and Jameson's own time was almost gone. He would have to get the comission to move while he could, and to move on its own, as it could but rarely did; and how would it move? Feng, who was not a decisive man, might easily be swayed to side with Petrov and al-Nimeury. The longer it went on the more people would insist on having a hand in it. He could not keep Hanna to himself legally or for long.

He said to the house, "Get me through to Andrella Murphy. Commission emergency, priority one override. As soon as I'm done with the call, do the same with Arthur Feng—hello, Stan. Satisfied I'm alive and well?"

Morisz looked at them doubtfully from the doorway. "I'd feel better if I could see her hands," he said.

Hanna turned and lifted them silently, palms up. The wound on her arm had begun to ooze blood.

Jameson said, "Stanislaw, it is essential to keep this quiet. Commissioners Murphy and Feng will be here within the hour—"

Andrella Murphy's voice said sleepily, "Starr? What's wrong?"

"Wait a minute, Andrella. Stan, keep your men where they're at. Don't let anybody in here except Murphy and Feng, don't let anybody get near *Heartworld II*, and don't report to anybody, anywhere, without checking with me."

Morisz said, "I can't do that without proper authorization." His hostility was so palpable that Hanna would not have to be a telepath to feel it. She sat upright, astonishment on her face.

Jameson said coldly, "I am your authority. I am still a member of the coordinating commission. This is a commission emergency. My word is enough. Do as I told you. That is an order."

Morisz's eyes glittered. For a moment Jameson thought he would refuse. Then he said, "Yes. Sir," and turned and left.

Hanna said, "What's happened to him? What haven't you told me?"

"Starr?" Murphy said. "Who's that? What is it?"

"Andrella, I need you at my home at once. Don't waste time talking. Just come."

"Starr, it's five o'clock in the morning!"

"I know," he said, although he had not known. "Just do it, Andrella. I don't have time to argue."

"All right," she said crossly, and was gone.

Hanna scrambled to her feet, her eyes wide and doubting. She said, "What is it? Tell me!"

He said evenly, "Your escape was too much for my council. I have perhaps a few hours left on the commission. There has been some disagreement about my successor, but it is nearly over. Murphy and Petrov and the rest will not have to deal with me in future. What I think no longer matters much to anyone. But I think you must go, and go quickly. If I am to get you what you need, there is only one thing left to try."

He stopped at the rush of sorrow he felt in her. She said, "I'm sorry. I'm so sorry. It's because of me, isn't it?"

Perhaps he ought to be angry with her. She was, in fact, the cause of it all. But for too many days he had seen only triumph, open or suppressed, on the faces around him. He bore it, he hoped, gracefully. But he was not proof against the understanding he felt in Hanna of what it meant to him.

He took her hands and said, "I'm not finished yet."

"What are you going to do?"

"Something marginally legal. If that."

She said with grave approval, "That's all right, then," and let her hands rest in his with simple trust as Feng's voice sounded in the room and Jameson began to talk very urgently.

CHAPTER XVII

Not even Arthur Feng's best friends counted intelligence among his virtues. His appointment to the Coordinating Commission was a compromise, a least-repugnant choice made to satisfy half a dozen Colony One political factions. Jameson had for two years made a conscious effort to avoid treating Feng with the tolerance he usually reserved for rather stupid dogs. Now he looked round his study, transformed to an emergency conference room, and thought perhaps he would have to think of something else after all. Feng still was trying to cope with the idea that Hanna ril-Koroth had returned to Earth of her own accord, and that the aliens she spoke of might be something more than a vast deadly mystery.

"But what do they call themselves?" said Feng, returning to the beginning yet again. "They have to call themselves something. We can't call them People. It's too confusing. We're people."

Hanna said, "But they don't call themselves anything. Words are phonetic. They don't use words."

"But they have to have a name."

Murphy said, "All right. All right, we'll name them." She was looking not at Feng but at Jameson, reading his worry from long practice. "Girritt was named after Captain Neil Girritt. Let's call them after Lady Hanna."

"No," Hanna said. "Please. Not after me. If you must give them a human name, call them after Charl Zeig and Anja Daru, who died contacting them. Call it Zeig-Daru, and talk of Zeigans."

"Zeigans," said Feng, trying it out. "But they didn't really discover it."

Jameson closed his eyes for a moment. "Suppose we use it as an interim term in an emergency situation," he suggested.

"A code name for unknown hostiles, applicable in situations calling for intelligence analysis."

The doubletalk satisfied Feng, but he had more ground to test, his bureaucratic instincts in full cry.

"What section are we convening under?" he said. "Appointment of an envoy? Can't you do that, as head of your committee?"

There were no commission by-laws specifically applicable to this situation, but that would be the wrong thing to tell Feng. Jameson said, "I can't act alone in this prior to the establishment of friendly relations. We are talking about a peace mission. Majority approval is required."

"This is a majority. But look here," Feng said warningly. "It's not the full commission."

"You noticed," Murphy murmured, and Jameson gave her a cold look.

"I don't think I can go along with this. Can I?" Feng said.

Jameson said warmly, "Of course you can."

"Let me think," Feng said, and Jameson thought there was some sort of contradiction in terms there.

It was nearly dawn, and the drip-drip of prematurely melting snow fell into the sudden silence. Hanna had left this temperate coast in the deep grip of winter and returned with the promise of an early spring. Jameson wished he could think it was an omen, but he was not a man to count on omens. And hope lay now in speed, and Feng had decided not to be rushed.

Hanna sat cross-legged before the fire, and Jameson was beginning to worry about her too. Her hair was loose about her shoulders, an unkempt tangle. Her face was drawn with fatigue, and he saw now that in the last few minutes she had torn off the end of one sleeve and was trying one-handed to wrap it around the gash in her arm. Murphy looked at her curiously. Andrella remembers her from the time of Goodhaven, he thought: poised, graceful, even elegant in her way. Now all her grace is gone, and she is a bleeding scarecrow. But Murphy herself looked entirely normal, fresh and decisive as if she were listening to an unusually interesting bit of testimony at some routine hearing.

Jameson stirred, composing himself to go on patiently and soothingly with Feng, but he was interrupted. His house now was tied to Morisz's communications system, and Morisz said into the room, "Commissioner Jameson? I think you'd better come out."

The voice was expressionless. It was more alarming than agitation could have been. Jameson said, "What is it?"

"Some visitors would like to see you."

"Who are they?"

Morisz said stubbornly, "I'd rather not say."

Hanna lifted her tired face and said, "They're important."

"Who?" Jameson said, just as Feng said, "How do you know that?"

Hanna did not answer. Jameson got up and went out with a sense of foreboding.

The light from the door was dim on the faces of al-Nimeury and Petrov and Struzik. Morisz stood nearby. He looked satisfied and unpleasant.

al-Nimeury said at once, "What are you trying to pull?"

Jameson shrugged, looking past him at the others. Petrov, like al-Nimeury, looked furious; Struzik had the face of a man in shock.

al-Nimeury said, "What the hell are you having a secret meeting for?"

"Lady Hanna came back in the night," Jameson said. "She brought valuable intelligence."

"I know," al-Nimeury said. "Morisz told us."

Petrov said, "Weren't we going to hear about it?"

"Eventually." Jameson knew when there was an end to the usefulness of evasion. There would be no quick secret mandate for Hanna, thanks to Morisz; he would have to salvage what he could from the wreckage of his plan. He said, "Come on in. You too, Stan. You'd better hear this."

He turned and went into the house and they followed him, talking loudly. He ignored them.

Murphy was kneeling by Hanna when they came in. She looked up and said calmly, "Hello. Starr, have you looked at this?"

"No. Why?"

"There's something wrong. Lady Hanna says she had medical supplies and used them. It shouldn't be infected."

"Compatible biology, then?"

"In some way."

Jameson frowned at Hanna, who looked back at him without expression. Something new to worry about now, and no way to tell how dangerous it was because no one had had an alien corpse to dissect, or visited the world in question, or even had the artificial environment of a captured spaceship to study. Environmental traces in Hanna's own body on her first return had been inconclusive. She was, however, alive after two contacts. That was encouraging, but the still-open wound could mean she was slowly being eaten alive by something nasty that might or might not remain confined to her. And there was no time to study her. She had already violated biosphere protective regulations by returning here, and ought to be quarantined. The fact clearly had occurred to Murphy. Jameson wished he could tell her privately not to mention it in front of Feng—and then saw her turn suddenly to Hanna, puzzled, and knew Hanna had told her.

He said, "Sit down, all of you. If you please."

"I want an explanation," al-Nimeury said.

"You're going to get one."

Only al-Nimeury remained standing, his eyes on Hanna. They had not met before, but there was no need for introductions. Hanna regarded him bleakly from her seat before the dying fire.

"A D'neeran," al-Nimeury said with contempt in his voice. "So much damage. One D'neeran!"

Hanna got up slowly. What he thought, what he meant, reverberated behind the scarcely heard words. Trouble. Difference. Separation. Arrogance. A whole history. But al-Nimeury could not know she was his sister; he had not seen the void that lay between human beings and the others. The strangeness. And he was strange to her as she to him. Her body felt curiously light. Sleeplessness, disorientation and her own urgent purpose kept the room at one remove from her. Her careful schooling in the uses of telepathy was confused by the functioning of Leader-in-her-thoughts, still here, still alive, crouching waiting watching while she tried to do what he and she together would do later somewhere else. Alliances. She and Leader. She and Jameson. She and al-Nimeury? She hardly saw the commissioners of the Polity. They were presences nearly without flesh, and only two of them counted. One was Jameson: steady, fearless, committed. And reckless, a thing she had thought never to find in him; but he had not much left to lose. The other was al-Nimeury, and his dislike, even disgust, was the strongest force in the room. It woke chords of hostility in her, the ancient emotional response to threat that fueled war within humanity and might now reach outside it if she could not, as she had said to Jameson, put an end to the dance. And she would have to end it here first to reach the People. On the edge of thought she heard or felt Jameson thinking, trying to find a way around his colleagues. Already he was separate from them. Already they saw him stripped of the power his office gave him. But there was a power in him that depended on no office, and she felt it with gratitude. Because there was no way around these others. The only way was through them.

She went to al-Nimeury, feeling that she floated. She stumbled and Jameson moved toward her, but she got balance back and took the last step. al-Nimeury was a short man, and stocky; her eyes were nearly level with his. They were deep brown, nearly black, and she might have thought there was fire in them, except the fire was behind them in the accumulated prejudice of generations.

She said, very softly, "I have to go back."

He took a step backward and opened his mouth. He was going to say: I won't listen. She held his eyes and it was not her eyes or her words that kept him silent so much as Jameson like a flame at her back. She drew on his strength as on a tangible current.

"Do you want war?" she said. "They're so delicate. So cruel. You could win it. They know nothing of war. They tried to keep up with human warfare, as the colonists of the Lost World knew it. But that was long ago, and the colonists had forgotten—"

"Wait," somebody said. The word slipped by her, but she felt Morisz's urgency and answered the question before he asked it.

"I don't know when it was." She still looked into al-Nimeury's eyes. "They have a stable written history, but I know nothing of it. I know only the common memory, which shapes time according to the importance of events. The great human exodus began seven hundred years ago and more, and lasted three centuries. Only in the first century and a half were fragments of humanity lost. Count back and you'll know what they thought our capability is, as the colonists' descendants remembered it. And then they got me and found that we'd learned—so much more. How to kill. How to destroy. They can't match you. You could destroy them—"

Leader seemed to explode in her head, in her whole body. The humans babbled at her but words melted into Leader's silent shocking clamor. *It is true it is true you must see it is true!* she cried to him. She felt hands on her shoulders, Jameson's hands. They drew her back to the light. She trembled violently. Leader read her conviction and her purpose and she said to him, *Trust me. Trust me!* He answered mournfully, *I must. You have the way Home.*

She could lift her head. She did, and saw they watched her warily but, except for Jameson, without understanding what had happened. The living presence of Leader was a thing she dared let no one else recognize. Jameson said quietly, "She is very tired. She has been with them and returned with news of . . . a willingness to open discussions."

She twisted under his hands at the lie, but they were suddenly attentive; skeptical, yet open to hope. al-Nimeury's eyes were on her and she said, "You could have them in thirteen days. I can show you how to reach their homeworld in thirteen days. They know where you are but that's all. They haven't got the program to get here. They will need weeks to reach you at least. You fear them for nothing, and all because they fear you."

al-Nimeury looked away from her, uneasy. She felt his uncertainty growing; he had not expected any of this. He said to Jameson, "Is that true? Why didn't you say so?"

Jameson said, evading it, "Listen to her."

Hanna said, as much to Leader as anyone, "They know nothing of wars. They have never had one. They know only the slaughter of dangerous beasts, and you are not beasts. Not unless you choose to be."

"Are you sure? Is this something you've guessed?"

It was Morisz's question, but she watched al-Nimeury, who was unwilling to meet her eyes. She said, "I know."

Morisz said, "What exactly have they got?"

"It doesn't matter."

"Doesn't matter—" Petrov sprang to her feet in vigorous denial. "Doesn't matter!"

"Doesn't matter," Hanna said. She glanced at Petrov and thought: She could be trouble. She is afraid. Earth-island and outside the blackness—

Hanna moved a little, so that she faced al-Nimeury and he could not ignore her.

"I want to go to them," she said. "I want to be appointed your envoy. They don't understand they can't win."

"You want to tell them they can't?" He was doubtful, suspicious.

"It won't matter to them. If you send anybody but me they'll attack anyway, because they won't understand anybody but me. They might do it even if I'm the one who goes, but nobody else has a chance of convincing them—not that war is futile, but that it's unnecessary."

al-Nimeury said to Jameson, "I thought you said—" but Petrov said violently, "Nonsense! She's lying. She came back to do something else for them, she came back to keep us from fighting. Starr, why did you not immediately call for help? She's still under control. Anyone can see it!"

"Do you really think so?" Hanna said. She swayed, sickened and dizzy from the power of Petrov's fear. Jameson put his arm around her quickly. He said to Petrov, "Hanna killed five of them to get away and bring us the way to their home."

"So she says!"

"I did," Hanna said faintly, and used everything she had learned from D'neera and from the People to take Petrov there. She leaned against Jameson and showed Petrov the chaos, the soundless screams and the thick blood and reality ending, and Leader-in-her-thoughts lived his death again, and Petrov recoiled in horror, and Hanna let her go.

Petrov sat down abruptly. Her face was haunted, her eyes inward. She did not try to speak.

The others had glimpsed some of it too. Jameson said close to Hanna's ear, "A demonstration of the usefulness of D'neerans, or at least of Hanna. After that, can you doubt her ability to communicate with the aliens?"

Someone moved restlessly. al-Nimeury said not to Hanna but to Jameson, "I don't care. Even if it's all true I want to send humans. Not her. The aliens are telepaths themselves, we don't need D'neera."

Hanna said flatly, "You can't shut us out any longer. You cripple yourselves with fear of us. *He* knows." She meant Jameson. "You think I will reach into your mind and know its secret places. All your shames, the dark hidden things you won't acknowledge even to yourselves . . . what can you do with these things, who can do that more surely than I can? You know they took me and tortured me—''

The Questioner came alive for an instant, and her voice caught. The effort of projecting to Petrov had drained her more than she thought. She turned her head and for a moment put her cheek against Jameson's shoulder, fixing herself in present reality, and went on.

''They took fear from my heart and used it. I showed them my own fracture points. Pain and mutilation, humiliation, all it took to make me a blind, screaming animal. I told them all unwilling how to destroy me and end my spirit. And they learned from the colonists too. Whom they slaughtered. Everything I most feared, the greatest terrors humans have, they learned from humans. Will you go to them yourself? But I have learned from them. I have some things no one else has. And you would send someone else, defenseless, to treat with them?''

She knew al-Nimeury acknowledged the logic; but disbelief fought logic.

Morisz muttered, ''If we can beat them so easily, why is there a chance they'll fight? You can just tell them what will happen. Won't they give up? What will happen?''

''Genocide,'' Hanna said.

There was a murmur of disbelief from Struzik.

''They would not give up,'' Hanna said. ''You would have to kill them. You would not kill all of them, but you would destroy them. All their culture. Every fragile thing they have built through the millennia. They are more vulnerable than you are, than we are. They may be a dead end like Girritt—or evolving toward something neither we nor they can guess. Perhaps they will become a group mind, a step maybe—'' she glanced up at Jameson— ''toward becoming adults. Now they are a fabric, and too great a rent will destroy them. They must be sheltered—''

''Sheltered!'' al-Nimeury said, and she felt his outrage. When she thought of The Questioner it was incongruous even to her, but she knew it was true.

She began, ''A moral choice—'' and the word made them look at her with distaste. Morisz said skeptically, ''Don't they know they're weak? You still haven't told us—why do they hate us? Why would they fight?''

"The colony," Hanna said. She let the words drop among them, and quite suddenly felt that she had reached the end of her strength.

She sagged against Jameson, indifferent to their eyes, and said nothing more. After a minute he said gently, "Explain. Explain to them as you did to me."

"I can't," Hanna said, and roused herself enough to turn to him. She wanted it to be over, she wanted him to hold her, she wanted to go to sleep in his arms in peace and safety, and what she wanted was clear to him. He was alarmed, but he held her, and she was happy. She did not, at this moment, care about the conflict she felt in him. Slowly he was coming to his senses. He would come to them in the end. This would do for now.

"Hanna," he said, and pushed the moment aside with an almost physical effort.

I want you to stop doing that, she thought, but not so that he could hear her, and looked up obediently.

"Show them," he said.

"Show them what?"

"What happened when they met the colonists. What they saw in us. You showed me a little. I don't think you knew you were doing it. It wasn't all in words."

She thought back slowly. Trying to concentrate on a single memory from the past hours, days, months, was a matter of slow drunken circling, an absent-minded bird looking for a landing place, distracted by currents that had nothing to do with its goal. She found it at last, and shook her head.

"I can't," she said. "I'm too tired."

"You can."

"It's not the same as with one person. It's harder. I'm not an Adept."

"I think you're something more than an Adept now. Something different. You can do it. Show them," he said, and she resented his certainty.

She bowed her head and said against his heart, "How often have you made me do things I did not want to do?"

"I have never 'made' you do anything," he said, and then could not hide the thought that if she pulled this off perhaps he would survive after all, and *Endeavor* would go out again.

You only want to use us for your dream, she said, or remembered saying, or he remembered it, and when she looked up he would not meet her eyes for the first time in all their acquaintance. But she stood groggily with her arms around him and knew she was going to do it anyway.

Behind her she heard Murphy speak anxiously. The words meant nothing, but she understood the vector of communication between Murphy and Jameson.

She has reached her limit, let her rest.

There is no time for rest, we must resolve this now.

It is not so urgent.

It is. If we do not immediately present a solid front to our governments and the military, I do not think we will ever do it. And if she is wrong about the timing, it could begin tomorrow, or today. We do not know their capabilities in unknown space.

But if she is right we have the firepower.

To attack. But we do not know what there is to defend against. I do not think she knows, except in the most general terms. And how many lives does that mean?

Yes. I see. I see.

They stood on a broad river plain and looked at the sky. The plain was fertile, washed annually by spring floods that left rich deposits of soil. They were not ill-fed. They had that much to thank the river for.

The thing in the sky had been there a day now, and sometimes seemed to move nearer. It was no longer a dot visible only to the sharpest-eyed of the young, but clearly an oval.

(Murphy moved uneasily. Is this apprehension what they felt, she wondered, or is it Lady Hanna's, knowing what happened? Or my own, guessing what is to come?)

Thc radio worked well enough, and was all they had. Some of its parts were pirated from the useless Inspace communications equipment that still bore Eden Unlimited's logotype. This third generation joked about the name; the company that had found this world, and dropped their grandparents here with (they discovered too late) second-hand, shoddy equipment, had passed into their jerry-rigged culture as Flybynight Inc.

This would not be Flybynight coming back. It had to be from Earth, or maybe Colony One or maybe another colony, maybe there were hundreds of colonies now. But if the radio worked, why did it not answer them?

(Hanna sat on the floor, so limp in Jameson's arms he knew she would topple if he let her go. He knew where he was, sheltered in his own invaded home, but the river was there too, and he was highly critical. Stupid to build there. No wonder they lost their computer. As sensible to build on a volcano's slope as on a flood plain.)

They swarmed from the stilted wooden houses, calling back and forth through the thick bright air. My God, it's coming closer. Oh, Jesus. Tell your mother, tell her to stay inside, no, come out, oh, Jesus.

Do you read, said the radio, come in Overhill, do you read. The UFO's descending, we'll keep in touch. Have you heard from N'Gomba's group, are they sending anybody, what, wait a minute, it's landing, I never heard of anything like, they must have changed the design.

(The air was hazy and Struzik blinked into the sunlight, trying to see. Featureless metal; it must be damned claustrophobic inside. No markings, nothing like that in the Polity, then or now or ever.)

They gave it plenty of room to land. As soon as it was down they started running toward it, laughing and crying. Sometimes they had been sure they were forgotten and now it was all right. They wouldn't leave, it was a good place to live, unless some of the youngsters, well kids are like that, even some of the adults, but it didn't matter, it was all right, they could get machines, a grant, a doctor, news, they could make a world, it was all right now.

There were two hundred of them here and when they were all quite close they waited for the crew to come out, but nothing happened. Nobody came out for a long time.

(al-Nimeury wiped sweat from his face. Is it really taking this long, he thought, or is she making it seem that way? The gray hull shimmered in the sunlight and through it he saw, very far away, the D'neeran woman. Jameson held her tightly and his eyes were closed, his face pressed against her hair. My God, al-Nimeury thought, he's in love with her, how extraordinary; but something began to open on the hull, and he waited to see what would come out.)

There was a hole of black nothingness in the sunlight and something huge and gray showed in the opening. The first ripple of fear struck it and was flung back redoubled. They thought it threatened them, not knowing they were the threat, and some screamed and ran, and others surged forward. Round and round went the loop accelerating in an instant of thought, a paradigm of cornered fang and claw. The People saw Renders, the first weapon was fired and it was confusion, warfare, death and dying, red blood in the hot hazy morning and happening so fast they had only time to hate and did not even know why they died, D'neera's time was just beginning and they knew nothing of telepathy and each felt the things' terror as his own, the instant response of murder to danger, savage animals spilling from the grayness, savage animals twisting on the grass, and the pleasure of their dying *proved* it—

(STOP, STOP—)

"Stop!" cried Katherine Petrov, weeping and gasping, rocking back and forth.

The vision shivered and was gone. al-Nimeury made an inarticulate noise, and into the frozen silence came other sounds: a sigh from Murphy, Petrov's sobs. Feng stared into space, ignoring Petrov moaning at his side. Morisz started to curse and changed his mind.

Jameson eased Hanna's head into his lap. He thought she was unconscious, but her eyelids fluttered and for a moment she looked at him. Then her eyes closed and she lay still.

He waited for the others to say something. Morisz said at last, "That's—that's what's going to happen every time we make contact?"

Jameson looked down at Hanna and saw that she could not or would not answer.

"Presumably," he said. "That's how they see us, you know. All of them, in a great collectivity. They've been searching for us as a deadly danger ever since that day."

"Then how in hell are we ever going to get anywhere with them?"

Jameson said, "Either Hanna will, or maybe nobody ever will."

Murphy's head was buried in her hands. She said indistinctly, "How is she going to do that?"

Jameson started to stroke Hanna's hair, hesitated, and went on with it. The hell with it, he thought; I've gone too far already.

He said, "She was in intimate contact with one of them for some time. You all understand, I think, that she was under the control of a non-human personality. I have learned tonight that it was not altogether non-human. It was partially created from elements of Hanna's own personality; it was not entirely imposed from outside. She succeeded in integrating it, in making herself a kind of hybrid. She hopes she will be able to forestall the instant-feedback effect."

al-Nimeury said, "What about—how did she get them to agree to negotiation anyway?"

Jameson said, treading a narrow divide between fact and fiction, "She has one important contact."

"I don't see why they won't just kill her on sight."

"They didn't the first time. They didn't kill all of the colonists immediately. They kept some alive long enough to interrogate and experiment with them. They found nothing but the hatred and fear they expected, of course, under the circumstances, and the same has been true for Hanna. If she can control her own reaction, perhaps. . . ." He left the thought unfinished.

Murphy said in an odd voice, "Perhaps?"

He said bluntly, "The only risk is hers."

Murphy stared at him, upright and indignant. "You'd send her to them again? After what they did before?"

Jameson shrugged. It cost him more than he would have cared to admit to her.

Petrov was recovering. She said querulously, "We'd better send the whole damned Fleet with her."

"No," Hanna said unexpectedly. "Nobody."

She tried to sit up and Jameson helped her. She held his hand and said without looking at any of them, "I've got to make them restructure reality. Not frighten them. All I need to do is convince a few we're not what they think, really convince them, and it'll spread through the whole population. They must have gone a lot faster than we did. No war, that kind of communication—it took us longer every time we did it."

Struzik said, "Did what?"

"Changed the shape of the universe. Like knowing Earth goes around the sun, like accepting evolution or the size of the Milky Way or meeting F'thal. It changes everything for a whole species."

Murphy said in astonishment, "*That's* what you're going to try to do?"

"Well," said Hanna, "what else is there to do? Except kill them?"

She listened to the voices drifting around her as if they were a kind of music, sense forgotten. The room was very bright now. They were arguing about her nebulous contact, about studying and waiting and the gathering of intelligence, about weaponry human and alien, about what Co-op would say and what Fleet would want, about the course to Home and—with Jameson picking a most delicate course—about Leader's impact on her.

They would go on arguing for a long time (humans talk so, she thought) and then they would let her do it. Jameson still was not sure of them, but he could not feel what she felt: the bare tilt of a balance to one side, the change in al-Nimeury's reality, at least, that would make the difference.

She struggled to her feet and found herself looking into Jameson's face. She said: *I'm going to sleep now.*

"Don't do that," he said, not meaning, don't sleep.

She could argue with his constraints later, if there was a later. She found her way back to his bedroom and opened it to the sunlight which had bred her ancestors and his, and fell into his bed and into sleep.

CHAPTER XVIII

Hanna slept so soundly she did not even wake when Melanie Ward came in with her flickering instruments and began the series of feather-touches that would tell her if Hanna was fit to go on or not. Hanna woke at last not because of pain but because of its cessation. The varying ache in her right arm, which had become part of the landscape of her body, was gone. She dreamed that she was well and whole and when she woke and turned her eyes to where the pain had been she thought for a moment it was true, she had never gotten in the way of the knife, the fight had never happened. But Leader-in-her-thoughts whispered to her and she saw in harsh noon light that the wound was only hidden under a neat strip of false human hide. Then she saw Ward, and behind her Jameson silhouetted against the light. They were talking as if Hanna were still asleep.

Jameson was saying, "But there is nothing immediately life-threatening?"

"Not immediately." Ward spoke with the irritation of a physician who already knows her advice will be ignored.

"Well, then. . . ."

"I won't be responsible for the consequences. And I won't be responsible for starting the sequence of stimulants."

"You will. Or must I have your commanding officer give you a direct order?"

They converged on Hanna, tall shadows, and she shrank away in irrational alarm. There was the slight pressure of an injection in her uninjured arm. After a moment her head cleared with a rush that threatened to suck her into the sky, she was sitting up and looking wide-eyed at Jameson, and Ward was gone. The immense relief of new energy seemed to touch every cell of her body.

She sighed with pleasure. She had forgotten what it was to feel well.

Jameson said, "The vote was four to one."

She had been admiring the new steadiness of her hands. She looked up, distracted.

"Who didn't—?"

"Petrov. Who still can see that you are stopped, if you don't leave at once."

"At once—" She stood up obediently. Artificial strength steadied her legs, and she nodded in satisfaction. She had never liked using stimulants, even when the need was urgent. Why? They were a fine thing.

She took a step, her head swimming, and he stopped her.

"Not this instant," he said. "*Heartworld II*'s not ready. And there are things you should hear."

"All right." The first burst of well-being was settling down, curling into the corners of her body. Her vision was sharper than usual. She saw that Jameson looked tired and careworn, and said, "You ought to've had Melanie give you some of that stuff."

"I'll be taking enough of it, I assure you. So will you. Ward advised against a direct booster implant, and you will have to be very careful about giving yourself injections at frequent intervals. You'll have no time to sleep. How do you feel? Can you attend to what I say?"

Leader-in-her-thoughts was singing some melody wrested from Hanna's memory. She made him shut up.

"I'm listening," she said.

Jameson was detached as she had ever seen him, and she stood with tilted head, entirely alert, and listened to a dry sequence of orders. The People's course program could not be used until it was translated into human mathematics. Hanna would work with Fleet to do that while she still traveled through human space. When she was finished the Fleet escort would leave her, but she would not be able to rest. She would program a powered projectile to return to human space. Into it she would dictate every scrap of information she had gotten from Leader-in-her-thoughts about the People's military capability, technology, biosphere, biology, history and cultural patterns. She would describe in detail their remarkable development of telepathy, especially their use of it to control machines, which had only a coincidental resemblance to human direct-control techniques, D'neeran or otherwise. She would continue reporting until the last possible moment, and send the projectile back just before she contacted the People.

She thought there were other things she had better be doing as contact approached, but she did not say so.

When Jameson was done giving orders he waited for her to comment on them. But she had lost interest in orders several minutes before. She had heard none of the latter instructions; she was caught up in the open strain in his voice, and sensed a new fragility in the surface he presented.

She would do him no favor by breaking it. But she could not help saying, "Are you going to be all right?"

His face changed in the instant before he turned away from her. It must have been a very long time since anyone had asked him such a question. She moved toward him too quickly and was light-headed again. The space around her was luminous and his shoulder when she touched it was the form and substance of warmth.

She whispered, "S-starr?"

He made the very slightest of movements, a fractional lessening of tension. He said, "You haven't got it right. You're not supposed to hiss." His head was bowed and she could not see his face, but there was something new in his voice.

She rubbed his arm gently, at a loss for words, and moved a little dizzily to face him. She leaned against him without looking up, and he made a sound of exasperation or defeat or desire and abruptly pulled her to him without restraint. They kissed with concentrated, mutual greed. Hanna had not even thought of lovemaking in so long that the violence of her physical reaction took her by surprise. But she did not think of it then; she did not think at all.

He raised his head after—it seemed—a very short time. She murmured a protest and leaned on him in earnest now because her knees were weak.

He said reluctantly, "They're waiting."

"In a minute. . . ."

She meant she could not face anyone else without time to pull herself together. She was sure she did not say all that, but he said, "Me too," and moved away a little. Inside her, newly roused, Leader mourned again for Sunrise. *Shut up shut up shut up,* she said, but it was too late. Jameson kept slipping with her over a border into a lovely unknown land, but she could not get him to stay there.

She said, "Ah, you have such discipline."

"Not enough." He folded his arms—possibly to prevent himself from reaching out to her again—and looked at her with bright eyes. The odd, irregular face was younger and no longer tired. The consciousness that half a dozen people expected them to appear annoyed her.

She said anxiously, "If I come back will you remember this?"

"I will."

"Promise me."

"I promise," he said without hesitation.

"Oh, good. Oh, I'm glad. What ever happened to that girl in Central Records?"

He said in some alarm, "How did you know about her?"

"I snooped. While I was here before. Where is she?"

He shrugged. "Back in Central Records, I suppose."

"And always will be?"

He looked at her carefully and said, "Unless she learns to distinguish between a setback and the end of a man's career, yes."

"Why," said Hanna, "do you have such a wall around yourself? What are you hiding from?"

They faced each other in the center of the room, and she saw the habitual shutter begin to drop over his face. He shook his head. "No questions, Hanna. Not now."

"I might not have another chance. Even if I come back. If you're gone."

He said heavily, "Does it really matter now?"

She sighed and said, "No. I suppose it doesn't. And if we knew each other better we might not get along at all."

"I wonder. I wonder about that sometimes."

He took her arm again before she could answer, and this time, knowing she would get no more from him now, she went out with him obediently.

Today air traffic froze by order of high authority. The river became a ribbon. The city shrank to invisibility and disappeared as Hanna rose into cloud and then the clouds were under her too, dazzling.

Entering black space meant re-entering a personal reality

from which she had briefly escaped, and it was more real than the one that had Jameson in it. If it were not for the Fleet vessel that trailed her, she would have thought her little time on Earth a dream. As a sleeper, waking, remembers sharp singular images shorn of context, Hanna remembered details: the color of al-Nimeury's eyes, the texture of Jameson's hair, the curve of Murphy's back as she knelt touching Hanna's arm. And as if she were waking from a dream, Hanna (as she spoke with Fleet and *Heartworld II*, slaved ship's systems to *Willowmeade*'s, prepared to analyze the precious course program) felt sorrow not sensibly connected to events, as sorrow ought to be, but the shadow of the sorrow of a dream, truncated and distant from consciousness.

They might have let her speak to Iledra, but she had not asked. She might have spoken to Jameson frankly of love, but she had not.

She was going back into the night, which was real, and on to a deeper night. Only this commanded her attention.

Heartworld II was half real, half not. Faces looked at her from every wall, voices echoed in chambers whose silence only she had broken for what seemed all her life.

She was busy at every moment. Leader would not be a translator. He did not have to be. She knew the People's notation as if she had learned it in infancy. She was no mathematician, but she did not have to be. The Fleet vessel threw mathematicians at her, summoned hastily to this flight not in body but through the skein of relays that filtered into every part of human space.

Hanna did not know any of them. Their faces ran together.

She did not sleep, ever. She did not need Leader, but he talked to her anyway. He meditated in a corner of her mind, content:

I will not die but live. Strangely. In thought and bone of generations past and those to come. Not memory, but real. No longer bearing precious burdens in my own true body; no life that you understand; not to act, but to advise. To love those past and those to come. And pass into history more than Self. Sacrifice less great than you think and payment and exchange for final value. Logical progression, natural act, next and last phase of life, and that for which I was most joyfully destined all my time.

Only those who die without this truly die.

Now Alta was nearer than Earth, but neither was near. The alien program cracked and broke. The mathematicians leapt upon the prize, the programmers and engineers went without sleep. The commander of the *Willowmeade,* a courteous man, thanked Hanna. She stared at his face, distracted, thinking him Erik.

It was not Erik. He talked like Erik. But, "We have met before," she said.

"Briefly," he said, smiling. "Rescue mission to the *Clara Mendoza*. I always wondered, did you scrap her?"

"We buried her," Hanna said. "With her crew."

"Funny thing to do," he said.

Yes, Leader agreed. Then he thought of the First Watchsetter and was not sure.

The commander—Tirel, she remembered suddenly—said, "We won't be with you much longer. I understand you've got plenty of power and fresh stores. Anything you need before we withdraw?"

She shook her head. She needed nothing more. She had had a great deal. She had been—

Lucky. Lucky to have had D'neera. The Mason Range Falls crash a kilometer down jutting rock and rainbows leap in sunlight mellow as Earth's, and clean. At B'ha the sea rocks gently only with the sweet star's motion. There is no moon. On no human world do stars shine more clearly. On no human world is freedom so friendly. I was shaped by no mold. Made myself. And chose my own loyalties.

Lucky. I have been so lucky, so fortunate, so happy!

Tears must have glittered in her eyes, because Tirel said, "What's wrong?"

"I was just remembering. . . ."

Willowmeade's next Jump would take it back into human space. Hanna's would start her on the path the People had charted.

Tirel knew the purpose of her mission, but neither he nor anyone except Leader knew what she expected at the end. He looked at her curiously and said, "Sure there's nothing you need?"

"No, thank you," Hanna said.

"Good luck," he said.

A little later, when *Willowmeade* was a light-year gone, Hanna wept. All the human faces had vanished, all the human voices. But the reason she mourned had to do with his last words to her; they seemed the sum and essence of what being human was, and her tears were not for herself.

Time ran on, shrinking. She had no time to watch it run. She had too much to do. Why? Why tatter her voice with talking, reciting facts, surmise, portraits of the People? Why work so for Fleet with its guns, or for Jameson who sent her again into night?

It is for the future, Leader answered, comforting her.

She was not comforted.

She went on with it, though. The stimulants drummed in her and distanced her from all save the tasks before her. The hard part was remembering human speech; and sorting out the knowledge Leader had given her in the days when she came scarcely human toward Earth. Singular concepts triggered hallucinatory visions that touched all her senses and forced her to think with precision of how she could describe them. Strange flowers filled the decks of *Heartworld II*, predatory fleshy living things whose massed shapes pleased the People. When she bathed, the water seemed a running stream, and the walls that surrounded her shifted to angles their designers had never intended. Leader, caught in the interstices of her self so that though he was a functioning unwelcome intruder it seemed he *ought* to have been there always, said of every moment: it should be *thus*.

It seemed to her she was more alien than human.

The theories of "Sentience" were nonsense. This was what she had meant, but she had not known it before. "Sentience" was a failure because neither she nor anyone else had fully understood what she was talking about.

Leader thought quietly in corners:

I too was most fortunate. Saw Sunrise, Heathkeeper's child, one rainy dawn in early youth and I too was a child, younger even than most at bonding and all of Us in your thinking children. The bond cannot be otherwise. There is no place for jealousy for doubt for dolor unknown to Us but known to me since known to you. There was no ceremony, nor need for one. Came I to her Nearhome. We grew and flowered together until time came. Sealed the bond in a space of time apart. Those who passed the Bower knew and took joy and strength from creation of love which was shaped from our bodies and selves. The future born anew with each bond.

She did not wish my leaving yet they called me: Explorers, Watchsetters: from the first waking, ever: she knew. Yet she is my rest and true Home and ever was. And ever is.

Hanna listened to Leader within her, and to the voices within him. They passed a halfway point in space, passed it again in time. Time was material. And shrinking.

She turned with more than human patience to the task of disentangling the People's written language, a tricky blend of mathematics and pictographs with all its own structural complexities. She analyzed flawlessly, drug-driven, the relationship of its precise, concrete symbolic structure to the ambiguity of the People's living mind/s. Behind her acute attention drifted shadows of lost futures, dreamlike. Might have built a city, guided Koroth, loved, learned to laugh. . . .

Might have grown wise. . . .

Living is, said Leader, *and will be. Different. Yet real.*

"For you, Not for me."

How do you know?

"I do not know. I hope. I do not want your future. I want only mine, and will not have it. There will be naught but the dispersion. And the ruined self and I think the body's death. And then nothing."

Not nothing. He wanted to ease her grief. *Even among Us it is said one can live for the Good. And die for it.*

"That is no comfort. I choose this, but I do not know why. I do not want it. But I choose it."

You will be remembered. The work of your hands and thought and self will live. You will live. Not as We do; as humans do.

"That is no comfort!"

When the last Jump was near, it was Leader who remembered to send back the return projectile, and to program it with messages for Iledra and Cosma and her parents and cousins.

She left no farewell for Jameson.

At the very last she programmed *Heartworld II* to begin broadcasting a plea for tolerance that would, she hoped, induce the People to consider some course besides blasting her to atoms at once.

She knew (from Leader-in-her-thoughts) that security around

Home was as tight as anything humans had ever produced in their most paranoid moments, and he could make a fair guess at their reaction to what they had found on the First Watchsetter.

They will not make for your Home, I think; for the others; the fleet flies toward them.

"Not much of a fleet, is it?"

Not much. Not like yours, for which we/they wait in readiness; they will think you the flagship. And fire.

"Will what I write now stop them?"

???

"Well?"

Hope!

The People's defenses, like humanity's long ready but unused, were not automatic. They had to be ordered into action. But even if they did not fire on her single small vessel immediately, what would they do when they sensed *her*? The crew of the *First Watchsetter*, she knew now, had brought every conceivable discipline and defense to stalking the *Endeavor* and examining the precious prisoner. They had shut themselves away from her. But *she* could not use the barrier, the wall, the absence of a connecting medium she had found when (who? Bladetree, Leader answered) came to meet her. With an effort that drained them the crew had, while they questioned her, operated in the Hunter's mode, subsuming the killing reflex into the purposefulness of stalking, though their prey was information. But that was an artificial state, an unnatural event, which drained and dismayed even the remarkable individuals who created it. What would happen when Hanna touched the edge of a whole population's awareness? It depended on her, and on Leader, of course. She could see no recourse except to distance herself from her own fear; with Leader's help—if he could help. She did not know if she could do it or how she would do it. Therefore she prepared *Heartworld II* to plead for her, to get her time, and at the final Jump was glad of it, because the first thing she saw was a Render.

It seemed painted, two-dimensional, though the texture of its shaggy brown fur was reproduced in detail. Its eyes were filled with red light. It floated in semi-darkness, bright against the shadows. She saw it clearly from the corner of one eye, but when she turned to look at it directly it was gone and the shadows fell again.

Hanna thought automatically: That's silly. What would a painted Render be doing here?

She was much closer to Home than she had expected to come with the last Jump, and the curve of it nearly filled the pilot's port with the fertile marbling of a terrestrial world.

Heartworld II's song went on, the binary version of Hanna's version of the People's binary version of their version of symbolic communication. It said: (This individual) is harmless flesh and blood, unclawed, not predator, not prey, not harmless, a quantity N. (This individual) stands outside reality strange as the nospace of Inspace, stands outside logic strange as We and I, stands—

It is a Lifetender with blood on its breath, someone remarked skeptically, and a Render sat in the empty and redundant co-pilot's seat, and the air crackled around it, and Hanna leapt to her feet and was alone again.

Heartworld II went on talking:

—with you in the unnamed haze, this time they see without fear, We have—they have no need to kill, inertia is reversed and—

It was a hand's width from her face, fur blurring into grayish scales, fangs glittering at her throat. She started to scream and strangled the sound and did not move. It disappeared. She shook with reaction and her legs were weak and the hammering of her heart frightened her.

—one being in this unit, harmless flesh and blood, unarmed, unclawed, requesting permission to land—

Does it lie? said a Render on the edge of sight, and another said: *Beasts lie.*

Then they said: *What is lie?*

Hanna stumbled back to her seat. Eyes closed, hands over her ears, she waited for the Renders to go away. They did not.

The value of
what We lost when
and one being
but blow it away
and lose the
Let it land

"I have," said *Heartworld II,* "a landing beacon."

Hanna opened her eyes and peered through more Renders. "Land," she muttered.

Heartworld II whistled quietly. "Awaiting orders," it said.

"Go on down," she said more clearly. "Land."

The fall was slow, the Renders whispered at her back and somewhere, everywhere, the equivalent of fingers rested on the equivalent of triggers. She had no illusion about what would happen if she tried to deviate from the course they set her, or why she was still alive. They wanted *Heartworld II,* the prize *XS-12* should have been to them if they had not clumsily destroyed most of its value to them. They wanted the data this ship carried. They must not be allowed to get it. Surely someone, Jameson, Petrov, somebody had thought of this?

She asked *Heartworld II* about it and got no answer. There were more devious ways to ask and she did so and found her suspicions were correct. While she slept *Heartworld II* had been programmed not to self-erase but to self-destruct if alien hands touched it.

So I get off and try to make peace and they come here and it blows them up, she thought. Me too, if I'm still aboard.

The Renders went on talking among themselves, paying no attention to her. Imaginary Renders. She wiped sweat off her face and listened intently to their talk of defense.

But Renders were dust and did not speak.

She was listening to the People. The Renders were her own creation, an objective referent for her fear, which she dared not direct toward the People themselves. Perhaps Leader-in-her-thoughts, who must share her fear but could not fear his own kind, helped her create them, had helped her find this brief precarious solution. They winked in and out as her eyes moved, but their numbers seemed to be growing.

She had stopped watching the monitors. She looked out the port and saw a civilized world. There was less green than she had expected, more brown and blue, and now she was close enough to see clusters of light past the terminator.

The Renders fell silent. A claw brushed her cheek and with an effort she remained still, biting at her fingers. She reminded herself they were an illusion, one possibility of many and that the most destructive. There were alternatives. There had to be alternatives. She was here to create them.

She said to *Heartworld II*, "I want to meet with one individual. Tell the Defenders—"

She stopped short. Was that the right word? *Yes*, whispered a Render, and the mutter began again. The southern hemisphere, the Nearhome of the Defenders, that was where she was going. Thousands of them there.

She started again, "One individual. The, the Hearthkeeper of the Nearhome of, of—" She stumbled and finished the thought: "Of the Leader of the First Watchsetter."

Heartworld II chuckled doubtfully and began the translation.

She knew then that Leader had been thinking of Sunrise all along; and he came suddenly to life and cried out with longing.

Heartworld II settled slowly to a city. It was white in the midday light, though other colors showed here and there. Its rooftops were landscaped and decorated and made into space for living or beauty to be seen from above, a convention inconsistently followed on human worlds but perhaps universal here. It was not large, but she had seen smaller towns clustered round it during her controlled fall.

Thousands of them here, she thought, and felt the Renders crowding round her, and licked her dry lips again and again. She was afraid, and her fear created the beasts. The cabin was hot, surely with their body heat. Yet it was the animal in the People she must fear, and the animal in herself, and the Renders could not harm her though they kept the truth before her eyes.

"They will bring you the individual you request," said *Heartworld II*.

So near, whispered Leader-in-her-thoughts, and Hanna shivered. Sunrise was indeed near. Among the Nearhomes scattered round Defense were two or three occupied mostly by Watchsetters, and one of them was Leader's.

Heartworld II drifted gently downward, under the rounded towers of the tallest buildings. In them, unlike the People's spacecraft, there were windows, transparent openings in immaculate walls; but she could not see anything through them. The Renders surrounded her, muttering. Beyond them on the edge of perception she seemed to hear a grim vibration of floodwater or landslide, a threat inescapable as an incoming tide complex and unpredictable under dancing moons. The Renders held it back. Behind their red eyes were hundreds, thousands, millions of eyes watching her. She hid behind draperies of coarse fur and hoped the Renders would not go away.

Heartworld II touched down at last. Automatically she checked monitors, rounding out the view the port gave her. This was clearly a landing field, though no other vessels showed around her. Its floor was brilliant white, and she saw that only *Heartworld II*'s compensation for light kept it from hurting her eyes. The nearest structure was a kilometer away; the work of the Defenders was carried on deep underground. Nothing moved, except once when a blood-red flash drew her eyes to something like a bird that vanished almost at once.

Heartworld II said, "You are to leave this vessel and walk to the building you see before you."

"All right," Hanna said. She was busy for a few minutes, modifying *Heartworld II*'s destruct program slightly. She said, "What is *Heartworld I*, anyway?"

"*Heartworld I*," said its sister, "is reserved for the president of the General Council."

"And the commissioner from Heartworld gets Two?"

"That is correct."

"Well, good-bye," she said.

"Good-bye," it answered without surprise.

She went out, accompanied by a rapidly multiplying retinue of Renders. Those nearest her had solidified, and jostled her now. Their odor was delicate and sweet—no. That was the warm lambent air. She scarcely saw her goal through the crowd, though the Renders thinned in substance at a distance so that even in their infinite numbers those on the horizon were only shapes of air, hollow spots in the atmosphere, which she could barely see by squinting because she had forgotten to protect her eyes and the light was indeed too bright. But all her memories of Home and the First Watchsetter were of spaces filled with dimness, and she did not understand this light.

Her footsteps made dull sounds on the shining ground, but the Renders made no sound at all. The structure ahead of her grew slowly. It was not large. She knew it was made for observation and maintenance, that was all. It was expendable.

She had miscalculated how long it would take her to reach the building, and before she got there *Heartworld II* blew itself up with a roar and a hot blast of wind that knocked her flat. Debris rained on her unshielded back and the arms clasped over her head. Before the roar was finished she looked up and saw that the Renders had gone, and one of the People said to her, invisible: *Why did you do that?*

His voice was clear over the roar that was also the relentless waiting flood. She answered: *I did it to protect both of us.*

He seized and examined the thought and she cried out aloud, remembering The Questioner; though to Bladetree she had said little so clearly, having been consciously obscure or blurred by madness.

The presence vanished, but it was not replaced by silence. The sound of the explosion must have ended, but still she heard it, a thunder of countless voices. The ground seemed to tremble and she dug her hands into it: earth now, not the flat whiteness. Bluish stalks came loose in her fingers, studded with tiny blue pinpoints of flowers. She cowered before an impending avalanche, but nothing happened, it was only their immanence she felt, the giant awareness of her presence.

She turned her head, licking dust from her lips. She had not given any thought ahead of time to how she would handle the minutes just past, because she had had no idea where to begin. The right response, by luck perhaps, had come from some deep unconscious well, and she had managed to distance herself from the People, transforming them into dangers she could understand. But the innumerable Renders, the tide, the landslide, the avalanche, all were ultimately irresistible and this was not good enough. She would have to succeed quickly in what she had come here for, or she would go under.

She remembered a moment from the struggle with Leader-in-her-thoughts and forced her attention to physical reality. The earth was warm, something had burnt through her clothing and there was patch of fire on one leg, there was dirt under her fingernails and the tiny blue flowers gave the air its odor. The People's sun shone on her indifferently.

She carefully relaxed all her muscles and lifted her head—and saw Sunrise standing over her.

CHAPTER XIX

Leader-in-her-thoughts cried *Lovely how lovely my love how long absent o stay with me!* and . . .

Hanna choked, her face in the dirt again because she wished to reach for Sunrise and draw back all at once and was helpless and . . .

In the stunning surge of longing and desire Sunrise took her shoulders and turned her without effort. The pressure of the thousand million voices was gone. Sunrise regarded her with eyes hidden behind the membrane that kept out the sun and said very intimately: *Thou art not truly my strength.*

Sunrise's headfeathers were intricately groomed and her face was decorated with stylized flowers. A flame-shape, symbol of her office, hung from a chain round her neck.

Hanna shook her head numbly, over and over. She spoke, and so did Leader.

I live. I live and love thee and—

I killed him. I killed him as he cried out for thee and for the little one who swims so swiftly—

I live—

He is dead, I his murderer—

Sunrise's face was a nightmare mask, vaguely reptilian, so cruel as to acknowledge no conscience Hanna could recognize; but it wore the hearthkeeper's dignity.

The great rending paws moved over her with a sadist's anticipation. And wavered and were tender hands with elegantly pointed nails, fingertops softly ridged, palms soothing and cool.

Thou art injured, my love?

Thine enemy. Thine enemy!

I cannot see my enemy. . . .

And through Sunrise's eyes Hanna saw herself, not alien

animal altogether, but shadowed by Leader's form, visible to eyes not her own. Her own hand, its knuckles scaled, reached for Sunrise.

The crystalline air reflected a thousand faces, which trembled and shattered with a long tinkling sigh. Her hand fell short, her arm was not long enough, her face was wet and The Questioner lifted her to her feet and she nearly fell and Sunrise held her up. She clung to the great arms and tried to hide from the shards of voices that pierced her eyes whispering

New, something new, this is new, o news. . . .

Something new, murmured the earth, and an arched dome of muted blue closed them in and fell to indigo and blackness, and when light came again she was walking.

She did not know why they were walking. She wished they were not, for she was tired. From the air she had seen elegant lines of roads for surface transport, arranged it seemed not for speed or convenience but for the patterns they made. But they walked, Sunrise shortening her stride awkwardly to Hanna's. Columns rose by the roadside at intervals, higher than Hanna's head, black, and heavily carved. It was high summer, and fruit hung swollen from the trees. *Drop*, whispered the trees. *Fall away, I shall cast you to the wind and increase.* Hanna dissolved into the landscape, bit into a red-gold globe and licked the juices from her hand. Very far away a voice screamed that this was dangerous. Never never *never* eat unknown vegetation or breathe unknown air or touch unknown herbs, lesson number one in the age of space. But this was not unknown. It tasted purple.

Here is something new, said Sunrise among stalks of grain-to-be, who wore their spent flowers proudly. Their roots drew on earthblood and sang. A swelling grainbud trembled at her brown fingertip and shrank toward Sunrise in fear. Under their feet a million invisible lives took up its cry and something, nothing, snake or scarab, centipede or dream, skimmed the uneasy earth and was silenced.

The grasses froze, the frame cracked and Hanna stepped outside, saw it whole and enclosed, the blue dome the sentient grain Sunrise all one. Fragile in the surface of her throat's tender skin was a recorder, tiny, a dot just big enough to see, in case they found her body someday. She started to speak to it and was inside again and time flowed, unstopped.

Tell me of thy death.
I died unchoosing—
No, my love!
none to comfort me last-kindness absent—
of all deaths the worst—
they died at my side and I saw myself die. . . .
This alien—

Hanna leapt at the touch like a startled bird.

did not know. They all die alone and forever.

Animals, said Sunrise, and Hanna shuddered at the hands on her throat, the great thumbs gouged its hollow and she choked.

No. I live in it, and fade. . . .

They are soulless—

Only new.

Here is something new, said the sky, but Hanna did not hear it, absorbed in a streamlet's speaking waters. She lay on her stomach and her head fell gently toward the water, nodding, looking for the faces. A silver streak whisked by her eyes, warning: *I am not good to eat, no no not I not for you*, and her belly hurt. Her head drooped lower. Pink and turquoise showed in shadows under stones. Her hand crept into the water and the colors vanished with a muted scream. Under the rocks—

No. Thou art careless as Swift.

Sunrise tugged at her hand. Something under the rock would strike, whether she would be good to eat or not.

Here was no one, except the two of them, but the air was full of voices. Faces showed in the clouds. Hanna sat in dust and listened to the flowers, which dreamt of dying at summer's end. Her blood stirred with their satisfaction. The communion of Leader and Sunrise went on without her. Vessel, seedpod, something new, a chariot for Leader and nothing more, she dreamed with the flowers of insignificance and thought of winter's stillness and waiting seeds. Her ring cast blue dazzles into her eyes. She pulled it off, lifted it, licked it, dropped it, forgot it. The tiny characters engraved inside said, *The first duty of the D'neeran citizen is to the integrity of the self*; stopped speaking, flickered, and went out.

* * *

Kill it, they said. *Now, instantly.*

The rest of them were Sunrise. Who said: *It is my love. Was and was not; is and is not. But is. He died but did not and dying yet not dead comes to Us for easeful proper death. He also she is of Us/not of Us. We cannot deny the kindness she refused him.*

They said (though only of Leader) *That is true.*

Alone as Hanna was, helpless as she was, still they feared her. She lived only because of Sunrise; because of Leader-in-her-thoughts, whom Sunrise would not harm; because the communion of bondmates was a whole within the whole, and the greater whole stretched to accommodate it.

Hanna or her avatar stood at the gates of her Nearhome. The gates rose into a sky grown pale in the late afternoon, traced with magical symbols in lapis and silver. The People had outgrown magic, and the designs were merely traditional, but in this world of softened edges the meaning of spear and dagger had not changed.

It was harder and harder to be Hanna. They were surging seawaves; she a soft bubble of foam.

The gates will not hold against death from the skies, someone said, and the human fleet rained death. Death also fell on Willow, on D'neera, on Earth, their peoples vanished. Cold and shining, past present and future, the handful of gray-brown boxes worked its way through the void, slow but unerring.

The voyage was happening now; in space and in the mind/s of the People. Hanna struggled with the vision, overwhelmed. Spearpoints danced with symbols of another world, a glowing sun, great cats yawning and thinking bloody thoughts of hunger and changing to Renders, and a murmur of astonishment surrounded her. She saw no one except Sunrise.

The gates were open, but seemed closed. They would not let her in, tiger, Render, alien form.

Held they, said a Hunter, *against Renders past.*

Yes, Hanna said, *but We did not.*

There was a great stillness of incomprehension. *No*, said Leader, but less strongly than he had argued by a fireside otherwhere.

Behold, Hanna said to the ghostly gates, and fell into memory; searched the persons she had been; watched (adamant now, alien and unmoved) a Render die. Pain destroyed it and the People ate its death, absorbing it

like air

like food

like flesh

thus must it be, they said strongly, but:

The Celebrant wore only a loincloth, which shimmered golden in the fading sun. Behind him in an age-long-past boiled a sea of dark blue cloud, and the wind blew hard. He said: *Felt Renders' power and channeled it to memory unending. Each time at unity was I new and all of Us and stronger. That was my being and purpose and that I fulfilled. Strong grew my Nearhome and fearless*

She sat on stone and its heat scorched the burned place on her thigh. Quartz sparkled in the spaces between stone. She summoned an early Explorer, one of the first of the age of space. He wore a uniform something like Leader's. Metal gleamed around him and he mastered it. *Saw We in my time the field of all-life and We its fulfillment and shaper. Saw We were not separate but part of Our world and it part of Us and knew Ourselves separate from beasts yet not. But then there were no Renders. We did not think of that. Naught vanishes, but is changed. But We did not think of Renders.*

Leader, wavering, drew on memory and Hanna. Renders died and died again. The years were the whirl of a kaleidoscope. In centuries of Rites the Renders died, and their passionate savagery passed again and again into the People.

"Thus is it," Hanna lectured them, "in all and each part of Our lives."

She was, oddly, speaking. The wind took her words and measured them and turned them about for meaning, and absorbed them.

"Look," Hanna said, urging.

Through her eyes looked Sunrise and Leader and a vast omnipresence. They saw:

The lapis which was stone and art all at once, and thought, and the shaping of hands, and before that the eons of creation, and all the years to come. So the artist's hands and his brain shaped the stone, and the stone and its color and texture shaped also his brain and the brains of all who saw it, and those in turn shaped others, and each was changed and returned refreshed and new to create what was real in the viewing and be created by it. Thus it was with sky and water, earth and stars, and always with each other, through the ages. And with Renders. For each that died, each principal in the Rite, dissolved indeed; but not into nothingness.

"Not here," Hanna said. "Not here, at least."

It seemed they listened, silent, holding breath.

"You made them part of you," Hanna said. "That was the purpose of the Rite. I know. He told me so. But did you not see that you were thereby changed?"

No, said the thickening air.

But Sunrise said: *It is We who speak. Taste truth.*

No, said the wind.

Truth was kernel and seed, though. It was hard. It would not go away. They could not make it not be. It was, and grew.

She tried to tell the recorder: Yes I was right I hear feel smell *see* truth acknowledged, one and one and ten and exponentially a shift a change I was right!

But her tongue was too thick.

(In deepest space and the wells of time a particle of dust pulls gently on another and it comes. To them, drawn, another. And another. Ruled by final forces galaxies form—)

You are right, whispered Leader-in-her-thoughts. Hanna did not hear him. She was in this moment at home, and the season was turning. The falseoaks at their peak shone even in the night, the shining dust fell on her upturned face from the shining sky.

Sunrise took her arm softly, softly, as if touching a lover grown frail and strange. Carefully Hanna stepped to the gates.

She thought the gates said that she was dangerous. She could not be dangerous. She lifted a hand to her head and felt feathery, delicate scales. The sunlight was warm as water, and she swam in it. Beyond the gate a maze of passages began, and hidden among them was Swift.

Leader said: *This creature is I, and not dangerous. I am the Leader of the First Watchsetter, and I tell you so.*

There was an authority in Leader-in-her-thoughts that Hanna had not heard before. He drew strength from Sunrise, from the People, from the persons of his Nearhome, and was completed by them, unmistakably himself. His assurance checked their doubt. An infinity of circles swept away and faded out of Hanna's perception, conflict resolving in harmony. And dizzily she saw that this would not have been possible if she had not in the first place accepted Leader's right to exist; because then he would not have accepted it, nor would those who watched him now—the knowledge was plucked from her thoughts and reverberated and faded outward through the dimming circles.

The wind said: *Enter*.

It was dark. Time played tricks. She had walked for hours through the People's debate, dreaming and bemused. She had been part of it, irresistibly, and now was not. The indefinable roar that had filled her was gone. She was apart in a circle of light, and there was a great silence.

She shook her head, hard, suddenly wakened to herself. She felt something in her hands and looked down to see that she held a stone knife. Its slender hilt was delicate as her hands, gold-chased, gem-encrusted. The jewels were bluish-green. They matched a leaf that bent low, shyly tapped her arm, and whispered welcome.

She jumped at the touch, and saw that Sunrise sat beside her on a stone bench. Copper-colored metal lay polished at her feet and stretched into the nearer darkness. Beyond that gray shapes of growing things rose against a wall, and the wall against a cloud-torn night sky. She was inside—just inside—the Nearhome of the Defenders.

"Why?" She was hoarse. She cleared her throat and said to Sunrise, "Why can't I hear them anymore?"

We are apart, you and I. . . . I wished to know with whom I walked. I think I cannot know. You are he, yet not. Nor are you altogether other. New, I said. New indeed. . . .

The surface of the bench somehow had been softened, though it looked and felt like stone. It was finely carved, and all its design (she knew, though human eyes alone would find no sense there) was the story of a far-famed Hunt. There were rituals for the completion of such works. There were rituals for everything. Ritual imbued all of life, a complex outer structure for the incomprehensibly complex inner structure of the People.

It pleased Hanna that she had thought of that. It meant she was still human, and still Hanna.

They had no ritual for anything like her. Except one, which she had endured.

She said kindly to Sunrise, taking up the debate anew, "You knew not how Renders changed you. How could you? Knowledge is the opening of doors in what is known, through which one walks to new dimensions. And you are enclosed."

Sunrise said, seeming very human: *We liked it that way. Yet time brings new truths; or reversal of the old. It has been long since there was a new truth. And did We then perceive it truly?*

Hanna rested comfortably in the silence, almost at home. She said, "What are they thinking of? Will they call back the ships?"

I do not know. If the threat is not real? But the threat is real.

"Only if it is made real. Willed real. Don't you see? You do see!" She meant all of them. "I know you do!"

Perceive the past, Sunrise said, and Hanna knew that the doubt she felt in Sunrise was an echo and reflection of a debate that still went on. And she perceived indeed the past and the weight of it, obstacle and illumination at once.

You ask a new thing, Sunrise said.

"It is new for the others as well," Hanna said, thinking of her last hours with humans, who had not understood that the balance of weapons would not sway the People, who had leapt at an idea of negotiation when nothing that could be done with the People resembled human notions of compromise even slightly.

She had not been honest with them, not even with Jameson, from whom she had learned the art of withholding full truth. They would not understand (she and Leader agreed) the strange new thing to be done. But the People understood it, and therefore the debate continued.

It is pity, Sunrise said, *that you-other must die too.*

Hanna thought of what was left of her future, and shivered.

"I must complete his death," she said.

No. The fullness of his life.

Nonetheless there was grief in Sunrise, deep and poignant. He would not come to her again in the union of their bodies, or dart through the waters in play with Swift. She would not look on his face again. She would have no other bondmate, and soon her own life must fail.

Why? —a human question. A sicentist's question. Sunrise was a fertile female; why must she waste and die when her love's end came?

Hanna saw the answer suddenly, unexpectedly. In the single organism that was the People, there was no room for internal competition for mates. The bond was permanent, imprinted, and exclusive. When it ended the reproductive function did too. There could be no instability in family structure, no intra-group source of stress. In murdering Leader, Hanna had condemned Sunrise as well.

She said in anguish, "I am sorry. So sorry, so sorry!"

Sunrise said nothing. Instead she took the dagger from Hanna, and drew a fingertip across the blade. The ages had dulled it. A thousand Celebrants touched it with her. It was a relic of times past, and Hanna did not know why a species on the edge of extinction would stop to contemplate truth, knowing they shaped it. She did not know how Sunrise kept her waked from the People's dream, nor why they were to her a dream, so that the passing hours were a series of fragments with blankness in between.

"I do not understand," said Hanna, and halted. She lifted a hand to her throat. The tiny recorder Ward had put in place still was there. She would go on speaking, while she could speak and think. Someone would hear this someday by the river. If not Jameson, someone else. It would not tell him much.

Sometimes you can't think very much about what you have to do. All you can do is to do it.

"Why, yes," Hanna said, wondering. "How did you know?"

So my love said to me of his travels.

Sunrise smiled. It was little enough like a human smile, but Leader had seen it before, and Hanna's human body warmed with delight.

Sunrise said, *You do not understand why We learned not these things from the Lost Ones.*

"Yes," Hanna said, thinking of their terrible end. She ought not think of it; she must maintain this precious equilibrium.

Sunrrise said, *They were different; or We did not know them. We knew Renders only, and Renders they became, and resonated with the Render in Ourselves. I think that is true.*

"But surely you knew there was a difference!"

There was none. Or else We would not see. . . . For We did not know, having never seen. We see in the part of you that is she an infinite variety. The Lost Ones knew it not. . . .

Hanna pressed cold hands to her hot cheeks. "They must have. They must have known F'thal, surely, even then."

They did not, Sunrise said.

Hanna shook her head, but she could not protest again; she could only accept. In the People's reality the colonists had known only—certain things.

They did not die as We would have them die, Sunrise said. *So we tampered with the brain itself, as with yours. And thus, if they would not be Renders, we made them Renders. . . .*

Hanna turned her head sharply at a whisper in the darkness. But there had been no audible sound. The great voice was beginning again, and whispered, though conditionally, though tentatively: *Yes. Yes. Yes.*

Leader said, *It is time.*

Time, Sunrise said; *time*, said the leaves.

"Time . . . ? Oh, no. . . ."

Hanna began to shiver. She said thickly, having scarcely had the courage to think of the question before, "Must I die in th-the pain? Again?"

Not, Leader said, *in my body.*

Sunrise stood and walked into the darkness. Light glimmered at her feet. When that faded too Hanna knew she was sinking back into the dream.

The passages were too dark for human eyes, and Sunrise guided her. Around her were walls of silence, the telepathic barrier with which Bladetree had met her when he took her from *XS-12*. It seemed tangible, so that she shrank away from physical walls with the sense that she would run into them. She stopped sometimes in the complexities of darkness, thinking Sunrise had gone on through solid substance, but always Sunrise turned and held out her hand and Hanna followed, trusting her. The barrier began to shiver; through it she heard whispers and sometimes identified those who made them, though in doubt and confusion. For their conceptual names were those of their tasks, or descriptive, or spoke of one person's relationship to one or more other People, and everyone had many such names, and everyone but Hanna always knew who was meant. She was herself an alien-too-small-Render-thing and many other things, none pleasant; but also she was form-of-Leader.

She knew dimly that she walked, but her consciousness was erratic and it seemed she was in one place or another without volition or movement. The empty rooms she crossed with Sunrise were bare of ornament, the rich imagery of many thoughts sufficing to fill them.

Not bare, said the People in surprise. *Do you not see beauty?* A wall of fine mosaic came to vivid life, and she admired it. Here was a column of pale light; but its final form depended on its union with other columns in other rooms. For a moment she saw the work whole. "Beautiful," she whispered.

Someone said, *That is no Render*; and others answered, *Yet it is. Yet he is. Yet We are.*

Here were more walls that danced with symbols waiting for a thought to rearrange them. All history was here. Hanna asked a question without knowing what she asked, and Sunrise paused and the symbols changed. Sunrise said: *In the long days when my love was gone, in the days when my duties permitted, in the nights when my Child slept, I studied these matters.*

A web of lines enclosed a globe of stars. Here was the People's sun, here the sun of the less-than-People, here the travels of generations. Hanna reached out to point, and did not have to. Sunrise knew the place she meant, and knew her question.

No others. Only the Lost Ones, the less-than-People; only your own kind.

"But why? Why go that way?"

Why not? It chanced to lie in Our path.

"If you had gone another way it might have been—"

Leader-in-her-thoughts took it up: *The slippery-thinkers or the uncarpenters, the tree-dwellers or the not-yets or others still unmet—*

And all of them shouted at her: *Are they all like you?*

"No. No. Yes." Hanna looked up at Sunrise's flat face with the noselike projection she knew, had known for some time, was a bony plate to protect the organ of telepathy, distinct and localized as Hanna's own eyes.

"They are all like me. They are all like you, too. They fear death and protect life, as I do, as you do. It is the first lesson life teaches any world, the first lesson life learns. It is life."

You teach Us, yet you know not soul, they sighed, and the deep vibration began again, a cavern of winds at her feet.

Hanna said with downcast eyes, "I cannot know its meaning."

We are soul, they said.

"But there is something else," she said, and Leader said, *That is true*.

What else? they said, and Hanna almost knew.

When Hanna looked at still another room Sunrise had vanished. Hanna was not in the room of records anymore; this was a dark and pleasant place with soft lights that flickered, light enough for the People's unveiled eyes, but she could not tell why the light was not steady. *Many lights are not*, they said. *It is pleasing this way*. She took an experimental step, and then another. The floor wavered before her eyes, from one substance and one level to another, and she knew she was seeing many floors through many eyes, and had not their perceptual adjuncts to tell her which she stood on. The walls had a calm and warming polish, though their color changed or seemed to, and sometimes she saw stone. She called on Leader, but he could not help her. *Your body*, he said, *is not mine. You must sort the flux yourself.*

Many hours had gone by since the last stimulant injection. She had not expected ever to need another one. There were weights on her feet, her chest and head hurt and the darkness was caught in her eyes. She stumbled on softness and the carpet made a hollow for her body and a cushion for her head. This was a room for children, scattered with bright toys, some of which a human child would take up at once. The room was empty because the alien-Render-thing had come. She crossed the rug and it flattened obediently. A couch offered to enfold her. She did not have to climb up on it—she dropped onto it—it was made for persons even smaller than she. She did not lie down. If she did she would go to sleep, and there was not much waking left.

She sensed Swift before she saw him, sleepy and compliant in Sunrise's arms. He rubbed at his eyes and Hanna felt the down of his child's plumage against Sunrise's cheek. Her body trembled with Leader's eagerness. Swift was big as a human six-year-old, but he did not seem heavy when Sunrise put him in her arms. She was abruptly isolated, watching tears stream down her own cheeks, and saw herself with amazement. That body, her body, was shaken with emotion. Bowed with fatigue and Swift's weight, it caressed the child and Sunrise and dimly, as if through a pane of solid substance, Hanna felt the joy of their reunion, and all their Nearhome rejoicing in it.

But dimly, dimly. And then not at all.

She was apart from them. There was no room for her. She had no power at all—Leader had it all—she would never have any again. To her eyes—but they were not her eyes—Swift seemed to grow larger. He filled the field of vision, he was the largest thing in the universe, he was its center, he *was* the universe. Green gentle eyes looked into hers, and he laughed soundlessly with pure infant mirth. His father held him like a treasure of innocence, unscathed.

Time to come. Time to come in my arms. Now truly it is my time!

I am not ready, Hanna cried, *I have no child!*—for she saw in Swift the something else she had almost known before.

But no one heard her. No one.

Fear clawed at her and would have clutched her throat, but it was not her throat anymore. There was a panic urge to try to seize control again.

She mastered it.

No. Let it be! I came here for this. . . .

She tried to say to Leader: *I knew it would be hard. I do not know if I have the strength.*

But he was still absorbed in Swift, and did not hear her.

Time is, said the voice of a wind astray in starlight; *time* echoed the sky, white again (night was gone); *time* whispered a tunnel of arching blue leaves whose thin flexible branches bent low to caress the heads of those who passed; *time* sang a moat of rushing water; *time* murmured flickering flame; *time time time* said the voices of a world, until:

Time evaporates. Past is ended and present ending, and only the future exists as Hanna hurries on from moment to moment. But she sees where Leader bears her: through passages of leaf and bough to a silver spire from whose peak a flame beckons like hope, and up, and up, and up, until she has ascended to the radiant sky.

Thus rejoice We that We share not the fate of all life else. . . .

They do not speak to Hanna anymore nor even, now, to Leader. The great thought has no subject nor any object. It is thought thinking itself.

(Do not think of what you have to do, thinks something-of-Hanna caught in a crevice of stone.)

What will last-kindness do to this alien form?

(What will it do to me!!!)

We do not know.

(I recline—)

Terror is a palpable thing. It is no stranger; it has an old companion's face; but now she is utterly contained with it. It does not touch her body. No heart beats faster, no breath is shorter, no muscle is weak with it. *He* is not afraid. She sees through eyes that were hers, and feels terror that is only hers. She wishes to report, report, report; to objectify; to become the observant scientist postponing the future moment by moment by reporting, reporting, reporting as if there were a future, as if it matters her voice will live on in the object in her throat. But she cannot speak.

(Think it then. Think my death. So that at the end it will pass into this great plurality and be remembered and someday somehow be returned—but how transmuted?—to those who ought to hear it. Survive. In some form, survive!

I lie, no, recline, not on the altar I feared—there never were altars, they needed no gods, there were laboratory tables not altars—at ease—*his* ease. Bondmate clasps my hand. She does not fear the alien flesh. The Child clings to me, now puzzled and lamenting. Knows his father. How can he among so many? How can he in such strange form?)

The sun rises, warming the vivid height. Such places do We choose when there is choice. This is the time We choose, when choice is given: the rising of the sun.

(The drink is cool and has no taste to my alien mouth—)

The cup of last-kindness thy father's own skull, carven, gemlike, polished. Last-kindness, like water, is tasteless. This path We choose (no others so choose) for saving, for peace and full joining. Drink! Like water is formless is shapeless: life gives it form: ever filling, ever bursting forth. Life shapes itself. You have shaped your time, your self, your Home and Us for the good or the ill of your days and those to come. Water purifies flesh. Flesh dissolves in sweet water. Now join the eternal completing!

The purpose, We affirm, for this is needful, and

The purpose, he affirms, and knows Us, each of the persons of his Nearhome and beyond them the persons of all others past and present, and in others at this very dawn those who like him wait for the sun to give up completed lives:

The purpose, he says, and Bondmate bows her head grieving and assenting:

The purpose, he says, and the Child is still, hands on his father's alien heart:

The purpose, he tells Us, *is life and the absence of death; life unending in the soul, life renewed in the Child.*

It is the true and proper answer and he fully freely gives it. And We ask: *What have you learned?*

He says: *I have learned that my love's eyes are green.*

Green. A wōrd. A thing a color We cannot see.

It is all of me which comes to you, he says. *That We know and that We do not know, save I; new lives, new deaths; the balance of a stranger's form, and worse: a stranger's death.*

We do not want this thing. To change Us?

Renders changed Us. It is no Render completes Us now, but one of Us.

We doubt. His limbs are weak, the alien strength is waning.

He says: *Think with pity (though We could not pity Renders) on their end. These are not beasts and yet they die: finally, irrevocably, beyond recourse. The sorrow! A race of sorrow, a species that knows its fate: they invent immortality, and invent belief in it: it bends and twists and warps them even the best. They are what We might have been; pity them!*

And this is what he has learned. And so We also learn. For this is how We learn.

The limbs come near to weightlessness in the morning light. They are no longer his nor anyone's. In each moment he is nearer. He looks back/We look back at the silent strange form, a rag of a thing, small and harmless. He is almost visible; We are always almost visible at this ending, almost on the edge of sight a puff of smoke, almost in clear dawn light. It is so always, and this is the same. One of Us. And each of Us always is different from all, and so with each death and new life We are changed, and changed all the more by the Great.

Therefore begins the final scrutiny and shaping, judgment and acknowledgment at once, and We pare to a structure of light his life and honor it: fear met with courage, suffering with duty fulfilled to final measure in the company and sharing of a beast.

Not beast, he says. *Returned she to grieve with Bondmate and Child. Beasts do not do that. Forswore she attack. Beasts do not do that. She is Ours. We are she.*

And the lives intertwined are a skein of light, he stretches thinning toward Bondmate once more, and is attenuated, and settles without fear or grief into each cell of each one of Us.

And the alien form is a wisp of darkness in the light of a sun no longer strange, and

It is done.

She dreams of water. Mist, really. The cool spray of falling water bathes her face. *Her* face. She lifts to it a hand that has a cobweb's weight and strength. *Her* hand. Strange thought.

Why strange?

Her eyes open, with effort. See the scaled gentle face, familiar as her own. She smiles, and whispers a question.

Sunrise cannot answer. She does not know why the human body lives. But she tends to it carefully as she tends Swift, and the food she puts into its mouth comes warmed and softened from her own. And is gratefully accepted.

The ships have been called back. They are not necessary.

The security module was not in Jameson's house anymore. The place where it had been was a cavity, the walls scarred and strange from amputation. He felt as if a part of his body had been removed. The transmitter was gone from his ear and it seemed he would never again know what was going on anywhere.

He slept drugged to the top of his skull and severed from the world and they almost had to break his house down before it sounded an alarm of intruders and he finally woke, sick with dread. The antidote to oblivion didn't really take effect until he was on his way to Admin in al-Nimeury's aircar. He had fallen on the way out his own front door, and he did not remember anything al-Nimeury had told him. He was too proud to ask for a repetition. He watched the night go by and waited for al-Nimeury to say something else. When it came it was a string of curses, but absentminded, as if al-Nimeury had been through it all before.

Jameson tried his dignity and found it, with relief, returning.

"Calm yourself," he said.

"You sonofabitch, you never answered me. Did you tell her not to talk to anybody but you?"

Jameson said vaguely, "You never know."

"I'm not sure she's all there anymore. Maybe Katherine was right—no. No, I take that back. I was there, she wasn't faking. But she sure as hell sounds strange."

Jameson knew who he meant then. al-Nimeury said, "Here, are you going to be sick?"

"No. Sorry."

"What the hell then?"

"Never mind. Shut up."

The aircar swooped down to a wet rooftop and al-Nimeury said, "We're here. Come on."

They ran through the labyrinth of Admin to al-Nimeury's rooms. Pain shot through Jameson's head at every step. al-Nimeury kept talking. "She's patched in through *Willowmeade*. How did she know Tirel was out there? Did you tell her? Or did she get it out of your head?"

"I don't know."

"Little bitch," al-Nimeury said inconsequentially, and a guard fell back and they were in his chambers. Morisz's replacement was there, and a dozen men from Fleet, and Murphy, who must have been roused from sleep too but was sleekly groomed as always. Her eyes were wider than usual, though.

Murphy said, "I thought she might talk to me, but she won't."

"Right. Well, he's here now. There's no video," al-Nimeury said to Jameson. "She can hear you."

Jameson said cautiously, "Hanna?"

The faintest of sighs filled the room. There was nothing else. After a minute Jameson looked uncertainly at the others. Murphy muttered, as if Hanna could not hear her, "She's very strange. Talk to her."

He said to thin air, feeling like a fool, "Hanna, are you all right?"

A voice said slowly, "Ye-es. Yes. All—right."

He sank into a chair, beginning to forget the others, all his attention concentrated on a faint sound from infinity. It might have been the voice of a ghost. But even if they had not already checked the identity with every means at their command—and they must have done that at once—he would have known the voice was Hanna's.

He said, trying to sound ordinary, "What happened?"

"It's all right," Hanna said.

"What's all right? Where are you?"

"Here," Hanna said.

"Are you on the aliens' homeworld?"

There was a long silence. "Yes," said Hanna.

"Have you come to an understanding with them?"

This time the silence was very long. Hanna said finally, "What?"

Oh dear God, Jameson thought, they have destroyed her mind. Desolation swept over him. He said very slowly and carefully, "Hanna, can you understand me?"

He waited. Nothing. His shoulders ached with tension; surely he listened for a voice from the dead. He had had time to think in the last terrible days, much too much time to think, while all he valued most was taken from him and he could not know if the great price had purchased anything. He had not been able to make Hanna's weary face disappear, except when he eradicated it in sleep. Now it seemed he might have bought something after all—and now the sound of Hanna's voice was more important to him personally than anything it might say. It was not a thought that fit in with anything in his life, anywhere. He thrust it aside.

"Hanna?"

She said suddenly, "Yes. Wait."

But he was nearly ready in his anxiety to speak again when she said, "Very difficult. This. Talking."

"All right. All right. What's wrong with you?"

"The interface," she said. "Wait!"

He was not even sure the command was addressed to him, but he waited. Presently she began to speak, slowly and awkwardly.

"It's all right. They won't attack. I'll come back. You shouldn't have sent the ship. To follow me."

"How did you know about *Willowmeade*?"

"I guessed. I know *you*," Hanna said. She said this strongly and without hesitation, and sounded irritated. He breathed again, weak with relief. It was Hanna, all right, and whatever had happened to her, she was herself.

"You're positive they won't attack?"

"Positive. They were going to. They aborted. It's all right. If you don't do anything stupid."

"What do you mean?"

Speaking more easily now, she said, "Don't frighten them. Pull *Willowmeade* back."

"Are they demanding that?"

"*I* am. Demanding it. I promised them."

He glanced at al-Nimeury, but it was Murphy who said, "Yes. Yes, we'll do it."

"You have to. They'll know. Look," Hanna said, "it's started. Now it's up to you."

Not me, he thought. Not any longer.

Someone else had come into the room. He knew who it was without looking around: the new commissioner from Heartworld.

He said, "You have to come back. We have to talk to you."

"I know. I'll come. Not yet."

"Why?"

"I have to, to, see some people. The others from—the ones who belonged with the people I killed. And find—I lost my ring."

He hesitated, and decided not to pursue it. He said, "I'd rather you came back right now."

"I can't. I have to show them—Starr?"

"Yes?"

"I didn't do much. He did it."

"What are you talking about?"

"The alien. Made the interface. In me. He was—he is one of their great ones. They know that. I miss him. I like his, his, wife," she added with apparent irrelevance.

Jameson, at a loss, said, "That's nice."

"They might not have any more—" There was a long pause. Then she said, "Watchsetters. They might have communicators instead. She'd be good at it."

"I'm sure she would. When can you come home?"

"But this—oh. Does Iledra want to know?"

"I mean here," he said to his own surprise.

"Oh. I don't—a few days. I was wrong."

She seemed to think he would know exactly what she meant. He said, "What were you wrong about?"

"I didn't go far enough."

"No?"

"No. It's not enough to . . . to . . . to think with them. To know what's real. You have to live with them too. And then—"

There was another long silence. The space and time between them disappeared and he could almost see her face, alight with wonder. He thought she reached out to touch him, and shook his head to make the vision disappear.

"Then?" he said. "What then, Hanna?"

"Why, then you have to die with them," she said.

CHAPTER XX

The room Tirel gave her on *Willowmeade* was small and cramped. There was a guard at the door. Tirel said she was an honored guest and the guard was there to keep curious crewmen from disturbing her. He lied. She was guarded because no one knew what to make of her yet; because suspicion lingered, and Tirel wanted no alien monster stalking his ship. If sometimes Hanna felt like a guest, it was because of the very crewmen who were kept away from her. Her room filled up quickly with their gifts: fresh flowers grown in cubicles cramped as hers; tapestries as carefully woven as the coverlet incinerated with *Heartworld II;* strange and beautiful animals carved by clever hands; presents of food from the galley; cherished garments from the women. The room took on the look of D'neera, crowded with beauties stacked and tumbling over one another. It was only later that Hanna wondered why the phenomenon had happened, and found that as the full story of her contacts with the People spread through *Willowmeade,* with it spread a wish not so much to honor as to comfort her.

She hardly left the room, because she was weary and sad and unwell and it was difficult to get used to human beings again. Still, she resented Tirel's strictures. She had been the prisoner of someone or other for a long time now—or maybe sometimes she had really been a guest—but she wished they would stop calling it one thing when it was the other.

A true-human mindhealer came to see her, and asked questions she would not answer, and proposed a moderate intake of drugs (a suggestion she rejected with some violence), and said that she ought to have the most normal regimen of living possible.

He must have forgotten to tell anyone else. Her other

visitors were not normal, they did not pay social calls; they asked questions about the People. They thought she must have all the answers and she did not. A lifetime of study would not be enough to get them all. She could not even answer simple questions with the expected yes or no. To do so was to disregard a world of connotations, implications, and interconnections, and a simple answer, being incomplete, was false. Her ambiguous answers satisfied no one, but they were all she had.

She talked to Jameson sometimes. The transmissions were clear; behind lurking *Willowmeade*, as Hanna moved toward the People's Home, other ships of Fleet had worked feverishly to set human relays in place. Whatever came next, the line was in place for communication with the People, and *Willowmeade* now followed it home. It was a remarkable achievement, Jameson told Hanna complacently, but she was not interested, and barely nodded in acknowledgment.

Their conversations sometimes were private, but Jameson was cool and impersonal. The caution with which she was treated must have his approval, and she asked him finally, bitterly, what she had to do to prove herself to him, and, indeed, what exactly she was supposed to prove. He was jolted for the first time from his abstraction. He said, "You must understand, Hanna, we still don't know how human you are."

"But he's gone. *Gone*."

"His memories are there, are they not? His knowledge?"

"Yes, but *he* isn't. I 'heard' him sometimes before I came away. . . ." She fumbled, searching for words to explain. "He's still *there*, in them. But it's a change. By the time I left he was already almost archetypal, like the others—the ones who'd been in him. They lose some individuality. . . . She'll die soon, his spouse. Not right away; in a year or so. Just slowly, gradually fade. I think I might too."

He gave her a very measured look. "I don't think so," he said. "Not if you're a human being. And you weren't united with him very long. I think you're just grieving, Hanna. Because you've lost him. . . . Did you love him?"

"I don't know. I don't think it matters. He was *me*. And I thought if I lived through it, somehow he'd still be there."

Jameson's explanation was insulting—who should know how human she was, if not Hanna herself? —but it explained the medtechs who swarmed about her. They examined her as soon as she came aboard *Willowmeade;* decontaminated her, corrected some nutritional imbalances, pounced on her still-bleeding arm with delight; and analyzed her skin, her hair, her nails, and every conceivable body fluid, along with the air that had been in her lungs when she arrived. After a day or two they came back and began scanning every cell of her brain. They talked enthusiastically of dendrites and axons while the traces of light that defined Hanna formed ambiguous amoebic shapes on portable video screens, and the mainframe computer in medical mode emitted strange gobbles and pings as comment on what Hanna had become.

They were on to something. They would not tell her what, so she read their thoughts, and was frightened. Perhaps Jameson was right after all; there were subtle physical changes in her brain. Interpreting them was difficult, but something, plainly, had happened to her.

''Give us just a little slice of cortical tissue,'' they coaxed her. ''Quick, simple, safe, painless—''

''No!'' she said. She had been tampered with enough. Her head ached at the very thought. ''Enough is enough!'' she cried in despair, and Jameson unexpectedly supported her.

''Should I thank you?'' she asked him.

''No. Why? What you are now works. Just the way it is.''

''Then you'd want to be able to replicate it. Replicate me.''

''It will be a long time before we can do that. I dislike using the word 'impossible,' but it just might be applicable.''

He was using holographic transmission, exceedingly rare for him; he said it was too difficult to remember that you were talking to an illusion. And indeed he appeared so substantial, seated at ease in Hanna's cabin, that she yearned to put out her hands to touch him, and restrained herself with difficulty. She brought her mind back to what he had said and asked, ''Why?''

He shifted a little in his unreal chair, and Hanna, recognizing the signs, prepared to be lectured.

''The theory postulates two elements that are too difficult to deal with,'' he said. ''One is the shaping of consciousness the aliens did when you were their prisoner. The other is the massive regeneration you went through on Earth. The changes probably were in place before you left, and were overlooked because no one recognized their significance. We might be able to modify the regenerative effect in a healthy subject. But the first part of the business . . . certainly we wouldn't reproduce it, even if we could. And we'll need the aliens to find an alternative means of producing the same effect. No, you're a synergistic product. Getting the same result, with due attention to the safety of the subjects, will take years. You've made it possible to proceed with contact along more conventional lines. I don't see why anyone should be permitted to dig around in your head."

Hanna thought rather doubtfully that it sounded like rationalization for a decision made on emotional grounds, but probably not; probably he meant just what he said.

She spent two weeks on *Willowmeade*, and through all of it, when she was not being questioned or examined, she grieved. Whether her brain's changes had anything to do with it or not, she was still more than half alien. Now she felt herself to be much as the persons of the First Watchsetter had seen her—a part of an organism severed from the whole, and bereft. Before Leader's final transition she had not looked beyond it, thinking there would be nothing, or still-Leader; if she had looked beyond it she could not have predicted this loneliness. She refused to talk to Iledra. She did not know if she wanted ever to go home. She had said farewell to D'neera, deeply and it seemed irrevocably. She could not easily undo the parting; and there was a question she sometimes contemplated, without daring yet to test it: whether or not she might have become so different that she belonged nowhere.

Presently *Willowmeade* came to Earth, and she was invited aboard a shuttle for the trip to the surface. The two men with her might have been an honor guard, or merely guards. They were not sure themselves—as Hanna discovered by shamelessly examining their thoughts. She had not asked anyone on *Willowmeade* what was going to happen to her next. Jameson had talked of "developing and implementing a plan of systematic contact with the Zeigans" —but she did not know how much choice she had about participating, what role was designed for her and how much pressure would be applied if she declined it, or what the official attitude might be concerning her humanity or lack of it.

The shuttle dropped to an Admin landing pad, and Hanna's

guards took her through a section of the maze she had never seen before. The place was nearly empty; it was a down-day, and she moved through the hushed corridors feeling like a ghost.

A door opened, and Jameson came out of it. The guards disappeared.

Hanna looked at him in silence, and saw that he regarded her speculatively. She shrank in on herself; felt herself grow smaller, tighter, harder. It had occurred to her that when she saw him she might throw herself into his arms. But not when he looked at her like this.

"Come in," he said suddenly, and she walked past him cautiously, stiff-legged, into a strange room from which she could see the river shining far below. It was very quiet. It was almost always very quiet wherever Jameson was, as if silence were something he created as an extension of himself. Hanna caught her breath; it was nearly irresistible.

She did not want to look at Jameson. She looked instead at an object in the room: the head of an alien animal, carved in wood. A memory came from months before of Jameson lifting it with careful hands to show it to Iledra. But this was not where she had seen it.

She said, "Where am I?"

"My offices," said the quiet voice behind her.

"No, it's not!"

He said carelessly, "New job, new rooms. They needed someone to head up the contact project. They're thinking about sending *Endeavor* out again, too. Gives me a chance to stay on Earth. Heartworld has a new commissioner; have you forgotten? He likes my old quarters very well."

His voice was entirely controlled. If she looked at him his face would be tranquil too. So she listened with the other, inward hearing, more sensitive and finely honed than it had ever been before her sojourn with the People, and felt his pain. Her head drooped.

He said, sounding merely curious, "Why are you angry?"

"I hardly know where to begin!"

It was not what she had meant to say; it came from Leader's empty place. She twisted her hands together nervously and said, "Why did you send *Willowmeade* to follow me? After the promise you made that I'd be alone?"

"It was necessary. It could have gone either way. By your own account the beginning was shaky—"

"You endangered everything I was trying to do!"

"Did we? *You* believed we would put nothing in position for an attack. It was worth the gamble that they therefore would believe it too—and not look too hard. If you failed, we had an alternative. It was necessary," he repeated.

"It wasn't." Hanna took a deep breath. Leader was gone, but she would speak for him. She said, "It was stupid and dangerous, and you cannot, you can *not*, behave with these beings the way you behave with each other. They're different. They play by different rules. You can threaten them without meaning to. If you behave like the beasts they remember you'll undo everything I've done. They know I'm an aberration. They could reject me as quickly as they took me in, if you can't give up something of yourselves the way they did, the way I did. If you can't understand that, then it was all for nothing!"

"Good," he said approvingly.

Astonished, she turned to him at last. He was smiling.

"Good?"

"That's exactly what we must learn from you, and through you."

She looked at him suspiciously, but he was serious. For once he was telling the whole truth. But if he thought it would soothe her, he was mistaken.

She said, "You mean you want to use me some more."

He said thoughtfully, "You can put it that way if you want to."

"Can't you go on without me? What do you want from me now?"

Jameson said slowly, "I want your recommendations on how best to establish regular communication with the aliens, with the exchange of knowledge to promote mutual understanding as your highest priority. I want you to organize a detailed plan of contact. I want to go back there, if need be; with companions, if that is best. If so, I want you to train the others. I do not think you should be questioned any longer. Our questions come from a human perspective entirely. I want to know what you will say when you are allowed to speak spontaneously, with due reference to 'Sentience.' I want you to be the guide for a future spent sharing the universe with these beings. . . . That will do for a start."

She felt sick. She said, "I don't want to do anything."

He looked at her for a long moment and then said, "All right."

She eyed him with disbelief. He added, "Trying to force you is futile. There is no weapon to use against you. I cannot threaten you, even with confinement. You're too important. You don't know anything about the kind of personal power that has its source in the way others perceive you, but you have it now, whether or not you know how to use it. I can't touch you. Not now. No one can. And if you don't care about power or riches, and I don't think you do, I have nothing to bribe you with. . . . What do you want? What is the dearest wish of your heart?"

She was taut as she listened, but it was all true. She felt—the lifting of a great weight? No, not its vanishing, it was too soon for that, but the first intimation that a burden she had long carried might, in time, be put down.

There was only one thing she wanted. She said simply, "Rest."

He nodded. "You can leave for D'neera today, if you like."

She shook her head abruptly. She was not ready to go home to D'neera. It was not time. She did not know why.

"No? Well, then, there are quarters for you if you want them; near here, near my home. You can be the guest of the Polity for as long as—"

"Not that!"

"What?" Her vehemence startled him.

"I don't much like the way the Polity treats its guests," she said, but she said it forlornly. Her vision was blurred. That happened often of late, but she could not remember the last time she had wept.

After a minute he said slowly, "You could come stay with me."

He spoke with an edge of reluctance, as if he were not sure what he was offering or if he should offer it at all. But the fireside and the warmth and the quiet of his home, the sense of enduring, solid-founded peace, were fully present to her mind.

"Yes, please," she said.

* * *

She slept; slept for three weeks; slept through the nights and half the days, waking to eat when Jameson insisted, waking sometimes to slip from his house by night or by day to walk a little in an endless spring rain. Her eyes were swollen with sleep, and she was slack as a broken bowstring. Jameson gave the house orders, and it guarded her. People came to it, but it would not let them in and sent them away. People called, but it let no one speak to her; and she slept. Her dreams were strange and restless and sometimes terrifying. She woke from a nightmare one evening and in a sort of daze made her way to Jameson's study, where he sat reading before a fire. He must have spoken to her, but she never remembered what he said. There was space for her beside him and she crept into it, easing her head onto his shoulder and pressing so close that she might have been trying to erase herself as a separate presence from the universe. He looked down at her for a long time, and finally laid down the reader he held and very gently put his arms around her. Hanna began to cry. She cried for a long time and he held her through it, until she was done and exhausted with weeping and lay down with her head in his lap and slept again. When she woke near morning he had not moved; he was sleeping too, and still held her hand.

A day or two later Peter Struzik said, "I don't care how you do it. Beat her, dope her, make love to her, tell her she can name her price—just get her going so we can get somewhere."

Jameson said nothing. They had just disconnected from an all-project conference that was another installment of the ongoing quarrel the whole endeavor had become. Hanna's reports from *Heartworld II* were rich in detail—too rich; there were no guidelines for interpreting them. If Hanna had died with Leader-in-her-thoughts, they would have made a hero of her and gratefully accepted the finite body of knowledge and speculation left to them. Since she had made the mistake of staying alive and only declining to cooperate, resentment had turned to suspicion. How much of what she said was true? Had she been mistaken in some places? Had she even lied? It was evolutionary nonsense for a child-bearing female to die soon after her spouse. It was ridiculous to suppose that objective reality could be altered by the consciousness of a species, that flora were in any way conscious, that a world's direction could turn on the shaping of a single mind. Why had Hanna's answers on *Willowmeade* been so unsatisfactory? If she had once translated the People's written language, as she claimed, why would she not do it again? Did she wish it to remain a mystery? Perhaps if they could read it, they would learn things that contradicted her testimony. Perhaps she knew it.

Struzik walked up and down Jameson's new office with small fussy steps. When he went out of this room he would walk through the project's main workspace, where the air was that of a battlefield. Most of Jameson's former staff still worked for the commissioner's office, assisting in the transition; but some, like Rodrigues, were here. They were not expert in the matter at hand, and personal loyalty prevented them from complaining of the project's direction or lack of it, except perhaps among themselves. But there was a larger group of specialists recruited just for this undertaking, and they were frustrated and angry, they could not get at Hanna, and they had begun to talk of her absence as deliberate sabotage performed, for inscrutable but probably political reasons, by Jameson. The two groups did not mix well.

Struzik looked down twenty stories at the river, an ice-blue ribbon today. He said, "You could get her to stop sulking."

"She is not sulking," Jameson said mildly.

"Well, what do you call it? Sleeping her life away when we need her."

"Peter. It has been almost a year since she went into space with the other two to meet the Zeigans. Do you need to be reminded why we named them that? She was present at the deaths of her friends, she was taken apart in body and spirit and intellect, she was rushed through regeneration and was conscious far too often while it was going on, she was kept a prisoner here and treated—not badly, but not particularly well; and all that was the easy part."

"I know, I know, I know. But she could be made useful anyway."

Struzik peered over his shoulder to see what Jameson made of the suggestion. Jameson knew exactly what he meant. He said, "She's had enough of chemical tampering. It's not a thing that has ever been accepted on D'neera in any case. She doesn't like it and she's not used to it."

"Living with you must be an education for her, then."

There was no response, and after a minute Struzik went on, "She wouldn't have to know about it, you know. She'd just feel better. Calm. Cooperative. Happy. If—"

"No."

"Maybe somebody else could make her see reason, anyway. If you won't. If you'd let one of us talk to her—"

"No."

"No?" Struzik swung around and said experimentally, "Look, you could be removed from the project. Not that I, that we want to do that. It's hard watching an old friend go under. We all got here more or less the same way. What happened to you—it could have been me or Kate or any of us. The point is, you're answerable to us. It's going to be our hides if you don't produce. Do I have to spell out what it means to you? Your own council dumped you and we grabbed you. For this. If you last a month and that's the end, with all the talk, what are you going to do then? I hear people say already you've been overrated all along, and that's when they're being nice. Now, think about it, Jamie. I know you can do it. It's her or you. You just decide."

He stared at Jameson. There was no reaction for a long moment, and then Jameson's right hand moved in a rude gesture. That was all.

The mists were thinning. She slept well for several nights running, and the half-heard echoes of Leader that made her anxiously turn her head, as if to hear better, were muted and vanishing. She communicated a little with Iledra, but not by holo or video or even voice; she wrote, as she had from *Endeavor;* it was easier that way to be cautious, to be sure of saying neither too much nor too little, to hide behind the shield of distance and make noncommittal answers to Iledra's fulminations on the Polity, whose occupation of D'neera was finished but far from forgotten.

"Don't you," Iledra asked again and again, "want to come home?"

"Not yet," Hanna answered each time.

She had no energy for going home. She felt she was at home, maybe as much at home as she would ever feel again, anywhere. Jameson's house emphatically was not D'neeran; it was uncluttered and largely unadorned; but it was luxurious for all its look of austerity, and suited Hanna better than the gaudier conventions of D'neera.

She absorbed the spaciousness and quiet gratefully. She liked the quiet especially, because there was no peace inside her. Leader's voice was fading, but others took its place. In one way or another they were all her own, but often enough the notes her spirit played were taken from elsewhere, from others. It amused her to put names to them.

You shirk your duty. You have come through fire and agony and now at the flowering and fruit you turn aside. Why then did you do it? What good will it be? What benefit?

Was that Iledra? Jameson?

See them, all the differences. Those in the higher classes have two mutually functioning brains. They move whitely gracefully. Swaying they mean—what do you think they mean? How do you think they think with two brains?

A teacher long-ago? Or H'ana Bassanio long-ago, a small girl contemplating pictures from F'thal?

Thus the turn and the shimmer that is faster than the eye or comprehension and we catch the facets sparkling and dance in our turn live die and know all or naught—

The Hierarchus, surely; yet it sounded like Leader.

Worth it all. Not much in this life worth it all. Transforming transcendent the will straight and sure worth the gift. Choose, and do not hesitate.

That was her own voice, and the cruelest of all. But she had learned some things since the black day of the *Clara*. She had thought that day a hard one. Now she knew it had not been hard at all.

She crept from the voices to Jameson, because there was nowhere else to go. Rock. *The universe is made of rock.* Here was rock, grim and immovable. She spent the evenings sleeping with her head on his knee, a most satisfactory resting place. He always held a reader propped on his other knee; he held it with his left hand, and his right lay on her waist. It did not wander, except sometimes, with restraint, to smooth her hair.

She is a sick child and so I will treat her, said his thought, stubbornly, and he declined to remember the kiss, far from a child's, that she had given him. But she was not a child and she was not, she discovered, the thing Bladetree had left for Fleet to find. Her face was unflawed, her breasts round and whole, her skin soft to the touch, the arc of her hips an invitation whether she wished to be inviting or not. And Jameson was not altogether rock, because she learned these things through his senses. And finally learned more; not willingly.

There was no fire tonight. The east-looking doors stood open to a mild wet evening, and when the last gray faded from the horizon the clouded sky was altogether black. A fragrant breeze whispered through the room, fretful, impatient. A new and unsatisfactory report on linguistic programming—the last perhaps that would be made to Jameson—still showed on the reader's face when he put it down. The movement woke Hanna from her half-sleep, but Jameson did not get up, so she only sighed and turned to settle her cheek more firmly on his thigh. The room was cool and she shivered a little, but she had no desire to move from Jameson's presence to somewhere warmer. Her arm hurt, no nearer healing than before; and the voices were very bad tonight.

I do not hide from you my grief and fate my love gone my end approaching my child left to kin's care and comfort; I/We in him yet not the same and grief to all though not what you know in like case; yet mourning I think is for all the same and universal, so it seems; though We are ignorant still; you, I, all of Us.

The room was very dark; the reader, half-hidden from Hanna's sight, a vivid spot of light.

Grief, that is all; defeat and bitterness. In Peter's place I would do the same. He knows the cost to me. I think he even cares, a little. In his place I would do the same.

Hanna's muscles tightened. She put her hand suddenly on Jameson's knee. She would not have spoken, but he said, drawn from his abstraction, "Hanna?" He meant: Is something wrong?

"Nothing," she murmured.

"All right. . . ."

But her eyes were wide open in the dark. Since coming to Jameson she had made no effort to tap into his thought. His kindness and the care he took of her were all she wanted and all she cared about. The conversation of confusion inside her had kept her from looking for more. She thought of it, when she thought of it, as a sign that she was more true-human now than otherwise—

They don't have to care for anyone, child; for anyone but themselves. We haven't got that luxury. True-humans, they call themselves. The authentic thing. What does that mean, "human?" What do you think it means?

Strange, this. . . .

Oh don't, Hanna said silently to herself, and almost sat up, almost spoke, to make him stop thinking. Or she could stop listening, break the contact inadvertently formed in her drowsiness, go quietly to the garden or her room; he did not know she heard him and wished her, undoubtedly, to remain ignorant of his thought.

A voice from the past said severely: *You turned away when you should have stayed. We are all of us entitled to our pain. You cannot deny another's truth. That's selfish. Don't do it again.*

Hanna stayed where she was, and listened. Jameson thought in words, and though bitterness attended it, his thought was clear and precise as his speech, stripped and pitiless.

. . . to feel that one cannot, and know one must and will. Hanna I suppose knows it well. But I had forgotten; so long has it been since the reek of tiger breath and pain forgotten too; the weight and the spear out of reach and the long knife slipping from my hand. When I was well, I had to hunt again. Had to. A Jameson of Arrenswood, of Starrbright. I could not but I did. No one knew I was afraid. They watched me close and hard. They saw no fear. No sign of breaking. . . .

Hanna closed her eyes and saw color. Green: deep shadowed forest paths. Russet, aquamarine: grain against an alien summer sky.

. . . and I will not break now, though I never loved it there. The girls' bright eyes see only Starrbright. Their mothers are worse. Arrenswood affairs; a council seat someday if I live this down long enough. The years run short and I die day by day into night. At the Capitol a tiger is caged. . . .

The dark closed in and split into bars. Shafts of sunlight between them warmed shabby fur. Hanna let another nightmare seize her, Jameson's nightmare; he lived it, waking. His hand stirred restlessly on her flesh, but he did not know what he touched.

Perhaps I have had enough, enough for any man. I thought always that I would know when it was time to give up the future and its shaping. Is this it? My heart says no. But I always knew need when I saw it, and I see nothing else, nothing left to command but myself. Well, then, I will. Turn away, let it go, diminish and meet the final test and prove I am master of myself; that at least. Hard to turn away from the turning, though. The furlcrum shifts, the balance changes and history with it. Immortality, of a sort. Should it be? Never mind; it will be. The question is only how—

In the depths of nightmare Hanna made a pitiful protesting sound. "Hanna?" he said in sudden alarm. She struggled to sit up and did it though she seemed weighted down with rock. A ghostly procession wound through the dark, humans and F'thalians seeking in the People some kind of survival. Nightmares of negotiation—

The lights came on. "You can't do that!" she said. She saw that Jameson looked at her with deep concern; he must think her mad and stumbling in painful memory.

"You can't!"

"Can't do what?"

The room was full of loud voices. There were only hers and his.

"What can you be thinking of? You have no right!"

He said with sudden comprehension. "You've been reading my mind."

"Yes. Yes. Who is doing this? Why are you doing it?"

"I do nothing. It will be out of my hands very soon."

"But you're planning—"

"No. Hush. Wait. There are no plans. Hush. . . ."

He reached for her but she moved away, avoiding his hands. She said, "Immortality. What do you mean? It can't be that. I must have got it wrong."

"I don't think so. The potential for survival as some kind of entity in the Zeigan mass mind is. . . ." He did not finish the sentence. He got up, not suddenly, but with one of the movements that always startled her when he ended a long stillness, and she saw him with new eyes. He was not part of the comforting background now, but singular and alive. It struck her for the first time how worn he looked; not by comparison with the recent past, but gauged against the icy and self-contained presence he had been when she met him on the *Endeavor*. He looked absently around the familiar room, as if he had not seen it before. He said, "Everything will be new, soon."

Everywhere We went was new.

"No," Hanna said to the trace of an old Apprentice, or perhaps it was Apprentice who spoke. Jameson thought she said it to him. He said, "It can't be helped. I don't know if what is coming is 'good' or 'bad' or even if those judgments are applicable. I don't think they are. What's going to happen—just is. Is exploration good or bad? It doesn't matter. It just is, inevitable. So is this. There'll be no hope of stopping it—even if stopping it might be good. All that will be left, all that is ever left, will be to minimize some evils that may come. There are some dreadful possibilities for exploitation, violence, enslavement, among ourselves or in conflict with them. . . . There are no plans, Hanna. None that I know of; though I might not know, now."

She said hopefully, "Has anyone but you even thought of it?"

"Oh, surely. Surely. I must," he said, thinking aloud now, "get Peter to institute a study of the questions. Secretly, of course. It can't be done too soon and they will put it off if they can."

They would rather put it off for a century or two, Iledra said. But she had been talking about something else. Or maybe not. *To have a telepath at a first contact—they must see what it could mean!* And this was what it meant.

Hanna ran. Pure instinct. She fled through the wide inviting doors, stumbled on a dark terrace, crushed barely nascent growth underfoot (there was no complaint; flowers here did not complain).

And stopped. There was nowhere to go this time.

Jameson came after her, picking his way more carefully. She gave him her arm and let him take her back to the house. They were silent. He was neither surprised nor distressed by her abortive flight. She thought he had expected it. Predictable.

He brought her, predictably, a tiny glass filled with brilliant red liquid. The chemical man; though his head had been clear these last weeks. She glanced up at him suspiciously—she was not entirely unaware of certain suggestions he had rejected on her behalf—but he said, "It's only Valentine brandy, Hanna," and she drank it. It was bitter.

He said, just as if there had been no interruption, "Individual survival has always been humankind's first dream. You accepted as self-evident—it has always been so accepted—that awareness of one's own inevitable death is an early mark of sentience. Did it never cross your mind on Zeig-Daru that in doing what you did you had found a kind of endless life for yourself?"

The questions would not go away. *Questions answer one another*, said an Explorer long-ago. Hanna said doggedly, "It did not. Anyway that wasn't me. It was *him*, just changed. I don't think I *want* to live forever."

"You'll change your mind when the end is closer." There was a sharp secret amusement in him that made her stare at him.

She said, abandoning right and wrong, "They'll never agree to it."

"Will they not? They're extraordinarily malleable. And maybe," he said very gently, "that is their function. You find the prospect unimaginable. But consider yourself: a new thing in the life of the human species. Unimaginable, until you were real. Did you know there was a time, before your people left Earth, before the oppression began, when telepaths were called new-humans? Then the rest of us became true-humans—a term coined in hostility toward what your ancestors were. Because they had been unimaginable, and were new, and perhaps better. You have indicated that the Zeigans regard themselves as instruments of life. In the strict sense all of us are—and this, perhaps, is one more step in its progress. Life experiments, you know. The Zeigans so far have been successful. Perhaps success for them means absorbing us, and the F'thalians, and others we will come to know together. Can you say this is untrue? When we don't even know—as you know better than anyone—what is real?"

His voice enchanted her. It had always enchanted her, resting her with its sureness, creating a spell in which she saw the universe he knew—or made. His eyes were distant, set on visions. But she saw with her fresh shock-born sight that they were the eyes of a very weary man.

She took a deep breath and stood up. The spell was broken.

"What you are thinking of is not real," she said.

He answered without resentment, "How do you know?"

She did not know. There was only her own inner insistence

that what he proposed somehow was not right, and against it his certainty that it was.

She said, "I don't want to believe that it can happen. You do. But I think in the end that what the People want to believe is what will be."

"That," he said, and after a pause: "That. I had forgotten that."

He bowed his head and she saw the direction of his thought. She said sadly, "Must it be war between us, then, to shape their reality?"

"What?" He looked up, scarcely seeing her. An odd expression touched his face. He said, "It won't be. We're both out of it."

"But I could—" Hanna said, and then the word struck her, and the pacing aging tiger and the prison of the fields and the dwindling days racing into night.

"Both?" she said. It was only a breath.

He looked as if she had caught him in the act of performing some unspeakable crime. She said, "What have you done? What are you going to do?"

"That's entirely my affair," he said, in an instant cold as stone.

He meant to stop her. But she said. "You're leaving the project. It's over for you. Everything's over. But *why?*"

"I'm in need of a rest too," he said, lying without a sign of guilt. "I should like to go home for a time."

"That is not true."

He said with a sigh, "I wish one could lie to you successfully. I ought to have learned better by now. Leave it, Hanna. Just leave it. The project is a shocking failure, and the responsibility is mine. That's true enough."

"But not the whole truth?"

"It's all the truth that matters," he said impatiently. "The failure is complete, and all mine. You'll drop it, if you have any kindness."

She said, remembering more, "I could ask Peter."

"You don't," he said, and the world split for her; he appeared angry but the appearance was a trick, a diversion, a ploy to cow her into silence, and underneath that was real anger, entirely controlled, but he adamantly would *not* let her know all the truth. "You don't," he said, "know when to give up, do you? But you never did. The subject is closed. Good night, Hanna."

He turned and started away, escaping. His footsteps echoed on hardwood, a nightmare of abandonment from the past. Hanna said, perhaps aloud, perhaps not: "Not this time." She slipped in front of him and blocked his way. She said, "Tell me. Tell me the rest of it or I will take it from your mind. I will tear it out by the roots." *Bluff.* "You owe me. I've died for you, yes, you! how many times? You owe me the truth. You owe me a little of your precious self! You can give it to me or I will take it."

How admirable the uses of deception! He believed her, and she had learned the trick from him.

If he thought there was only one thing to do he would do it, however distasteful. He told her about Struzik, the threats, the ultimatum, the coming end. She stood before him, small and immovable, and listened. He could not bring himself to say: I did this, I gave it all up, for your peace. But it was manifest in everything he said.

Yet still in the short recital there were things he did not say. He had been this way at their first meeting, layered, giving up what he must in order to hide another thing and yet another. She had been his match even then. She was stronger now, and bolder. When he was finished she put out her hands and touched him. His heart beat under her right hand. He made a sharp movement as if to turn away, but he did not. His eyes rested on her face curiously now, and with, she thought, a kind of fatalism. She thought he knew what was coming.

She said softly, "More. The rest."

There is no more.

She heard the words form, but he did not say them. He was caught in suspense and watched himself through a stranger's eyes. It had been hard for him always to resist her touch. This time he could not. Something hurt, wavered, and broke. It was so nearly audible that she started and stepped closer protectively.

All over. It will not matter to anyone. Why not?

He said without any expression at all, "Are you familiar with the term 'profound geriatric failure'?"

"Yes. . . ." She looked up into his face without comprehension, distracted by the irrelevance.

"What do you think it is?"

She said, puzzled, "The standard techniques of cellular and hormonal regeneration and toxin removal don't work and they have to use a modified procedure. Everyone knows that."

"No. That's the popular understanding of the term. The medical definition is quite different."

She had gotten very good at disentangling Jameson's substance from his style, and she remembered that he was never irrelevant. She stood very still, except that her hands moved a little, not to caress him but to touch while she could the solid warm flesh, strong and unchanging. She did not want the moment to end. She did not want to go on to the next one. Jameson's face was a mask and she knew past any doubt that she was going to hear something she did not want to hear. But she said, compelled, "What is the medical definition?"

He did not answer at once. He drew her back into the room and to a seat before the cold fireplace. He sat close beside her. Even now, she thought, it was for her comfort, not his.

He said, "It is the rare inadequacy of *all* anti-senescence techniques. Occasionally a victim who continues standard treatment will begin to respond normally. More often, at some unpredictable point, treatment accelerates aging without warning or recourse. The failure is so rapid and overwhelming that no treatment is of any use. The victim dies, of old age or something else, within a year of the last treatment, regardless of his chronological age."

I cannot bear this, Hanna thought.

To feel that one cannot, and know one must and will. . . .

Jameson said softly, "The Heartworld political arena is an exciting milieu," and Hanna listened through a blur of pain. "I was involved in it from the time I could talk—earlier perhaps. My grandfather might have been commissioner at one time, but Progressive fortunes were low in those years. My father for many years headed the Provincial Court. He's dead now; he was one hundred and forty when I was born. My sister married a man of another province and perpetually runs for a council seat. Someday she'll win, I suppose. . . . I was very happy. Full of plans, full of ideas, eager for power and it came year by year, always growing. . . . There was so much I wanted to do. A world was not enough. I thought two centuries would be too short. I wanted to get to the top early.

Later I wanted to do so even more badly, though for other reasons. But even at the start I thought of little else."

His voice was very quiet, but he spoke without hesitation. His skin was faintly golden in the soft light and etched with fine lines Hanna had hardly noticed before. She thought: *You can't do this. I love you.*

"Nothing," he said, "is constant except change. I came to want another thing. My family helped found Heartworld seven hundred years ago. Starrbright has descended in the direct male line ever since that time, and I could take you today to Southwest Namerica and show you where my ancestors lived before the Explosion. Starr is a family name; it has been borne by many men through the centuries, and some women. I wanted to continue the line. It was time. In my twenties I thought an entire world of attractive women had been created just for me; at thirty I looked for a wife. I wanted a great deal. Beauty, intelligence, breeding, education, character—I don't remember all the list. I have not thought about it for years. No one suited me, but there was plenty of time. I thought it was time to prepare for the long fine future. You haven't started anti-senescence treatments yet, have you?"

"No," she said, startled into speech. "In a few years, I guess. There's—" She nearly choked on the next words, but said them anyway: "No hurry."

"I got around to it at thirty-two, in Standard years. You'll find that before the initial treatment they do the most extraordinary battery of tests. Before they let you go they tell you to come back in thirty days and again in six months for more tests. The six-month visit helps them determine what modifications need to be made in future treatment. Most people think the thirty-day visit is required for the same reason, but it is not. It's because the infinitesimal fraction of the population for whom the procedure fails react predictably—with a massive immunological failure that will kill if it is not caught at once. I didn't even last the thirty days. I was extremely ill before the time was up. I had never been ill before. I was appalled, even before I knew what had happened. I suppose I thought I was immune to death. . . . Afterward I changed my plans."

She waited for him to go on, but he did not. He had said what was necessary. He would not embellish it. Presently she said unevenly, knowing the answer, "You have kept trying?"

"Yes. Each time it does not kill me I gain a little time. There has always been talk about the obscene length of some of my vacations. It takes time to treat widespread carcinoma."

There was not a trace of self-pity in the way he said it. He presented it as a matter of fact, dispassionately. Hanna lifted her hands to her face. They were icy. Everything she knew about him and everything she had not understood was in place now. The mosaic was complete. *There was so much I wanted to do.* So little time for intellect and ambition to mark the passing years, leave an imprint or a legacy. The gamble! Time after time—! For an instant she saw his world as, perhaps, he saw it—a shadowy place of uncertain values, where he stood over an abyss and made what he could from whatever was at hand, building for eternity in spite of time.

She said—with difficulty, because her throat was tight—"I've never heard a word about this. It must be almost unknown."

"It is. It's limited to a handful of medical personnel on Heartworld and at the Beyle Center here, and a very few other persons. My sister. . . . I suppose Morisz knows. He knows everything about everybody. The last time I spoke of it was five years ago to Andrella Murphy."

He leaned back, exhausted. She could not guess what these few minutes had cost him.

And all the past weeks? What of them?

The enormity of his sacrifice gained on her comprehension, but only slowly; it was too large to see all at once. All debts were cleared forever. He could owe her nothing more. He had paid back everything at once, magnificently, with everything he had and everything he wanted; with all of himself.

She found her voice somewhere. There was one question more that must be asked.

"Why . . . ?"

"Why what?" He looked at her finally. He was exhausted beyond fear or need of defense.

"Why did you—do what you did for me?"

He said, "I don't know why."

"You never do anything without a reason!"

He said with the ghost of a smile, "No doubt there is one."

"You must . . . you must have said something to yourself." She touched him at last. He took her hand; automatically, it seemed. She said, "You must have told yourself something. What did you say? When you decided?"

"Just that—I couldn't." He was mystified by it still. "I couldn't press you, persuade you, work on your sense of duty, seize on your—your frightening generosity—let the others try to do it, coerce you into service—or 'adjust' you, as Peter suggested—I couldn't. You'd earned freedom many times over. I couldn't do anything to keep it from you. I just could not."

Why? But she did not say it again. He really did not know. Something dormant and forgotten had been forced to new life by circumstance, or by Hanna herself. He had said: No more. I will not buy power with her pain. I will not.

She got up and drifted away from him, thinking she ought to speak and unable to say a word. What was there to say? She could not talk of gratitude. He did not want her gratitude. He would not like it. The wind from the garden whispered round her head. She felt curiously light: light and free.

Freedom. It had an odd taste. Her life was her own. He would let no one else shape it. He stood between her and all the massed moral force of the Polity, unbending.

"What will they do without us?" she said.

"Damned if I know. . . ."

"Try to live forever?"

"Yes. Oh, yes."

"Was that why you—?"

She looked around hesitantly. He was standing now, wrapped in all his old dignity in spite of weariness.

"That is not for me," he said. "It could never be for me."

Truth. Whole truth.

She wandered uncertainly toward the outer door and looked into the dark. "Will they think of the evils that may come?"

"Some. Not much. The reward is potent."

The future on his shoulders—

I have too. . . .

"You know," she said slowly, "I thought that you would be in charge. That everything was safe. Even if we didn't agree on what should come you would listen. Even tonight. You would judge. You wouldn't decide lightly. I could leave it to you."

He said, "They're not evil. They'll manage without me. . . . I must learn to believe that."

"But will they think of the People?" she said. "Someone must."

Free, oh, free! To go home and build a city, arbitrate the Riverine dispute which surely went on still, prod a university to action, play sweet starlit games with laughing boys. . . .

He said at her back, certain as ever: "There is nothing you could do. Even if you were willing to participate, what could you do against all the rest?"

She saw D'neera suddenly and clearly, as if all her life there had been compressed to crystal and brought to this room for her pleasure. Flowers, laughter, light, beloved sea, star-powdered nights; but it did not need her—it receded as she watched—the laughter faded.

She said, "I could do more than you think." It was true. She did not know all her own potential yet, but it was true. "I'm unique. We haven't talked about it much, but you know it. Unless you create another like me—years away, you said—there will be no one who can do what I could do. And I could—be their guard and sentinel. They shouldn't be our servants. Or maybe we would become theirs, and maybe that would be wrong too. Or maybe not. But they must see all of it, all the possibilities. That they must shape themselves as they want. And we must see it too. And if I were to—when you told me all the things you wanted me to do, that first day—if I were to—"

She turned and saw that he seemed to have stopped breathing. There was no color in his face. She went on with difficulty, "If I were to do all that, it would be . . . you were giving me more than tasks to do, weren't you? You were asking me to . . . when you said I would be the guide—you meant, did you know it? that all the project would be in, in my image, our future with them—and yours, if we worked together—"

The words came very hard. She was so tired of decision and labor, someone, someone, must instruct the People not to permit themselves to be bent to human self-serving, there was no one else but it was so hard to give herself freely, even for this. She wanted Jameson to say something, but he did not. He was utterly still, remote as the People's star. Her hands crept together and her fingers sought the Heir's Ring of Koroth, but it was not there. She had searched, but never found it. It was lost in the dust of Home.

"And you could—you would—if I came to the project, the way you wanted—then you could be there too, and—would it have to be war between us?"

He shook his head abruptly, and suddenly sat down. He put a hand over his eyes. She looked down at him with compassion and a profound regret. She was giving back the gift, and it was a terrible gift to make to one so proud. She thought: Perhaps I have just lost whatever chance there was for love in his strange code. But no one else will ever see again what I see now. But I wish it could be the other way.

"I will do it," she said. The voice sounded strange in her ears, as if it were someone else's. But at last she knew it, clearly, for her own.